Times
bestse... **...sey Yates**

"Fans of Robyn Carr and RaeAnne Thayne will enjoy [Yates's] small-town romance."
—*Booklist* on *Part Time Cowboy*

"Passionate, energetic and jam-packed with personality."
—*USATODAY.com*'s *Happy Ever After* blog on *Part Time Cowboy*

"Yates writes a story with emotional depth, intense heartache and love that is hard fought for and eventually won in the second Copper Ridge installment... This is a book readers will be telling their friends about."
—*RT Book Reviews* on *Brokedown Cowboy*

"Wraps up nicely, leaving readers with a desire to read more about the feisty duo."
—*Publishers Weekly* on *Bad News Cowboy*

"The setting is vivid, the secondary characters charming, and the plot has depth and interesting twists. But it is the hero and heroine who truly drive this story."
—*BookPage* on *Bad News Cowboy*

In Copper Ridge, Oregon, lasting love
with a cowboy is only a happily-ever-after away.
Don't miss any of Maisey Yates's
Copper Ridge tales, available now!

HQN Books

Shoulda Been a Cowboy (prequel novella)
Part Time Cowboy
Brokedown Cowboy
Bad News Cowboy
A Copper Ridge Christmas (ebook novella)
The Cowboy Way
Hometown Heartbreaker (ebook novella)
One Night Charmer
Tough Luck Hero

Harlequin Desire

Take Me, Cowboy

Look for more Copper Ridge

Last Chance Rebel
Hold Me, Cowboy (Harlequin Desire)

For more books by Maisey Yates,
visit www.maiseyyates.com.

MAISEY YATES

Tough Luck Hero

ISBN-13: 978-0-373-78981-8

Tough Luck Hero

Recycling programs for this product may not exist in your area.

Copyright © 2016 by Maisey Yates

www.HQNBooks.com

Printed in U.S.A.

Tough Luck
Hero

CHAPTER ONE

SHE DIDN'T HAVE a chandelier hanging from her bedroom ceiling. But somehow, when she opened her eyes, that was what she saw.

Lydia Carpenter's bedroom ceiling was sedate, and mostly nondescript. White. It was not bright yellow with diamonds painted around a—well, yes, it was still a chandelier.

She squinted in the dim light and looked to the left, at the curtains—bearing a similar pattern to the ceiling—and the near-blinding shaft of light they let into the room.

Wind from a vent somewhere shifted the curtains and let in more light. Light that promptly stabbed her in the eyeballs.

She hissed and rolled onto her back, her head pounding, the room spinning slightly.

She wasn't at home. Where else would she be?

The wedding.

Oh right. The wedding of the century, at least according to the town of Copper Ridge, Oregon. The wedding that hadn't happened. The wedding of her ex–best friend Natalie Bailey to Colton…

His name hit her like a brick. A brick thrown directly at her head. She turned away from the window and looked across the bed. She covered her mouth with both hands, trying to prevent the horrified squeak from escaping and disturbing the man that was lying there. The very beautiful man, whose brown hair was shot through with gold, and looked perfect, even in sleep. The man with the exquisitely square jaw, and lips that looked like they existed to kiss a woman. The man who was barely covered by a very brightly colored hotel bedspread.

She had never, ever, ever done anything like this in her life. Ever. Ever.

At least, she was pretty sure they had done this. Her memory could not be trusted at the moment. How was that even fair? She was in bed with Colton West and she didn't even remember what had happened.

She was… She lifted the sheets and cringed in horror. Well, she wasn't dressed, either. So there was no way to deny the very likely happenings of the night before.

What kind of friend was she? What kind of bridesmaid slept with the groom?

Though, in fairness to her, Natalie hadn't shown up to the wedding, so the groom hadn't really had a bride. And also in fairness to her, her friendship with Natalie was already splintered and—according to her friend— Lydia had already committed a heinous betrayal by running for mayor against Natalie's father.

But the bridesmaid dresses had already been ordered and fitted, and there had been no way to shuffle things without creating ripples in the community. And both Lydia and Natalie had wanted to avoid ripples.

Lydia nearly laughed. At the moment she wasn't experiencing a ripple. Right now she was in the middle of a tidal wave.

She got out of bed, dragging the sheet with her while making sure the thin bedspread stayed in place to keep

Colton covered, and started to tiptoe around the hotel room. She assumed it was a hotel room. Unless Colton's bedroom was very strangely decorated.

Her hideous bridesmaid dress was on the bar. The hideous bridesmaid dress her mother had pointed out was her *unlucky number three bridesmaid dress.*

"Three times a bridesmaid, Lydia. You know what they say."

Well. She had not actually been a bridesmaid. So her mother's fears were unfounded. At least, that specific fear.

The bar was huge, with a wide selection of alcohol her dress was currently draped over. This wasn't just a hotel room. It was a suite of some kind.

In Copper Ridge? There wasn't a place like this that she could think of.

She wandered across the room and grabbed the edge of the violet-colored dress, then dropped the sheet as she quickly put it on, the tulle and netting rustling as she tugged it up over her bare curves.

There. Now her dignity was restored.

She laughed, a kind of short, hysterical sound that she quickly tried to tamp down. She did not want him to wake up. Not now.

Sanity. She needed sanity. And coffee. And to figure out what had happened to bring them to this point.

Lydia had never, ever gotten drunk enough to leave the previous night a total blank space in her mind. She had never even been hungover. It wasn't fun. Not at all.

From across the room, Colton groaned and rolled onto his back and Lydia froze.

Please, don't wake up. Please, don't wake up.

She tiptoed across the room and over to the window,

because she needed to try and get her bearings so she could figure out how she was going to get home. Without involving Colton in any way.

Maybe they would never even have to speak of this. Maybe they could pretend it hadn't happened.

She paused in front of the curtains and steeled herself for more sunlight. It looked awfully bright out there beyond the curtains for their misty Pacific Northwest mornings. Maybe it wasn't even morning. How would she know? She was disoriented. And fuzzy. And she'd had sex for the first time in way longer than she wanted to admit and she didn't even remember the sex.

Today was not going to be a good day.

Taking a bracing breath, she pulled the edge of the curtains back and poked her head past them, trying to minimize the amount of light she let in so she didn't wake her partner in licentiousness.

And her stomach dropped straight into her feet.

The view in front of her was a sun-washed contrast to the misty green of Copper Ridge. The sky was pale and clear, the mountains in the distance brushed a hazy tan color that made them look thin and faded. Like the sun had burned the intensity out of everything it touched, leaving only a husk behind.

Then she started soaking in the rest of the view. A concrete sprawl rising up out of a desert and—and the Eiffel Tower.

"Oh," she said, suddenly not caring if she woke Colton up at all. "Oh no."

She heard rustling behind her, a very masculine groan that skittered along her already frayed nerves.

The view didn't look like Copper Ridge, because they weren't in Copper Ridge.

Another piece of the puzzle locked into place, and when it did, it hit hard.

They were in Las Vegas. She put her hand on her forehead, trying to remember exactly what had happened.

She'd been at the front of the aisle. And Colton had been too. Then the music for the bride had played. And played. And played.

But there was no Natalie.

Colton had taken charge and told everyone to go ahead to the reception. Natalie's parents had been frantic. And then…well, then Colton had gotten a text and it had become clear that Natalie had chosen not to show up.

The reception had been overtaken by manic energy. Colton's father had been holding court, trying to take control of the situation, while his mother had started drinking.

Natalie's parents had been fighting.

Colton's brother-in-law Ace had been worrying over Colton's very pregnant sister, and his other sister, Madison, had been nowhere to be seen.

And then she'd seen Colton slip off by himself.

For some reason—a moment of insanity, of compassion—she'd followed after him.

Let the sound of the reception fade into the background.

"You want to get out of here?"

He turned his head, his brows lifting in surprise. "With you?"

"Why not? The alternative is hanging out and waiting for Natalie to decide to come back." For some reason, she hadn't been able to stand the idea of him doing that. "Do you want to be here if she does?"

"Hell no."

"Well...almost everyone is here. So no one will know if we make an escape."

And they had. They'd gone to Ace's bar—where Ace was not since he was still at the non-wedding—and started ordering shots.

From there, Colton had called the airport. And after that, things were a little blurry.

She knew they'd had a discussion about where they could get to quickly, and she knew they'd had more to drink on the plane and landed and...and...

She couldn't remember much more after that. But hey, they were naked in a hotel suite. The blanks sort of filled themselves in.

She heard the covers rustle behind her and she realized that her chance to process this alone was coming to an end. She had to face the music. And the naked guy that was in her bed.

She swallowed hard, turning away from the window and looking very determinedly past the bed at the back wall. Whatever had happened last night, she didn't remember it. She was not about to refresh her memory.

No. Some things were better left buried.

"Good morning," she said, doing her best to keep her voice crisp and even. A sharp stab of pain answered immediately. Her hangover obviously didn't appreciate her tone.

"What?" His voice was very male, very husky. Unfamiliar. She did not often wake up with men, so she didn't usually hear their rusty morning voices. And she had never, ever, heard Colton West's rusty morning voice.

First time for everything.

"We're in Las Vegas, Colton," she said, sounding a little harsh even to her own ears.

He sat up, the motion drawing her eye to him and she gave thanks that the sheet was firmly over his lap. "I..." He studied her. "I'm not supposed to be in...Vegas. What the hell?"

"Well," she said, "I'm not supposed to be in Las Vegas, either. I don't gamble. I don't really drink, for that matter."

He laughed, then winced. "If you have a headache like mine I'm pretty sure we both had something to drink last night."

"I have a feeling last night contained more than one aberration."

"Right." He looked around the room. "How did you get into my room?"

She snapped her mouth shut. She was wearing the dress from last night, and, ever since he had been conscious, she had been standing. Which meant he didn't realize... She considered, for a couple of seconds, allowing him to maintain the illusion. But, ultimately, she kind of wanted him to be horrified by his behavior right along with her.

Assuming they had behaved as badly as it had appeared when she had first woken up.

"I slept here."

He didn't say anything. In the dim light, she could make out a slow shift in his facial expression. "We left the wedding together."

"Yes," she said, speaking slowly and softly for both of their benefits. "Natalie didn't show up, Colton."

He nodded slowly. "Right."

"And then we…" She scrunched her face. "Obviously we ended up here."

She heard a loud, low vibration coming from the nightstand by the bed. "Text," he said, picking up the phone.

Her phone. She needed to find her phone.

"I have to turn on the light. I'm sorry. I'm sorry to both of us." She moved to the lamp next to the window and flicked it on, then she scanned the expanse of the room. "I had to have a purse, because it has my ID. And I couldn't get on a plane without my ID."

"Do you have to think out loud?" he asked, wincing.

"Right now, yes," she said.

She was starting to remember why she and Colton didn't often have conversations. He was so bossy and obnoxious. High-handed, irritating as hell.

Which was why she felt a little bit like her skin was too tight for her body when she was near him. And nothing else and no other reason at all.

She spotted her purse finally, shoved into a dark corner of the room. She never did things like that. She did not *shove* her possessions.

Everything had a place. *Everything.*

Just not in this room.

She growled and took a small amount of satisfaction when the sound made Colton flinch. Then she walked across the room and sank to her knees, grabbing her purse and frantically digging for her phone. Thankfully, it was there.

She picked it up and clicked the home button, her heart hammering hard when she saw the screen filled with texts.

So, some people knew she was gone. Great.

She entered in her passcode and for the first time noticed that something on her hand felt weird. She hadn't noticed before because her whole body felt messed up. Her head, her balance, her mouth. And she was tingling. With some kind of strange, euphoric feeling leftover from the night before. One she'd certainly never associated with sex, but these were strange and interesting times, so really, how could she tell what it was from?

She looked down at her left hand and froze. There was a band there. White gold with diamonds. Or some cheap metal with cubic zirconia, for all she knew.

"No," she muttered, unable to tear her gaze away. "No, no no no."

"I think yes."

She turned to face Colton. "What?"

He held his phone out, the bright screen facing her. "Apparently I spent some time texting Natalie last night about her failure to appear."

She squinted from her position on the floor. "I can't… Is that a picture?"

"Yes. Of us."

She sprang into action then. She jumped up and crossed the room in three large steps, leaning into the screen. There she was. Her arms around Colton's neck, with what looked like Ace's bar in the background and a couple of empty shot glasses in front of them.

She couldn't imagine putting her arms around Colton. And yet, clearly she had.

She had also undressed with him. And very likely…

She looked down at her hand. Right. At the moment sex was the least of her worries. She held her hand up so that he could see. "What. The hell. Happened last night?" she asked.

It was her phone's turn to buzz, and that reminded her of the texts. She looked down at the phone. She had several from Sadie Garrett; a couple from Marlene at the Chamber of Commerce, where Lydia was president; and a couple more from coworkers.

She touched the line with Sadie's first.

LYDIA I AM ALL CAPS YOU NEED TO RESPOND

Lydia blinked and scrolled up, to see Sadie had texted several times. Each time a little bit more frantic. It had graduated from *what are you doing?* to *are you dead in a ditch?* since last night. Or rather, early this morning.

And when she reached the top she saw exactly why.

There were texts explaining the photograph, but Lydia didn't need to read them. Because a picture was worth a thousand drunk texts.

There she was with Colton, arms around his neck, but it wasn't Ace's in the background of this picture. Nope. It was a chapel. A tacky, Vegas chapel. She was in her bridesmaid dress and Colton was wearing jeans and a T-shirt.

Picture Lydia was holding her hand partly in front of the screen, displaying the very ring that was on real Lydia's finger, up close and blurry. She was grinning like—well, like an idiot. Colton's eyes were half-closed, a big smile on his face, and his hand was resting high on her waist, perilously close to her breast.

"I guess…" She sat there, completely stunned, feeling dazed and more than a little confused. "I guess there was a wedding yesterday after all."

As she stared at the picture, it all started coming back

in a full color blur. They'd gambled, they'd drunk, and it had all gotten increasingly…hilarious.

They were in Vegas! She was supposed to be the bridesmaid in a wedding that hadn't happened! He was a groom with no bride, and he had spent half the day in a *damned tux*—his words exactly—and that was just wrong.

So they'd thought the discrepancy should be remedied. And then…sometime, just before midnight, she had stumbled into a chapel on the Las Vegas strip, and she, Lydia Carpenter, front-running candidate for mayor of Copper Ridge, levelheaded community pillar and responsible citizen, had not been a bridesmaid for the third time. No, instead, she had been a bride. And she had married Colton West.

CHAPTER TWO

COLTON WEST COULDN'T remember the last time he had gotten blackout drunk. Maybe college? Maybe. It was hard to say if in those scenarios he had passed out because of the alcohol or because they were still awake at five in the morning after some ridiculous party.

Though at none of those ridiculous parties had he married anyone.

And, judging by the messages overflowing his phone, he had gotten married last night.

Which wouldn't be that weird since yesterday was supposed to be his wedding day. The weird part about it was that he had married a bridesmaid. Not the bride.

And not just any bridesmaid.

Lydia Carpenter.

There were three other bridesmaids. All of whom he was more likely to get drunk and marry in Vegas than Lydia. Or at least, he would have thought so if asked prior to his hasty Vegas marriage.

Actually, had he been asked prior to his hasty Vegas marriage he would have said there was no way on earth he would ever get drunk and marry anyone spur of the moment. He was not a spur-of-the-moment kind of guy. Colton was a planner. Colton had never set one foot out of line.

After his older brother had taken off and completely abandoned the family, it had been up to Colton to establish himself as the likely heir to his father's business. It had been up to him to be the son his father needed. And he had taken that duty very seriously.

Hell, the wedding yesterday was a prime example of that.

The wedding that had originally been scheduled, not the wedding that had ultimately taken place.

This was a nightmare. Unacceptable in every way.

So take it back.

It was the only thing to do. Unlike his brother, who had run when he didn't want to deal with his life, and unlike his father, who had buried his mistakes, Colton would meet his head-on.

He looked up from his phone at his scowling—he winced—wife.

"Well, I can honestly say this is the last situation I ever expected to find myself in," he said.

"No way," she said. "You do not get to look this annoyed about the situation. This is your fault."

"*How* is this my fault?"

"Granted my memory is questionable, but if I remember right, we were drinking in Ace's. Then you were the one who suggested we go somewhere. You were the one who said you had the time off and wanted an escape. You were the one that facilitated the car to take us to the airport and said we needed to get a nonstop flight to somewhere that would be *fun*. And lo, we boarded a plane to Vegas."

"At no point did you say no," he said, wishing he could remember the events a little bit clearer. Maybe she had been hesitant. Maybe she had said no and he'd talked her into it.

But he was going to bluff his way straight through, dammit.

She folded her arms across her chest, crinkling the ridiculous lavender fabric of the bridesmaid dress she was wearing. One of Natalie's choices. And honestly, he hadn't cared. Not about the entire spectacle that she had put together with his mother from top to bottom. It hadn't concerned him at all. The only thing that mattered to him was that Natalie was an appropriate choice. She'd been raised in a family like his. Highly visible in the community, with a lot of concern given to appearances. There were expectations placed on her as the daughter of the long-term mayor, and they matched the expectations placed on him. Plus, he was attracted to her. He liked her. A lot.

He'd liked her more before the wedding plans had started to get really intense. But, ultimately he had been confident in her as his choice of bride. So, the wedding had seemed like an incidental detail to him. Something that would have to take place to appease his mother, Natalie's family and the populace of Copper Ridge, before he could get on with his life.

He hadn't paid attention to things like bridesmaid dresses. And now he wondered if he hadn't paid enough attention to Natalie, either. Well, obviously, since she had left him standing there at the altar without anything other than a quick apology text.

Actually, it hadn't even really been an apology.

One line, obliterating a relationship that he had spent two years building. A relationship that was supposed to shore up the foundation of his life. And she'd just knocked it all down.

I can't do this.

That was all she'd said.

Fast-forward a little bit—through scenes he couldn't even remember—and here they were.

He swung his legs down over the side of the bed, something beneath his foot crinkling as he did. He shifted it, groaning when he saw what was there. "You didn't happen to wake up fully clothed, did you?" he asked Lydia.

Her mouth was a flat, angry line, which was par for the course with her. At least when he was talking to her. "No," she said.

"Dammit," he said, looking down at the condom wrapper that stood as pretty hard evidence as to what had happened after their hasty wedding. He couldn't remember that portion of the evening any better than he could the hours before.

It had been...well, it had been a long damn time since he'd had sex. Something to do with Natalie wanting their wedding night to be special.

Well, his wedding night had certainly been *something*.

He just couldn't remember what. And here he was, looking at a very rumpled, rather attractive woman, not having a clue in hell what had happened between them.

She shifted uncomfortably beneath his gaze. "*What?*"

"I don't suppose you remember last night?" he asked. "After we got here, I mean?"

"No," she said, her voice tight.

That was very Lydia. Rigid. Tight. Determined and single-minded in ways that were designed to dig beneath your skin and keep digging until you crawled out of said skin and left it behind. Something about the way she was made him feel like he needed to take a step back from her. And even then, that space between them always felt alive. He didn't like it.

"Maybe we used a condom to make balloon animals?" he suggested.

Her face turned bright red. He wasn't entirely certain he had ever seen Lydia flustered, but that was the only word for what she was right now. And something about that grabbed him, hard and fast, low in his gut.

A memory of something. Or maybe just a fleeting reminder of fantasies he didn't let himself have. Images that pushed at the back of his brain. That he never, ever let come forward.

Just what it would be like to see her lose all that control. To him.

He gritted his teeth, ignoring the fact that his dick was deciding to wake up. Ignoring those thoughts that he couldn't afford to have. Not now. Not ever.

"Somehow, I doubt it," she said, clipped. "Did you find…"

He bent over and picked up the wrapper, holding it up.

Lydia's entire frame seemed to sag. She clutched her head, a low moan escaping her lips. "I don't *do* things like this," she said.

"You think *I* do?"

"No. But I *really* don't do things like this. I am not spontaneous. I am not irresponsible. I do not…sleep with men that I don't like."

He snorted. "I don't usually sleep with women with superiority complexes."

And he'd ended up with Natalie *how*? But she didn't ask that out loud because she thought it best not to poke that particular beehive. "Why? In case they conflict with yours?"

This was a return to form for her. Rumpled she might be, in yesterday's dress, with her makeup drifting down her cheeks and her dark hair fluffier than usual, but she was buttoned-down inside. Completely. Thoroughly.

He'd damn well let her stay that way.

"Listen, I think it's pretty easy to get an annulment," he said. "Especially here."

She looked stricken. "You can't get an annulment if you...*consummated*, can you?"

"We don't have to tell them that we consummated," he said. "Hell, you don't even remember. Maybe we didn't."

"There is a *condom wrapper*," she said, her cheeks getting even redder. "And you are...you are *naked*."

He looked down at the blanket that was covering his lap. He was suddenly very aware of how little was between them. No one was here. He wasn't wearing clothes. And Natalie had run off, so he didn't even have a fiancée as a buffer.

No, you have a wife now. Good job.

"Turn around," he bit out.

She obeyed with no argument. He stood, holding the sheet up in front of himself and surveying the room, in search of his clothes.

"If it helps," she said, "I found my dress on top of the bar."

He rubbed his hand over his forehead. He didn't do

this. He didn't drink to excess, and he didn't have casual sex. When his brother had abandoned the family it had been up to Colton to hold it all together. To hold the people he loved most together.

Then, a few weeks before his wedding he'd found out that his father had had an affair that had resulted in a child who was now Colton's age.

Now he was holding everyone together from that latest blow, too. His mother was so fragile one more thing would break her completely.

And this morning was evidence of why he had to live life the way he did. With control. With a code. Without it, he wasn't much better than the other men in his family.

"We can't get an annulment," Lydia continued.

"We sure as hell can." He spotted his pants and dropped the sheet, striding across the room and taking hold of them, tugging them on as quickly as possible.

"We sure as hell *can't*," Lydia said, turning around, her eyes going to his chest, then determinedly to his face. "I don't know about you, but I texted quite a few people last night to let them know about our happy news."

"Well, that isn't my problem, princess."

Seriously, he must still be a little bit drunk. He had no idea where the endearment had come from. Not that he was using it as an endearment.

"So, your plan is to return to town and let everybody know that we got married by accident? Tell them that we got drunk and made a mistake? People are going to assume we hooked up. Correctly, if the evidence is any indication."

"What's your plan?" he asked. "Staying married?"

"Yes. That's exactly my plan."

"Maybe you hit your head last night."

She treated him to a withering glare, her brown eyes full of scorn. "Obviously I sustained some kind of head injury, Colton, if I slept with *you*," she said.

He offered her a tight smile. "Maybe we both hit our heads."

"Whatever. I don't know if it's escaped your notice but I'm currently running for mayor."

He laughed. "Oh, I know. There's no possible way I could have missed that, since that little stunt almost ruined the wedding."

It was her turn to laugh. Hysterically. "First of all, it's hardly a stunt. Second, I only *almost* ruined your wedding. Natalie *actually* ruined your wedding by not showing up."

"You are her bridesmaid—her *friend*—and you started a campaign against her father."

"Can you honestly tell me you think an…institution like Richard Bailey is the best thing for Copper Ridge? He's entrenched in old-school ideas. He doesn't know the new, vibrant economy the way that I do—"

"Are you actually stumping for votes right now?"

"No," she said, her tone fierce. "I'm trying to explain to you why this annulment can't happen. We have to find a way to spin the marriage, Colton, otherwise my campaign is doomed. I cannot come out of this looking flighty or like marriage is a joke to me or something." She let out an exasperated sigh. "This kind of thing would be serious for anyone, but as a woman it's even worse. The fact that I was single was never in my favor, because people questioned if I was cold or somehow felt above marriage and family and I just… This is the worst. I have to somehow manage to not look like a crazy person or I'm doomed."

"Uh-huh." He shoved his hands in his pockets. "And can you explain to me why I should care about the state of your campaign?"

"Well, I don't know. It could be because I am the best thing for the town, and that isn't me being full of myself. It's a fact."

"I'll reserve my judgment on that."

"Go ahead. While you're at it go ahead and reserve judgment on whether or not the sky is blue."

"Honey, we live on the Oregon coast. The sky is usually gray."

"Bite me."

The command, which was really very immature, simmered between them. It did more than that. It caught fire. Sparks racing over his skin, prickling at the back of his neck. Being around her was always unsettling. But this was something else.

He gritted his teeth. "I very well might have last night. Neither of us remember, though, so I can't be sure."

He needed to get out of this hotel room. He needed to get out of this situation. Talking to Lydia, being *near* Lydia, it always made him feel edgy. Of all Natalie's friends, she was his least favorite to deal with. There was just something about her that bothered him. And it was definitely mutual.

Right now, so was this other thing. That was a pretty serious problem.

She closed her eyes. "I'm going to ignore that." She took a deep breath and opened her eyes, staring him down.

She moved mutely around the room, straightening

things that didn't need to be straightened, vibrating with unspent energy. He knew she was holding back a rant, which suited him just fine. He didn't have any desire to hear it. Not at all.

He silently finished doing a sweep for his things, then looked back at his phone.

He had not sent any photos of Lydia and himself to his parents or to his sisters, thank God. He didn't seem to have texted them at all, other than that one placating response to his mother.

Sierra had texted to ask if he was okay. And he also had two missed calls from her. His youngest sister was obviously very concerned. While Maddy, his other sister, had sent a text commanding him not to do anything stupid.

He looked across the room at the very, very stupid thing he'd done.

Too late for that.

"Here's the thing," Lydia said, as though sensing his attention shifting to her. "Natalie left you at the altar. She could have told you she was having second thoughts anytime, and she didn't. She humiliated you in front of the entire town. And now you have a chance to get revenge."

The damn woman was like a dog with a bone.

"You want us to stay married so that I can get revenge on her?"

She shook her head, dark hair cascading over her shoulders. "No, I want us to stay married because a scandal like a divorce is going to completely ruin my chances. If we tell people that we've always had feelings for each other and Natalie not showing up at the wedding gave you the perfect chance to fully realize those feelings…"

"Anybody who knows us will know that is not true."

She lifted her hands up in the air and brought them back down hard, slapping her thighs. "And yet, we're married. So, what does it matter what they know?"

He grabbed his phone off the bed and looked back down at it. He had a text from Natalie, response to the picture he had sent of Lydia and himself hanging all over each other in the bar.

What the hell is going on, Colton?

That was a good question, though he didn't feel like the woman who left him at the altar had the right to question *him*. But even if she did, he didn't have the answer.

He couldn't remember being that person. Couldn't remember that moment. And he certainly couldn't reconcile the woman in the picture with the one standing in front of him glaring like he was something she had stepped in in a pasture.

He went back to the main screen in his messages. He had sent a few pictures of the impromptu wedding to some of the guys who worked for his construction company and hadn't received any responses. A few of them probably had phones that were too old to view pictures. He had a feeling he had been intending to send them to Natalie, but had failed, thanks to his advanced state of inebriation.

And further down there was a text from his mother. He almost didn't want to look. He knew it would be full of hysterics—since she often was. And he also knew that he would have to calm her. As he always did.

"Who did you text?" he asked.

Lydia fidgeted. "Sadie Garrett."

"Dammit. Who else?" Sadie Garrett, owner of Copper Ridge's most popular B and B, was like a small blond explosion. She did nothing quietly, and she tended to throw parties on a whim.

Lydia winced. "A few of the ladies at the Chamber. Who are probably already making...banners and things."

Great. News would be spreading already. He wondered if it had gotten to his family yet.

His mother, who was likely apoplectic over the abandonment of Natalie and the utter destruction of the wedding she had spent months working on.

He let his thumb hover over the message from her, and then he touched it.

Colton, please tell me you know where Natalie is. Please tell me there will be a wedding.

Oh, shit. Finding out about his dad, the fact he'd fathered a child out of wedlock more than thirty years earlier, had shaken her already fragile foundation. This on top of it would be so difficult for her.

He wasn't the one who broke things. He repaired them. That's what he'd always done. And he would fix this, too.

Everything will be fine. Don't worry.

He sent the message, then put his phone back down.

He took a quick scan of the room and saw his T-shirt wadded up in a corner several feet from where he had found his jeans. He had changed before going to Ace's, that much was obvious, though, he couldn't exactly remember that. There were large gaps in all of his memories from yesterday, then suddenly something would hit, blindingly bright and clear.

He pulled his shirt on over his head, fighting against one such memory as he did. Standing at the head of the aisle, waiting for Natalie to appear in the flowered archway she had spent weeks worrying about, debating which blossoms would look the most effective, the most bridal. He'd stared at it, expecting her to appear any moment, even long after the bridal march had stopped playing. Because she had chosen each and every one of those flowers, so how could she fail to come and stand beneath that damn archway?

He sighed heavily and pulled up his email, taking a look at the receipt for the tickets he'd bought for Lydia and himself. Dammit to hell, they were booked to stay in Vegas through next weekend. What the hell?

Drunk Colton was an ass.

"Coffee," he said, shoving that memory to the back of his mind.

"What?" She blinked rapidly.

"We're going out for coffee. And then we're going to get our tickets changed and get back to Copper Ridge."

Lydia hesitated, her hands clasped in front of her, making her look vaguely mouse-like. "We're going back already?"

"Unless you want to stay and play the slots."

"Of course I don't," she said, smoothing her hair.

"I think your hair is a lost cause." He reached out and

brushed a strand from her face. Too late, he realized that was a damned mistake.

Lightning shot from where his fingertips brushed against her, straight down to his cock. His unrest around Lydia had always been a vague, unsettling thing. Like static just beneath his skin. But all at once it was like the veil had been torn away and he saw it for what it was.

Attraction. Desire.

Hell no.

He pulled his hand away.

She turned, looking into a mirror that hung on the far wall, her eyes round, her hand shaking as she brushed her hair away from her face. She was just as affected by this. By him. "I need...probably to be dipped in a vat of mousse."

"No time for that." He needed to get out of this hotel room. Away from her.

He was going to leave these strange feelings in Vegas and never look back. The marriage might not be something they could leave behind, but this insanity was staying in Nevada, where it belonged.

She looked around. "I'm wearing last night's dress."

"And that's another thing we can take care of. Unless you want to wear it on the plane ride back."

She cringed. "No thank you."

"Then come on."

She made a low whining sound, but ultimately followed him out of the room. "Please slow down. The room is spinning and I'm wearing high heels."

He continued to stride down the hall, paying as little attention as possible to the tacky decor. Natalie would be appalled. She had planned for them to honeymoon in New York and spend some time in a posh hotel in

Manhattan. He'd just been along for the ride, because he failed to see the appeal in the rush of a city that size.

But then, he'd ended up in Vegas when drunk and left to his own devices, so he supposed he had no room to judge.

"You're so mean." She stepped into the elevator with him.

"I'm efficient," he said, hitting the button that would take them to the lobby.

"Is that the positive spin that assholes put on their inconsiderate behavior?"

"Yes," he said, not really feeling the need to defend himself. What would be the point? Lydia didn't like him anyway. He had never liked her. He didn't have to explain himself to her.

She let out a long, slow sigh, no doubt designed to demonstrate just how deeply she disapproved of him. Finally, the doors to the elevator slid open and he walked out ahead of her. He could hear her clicking along behind him, her steps unsteady on the high-gloss marble in the lobby.

He paused, turning to face her. "First coffee. Then we'll do something about that."

"About what?"

"That," he said, indicating her attire.

"You're going to make me hobble to get coffee first?"

"We can fix your head or your feet first. Choose."

She grumbled. "Coffee. Fix my head. Please fix my head."

There was a coffee shop down at the other end of the lobby, and fortunately, since it was getting to be the middle of the day, it wasn't all that crowded. He quickly procured them two very strong Americanos.

"Do you need sugar or anything?" he asked, pointing to the stand in the corner that held half-and-half, cinnamon and any other items you could possibly want to doctor up a coffee.

"I just need you to stop talking. And some sunglasses." She squinted, looking a little bit like a pathetic rodent that had been prematurely rooted out of her burrow.

"*One* of those I can get you."

"I can buy my own sunglasses, thank you, Colton."

"It's our honeymoon, dear. The least I can do is buy you a new outfit."

Color washed over her face. "It is not our honeymoon."

"Yes," he said, "it is. Especially since you're insisting that we stay married."

"It's the only thing we can do."

"I guess I see your point," he said, turning toward the gift shop that was located across from the café.

He didn't want to see her point, but he did. His mother was already on the verge of a breakdown, and he was going to be the primary topic of town gossip for months. Adding to it all with this weird marriage and a quick divorce seemed...well, it seemed like the path of most resistance.

Lydia clicked after him. "You do?"

"I have a reputation in the community that I need to maintain."

"I suppose drunkenly marrying your former fiancée's bridesmaid doesn't really jibe with that."

"Less so quickly divorcing her. I'm not sure if Natalie told you about my father."

Lydia blinked. "It may have escaped your notice that

Natalie and I weren't exactly on fantastic terms there in the end."

"Oh, it did not escape my notice." He began to rifle through the clothing racks. There wasn't anything normal in this place. It all had dice and glitter on it. Lydia didn't seem like the sort of woman who would wear either. "What size do you wear?" he asked. He was happy enough to change the subject away from his family.

"I can find my own clothes," she said, grabbing hold of a large pair of sunglasses that had small glittery dice on the earpieces and putting them on quickly. She turned around, grabbing a fuzzy black zip-up hoodie off a rack, followed by a matching pair of pants. "These will do fine."

He turned around, snagging a white T-shirt from a nearby rack and holding it out. It just so happened to say Bride across the chest in rhinestones. "You might want something short-sleeved," he said.

She frowned. "That's tacky."

"But true," he said.

Lydia scowled, taking a pair of black shoes with gold dice on them that looked an awful lot like men's smoking slippers. Then she took everything over to the counter, where a young woman was waiting to check them out.

"So," the girl said, taking the sunglasses from Lydia and scanning them. "You just got married?"

Lydia smiled, and it might have looked genuine if he was standing a little farther away. If it wasn't so apparent to him how intensely she was grinding her teeth together. "Yes. I bet you don't get a lot of newlyweds in here."

Lydia's dry tone completely went over the woman's

head. "Oh, we do. Getting married is a pretty popular pastime here."

"What else are you going to do in a desert?" Colton asked.

"Pretty much nothing," the girl responded, folding up the sweatshirt and then starting on the pants.

"Actually," Lydia said, "I kind of want to change now."

"Must have had some party after the wedding, huh?" the checker asked.

Lydia touched her hair again. "Or something."

"She's dressed a lot fancier than you," the woman said, this time directing her comment at Colton.

"Yes, well she was standing outside a chapel waiting around for her groom. I just happened to show up."

"I should have been waiting where you were waiting," the checker said, winking at Lydia.

"If only you had been," Lydia responded drily. "I'm just going to go change."

Lydia disappeared for a few moments and Colton pretended to look at the merchandise in the store. Merchandise he would never in a million years consider buying. But it was better than attempting conversation with the woman at the counter. When Lydia reappeared her hair was still a disaster, and she looked a little like a Real Housewife of Somewhere. All she was missing was a small dog.

"Are you checking out?" the sales clerk asked.

"Yes," Lydia said emphatically.

"In a hurry to start the honeymoon?" the woman asked with a grin.

"Something like that," Colton said as they left the store.

While they waited in line to check out, Colton took his phone out of his pocket and dialed the airline. After giving all of the relevant information, he made a request for a change of flight.

"Mr. West, that is going to be an expensive fee," the woman on the other end of the line—Julia, according to her initial introduction—said.

"I don't care," he responded.

"Four hundred dollars a ticket," Julia continued.

He gritted his teeth. It didn't really matter to him, in any way beyond principle, anyway. "I understand. But my new wife and I need to get back as quickly as possible."

Lydia shot him a deadly glare. He shrugged.

"You're on your honeymoon?" Julia asked, sounding surprised and delighted now.

"Yes. But regrettably we have to cut it short."

"When you get to the airport, explain the situation," she continued. "I can't make any guarantees, but let's see what they can do."

He hung up after that, then smiled at the man behind the counter. This was an awful lot of human interaction for being this hungover. "Just checking out," Colton said.

"Oh yes, Callie from the gift shop called over to let me know you would be over here. Newlyweds."

He rubbed his hand over his forehead. "Yes."

"Do you need transportation to the airport?"

"Yes," Lydia supplied for him. "A taxi would be great."

"I think," the guy said, smiling as though he had just managed to procure them heaven and earth, "I can make that a little bit more special for you. The car will be waiting at the curb in a few moments."

"That isn't necessary," Colton said.

"Of course it is, Mr. West," he said. "We want to make sure you have the best possible service during this special time."

Colton supplied his credit card and everything else, signing the bill before handing it back to the man.

"Thank you," Colton said, keeping a tight leash on his temper.

Because that was what he did. Regardless of how he felt. Even when all was right with the world.

Then he walked toward the automatic doors that would lead them outside into the bright midafternoon sunlight. And when they arrived outside, they both stopped in their tracks.

CHAPTER THREE

"No way," Lydia said, looking around the inside of the Hummer limousine they were currently taking to the airport. "There's a stripper pole over there. In the limo."

"Maybe it's just so people have something to hold on to."

"Well, that's all *I* would be using it for."

"This is our honeymoon," he pointed out, probably just to rile her because there was no way in all the world Colton was sincerely suggesting she get up and dance.

"Does that mean you're going to get up on the pole for me?" Lydia asked, leaning back in her seat and stretching her legs out in front of her. She was doing her very best to keep her tone casual, to keep from blushing. To keep from remembering anything that might have happened last night.

This entire morning—afternoon—had been a study in walking through the deepest darkest pit of hell as far as she was concerned.

A hangover like she hadn't experienced in ever, a walk of shame in a ridiculously fluffy bridesmaid dress and rhinestone-encrusted high heels along with hair so large she would inspire envy in beauty pageant contestants everywhere.

But that wasn't the worst part. Experiencing this with any guy would be traumatic. Experiencing it with Colton

West was just too much. Her dignity was now a rare and endangered species. Like a spotted owl or snowy plover. She needed someone to come and protect it. Maybe if she had feathers people would be more concerned for her well-being.

Her dignity might have been damaged, but her sense of self-pity had never been healthier.

"You say that, Lydia, but I have a feeling you would actually pay me good money to stay off the pole."

"True," she said, gripping her purse tightly, as though it might shield her from yet more embarrassment. Plus, focusing on clinging to that specific item helped keep her brain busy so it didn't do anything stupid like imagine how Colton might look if he were to engage in any sort of striptease.

Nope. No.

She might not be able to remember last night, but her memories of him shirtless in the hotel room were still way too vivid for comfort.

He was…he was everything a man should be. Broad-shouldered and lean. A chest and stomach so defined he looked like he belonged on the cover of a men's magazine, making other men feel insecure about their lack of abs.

Except, in order to be on a men's magazine he would have to be waxed bare. And Colton was not.

She swallowed hard, her throat dry. She did not need to be pondering his chest hair. Or his muscles. Or anything at all except the predicament they were in.

The drive to the airport seemed interminable. She could only hope they would be able to get seats far, far away from each other on the plane.

Of course, that turned out not to be the case. When

they arrived at the airport check-in the very helpful, *very* friendly man at the counter offered them a free ticket exchange, and a bump up to first class. For the newly-weds, he'd said, overly cheerful.

Why was it that today of all days they were experiencing the height of customer service everywhere they went?

She was so accustomed to people not giving a damn, and in this situation she would have preferred it.

But no. Everyone was doing their best to make sure that Colton and Lydia got to spend as much time together as possible.

Still, she thought ruefully, as they sat on the small plane waiting to take off and the stewardess poured champagne into a real glass, it could be worse. She lifted the bubbly to her lips, needing a little bit of a crutch to boost her for the journey.

"Your attempt at a hangover cure?" Colton asked, nodding toward her glass.

"At this point there's no making it worse, really." Her head still hurt, in spite of the coffee.

"Don't drink too much," he said.

"You're not the boss of me," she muttered.

"No, but when you start drinking you find it difficult to keep your hands off me."

She scrunched her face. "Colton, me being a little bit buzzed is the only way we're going to make it through this flight without me doing you serious bodily harm."

"So you're saying there's a happy alcohol medium you're reaching for?"

"Yes. Totally sober I would like to strangle you. Completely trashed I apparently..." She let that sentence die as her face heated. "But a glass of champagne or two might just take the edge off."

"The *edge*? Because I'm so horrible."

"You aren't horrible." She looked down at her glass. "You're…you know…well, you're you."

"That's very informative, Lydia."

She gritted her teeth. "You're high-handed. A bit bossy."

He laughed. "That's funny coming from you."

"I already know I don't want to know why you think that's funny," she bit out, determined to ignore him now.

Thankfully, the flight from Las Vegas back up to Portland wasn't terribly long, and she busied herself answering texts thanks to the onboard Wi-Fi. Though she wasn't entirely certain answering those texts was any less uncomfortable than making conversation with her groom.

Because people wanted explanations. And in all honesty, she couldn't give them one. She didn't have an explanation.

She breathed a sigh of relief when the plane touched down, but that was short-lived when she fully realized that they now had to make their way back to Copper Ridge.

Their town was too small to have its own airport. Which meant they had to make an hour and a half drive over to Portland's whenever they wanted to go anywhere.

"We have to rent a car," she said, feeling extremely persecuted.

"I'll handle it," he said.

"I know you're a West, Colton," she said, following after him. "Success leaks from your pores, lightning from your fingertips and all that hyperbole. But I do have my own money."

"Yes. I know you do. Don't worry about it. Why don't you hang out? Spend some time admiring the carpet, I hear it's famous."

"No, the carpet they ripped out was famous. *This* carpet isn't famous."

He lifted a shoulder, his expression one of supreme disinterest. "I only caught part of the news story."

"The carpet was the Grand Marshal in a parade," she continued, because she knew about it and he didn't. And it felt important to exert superior knowledge, even if it was about an old airport carpet and the general strangeness of the Portland area.

His eyebrows shot upward. "We really need to get the hell out of Portland."

They were sorted into their rental car quickly and on the road only a half hour later. They headed out of the city, taking a winding two-lane road that led to the coast.

"I haven't been on a road trip in a while," she said. "Well, not since we went to the airport yesterday."

"But we had a driver," he pointed out. "That isn't the same."

"True. So," she said, taking a deep breath, "what... are we going to do?"

It occurred to her then, now that the earlier fog was wearing off, that she and Colton had never actually had a conversation when they were alone. They were usually in groups, or standing somewhere where they had friends nearby. Because they never willingly interacted. It was always circumstantial. Always something they had to partake in to be polite. Definitely not something either of them would ever do on purpose. And now they were trapped in a car together.

Now they were trapped in a marriage together.

Lydia's heart started beating faster. Her palms were sweating. She was officially starting to panic.

Then suddenly, a hysterical bubble of laughter exploded from her lips.

"Something funny?" he asked.

"All of this," she said, the words coming out as half a screech. "We hate each other. And yet…we're married."

"I still don't think it's very funny."

"It's hilarious," she said. "Made even more hilarious by the fact that we made it impossible to fix this. Because we texted the whole world. And even then… if we were anyone else…it wouldn't matter, would it?"

"Maybe not."

The hysteria subsided, and suddenly she felt just… much less. Much less everything. Small and weak sitting next to Colton. Unsure of what to do with what had happened. Unsure of how to cope with the reality of the situation they were in.

And she was never unsure. Not anymore. She'd found her place. Her people. And she knew what to do with that.

She hated this. She had to get it together.

She took a shaky breath. "The election is in four months," she said. "I can't have anything messing up my chances."

"Of course not," he said, sounding resigned.

"Why did Natalie… I mean, maybe we talked about this last night, but I honestly don't remember. Why did she leave?"

"Hell if I know," he said, the words harsh. "She did

nothing but obsess about this wedding for the past eight months. She was…I would say overly invested in the idea of marrying into a family like mine."

"You mentioned…you mentioned something about your dad."

There was a slight pause, and she turned to look at him. His arms were tense, his hands gripping the wheel tight. "My dad, it turned out, had a bastard child some thirty-two years ago," Colton said, his tone dry. "That may have had something to do with her deciding not to show up, it's true."

She tried her best to process that bit of information. But it was a lot. Nathan West had never seemed like anything but the perfect husband, father and role model for the community, at least not from her point of view. It was difficult to imagine him betraying his legacy like that.

"But," Colton continued, "since causing a scandal was her primary issue with that bit of information about my dad, I can't really imagine she would have abandoned me at the altar to try and avoid gossip."

"You have a point." She worried her lip. "Wait… Do we know who…"

"Jack Monaghan."

Lydia nearly choked. "Jack Monaghan is your half brother?"

She had gotten to know Jack in passing over the years. Really, every woman in town was aware of him on some level. Most of them on an intimate level, prior to his getting engaged to Kate Garrett.

Lydia didn't know him *that* way. Lydia had never gone there. She wasn't one for bad boys with wicked blue eyes and charming smiles. Well, she noticed them. She thought they were hot, and spent a little bit of time staring at them, but she didn't pursue one-night stands. Not with anyone.

She remembered last night and groaned.

There was nothing wicked about Colton's blue eyes, nothing particularly charming about his smile. Yet, even while she thought of that, she realized that his eyes were the same color as Jack's.

But they seemed cold. And he didn't have that easy way about him. That breezy charm that seemed to roll off of Jack in waves. No, Colton was rigid. He was controlled. He was inflexible.

"I was going to say that I can't believe it," she said, "except, you do sort of look like him."

"I guess," Colton said, his words clipped. "Lord knows how long before this gets spread around. I think it's kind of a miracle it hasn't already. But then, it isn't just my dad making waves. There's Sierra, taking up with a bartender."

"Ace owns the bar, so it isn't quite like you're making it sound."

"Pregnant out of wedlock," he pointed out.

"Didn't they get married after?"

He shrugged. "I guess so. I'm just listing my family's sins. Of course, there's Madison. And her little indiscretion, but she was seventeen. Still, people tend to blame her for what happened with that dick because she was painted as some kind of home wrecker, even though she was still a kid."

"For respectable pillars of the community you do have a lot of skeletons."

"I think respectable pillars of the community do tend to have more than their fair share. Respectability makes a wonderful smoke screen."

"And what about you?"

He laughed, a rueful sound. "I'm *actually* respectable."

"Me too," she said.

Common ground with Colton. That was almost as weird as being married to him. *Almost.*

"I guess we just blew all that to hell."

"No. We didn't," she said. "Because true love."

He took his focus off the road for a moment, the electric blue of his eyes sending a shock straight down through her system. "True love?"

"That's how we're going to spin it."

"Definitely better than the truth."

They were silent for the rest of the drive. She was too exhausted to think of anything logical to say. She had a feeling that if she tried to continue making conversation with him they would only fight. She didn't have the energy for that, either. So she kept her focus pinned on the scenery. The trees that grew thicker and taller as they drove farther out from the city. The mountains shrouded them on either side, making it feel darker here. As though they were shielded from the sun, a canopy of lush greens protecting them from the harshest rays.

Unlike most of the locals in her age group, she was not originally from Copper Ridge. She had moved there from Seattle eight years ago.

Most people left for a while, came back later to settle down. Or, if they were first-time residents of Copper Ridge, they were usually retirees. She was the odd one out. But she loved her adopted home more than anything. Expanding the tourism there was a passion of hers, and had been from the moment she had arrived. Strengthening the economy, making it more viable for people to stay. For people to raise families and thrive doing something other than working hard in the mills, or deep-sea fishing. She had carved out a place for herself there. The place she had never had anywhere else. She couldn't face the idea of losing it now.

"Do you know where I live?" she asked, as they entered town finally.

She looked at all the beautiful brick buildings, their facade like something out of an old Western, made completely and wholly unique by the nautical details that clung to the exteriors like ornate barnacles. And again by the ocean beyond them, gray with whitecaps rising and falling with the tide. That was Copper Ridge.

In case you needed to escape some sort of high-pressure situation you could scurry into the mountains or float away in the sea. It was one of the things she liked about it. Multiple escape routes. Not that she was paranoid, she was just a planner.

"No," he said. He said it almost like he was pleased.

"I'm here in town," she said. "Just past where the buildings end. On Hyacinth."

She loved her sweet little home by the ocean. She had spent a good amount of time cultivating a nice garden, making sure every bit of it was cozy and comfortable, and absolutely for her.

"You won't be able to stay at your house," he said. "You know that, right?"

"What?"

"You're going to have to move in with me," he said, his voice steady as the road they were driving on.

"I…" Oh, well, she hadn't thought of that.

"We can't live separately. That negates the whole thing."

"But we…we don't even… We can't even have a conversation without swinging wildly between stilted and hostile. How are we supposed to live together?"

"We just will," he said, his tone shot through with steel. "I don't run from my mistakes, Lydia. I own them. I fix them."

"If by *own* you mean *obscure* with a more convenient version of the truth."

"My mother can't know this isn't real," he said.

"Your mother…"

"Is still reeling from finding out about my dad. She was very close to Natalie. She poured everything into this wedding. It's been her therapy. So yeah, I'm with you. For now, this has to look as real as possible. That means you're moving in with me."

She hated him and his infallible logic. "Why do we have to do that? Why can't you move in with me?"

Just as she said that, they pulled up to the front of her house. That at least was exactly as it should be. Pristine and well kept, the lawn green and freshly mown, the white fence newly painted, flowers matching the name of the street growing through the slats.

Her front porch was cheery, a wreath made of sunflowers hanging on the door, a bright red ribbon wound through the blossoms. There was a chair and table in a matching red that was just her style. She liked to sit out there in the evenings, with a blanket over her lap, listening to the sound of the waves on the rocks. This was her place. The most important place in the entire world to her.

"Because it's tiny," he said, effectively dismissing the most important thing in her world with incredible ease.

"But it's my home," she said.

"I have a ranch," he said. "Not a huge operation, but I have livestock. And yes, I do have men to come work on the property, but I can't leave it abandoned. My property is big, my house is big. It will accommodate both of us better."

She looked longingly back at her little two-bedroom. She couldn't really deny the wisdom of what he was saying.

Mostly because when she thought of Colton West's large, muscular frame filling up the tiny rooms of her house she got hot all over. She didn't need that. Didn't need memories of cohabiting with him there. That was one of the beautiful things about her house. It was a clean slate. It was all hers. She had never lived in it with anyone else, had never had to make any concessions to another human being within those walls. And she didn't intend to start.

So, on this, she had to reluctantly concede he was right.

"I can't… Not tonight," she said.

He nodded once. "I have to figure out what to do about Natalie's things, anyway. My house has a few bedrooms, and she was using one of them. Tomorrow's soon enough."

"Oh," she said, slightly puzzled by what he was saying. But she imagined that when Natalie had moved out of whichever home she'd been living in before, she'd had to put some of her extra furniture somewhere. "I guess you have to get a hold of her."

"Or, I just throw her shit out on the lawn," he said, sounding cheerier than he had all day. The coarse language on his lips was odd, slightly jarring. He was usually much more…appropriate. Even when she'd first met him at Ace's he hadn't talked like a lot of the men in the group who used profanity like a comma. It just wasn't him.

"I don't think you should do that. Especially since you're trying to look like you're in control of the situation."

"It might be worth it."

"You won't think so later." She had no idea. She had never felt passionately enough about someone to consider throwing their things outside and leaving them to rot.

For a while, she had had some feelings for Eli Garrett, Copper Ridge's sheriff. Those had been pretty strong. So she thought. But when Sadie had come into the picture she had fully realized just how little he liked her, by watching him interact with the other woman.

There had been no reason to keep after him at that point. She had her pride. And she had never seen the point of making yourself a crazy person over attraction.

It was funny, because on the surface Colton seemed a lot like Eli. Tall, broad, dark-haired and responsible. But whenever she had been around Eli a sense of serene calm had come over her. Whenever she was around Colton she wanted to punch him in the face.

"I'll… I guess I'll see you tomorrow," she said, still feeling dazed when she got out of the car and stumbled up to the front walk. Her hands shook as she shoved the key in the lock, and they didn't stop shaking, even when she went inside and closed the door behind her.

She leaned against it, her heart pounding heavily. It was strange. Everything here was undisturbed. Everything here seemed the same. But in reality, everything had changed. And in that moment, she sort of resented her house for maintaining its calm, cozy order when everything inside of her was thrown completely out of whack.

She walked back toward her bedroom in a daze, staring down at the extremely feminine, floral bedspread and the matching curtains. She wondered what Colton's bed would look like.

"That," she said out loud, "doesn't matter. Because you're not going to sleep in his bed."

Just the thought made her stomach turn over violently.

They would get through this. Basically, they would be roommates. Roommates until everything with the election was sorted, and until all of the gossip over the Wedding That Wasn't died down.

And yes, then they would have to go through the very public process of a divorce, and that wouldn't be pleasant. But as long as they could remain amicable, she imagined the town could, too. By then, they would trust her in her position as mayor, and it wouldn't be so dependent on everything in her life looking stable.

Maybe. She hoped.

She flopped down onto the bed. "You are insane," she said, her face muffled against the mattress.

She turned over onto her back and took a deep breath. No. She wasn't insane. She was in an insane situation; that much was true. But everything would be okay. Because she had a plan.

CHAPTER FOUR

"How is Mom?" Colton asked, settling across the small wooden table from both of his sisters. The Grind, Copper Ridge's coffeehouse, was in a lull between the early-morning, before-work crowd, and the retired set that would come and fill the tables sometime around nine. Which made it a safe enough place to have this conversation.

"Catatonic."

If Colton was hoping to get reassurance from his younger sister Madison, he should have known he was looking in the wrong place. Sierra, the youngest West, was a better bet for reassurance—false or otherwise.

Evidenced by the fact she was currently glaring at Maddy as though Maddy had just stabbed Colton in the eye with the stir stick she was using in her coffee.

"It's not that bad," Sierra said, lifting her tea to her lips, then frowning. "Cutting down on caffeine sucks."

At nearly eight months pregnant, Sierra was in the throes of pregnancy discomfort. And making her husband fully aware of it, Colton imagined.

It still screwed with his head. That the baby of the family was the first one of them to turn into an actual adult.

"Well," Maddy said, her voice crisp. "There you have

it. Mom isn't that bad. Sierra's caffeine consumption however—"

"I'm round, Maddy," Sierra said, her pale brows locking together. "Spherical. I'm entitled to complaints."

"I'm sorry for your roundness," Colton said. "But can we get back to my situation?"

"Your fiancée was horrible," Maddy said.

"She was," Sierra added. "Like...basically one of the servants of hell. And I'm sorry you got left at the altar, but it's really just more evidence of the fact that she's the worst."

"The actual worst."

"So forget about Mom," Sierra said. "How are you?"

Both of his sisters had grown large-eyed. He shifted beneath their uncomfortably dewy gazes. "I'm fine," he said.

He realized how true it was the moment he said it. He really was fine. Pissed, sure. Sierra was right. Leaving someone at the altar was a low move. There were any number of ways Natalie could have gone about ending things with him, and not ending them until the entire town had watched him get stood up was about the worst way to do it.

He was angry. Completely, justifiably so. But otherwise he really was fine.

"Right. That's why you flew to Vegas for one night." Maddy was looking at him skeptically.

He gritted his teeth. He had to do this. There was no other option. And right then and there, he knew he had to lie to his sisters too. He didn't like it, but there really wasn't another way to play it. He didn't need them opposing him when it came to dealing with their mother. And, since his youngest sister was married to the town bartender, who was the commander of the town gossip hub, he had to be even more careful than he might have been otherwise.

"Well, I didn't just go to Vegas overnight for no reason. I went to Vegas to get married."

"You're having a psychotic episode, aren't you?" Maddy's face contorted. "Please don't tell me that you married a stripper. If some Las Vegas stripper ends up with a portion of our inheritance because you married her without a prenup..."

"I did not marry a stripper. I went to Vegas with Lydia Carpenter."

"You did what?" Sierra's voice had risen several octaves.

"I'm kind of surprised you didn't hear about it already." He watched their faces closely, using their responses as a primer for what it would look like to confess all of this to his mother. Not to mention his father.

Though he didn't really care about his father's response. His father's sins were part of why he was in this mess. He had a feeling the scandal had influenced Natalie's behavior. More than that, it was one of the biggest reasons he couldn't afford to disappoint his mother.

"Why would we have heard about it? Did you print an announcement in the paper?" Maddy asked.

"Lydia may have...sent some texts." He cleared his throat. "And I might have sent one or two myself."

Maddy arched a brow. "And you didn't text your sisters. You got married in Las Vegas to someone that we barely know and texted a bunch of random people to tell them?"

"Texting decisions were made. They were not made entirely sober."

"So, you got drunk and you got married in Las Vegas," Maddy said, her gaze pointed.

"It doesn't matter if I was drunk or not. I'm married."

"Wow," Sierra said. "I really didn't expect you..."

He looked down at her rounded belly pointedly. "I'm not sure you're in a position to judge about drunken actions."

Sierra's pregnancy hadn't exactly been planned. But then, her entire relationship with Ace Thompson had been more or less unplanned. And though Colton would never have thought his sister, the town's rodeo princess, would have worked with the flannel-wearing once-confirmed bachelor, he had to admit that they did.

"I'm in love," Sierra said, flipping her hair.

"And I stand by my decision," he said.

He wasn't going to go throwing around the word *love*. He hadn't done so even when he'd been engaged to Natalie; he was hardly going to do so now.

Maddy noticed. "So, you marrying the woman running against Natalie's father has nothing to do with...I don't know, revenge?"

Lost somewhere in the murky mists of time was the reasoning behind his decision to marry Lydia. Maybe it had been about revenge. He had a feeling when they'd started taking shots together in Ace's that it had absolutely been about revenge.

But after that? He couldn't remember a damn thing.

So he could pretty much give her whatever answer he wanted to and it wouldn't really be a lie. As long as it sounded reasonable.

"No. I've known Lydia for a long time. It's just that I was involved with Natalie and..."

"And you were going to marry another woman anyway? But then Natalie just so happened to leave you at the altar?" Maddy asked.

"I was committed to Natalie. But then she didn't show up for the wedding. And Lydia and I..."

"You were overcome?" Maddy pressed.

"Yes," he said, turning his cup in a circle. "I was overcome."

Colton had never been overcome by anything in his entire life, but if that was what Maddy needed to hear to accept the situation, then that was what he was going to tell her.

He was not going to tell her this was only temporary. He was not going to tell her that he had never felt much of anything but irritation for Lydia, and for some reason a little alcohol added to that mix had resulted in the two of them ending up in bed together.

Maybe he had been overcome. But not by emotion. And he wasn't about to explain that to either of his sisters.

Even with Sierra visibly pregnant, and married, he preferred to pretend that neither of them would have any idea of what he was talking about.

He didn't really have any idea of what he was talking about. Because he still couldn't remember.

"Anyway, obviously I'm going to have to have a talk with Mom," he continued.

"Obviously. And maybe a therapist."

"Thank you, Madison. Would you kindly refer me to yours?" he asked, a little bit of bite in his tone.

"My therapist quit and retired to the Bahamas with all of the money I paid him. He said it was really nice that working with me was so financially successful for him, but unfortunately he was going to have to use a good portion of that money to pay for his own therapy," his sister said drily.

"Maybe it's just as well. Lydia is going to be moving into my house today. So I'll be a little busy."

"This is borderline scandalous behavior," Maddy said, her lips curling up into a smile. "How nice of you to join the rest of us in disgrace."

"You know, you could work a little harder to look concerned for my well-being."

"I'm just saying," she said, lifting her shoulder, "it is a bit daunting to be the sister of Saint Colton West. And more than a little satisfying to see your halo get tarnished."

He looked at Sierra. "Sorry," she said, not sounding apologetic at all. "It is kind of nice to know that you can make impulsive decisions."

"Impulsive, maybe. But I stand by it," he reiterated.

"You're too stubborn to do anything else," Sierra said.

It was easy for Sierra and Madison to sit there and give him side eye. Yes, Madison knew what it was like to be the center of a scandal. And the town, their parents and the dressage riding community had all been unkind to her when she had been caught in an affair with an older man when she was seventeen.

Colton had wanted nothing more than to break the other man's jaw. Before he killed him. Slowly. But far too many people had held his underage sister responsible for the whole thing.

Madison made a practice of laughing it off now, but Colton knew that she didn't really find it all that funny.

"I'm steady. All things considered, you should appreciate that. I'm not the kind of person to run for the hills when things get difficult." It was always easiest to turn the condemnation to Gage. Their oldest brother had left town under a cloud years ago.

"So instead you ran off and married a near stranger."

"I told you, Lydia isn't a stranger."

The moment he said that he realized what a lie it was. He had seen Lydia out of the corner of his eye at events for years. Hadn't really started speaking to her until he'd gotten involved with Natalie. And then, every time they'd spoken, it had ended pretty badly.

He always managed to get her hackles up, and he didn't feel a whole lot more sanguine about her.

Of course, now he was going to be dealing with her long-term. In close proximity.

Maybe this was what happened when you spent years being responsible. Eventually, it all imploded and you made one decision that was *so* bad it rendered all the others useless.

And, thinking of said bad decision, he had to go yank it out of its den and force it over to his place. And he was imagining that was going to go over well, even though they had agreed on it yesterday. Why? Because he and Lydia couldn't seem to have an interaction that went well.

Actually, they either didn't go well, or they went *too* well.

He had the sudden impression of fingertips trailing over his bare chest and the sensation shocked his system like a bolt of lightning.

"Are you okay?" Madison asked. "You look like someone just let a hamster loose in your shorts."

He frowned. "Thanks for that. I have to go."

"In all seriousness," Maddy said, standing as he did. "If this is a hostage situation, blink twice."

"It is not a hostage situation. And that wasn't serious."

"Really seriously now. You aren't having a crisis, are you?"

"I know what it's like," Sierra said, rising slowly and unsteadily. "That feeling of just being…lost. This—" she pointed to her stomach "—this is where that ends."

His entire face felt like it had been pushed into a barrel of bees. "This is different. Lydia is a completely sensible choice."

"And is that all marriage is to you? A sensible choice?" Sierra asked.

"Why else would you get married?"

Sierra practically flailed. "Love?"

"Not you," he said, looking at Sierra, then to Maddy. "You. Why else would *you* get married?"

"I wouldn't. So you're on your own here."

"But if you did…"

"Obviously it would be for money," Maddy replied. "And a big penis."

Sierra snorted. "Nice."

"Thanks for that," he said.

"If you can't stand the heat, don't come into my kitchen," Maddy said. "Or something."

"I'll keep that in mind. Look, I'm going to make time to come by and see Mom. Until then, don't tell her anything."

"Don't you think the news is going to make it through the gossip chain?" asked Sierra.

"The odds are high. But you said Mom was catatonic, so I'm assuming she's avoiding the garden club at the moment."

"She's avoiding anything that isn't prescribed by her doctor at the moment," said Maddy.

"That will probably buy me some time. Until I get a chance to sit down with her. And figure out how to spin this in a way that isn't going to cause even more trouble."

"And until then?" Maddy tilted her head to the side, her golden-brown ponytail swinging with the motion.

"Until then…I have to deal with my wife."

LYDIA HAD JUST hung her purse on the peg in her office at the Chamber when Sadie Garrett burst through the door.

"So. I'm going to need to hear this entire story from the beginning, with no detail spared." She plopped down into the seat across from Lydia's desk, her blue eyes a little too keen for Lydia's liking.

"Good morning to you, too," Lydia said.

"The greeting was implied."

"We couldn't have done this over the phone?"

Over the past year and a half she and Sadie had become fairly close, which was surprising considering they had started out as romantic rivals. Okay, they hadn't really been romantic rivals. That implied that Lydia had ever had a fighting chance with Sadie's gorgeous sheriff.

All she'd ever done was pine. Without any subtlety. But she didn't want to remember that whole chapter of her life.

She was happy with the way things had turned out. She needed a friend more than she needed a boyfriend.

"No," Sadie said, her voice getting shrill. "We cannot discuss your hasty Vegas marriage over the phone."

"It's way too early in the morning to discuss my hasty Vegas marriage."

"That's why I brought coffee." Sadie smiled broadly, pushing a large white cup halfway across Lydia's desk. "It's a peppermint mocha. Full fat. The good stuff."

"With whipped cream?"

"I'm not an animal. There is both whipped cream and little candy cane pieces."

Lydia sat down grudgingly, pulling the cup toward herself, curling her fingers around it. It was warm, and she hadn't realized she was cold until the heat from the cup began to seep into her skin.

She lifted the cup to her lips, the minty sweetness exploding on her tongue. "Okay," she said, swallowing her first sip, "you have earned details."

"Excellent. When I say details I mean…below the belt details. Details about the interior of his pants."

Lydia winced. "Sorry. I don't have those."

Sadie frowned. "What?" She tilted her head to the side. "Is this one of those moments where you tell me you're too much of a lady to do this kind of back-and-forth? Because it occurs to me that we haven't ever talked sexual details."

Mostly because Lydia had not had any sexual details to share with Sadie over the time they'd been friends. But she didn't want to admit that.

"No. I'm not too much of a lady. It's just…in order to get married in Vegas I had to get blackout drunk. Which means…"

"You don't remember."

"No. I don't remember. I don't remember anything. I don't even know what I was thinking. I don't like Colton. I think he's an arrogant son of a bitch."

"Well, that's because he always is to *you*."

"I know!" Lydia took another sip of coffee. "But… when I was standing up there with all of the other brides-maids, and the groomsmen, and there he was… I did feel bad for him. And…what was Natalie thinking? It was her wedding, for heaven's sake. Everyone was there. The entire town. And she just…left him there."

"I get pity sex, Lydia. Trust me, a guy in his position really needed some, but a pity marriage I get less."

"It just started as pity shots. We went to Ace's and started drinking. And one thing led to another."

Sadie held up a hand. "Again, when most people say that, they mean they went back to his place and had sex. You two went to Vegas and got married."

"I guess that's what happens when the person you end up taking shots with is stupid rich."

Sadie's eyes went round. "Oh, that's right. He is. I bet you he didn't sign a prenup before this quickie marriage."

"I don't want his money. I don't need his money. I earn my own. I don't want to owe anyone anything, least of all Colton West. But I still kind of have to stay married to him."

"Why?"

Lydia let out an exasperated sigh. "You can't tell anybody. Because Colton is busily telling his family that this is the secret love match of the century."

Sadie laughed, allowing a crack of sound in the small space. "And they're going to believe that?"

"He seems to think so. But I know that you won't believe it. You know too much."

"I do. I'm extremely perceptive."

"Not really so much that as I've told you a little too much about my feelings for Colton."

"Fair enough. But you have to stay married to him… Why?"

"My campaign," she said, tightening her hold on her cup. "Can you imagine? Lydia Carpenter goes to Las

Vegas for a drunk quickie marriage, divorced already! It would be in the *Copper Ridge Daily Tidings*, and you know it."

"Was that supposed to be the headline? Because that isn't a good headline. It would have to be like Mayoral Candidate's Marriage Didn't Stay in Vegas!"

"Okay, that's a cliché."

Sadie shrugged. "It's a small-town newspaper. You're not going to get much better than cliché."

"That's beside the point. I'm up against an incumbent that makes this place look like it's a monarchy."

"Close enough," Sadie said. "He's been mayor for as long as I can remember."

"He usually runs unopposed. Well, I'm opposing. And I know that I would be better for the job. I understand where the town is going…" Suddenly, she remembered Colton looking at her in the hotel room, his expression filled with disbelief as he asked her if she was stumping for votes. Maybe she had a little bit of a problem. But she had spent the past few years as a workaholic, and she didn't really know what else to focus on. Particularly when things were chaotic. She tended to fall right back onto the topics she found easy. Right now, that was her campaign. And since her marriage, or rather, the continuation of it, was directly related to that campaign, it was particularly easy to do now.

"You know you have my support," Sadie said. "And Eli's. I mean, he can't actually force people to vote for you under threat of arrest—I asked—but if anyone talks to him about it he makes his preferences pretty clear."

"And I appreciate that. I appreciate the support that he's given me, always. Which I mean in a nonsexual way."

"I know."

"Eli, in my opinion, is Copper Ridge. You two. The best, the future."

"I feel like you're avoiding giving details."

Lydia let out an exasperated sigh. "I'm running against an institution. Not only that, he's a man. It seems like the personal lives of women are always more scrutinized in these types of situations. I was single, which already made me somewhat unapproachable. I mean, people wonder why. They want to know if I even care about family. If I throw a quickie marriage and even faster divorce onto the pile…well, that's it. I'm done."

Sadie nodded slowly. "Okay. I see your point. So… what's the plan? You stay married to him forever?"

"No. I stay married to him until I get elected. But, basically we're just going to pretend to be married. I mean, we're going to actually be married, but without the love, or the sex."

Sadie frowned. "So, marriage with all of the annoying things like compromise, cohabitation and having to eat what he wants for dinner, without the things that make it fun?"

"For a limited time. We're going to be roommates. Roommates who don't like each other and who probably had sex and don't remember it."

"Wow. Good luck with that."

"That is not helpful to me, Sadie. You're an optimist. You're supposed to be optimistic about this."

"Sorry. Realist Sadie is the one who feels like weighing in. This is going to be a giant pain in your butt."

It was Lydia's turn to frown. "I think Realist Sadie is a pain in my butt."

"She's a pain in mine, too. I'm just saying, you honestly think that you're going to live with Colton West for the next few months and pretend to be his wife and that isn't going to be…awkward?"

"Oh, it's going to be awkward."

"Let me rephrase. You *aren't* going to sleep with him?"

"No," Lydia said, feeling each and every one of her muscles begin to tense up. "I'm not. The situation is complicated enough. We're not going to mess it up further. It's a blessing that we don't remember what happened."

"Okay."

"You don't believe me."

"I believe that sex often overrules common sense."

"Well," Lydia said, "that has never been the case for me."

"Except with Colton."

Lydia set her cup down on the desk and threw her hands up. "I don't remember it. It's basically the same as it not happening."

"Except that it did."

"It isn't happening again." She picked her cup back up again, then set it back down. "You know what? I haven't had sex in four years."

Sadie's mouth dropped open. "Excuse me?"

"So celibate, Sadie. *So* celibate. I don't think a couple of months sharing a very large space with Colton is going to undo my willpower."

"Except, you did… A couple of days ago. With him. He was the one that broke the celibacy."

"Whiskey broke the celibacy. Alcohol is to blame. I'll just…stay sober. Which is fine, because I usually am."

"I support you."

"But you don't believe in me."

Sadie shook her head. "Two different things."

"You just can't tell anyone that our marriage isn't a real marriage."

"Well, I'm going to tell Eli."

Lydia scrunched up her face. "Do you have to?"

"Sorry. Husbands before... Well, nothing rhymes with husbands. But, I don't keep secrets from him."

The fact that it was Eli made it slightly worse. Lydia was over her Eli crush, but since she had been occasionally pathetic in his presence already, she didn't want to add to it by having him fully aware that her marriage wasn't real.

A very unsettling thought occurred to her. Even if people believed the marriage was real, she still looked kind of pathetic. The bride hadn't shown up, so Colton had snagged the nearest bridesmaid.

But you weren't the nearest bridesmaid. You were on the other end. So, he passed over like three bridesmaids to get to you.

The thought made her scowl.

Sadie clearly thought the scowl was directed at her. "He won't tell. Not anyone. Not even Connor."

"I believe you." She couldn't imagine the very serious, upright sheriff gossiping to his brother like a couple of hens. If there was one thing she trusted in, it was Eli's goodness. He was one of the most truly responsible and decent people she had ever known. Which, really, explained her attraction. That and the fact that he was an integral part of the community that had become so important to her. The community that she wanted so desperately to be part of.

In a deep way. Not just a superficial way. She wanted

Copper Ridge to be hers. Not out of a thirst for power; that wasn't why she was running for mayor. It was just that she cared. She cared so deeply about this place, this place that was perfect in ways she could not begin to describe.

The sharp, salt air; the fresh scent of the pines; the way the mist hung low over the mountains. It was in her blood. It was part of her. When she had first driven into town with her car full of her earthly possessions eight years ago, ready to make a fresh start, she had felt like she'd crossed the earth, not just into the next state.

Had felt for the first time like something was hers. For her.

And she wanted more. Something that couldn't be taken from her. It was an ache, a longing that she had a difficult time articulating, even to herself.

"So, where do you go from here? What's next?"

"I guess…I'm moving."

CHAPTER FIVE

LYDIA HAD NO idea what she should bring with her. Obviously, she wasn't going to bring her furniture. She was going to have to forward her mail. She would need clothes, but mostly early fall clothes. Maybe a winter jacket. Definitely nothing for the late-coming spring. Because they weren't going to be married that long.

She was standing in her living room pondering these things when there was a knock on her door.

She wondered if it was Sadie with more mochas, or perhaps that was more of a fantasy than a wonderment.

"Just a second." She turned, moving to the door and jerking it open without checking to see who was on the other side. "Hi," she said, trying to ignore the fluttering in her stomach when she came face-to-midchest with Colton.

He was so tall. It was borderline obscene. Tall and broad and extremely muscular. Utterly masculine, with just a few days growth of gold-tinted whiskers covering his square jaw. And it made her feel a little bit regretful that she didn't have any memories about the interior of his pants.

No. No, she was not going to go there.

"I just came to see if you needed help with anything," he said, stuffing his hands into his pockets.

"I'm fine," she said, very aware of the fact that she didn't have everything together at all.

"So, are you about ready?"

"I mean, I'm ready kind of. Mostly. Also, you didn't have to come and pick me up."

"Sorry, I'm a little rusty on the protocol of how exactly you help your fake wife move into your house for a temporary period of time."

"Yeah," she said, "we may have to pioneer that."

"Do you need any help?"

Absurdly, she was ridiculously edgy about the idea of him coming into her house. Possibly because when all was said and done, she kind of wanted to go back to life as it had been before she had decided to make a Colton-sized mistake.

"No. I have it. Just wait there. You can sit in…" She didn't really want him sitting in her porch chair, either. But denying him a spot to wait was a little bit shrewish. "You can sit in the chair," she said finally.

"Okay," he replied, looking rather like he thought she was insane.

Well, maybe she was. But he had married her. So, that didn't say anything good about him.

"Just a—" She held up a finger. "Just a second."

She slammed the door shut and turned back around, looking at her half-packed duffel bag. She picked it up, turning quickly into her bedroom, then grabbing some clothes that were hanging in the closet and stuffing them into the bag. They didn't fit. She was going to have to get a suitcase.

Several suitcases, probably.

What had she been thinking? She had been thoroughly convinced that this was some kind of overnight trip, and she was going to pack a bag, and then she was going to return to her house as though nothing had happened. She was moving in with him. That was completely different. It was… Okay, now she felt like she was going crazy.

"I was tired of waiting out on the porch. I thought the entire point was that we minimize gossip."

She turned around, starting when she saw him standing in the doorway. "I did not invite you in. I, in fact, did the opposite of that."

"Do you really want people to start talking about how your husband was standing on the porch looking lonely only hours after your wedding?"

"That's so dramatic," she said, attempting to look less perturbed than she felt.

"You're the one with a lot of concern about appearances."

"You're not…disinterested in appearances, yourself. I have to find a suitcase."

"I thought you were almost ready."

"Okay, let's not stand around acting like you would be fully on top of the procedure for going about all of this. I admit, I was feeling a little shortsighted. Like, I was kind of thinking of packing an overnight bag. And then I realized that we're going to be living together for a few months."

She could have sworn that Colton paled slightly when she spoke the words. "More like a month and a half."

"Semantics. But we have to stay together until after the election. And presumably you need some time to allow your mother to adjust… Or whatever it is exactly that you're waiting for her to do."

"I would like to avoid giving her a mental break-down," he said, sounding exasperated.

"Right. Well, I don't really know your mother, so I don't really understand the situation. But I do understand that it's kind of complicated. But all that means is that it's not going to be a quick weekend stay at your place. And maybe I was in denial about that."

"It's not that big of a deal," he said, while his expression said something else entirely.

"No," she said, "not at all. We just have to learn to coexist." She opened up her closet and began to rummage around, digging in the bottom until she produced her suitcase, which she hadn't used in years.

"How hard can it be?"

Neither of them spoke the obvious, which was that they had a difficult enough time coexisting when they lived in the same small town, let alone the same house.

"I'm sure it will be super easy," she said, hefting her suitcase up onto the bed and throwing it open. "Super, super easy." She continued muttering as she walked into the bathroom.

She looked around at all of her things. Her makeup, put away neatly in the dark purple case that she kept on the left-hand corner of the counter. Her flat iron, snapped into its sparkly holder, which kept it and its cord carefully contained. Then she turned and looked at the shower, at the carefully organized caddy that contained her shampoo, conditioner and oil treatments.

Everything was right where she wanted it to be. Organized exactly the way it made sense to her. She didn't have to compromise. Didn't have to modify herself to be different for anyone. Didn't have to contort so that she wouldn't be in the way.

Darn it, she liked having her own space. Needed it, even. And maybe she was being really, really dramatic about the fact that she was going to be sharing a house with somebody for a couple of months. Maybe.

"It's a vacation," she muttered, picking up her various items. "A vacation on a ranch. With a surly roommate that will maybe cook breakfast?"

She walked out of the bathroom, back into the bedroom, where Colton was still standing in the doorway, his arms crossed over his broad chest.

"I thought you came in to help me."

"You didn't give me a directive. Did you want me to just aimlessly go through your things and try to decide what you needed?"

She made a scoffing noise in the back of her throat. "Obviously not."

Silence stretched between them, along with a thick band of tension that seemed to wrap itself around her, more specifically, her throat. She found it difficult to breathe all of a sudden. For some reason, the air seemed to reduce around them. For some reason, she was unbearably conscious of the scent of the soap that he used, and just how familiar it was.

It was a reminder. A reminder that—whether she remembered it or not—she had absolutely smelled it on his skin before. Her brain didn't remember, but right now, her body seemed to.

"Do you have a food processor?" she asked, because talking about food processors seemed as good a method as any for diffusing the unwanted crackle of tension in the room.

"Of course."

"There's no *of course* about that. A lot of men wouldn't have one."

"Well, I have a housekeeper. She cooks a lot of my food."

Lydia's eyebrows shot up. "A housekeeper?"

"You feel a little less victimized now, don't you?"

"No. Thoroughly victimized." She added as many clothes as she could to her bag, followed by shoes.

"It isn't like you can't come back to the house. You can make vague noises about how you intend to rent it out if anyone asks. But we'll never get around to it."

"You know, I hear some people live in cities, where nobody knows their name, or pays attention to what they're doing."

The corner of his mouth curved upward. "What must that be like?"

"I don't know. Do you have a juicer? Because I juice." She had juiced twice. Once right after she had bought the juicer, and another time when her pants had refused to zip after the holidays last year. But then, she had just bought new pants because juice with kale in it was an abomination.

Colton treated her to a baleful look. "Nobody juices."

She scoffed. "Well, okay, I don't do it every day. But I *do* stop at the store on the way to work and buy a bottle of juice sometimes."

"Do you?" he asked, his tone rife with skepticism.

"I mean, I don't always have time to stop on the way to work. But I do stop at the store on the way home. For a bottle. Of wine. But it's almost grape juice."

"I have wine, and several corkscrews. So why don't you just leave your juicer here."

She wanted to run through a list of yet more appliances that she would probably never use in his house, because she wanted to do something to delay the inevitable.

"Did you get Natalie's things out of your house?" she asked.

"I paid some movers to come by this morning and take care of it. I think they took it back to her parents' house."

"Is that where she is?"

"You know, I didn't make it my mission to figure out where the woman who left me at the altar was. But, seeing as she's your friend, you might know."

Lydia swallowed. "I didn't exactly think she would want to hear from the bridesmaid who ended up marrying the groom."

He laughed. "Coward."

"So are you."

"No, I just don't think she's my problem anymore. That woman is a project. And I did my very best to make her happy."

Lydia should not feel at all like she had to defend her friend. Natalie had abandoned Colton at the altar. Not only that, the relationship between the two of them had been borderline toxic during the planning of the wedding. The only reason that Lydia had continued to be involved was for appearances. Which is what her entire life was beginning to feel like it came down to.

Still, Natalie had been the first friend she had made in Copper Ridge. And things might have been rocky in the ensuing years, but she still didn't think that Colton had a right to act like he had no stake in what had happened. Natalie cared more about appearances than Lydia did. Possibly more than Lydia and Colton combined.

"Right. You had nothing to do with her running out on the wedding."

"I told you, I was totally shocked."

"Totally. Completely. There were no indicators that things were perhaps not completely healthy?"

"I didn't know. If I'd known I would not have submitted to standing up in front of the entire town with my dick in my hand."

Heat flooded her face, which was stupid, because he was being crass on purpose, and not talking about his actual...that. Still, it forced her mind there. And that, in combination with the scent of the soap, was a little too real.

"Fine. I'm just saying. It's clear to me the relationship wasn't perfect. And I sincerely doubt that she's the only one at fault here."

"Oh, are you a relationship expert? Does that mean that this marriage is getting in the way of a close, intimate relationship you're in?"

She shot him her deadliest glare. "Yes. The relationship I hold most dear. The one I share with my personal space."

"Well, as the more experienced party, I'll just say this. There is no justification for leaving someone at the altar."

"Did you cheat on her?" She didn't know what was driving her just now, why she wanted to push him. But then, that was kind of the story of her entire history with Colton. From the moment they had been introduced they had pushed each other's buttons. And that didn't happen to her. Everyone liked her. She was diplomatic by nature. It was one reason she was going into politics.

More than that, she just liked people.

But him, she didn't like. She just hadn't. Not from the first moment they had been introduced. They had been at Ace's, and Natalie had been chomping at the bit to introduce Lydia to the man she had been dating for a couple of months. It was serious, according to Natalie, so it was time to see if he passed the friend test.

She could remember it clearly because she'd had such a visceral, intense reaction to the sight of him. Like a hand had wrapped itself around her spinal cord, squeezing hard, tension climbing up from that point and up to the base of her neck.

"This is my boyfriend, Colton West." Natalie smiled like she was holding a winning lottery ticket.

Lydia knew the name Colton West. Everyone in Copper Ridge did. But she'd never met him before. And she hadn't realized he was quite so good-looking.

Lydia stuck out her hand and he grasped it tightly. Immediate discomfort rolled over her like a wave and she let go of him, taking a step back.

"I'm Lydia," she said. "Nice to meet you."

Her throat felt scratchy and dry and she felt uncertain. Insecure. She never felt uncertain or insecure.

The corners of his mouth had turned up slightly before flatlining again. "You too."

She attempted conversation with him all night, only to have every topic killed after a couple of one word answers.

She wandered to the bar, hoping to get another diet soda, since she was driving. And after placing her order she turned and brushed right up against Colton West's hard chest.

Something raced through her that felt a whole lot

like an electric shock, and his already stoic expression turned to granite.

"Had too much to drink?"

"I never drink too much."

"Then I guess you just need to be a little more careful."

Anger spiked through her, canceling out that electrified feeling. "I'm always careful." *She didn't need to be scolded, not by anyone.*

"Except for now."

"Maybe you should make sure you aren't standing so close to people."

He looked slightly stricken. "I wasn't close to you."

"Close enough for me to run into you when I turned around." *What was happening to her? She didn't talk to people this way. She took a deep, calming breath.* "For which I'm sorry."

"Good."

He brushed past her and went to the bar. And the two proceeded to ignore each other for the rest of the night.

He had been arrogant and impossible from the moment she'd met him.

Yes, she liked people. Most of them. Not so much him.

"No," he said now, through gritted teeth, "I did not cheat on her."

"I just think that…"

"I think that you should maybe acknowledge the fact that you don't actually know very much about my relationship with Natalie. You know how she is about appearances. She kept you in her wedding when she was pretty angry with you."

"That's just somebody standing next to you at a wedding. You're the person she was supposed to be married to for the rest of her life. So of course she would go through with keeping me in the wedding to minimize stress and gossip. I don't think there's an equivalent to the two."

"It doesn't matter. It doesn't matter why she left."

"It doesn't? I feel like I would need to know why my fiancé ditched me at the altar. But to each his own."

"Well, when you get ditched at the altar you can make that decision for yourself."

She sputtered, and he ignored her indignant rage, moving over to the bed to zip the suitcase shut before picking it up, throwing it over his shoulder, then grabbing the duffel bag in what was definitely an over-the-top display of masculine strength.

"Are you ready?"

"I guess so."

"Do you know where I live?"

It occurred to Lydia then that Natalie had never once invited her out to Colton's. The two of them had lived together for the past eight months and yet she had never been to Colton's house.

"No," she said, knowing she sounded slightly mystified. She felt slightly mystified.

"What?"

"Okay, I think it's pretty safe to say that Natalie doesn't do interpersonal relationships the way everyone else does."

"And what makes you say that?"

Lydia lifted a shoulder. "She never invited me out to your house. She came over to mine. Well, until I announced my bid for mayor."

"I think that proves my point pretty well. But it's nice

to know that you were only willing to take it on board when the focus was moved to your relationship."

"Whatever. I'll follow you to your house. Just load my stuff into the trunk of my car."

"Saying please wouldn't kill you, Lydia."

She just sort of stared at him, feeling that band of tension stretch even tighter between them. It was impossible not to notice the way his forearm muscles shifted as he worked to keep his hold on all of her luggage. The way the muscles in his broad shoulders looked even more pronounced when bearing all that weight.

Tightness crept down her spine, reminiscent of that feeling she'd had the first moment she'd met him. A kind of deep discomfort that overtook her entire body. Like something other than the normal rules of physics was suddenly in charge. And none of it made any sense. She couldn't anticipate what she might feel next, or how she might respond if he moved just a little bit, just a fraction closer.

Couldn't decide if she was angry at him, or if she wanted to trace the firm line of his jaw to see if it was as sharp as it looked. To feel that light beard beneath her fingertips, to see if it was as rough as it looked.

She swallowed hard, trying to ignore the insanity currently crawling through her. "Let's go."

"Please," he said, his blue eyes glinting.

He was so hardheaded. Saying please was good manners. That was just the truth. But she did not like being told what to do. "I can carry my own things," she said.

He shrugged, setting her suitcase roughly on the ground, followed by the duffel bag. "Suit yourself."

"Really?" she asked.

"It's that difficult for you to say please?"

"You're being a jerk."

The corner of his mouth curved upward. "And you're being petulant."

She growled, reaching out and grabbing hold of her suitcase, clinging to the handle as she hefted her duffel bag up and looped it over her shoulder. Then she began to walk toward the front door, her every step weighted by her things.

She turned and looked behind her, saw Colton standing there, his muscular arms crossed over his broad chest, one dark brow raised. Then she turned away from him, continuing on toward the door.

"Oh, for God's sake," he muttered, walking toward her before taking her suitcase out of her grip. "I'm not going to make you carry that bag down to the car."

He went on ahead of her, throwing open the front door and taking the porch steps two at a time out to where her little red sedan was parked.

She busied herself locking her door, and trying to ignore the weird sinking feeling in her stomach. Like she was leaving something behind. Like things were changing in a way she would never be able to change back. Maybe because the last time she had left her place, she hadn't gone back.

But that was dramatic. She was going ten minutes down the road.

She turned and looked to the side, at her little slice of ocean view, taking in a deep breath.

"In addition to not saying please, are you also going to leave me standing here with your bag for the next hour?"

She shot him a deadly glare. "I'm saying goodbye to my house."

"As mentioned, you're welcome to come back to your house at any time. You just can't inhabit it. The neighbors would talk."

"And you don't think they're going to talk about you standing out here looking at me like I'm a particularly distasteful vegetable you just found on your plate?"

"Yes," he said, a smile curving his lips upward. "You, Lydia Carpenter, are my broccoli."

"I guess that makes you my peaches."

"Who doesn't like peaches? That's ridiculous."

"I don't." She headed down the stairs, digging in her purse for her keys. "It isn't ridiculous to dislike something."

"I mean, you dislike something sweet, delicious, and almost universally enjoyed by the rest of the world. But sure."

She scowled, pushing the button that popped her trunk, breezing past him. She threw the duffel bag inside, then stood, looking at him expectantly. He put the suitcase in and closed it, a little too roughly for her liking.

"I think maybe peaches are not as awesome as they think they are."

She sniffed, getting into her car and starting the engine. Then she waited for Colton to get into his truck and pull away from the curb.

She did her best to subdue her panic by focusing on the details of town as they drove down Main Street. Rebecca Bear was outside the Trading Post, her knick-knack store, closing shop for the day, taking down the American flag and bringing in the plants that were out on the doorstep.

Cassie Caldwell had already closed The Grind for

the day, the little Open sign dim in the large picture window. Most businesses on Main closed early. Copper Ridge wasn't known for its exciting nightlife. But that was one of the things that Lydia loved about it. It was traditional. It was friendly. Well, for the most part.

It was true that a lot of people moved to a small town because they wanted to be left alone. So far from being the Thomas Kinkade painting that a lot of people imagined, small-town life was full of challenging dynamics. But overall, people were more relaxed and in general they were nicer than in big cities.

A difficult commute in Copper Ridge might mean that a deer ran out in front of you, rather than getting stuck in any kind of bottleneck traffic.

As she let these thoughts wash over her, she felt the stress of the past few minutes with Colton begin to drain away.

Yeah, essentially, this whole marriage would be her lying back and thinking of Copper Ridge.

That was why she was doing this. For her position in the community that she had come to love more than anything else.

The route to Colton's house wound out of town on a dirt road and into the mountains. She had to admit, she liked that. If there was one thing that she loved at least as much as the bustling main street of town, it was the thick, dark green silence of the mountains that surrounded Copper Ridge.

Colton stopped his truck in front of a large wrought-iron gate with an ornate design on it. A bear, pine trees and what looked like a river were skillfully shaped into the metal. She wondered if that was the work of Sam McCormack. She imagined it was. The McCormack brothers were two of the most skilled metalworkers in town, if not in the whole state. They were also built from all that time spent doing physical labor.

Lydia had been working with them to arrange tours of their forge for visitors to the town. She was always on the lookout for new ways to entice tourists to come to Copper Ridge, and along with that, ways to improve income for small businesses.

That was one of the reasons she and Sadie Garrett had grown so close. Sadie hosted a lot of events at her bed-and-breakfast, which had become one of the most popular places for people to stay. The whole Garrett Ranch put on a Fourth of July picnic that had become a can't-miss event for Copper Ridge and surrounding communities.

Yes, everything she did, she did for her town.

Colton entered a code on the brick pillar next to the gate, and it swung open. She drove in behind him, trying not to feel too awed by the sight of his house. She had known the West family had a compelling amount of money, but this was evidence she hadn't exactly been confronted with yet.

The simplistic description of Colton's home was log cabin. Because it was built entirely of logs. But that did the large, impressive structure a disservice.

If it was rustic, it was in a very intentional way.

It had a green metal roof, built to withstand whatever weather was dumped upon it, and a wide covered porch with some wrought-iron details that echoed the gate they had just driven through.

The door was a dark wood, the natural grain and beauty emphasized by a glossy stain that didn't disguise any of the imperfections. It was beautiful, but Lydia had a difficult time imagining Natalie living here. Rustic, Natalie was not.

Lydia supposed that love made you do crazy things. She wouldn't really know.

She parked her car and got out, attempting to minimize the impressed expression on her face.

"Home sweet home," Colton said, his tone dry.

"I feel like I can deal with it."

He arched a brow. "Compared to that little shoe box house you live in?"

Heat stung her cheeks, anger a reckless and unreasonable tide inside of her. "My house is not a shoe box. It's small. And it's perfect." *And it's mine.*

"I have an idea," he said. "Why don't we practice talking to each other like we aren't enemies. Your house is fine. And mine…"

"Is fine if you're into luxury and custom details," she said grudgingly.

Why was it so hard to…unclench around him?

She had the feeling the answer was buried somewhere in the night she couldn't remember. Because she most definitely hadn't been *clenched* then.

"From you, I'll take that as a compliment."

Oh great, now he felt like he was on the moral high ground. Now he felt like he had won the exchange.

She followed him up the steps. "It's beautiful. Literally one of the most gorgeous homes I have ever seen. And the fact that Natalie left you at the altar has now become one of the great mysteries of our time. Because she didn't only leave you, she left this house."

He treated her to a baleful look. Then he unlocked the door and pushed inside. She followed him, completely unable to look unimpressed now. Because, as glorious as the exterior of the home was, the interior was even more amazing. The front room was open, a large, vaulted ceiling adding the impression of endless space. Which paired nicely with the beautiful light cascading into the floor-to-ceiling windows that offered a view of the dense green timber that surrounded his property.

"It's so… There are so many trees. How do you have animals and a barn?"

"They're up the road. There's a field, a clearing."

"I didn't realize you had such a big spread. Natalie never mentioned it."

"Natalie didn't really care. I don't think she loved being up out of town. In truth, she probably would enjoy living in Portland better than living in Copper Ridge. But outside of Copper Ridge, neither my name nor hers carries very much weight."

Lydia laughed. "Well, she wouldn't like that."

"Where does your family live?"

She was taken aback by the question. "Why?"

"Because. It's a funny thing. Natalie and I are a product of our family name. I built what I have from what my dad started. I'm a West. For better or for worse. For Natalie it's the same. Her father has been the mayor since she was born. We have roots here that go all the way down. But you…you haven't been here all that long, and you've made your mark on every part of the place. I've never known anyone else to do that."

She swallowed, her throat getting tight. She didn't really like talking about her family, but she knew that avoidance was a lot more trouble than working out the most straightforward answer. Just enough information to answer without getting into the details was always better.

"I was raised in Seattle. Went to school there, was born there. My family is still there. It's a beautiful city, but I like Copper Ridge because it's small. It's more personal. I guess I'm a little bit of an old lady trapped in a younger body. Most people that move to Copper Ridge do it to retire, I did it to work. To feel part of something. You don't get that in bigger places."

"But your family is there. Are you close to your parents?"

She gritted her teeth. "Not especially."

"I seem to be close to mine. Even though it isn't easy. My mom is…well, she's a project. And the whole bastard child thing kind of put a damper on my relationship with my dad."

Lydia's heart twisted. For whatever reason, they seemed to be having a cease-fire right now, and she was going to go ahead and honor it. "I bet. Were you close before?"

"I'm the only son he has around. So yeah, I guess we were." He shook his head. "I'm not the only son he has around. He has Jack Monaghan. He just spent thirty-five years ignoring him."

"Family is terrible."

"You think so?"

"I just told you I don't see my parents who live one state over. Family is a terrible, complicated thing."

"On that we can agree." He lifted a hand. "But, we're never going to agree about peaches."

"I'm okay with that."

"I'll grab your things, and then you can start settling in."

Colton headed outside, leaving Lydia alone with her thoughts. She turned a circle in the room, examining the fine details of the space. The rich fabrics on the couch and chair, the rustic coffee table that appeared to be made out of the same logs that had been used to form the bulk of the house, and a piece of sheet metal. Again, something that looked old, but probably cost more than her last paycheck.

She was going to have to live here with Colton, live here and not spend the next few months tripping over him. Not spend the next month clashing with him. She felt like she was being crushed down into a little ball, and that made it difficult to breathe.

She was imagining spending the next few months tiptoeing through this space, doing her best to make sure her footsteps didn't sound on the hardwood floor.

It reminded her too much of other things. Too much of her childhood home.

Of being the least important person in a space. She swallowed hard, shaking her head, brushing her hair out of her eyes. No, she wasn't going to do that. Because she didn't do that anymore. She had driven into Copper Ridge at the age of twenty-two and started carving out niches for herself all over the place. Had made sure that she had effected change in the place, that she didn't tiptoe, that she wasn't quiet.

She wasn't about to behave any other way. Not for anyone. And certainly not for Colton West.

CHAPTER SIX

SHE WAS IN his house. He could feel her moving around.
Metaphorically. He blamed the fact that Lydia Carpenter
was terminally uptight. And he could feel that tightness
following her around wherever she went.

He could feel it in the air the moment he had walked
in the place after tending to his horses. He kicked his
boots off, pushing them up against the wall by the door
before walking into the living area. She had started a fire
in the fireplace, which was actually considerate, but he
was going to go ahead and take it as an invasion instead.

He had a feeling that the key to sanity when it came
to enduring Lydia's presence was to keep focusing on
how irritating she was. Not that it was difficult to do.

The issue was that her ass also looked nice in the
tight pencil skirt she was wearing today. He had the
passing thought that maybe looking at it could be an excuse to make a word association game. She was a tight
ass, with a tight ass. And if he looked at it, he could remember that...

Okay, not even he was buying that.

This entire situation was a ridiculous mess. She didn't
want to be here any more than he wanted her here, but
there wasn't much of anything they could do about it.

His phone buzzed in his pocket and he took it out,

grimacing when he saw it was his mother. He couldn't ignore her. Not given the circumstances.

"Hello?"

"You haven't called me since you got back into town."

He took a deep breath. "No. Sorry. But I had to get back to work, and I have the small matter of moving Natalie's things out of my place."

"I'm so sorry about what happened," his mother said, clearly not so much sorry because of his feelings, but terribly sorry about the wedding being ruined.

"Me too. But, for whatever reason, Natalie felt like she couldn't go through with it. And all in all it's better that she decide that before the marriage, isn't it?"

"I suppose so," she said.

He could tell that she wasn't at all convinced divorce would have been worse than a very public event like what had just happened. Fifty percent of marriages ended in divorce. The statistic of grooms left at the altar was likely much lower.

He heard light footsteps on the wooden floor, and looked up. Lydia was standing in the doorway, looking at him like she was a deer caught in the high beams. For a second, he had forgotten she was here.

He'd lived with Natalie for eight months. Any other time he'd heard footsteps in the house at this hour he would have expected to see Natalie appear. But Natalie wasn't here. Lydia was.

It was jarring.

In two days, his life had changed completely. He had been planning on being a husband. He had lived with one woman, and now he suddenly lived with another. He supposed he was a husband still. But not really the kind he had planned on being.

"Colton?" For a moment, he had forgotten he was on the phone with his mother.

"Yes, I'm sorry, I just spaced out for a second."

There was the small matter of Lydia, whom he had not told his mother about. But Sierra and Madison knew. Of course, he had made them promise not to tell, but his sisters never did what he told them to.

"Your father has been in a rage ever since it happened. He's dropping all of his support from Richard Bailey's campaign."

Colton looked back up at Lydia. "That's interesting."

"It's caused waves at the country club, or so my friends tell me."

Colton had no doubt it had. Probably bigger waves than when whispers had started moving through that Nathan West had an illegitimate child. Political contributions were a much bigger deal. Anyway, he imagined that particular group had several bastard children to their names.

"I'm sure it did."

"Your father is humiliated by all of this."

Colton closed his eyes, sucking a deep breath in through his teeth. Of course his failed wedding was a source of embarrassment to his father.

"I'm sorry for his humiliation."

"He's never had any trouble with you before, Colton."

There really wasn't a response to that. "Why don't we meet for lunch tomorrow?"

There was no good way to break the news of his *other* wedding to his mother. Certainly not over the phone. So, in person it would be.

She sighed. "That would be nice."

"Let's meet at Beaches around noon. I'll see you at

your usual table." He ended the phone call quickly after that, then looked up at Lydia again. "We're meeting my mother for lunch tomorrow."

"What if I have plans?"

"Cancel them. It's very important to the health of your marriage that you do this for me."

"I'm not really all that invested in the health of my marriage. In fact, if it were a horse I would probably take it out back behind the barn and shoot it."

"You would not shoot a horse, wounded or otherwise."

"Fine," she said, exasperated. "I'm much more likely to feed it sugar cubes and pat it until the vet arrives. But that's a *literal* horse. This was a metaphorical horse, wherein the horse represented our marriage. And that horse I would shoot."

He threw his phone down onto the couch, then followed its trajectory, plopping down in front of the fireplace. "Did you start a fire?"

She arched a brow. "No. The elves did it."

"I didn't know you came with elves."

"There are a lot of things you don't know about me."

He appraised her slowly, watching the color rise in her cheeks. He couldn't remember the last time a woman had responded to him in this way. Sure, women found him attractive, but he wasn't the kind of guy to engage in flirtations. He did long-term relationships.

He had a high school sweetheart he'd parted ways with the first year of college, then a girl he had dated until graduation had sent them their different ways. After that, he had been in relationships off and on with women who were practical. Suitable. Potential wife material.

He didn't do one-night stands. He didn't do…whatever *this* was.

But he couldn't deny there was something a little bit fascinating about it.

"Actually," he said, giving in to the completely reckless desire to heighten the color in her cheeks even further, "you don't have all that many secrets from me."

She stiffened, her dark eyes going wide. "You don't remember."

"Maybe I do," he said, smiling at her for effect.

"No," she said, narrowing her eyes, "you don't. I know you don't."

"How can you be so sure?"

"Because I can tell. I can…read it. If you had seen me naked I would be able to see it in your eyes."

He lifted his hand, rubbing it slowly over his chin. "But I have seen you naked, Lydia. We both know that."

"No, we don't. For all you know I got undressed underneath the covers. Actually, maybe nothing happened. We don't know."

Heat began to gather in his chest, a ball of fire that spread downward, a streak of flame that combusted in his gut. "I know. Trust me, I know."

He did, dammit. As much as he wanted to forget. Last night had been a study in torture. He'd been at the mercy of vague impressions of memory he couldn't quite gain a hold on.

Soft fingertips on his skin, faint, floral perfume mingling with the smell of whiskey and chocolate. Because they had eaten chocolate. He couldn't remember eating it, but he could remember tasting it on her tongue, mingling with the rich alcohol.

So no, he didn't remember what happened. Not totally. Only enough to wake up this morning with a hard-on that wouldn't quit.

He was suffering. She might as well suffer, too.

She was just so damn prickly all the time, and those prickles never failed to embed themselves beneath his skin. The one exception was the night of the wedding that wasn't.

Colton was going to get blind drunk and he didn't care. He never got drunk. But he'd never been left at the altar before either, so that seemed fair enough.

"I'm glad we decided to come here."

His muscles tensed as that familiar voice rolled over him. For a moment, he'd forgotten about his unexpected companion.

Then he turned and that already hollow feeling in his stomach turned into a yawning pit.

Lydia was still in that ridiculous bridesmaid dress, her dark hair curling and falling loosely around her shoulders, a little bunch of flowers holding part of it back. Just the sight of her was enraging. Like she'd brought his aborted wedding in with her.

But there was something else to that feeling, too. Something dark and hungry that he never liked to think about. Something that only ever roared to life when Lydia was around.

It made him angry at the best of times. But it was the worst of times now, and he was halfway to wasted. That combination made it something else entirely.

"Do you feel sorry for me?" he asked.

"Well, kind of. But really, only a cold-hearted jerk wouldn't."

"Feel guilty for anything?"

"What?" she asked.

"Did you have any idea she was going to do this?"

"No," Lydia said. *"She never said anything to me. And I had absolutely no idea she was going to stand you up."*

"You sound upset."

"I am. No one deserves that. I know that we don't—" She took a deep breath. *"I know that we haven't always seen eye to eye. Or ever seen eye to eye. But that doesn't mean I thought she should leave you like that."*

"And that's why you told me to ditch the reception? Why you came out after me? Out of...all of the people at the wedding, you're the one who came?"

"I couldn't stop thinking about how bad you must feel." The words made his stomach bottom out. She frowned. *"Do not let that go to your head. I also can't stop thinking about those ASPCA commercials with sad dogs."*

"So this is all because of your overdeveloped sense of pity?"

She tucked her hair behind her ear, her shoulder brushing his, sending an unwelcome bolt of lightning straight through him. *"Mostly, I just think people shouldn't be left alone when they're sad."*

"If you expect me to cry you're going to be sadly disappointed. I intend to get hammered." He picked up the shot glass in front of him and held it out toward her. *"If you want to join me in that, you're welcome to."*

She hesitated. He expected her to get that pinched look on her face. To lecture him.

Instead, she reached out, grabbing hold of the shot glass. Her fingers brushed his, and he felt that all the way down to his dick.

Then she put the glass to her lips, her tongue touching the rim. He felt that, too.

She tilted it back, taking a long swallow, gasping when she set it back down on the counter. "All right," she said. *"Let's do it."*

He was supposed to be a married man tonight. Committed and firmly arrived at the place his straight-and-narrow path had been leading him.

But his intended bride hadn't showed up.

Suddenly all of the tension he'd felt from the first time he'd met Lydia Carpenter exploded inside of him. He wanted her fingers on him. Wanted her tongue on him.

Tonight was supposed to be the finish line. But it hadn't been.

Now he wanted to make it something else entirely.

That was when the memory got fuzzy. His night to remember, his night of rebellion, had turned into a completely forgotten night with far-reaching consequences.

That figured.

"Back to the topic at hand," she said, her tone authoritarian, arch, as though she had been reading his thoughts, "why exactly do you need me to join you for lunch with your mother?"

"Because. I'm not going to tell her that we got married over the phone. And I need to tell her before it makes it back to her through the rumor mill. Because it will."

"All right. Though I'm not sure how it hasn't already."

"I'm not, either. Mainly, I imagine it's because she hasn't left the house in a few days. It's possible my dad knows, but even if he does, he might not have gotten around to telling her. I don't think they talk much."

"Had I known that this was how the West family

conducted their marriages I might have gotten on board with this sooner. It sounds exactly like the kind of marriage the two of us could have. Never speaking. Never touching."

Touching. That word pushed to the back of his mind. Ruffled the gauzy veil that had been drawn over the night they had spent in Las Vegas.

He could feel it. That's how strong it was. Could feel delicate fingertips wrapping around him. It hit him hard, left him breathless.

"Not never," he said, his voice sounding rough to his own ears.

"Are you going to be a lecherous tool bag when we have lunch with your mother?"

"If she takes enough pills before we order she won't notice if I am." He nearly winced at his own words. He was just being an ass now.

Lydia frowned. "I've met your mother at different fund-raising luncheons. She seems…nice."

"I'm not sure that's the word I would use. But I love my mother. She's been through enough. And yeah, it's easy for me to make dry comments about how she does and doesn't cope, but the truth is it worries me."

"I'm sure finding out that your father had an illegitimate child with someone was hard on her."

He leaned back, closing his eyes and resting his head on the back of the couch. "That was just the latest hard thing."

"Oh."

"I have a brother." He opened his eyes again, just so he could get a look at her expression.

"Oh," she said, her hands clasped in front of her, twitching nervously. "I didn't know that."

"I figured you didn't. Most people do, since they've lived here their whole lives. You're that rare outsider."

That made her frown. "I'm not an outsider."

Yet again, he'd managed to divert her right when he'd cut open a vein of ancient West history. And again, he was going to go with it rather than continuing to talk about family stuff. "You aren't really a local."

Color flooded her cheeks, except this time, it was angry. "This is my home. I have lived here for the past eight years. And I damn sure am a local, Colton West. I'm running for mayor. I don't think you can be more… Copper Ridgian than that."

"That doesn't make you a local. Being a *local* makes you a local."

"Why are you so invested in this?"

"Why are *you*?"

She frowned. "That isn't your business. We might be sharing space, but we don't have to share secrets and braid each other's hair."

"The only kind of slumber party we're going to have is a repeat performance of our wedding night, Lydia, so I would be careful what you suggest."

The moment the words left his lips, he regretted them. He had no intention of ever touching her again. He just wanted to get a rise out of her.

"I would be careful what you said, Colton," she returned, her words clipped. "Unless of course you want to get punched in the face."

"Are you resorting to playground tactics? Are you going to steal my jacket and make me chase you to get it back next?" He pushed up from the couch, taking a step toward her. "All to get me to pay attention to you?"

"Please," she said, the word coming out a disbelieving laugh. "I do not want you to chase me."

"Fine. Lunch. Tomorrow. Don't make me chase you."

Those eyes, brown, shot through with gold, glistening like whiskey in a shot glass, gazed straight into him as though they were wishing him a swift and painful death. "Fine," she parroted him, her tone so crystal he thought it might cut him. "I'll see you then. Beaches. Noon."

"You'll probably see me before then."

"I'm tired. I'm probably going to go to bed."

"It's eight o'clock."

She crossed her arms, straightening her posture. "So I may not have demonstrated this over the course of the past few days, but I am actually a very responsible person. Early to bed. Early to rise."

"I think I might have heard my grandmother say that once."

"She was a wise woman. Good night."

And Lydia turned on her heel and walked out of the room, leaving him alone with the fire, the memories and a vague feeling of dissatisfaction that he was not going to do anything to alleviate.

SHE WAS STARVING. Starving and trying to pretend that she was going to get some sleep in her current state. She had skipped eating dinner because she had just wanted to barricade herself in her own space and get some distance between herself and Colton, and now she was made of grumbling and regret.

She rolled out of bed, tugging her T-shirt down in place.

This room was so different than her own. The bed had a rather plain comforter on it, a deep green with no extraneous details. The bed itself was fashioned from natural wood, in keeping with the theme and the rest of the house.

Again, she could see no piece of Natalie here. Couldn't begin to imagine her friend—or rather, her former friend—inhabiting this place.

But then, she would never have been able to imagine herself living here, and yet, here she was.

"Maybe this is what he does," she muttered. "Maybe he just marries people and spirits them off to his house."

Well, in fairness, he hadn't *married* Natalie.

That she knew of. She supposed it was possible that he had yet another secret marriage. Though that would make theirs illegal. Which would potentially alleviate some problems.

Lydia Carpenter: Victim of Bigamy Scandal was a lot less damning than Lydia Carpenter: Quickie Marriage and Divorce with her Ex-Friend's Almost Husband.

Of course, the actual headline was about to be Lydia Carpenter: Found Dead of Starvation in Colton West's Home if she didn't find some food.

It was after ten, so she could only hope that Colton had retired to his room. She hadn't heard him move around for a while.

She crept out of the bedroom, walking on soft socked feet into the kitchen. She opened up his fridge and nearly sagged with relief.

It was full of food. Food in neat little Tupperware containers, likely provided by his housekeeper. Okay, that she could get used to. Sharing space with that…that *man*, was a different story entirely.

He was just entirely too there. Too big. Oh yeah, and too much of an asshole.

She thought back to the way he had been winding her up. The way he had looked at her with that confident gleam in his eye, the smile curving his mouth as he had told her that he remembered what they had done that night.

He didn't remember.

She took out a container that seemed to be full of enchiladas and huffed as she shut the door. "He doesn't remember," she muttered into the empty space, reiterating it herself.

"You don't think so?"

She jumped, and an elegant shriek escaped her lips. She whirled around, pressing the container tightly to her chest, the cold from the fridge bleeding through her top. "What are you doing?"

"I heard an intruder in my kitchen."

She waved a hand. "Not an intruder. Just me."

"So, that all depends on your definition of *intruder*."

"Oh no," she grumped, "don't act like I *chose* to move in here."

He folded his arms over his broad chest, leaning against the door frame. "You didn't? Because I seem to recall you being deeply concerned about appearances."

"I was *compelled* to move in. Compelled by the expectations of the community. And your family, I might add."

"Mostly your own ambition. What do you have there?"

"It appears to be enchiladas. I'm hoping they're chicken."

"You're in luck. I think they are. And my housekeeper makes amazing enchiladas, so it was a very good choice."

She suddenly realized she hadn't exactly asked for permission to have access to his food. She also realized that she couldn't exactly live with him and not contribute to the cost of groceries and electricity. There were so many logistics. Logistics that were just now dawning on her, because she was still overwhelmed by the whole moving in with him in the first place thing.

"Can I have the enchiladas?" she asked, sounding much more hopeful and feeble than she'd intended.

He pushed off the door frame. "Don't look at me like that."

"Like what?"

"Like you're afraid I'm going to snatch the Mexican food out of your hand. I might be kind of a dick, Lydia, but even I have my limits."

She eyed him warily as she crossed the room, popping the lid on the container slightly before sticking it into the microwave. "It's nice to know that you draw the line at starving me."

"I have no intention of starving you."

"Nice. Thanks for stating intent to keep me...well, living. But that does make me think. We need to work out a system. Because you can't possibly pay for all the food."

He shrugged, walking deeper into the kitchen. "I don't know. I'll ask Sandra what her budget is for the food, and I'll have you pay for some of it. But I don't do my own grocery shopping, so I can't really work it out."

He said it so casually. Having this sort of thing done for him was mundane, everyday, for the likes of him.

"Okay, noted."

He lifted his arms, bracing his hands on the back of his head, stretching. His T-shirt went tight across his chest, highlighting the fine musculature there. Then he made a low, masculine sound that seemed to rumble through him, and her at the same time. The shirt rode up a bit as his pants dipped indecently low, giving her a slight peek at bare, enticing skin.

She quickly turned her attention back to the microwave. "Do you not want me to light fires in your fireplace?" she asked, somewhat absurdly. Because there was nothing else to say, really. Maybe that wasn't even a thing to say, but she had needed to say something.

His dark brows shot upward. "Is that a euphemism?"

"No," she said, stomping her foot, the gesture completely useless and mute thanks to her thick cotton socks. "It is not a euphemism. I meant the literal fire. You seemed kind of…perturbed about it. And I just wanted to make sure that we establish some boundaries."

"You like boundaries, don't you?"

"I love them. Boundaries are practical. They keep people safe. I think of a boundary as being something like a guardrail."

"Is that so?"

"Yes. You know, they keep your car from plummeting over the precipice into the sea. I think we should all be a little more appreciative of boundaries."

He shifted his stance and for the first time she noticed his feet were bare. That shouldn't matter. And for some reason, it did. It mattered in some deep place inside of her that went tight. "That's a little dramatic," he said, his tone dry.

"I'm not dramatic. I'm actually very practical."

"Well, that's good."

"The fact that I moved in here is evidence of my practicality." She nodded definitively, more for herself than for him. "I'm willing to be uncomfortable for a short time in order to serve the greater good. Practical."

"I'm in awe."

"Somehow, I don't think you are."

He shrugged again. "It isn't my fault if you can't tell."

"Are you going to stand around and harass me or do I get to eat my enchiladas in peace?"

"I thought we might talk about tomorrow," he said. "Since you're up."

"Yeah, up for food." She tapped the countertop. "Not necessarily a strategic planning session."

"Too bad. We need a strategy. You need us to pretend to be married until the end of this election. That means there's no way to keep my family out of this. I made light of it earlier, but my mother is fragile. I mentioned that I had a brother. No one has seen him in over fifteen years."

"He's...missing?" The microwave beeped and she looked toward it, not entirely certain if it was appropriate to dive upon a container of enchiladas when someone was bringing up the topic of their missing sibling. Probably best to wait a second.

"I mean, not really. He's not on a milk carton or anything. He just left. He left like he didn't have a family. Like there wasn't an entire empire to look after. So I took over the construction company that my father started years ago, like Gage was supposed to do. And when my dad is unable to see to the business with the horses, I'll do that, too." He planted his hands on the counter, leaning across toward her. "I'm the only son my parents have left. I have to pick up the slack."

Siblings were a difficult subject for her. In fact, they were difficult enough that it usually took her a minute to personalize it. He had mentioned a brother, and it hadn't immediately made her think of her twin. She had a lot of practice just not thinking about her family at all.

Even now, she shoved it to the back of her mind. She wanted to hear what he had to say, but that didn't mean it needed to accompany any personal soul-searching on her part.

"Okay, I think I didn't fully appreciate the fact that our situation does force you to drag your family into this. I'm sorry about that. I don't have family in town, so it's different for me."

"But haven't you talked to them?"

She shifted uncomfortably. "Not yet."

"Do you talk to them?"

"Not often. Sometimes I go up to Seattle for holidays. Sometimes. I mean, the last couple of years I've been really busy doing events with the Chamber around Christmas, so I haven't made it home for that. But Thanksgiving."

She could sense the judgment coming off of him, and she had a fair idea he was conflating her with his brother who had taken off.

But that wasn't really her problem. She didn't owe him an explanation.

"It impacts me differently," she said. "Let's just leave it at that."

"Fair enough. I appreciate the concession." He let out a long, slow breath. "You know, tomorrow we're going to have to share a meal together with an audience. And we are going to have to pretend that you don't want to disembowel me with a fork."

"I don't want to do that. It sounds disgusting. I would

pay hit men to take care of you if I really wanted you gone."

"Remind me not to add you to my life insurance policy." He nodded toward the microwave. "Aren't you going to get your enchiladas?"

"Oh!" She turned, opening the door and pulling out the Tupperware, taking off the lid and fanning the steam away. "You have diet soda?"

"No wine? No beer?"

"I'm keeping off of hard beverages around you."

He chuckled. "It should be in the fridge."

She went rooting around for a drink and emerged victorious with a chilled can. "Okay," she said, "I have fortification. Now, about tomorrow."

"It's more than just not insulting each other every five minutes," he said as though he were explaining something to a small child. "We have to actually look like we want to be together."

She frowned. "That sounds hard."

"Sorry to inflict myself on you."

"Apology accepted."

The glint in his eyes sharpened. He took a step toward her, and her breath hitched. She was so touchy around him. Mostly because there was no denying the fact that he felt like a guy she had slept with, even if she couldn't remember the activity.

She wasn't very experienced. One boyfriend just after high school and another when she had moved to Copper Ridge. It had been nice. Comforting. But, even sex she remembered hadn't made her feel quite like this.

She swallowed hard, picking up the container with her enchilada in it and holding it up against her chest like a shield.

"You really can't look at me like that," he said.

"Like what?"

"Like you're a small frightened rodent suspicious about a predator."

She set the enchiladas down, glaring up at him. "I have reason to be suspicious."

"I promise I'm not going to eat you."

Those words sent a rush of longing through her, one that started in her chest, knocking the breath out of her, and spiked down between her thighs.

There was something erotic about the way he said the words. Something rough and unsophisticated, standing at sharp odds with the way she normally thought of him. A man who was born with a silver spoon in his mouth wouldn't have been able to speak those words around it. Surely.

They are innocuous words. You are being a pervert.

Yes, she was.

"Good to know," she said, wishing that her voice didn't sound so scratchy and thin.

"We're going to have to hold hands when we walk in."

She swallowed hard. And suddenly, she was tired of feeling like a cornered rodent. She was going to claim a little of her own back. Since when did she behave this way? Since when did she allow Colton to call the shots? Since when did she allow anyone to call the shots? She was allowing herself to get thrown off-kilter because she was out of her depth. Because he was undoubtedly the more experienced party here. Because, in spite of herself, she did have to acknowledge that he was sort of attractive, and she was not unaffected by that attractiveness.

But it was not going to win. It was no more powerful than she was.

She was an independent woman, gosh darnit.

She reached out, locking eyes with him. "That's fine with me. Let's practice."

His body jerked, a little like he had made contact with an exposed wire. He recovered quickly. "Sounds good to me."

He closed the distance between their hands, lacing warm fingers through hers. Her breath shortened, her heart pounding hard in her chest, in her throat, in her head.

Oh yes, she did remember this. Except, right now, she was sober. So it didn't seem hazy, didn't seem like a harmless bit of fun. It was sharp, slicing into her like a knife. And she was very afraid that he could see her bleeding need helplessly in front of him.

His palm pressed against hers, his touch hot and firm. And they just stood like that for a moment, her breathing slowly getting a little bit easier. She could do this. She was already getting used to touching him.

But then he changed the game.

He tugged her toward him, pressing her hand flat against his chest. He curved his other arm around her waist, his hand resting on the curve of her spine.

"What are you doing?" she asked. Her voice sounded foreign, scratchy. Definitely not unaffected, as she would have liked.

"Practicing," he said, his voice rough, a caress that skated over her skin, down her spine. And here, in one blinding moment of clarity she realized what the tension had always been. That gradual tightening of her

muscles, that twist in her stomach, that sensation that
her skin was too tight, too hot, to wear anymore.

Attraction.

Dammit.

"That seems like a little much," she said.

"We have to be comfortable with each other," he said.

"I don't feel comfortable."

"What's it going to take?" He smoothed his hand up
the line of her spine, his fingers digging into her tight
muscles, sending a wave of…something, something she
didn't want to analyze, coursing through her.

"I don't think I'm ever going to feel comfortable with
this."

"Well, this is extreme. If you can weather this, a little
bit of hand-holding shouldn't be an issue."

"Okay," she said, both reluctant to pull away and desperate to do it at the same time.

His breathing had grown shallow, matching hers, and
she wondered if his heart was thundering up against his
rib cage the same way hers was. She wondered if his
palms were sweating, and then came to the conclusion
they probably weren't. Because, while this was out of
the ordinary for her, it was certainly not for him.

He had been in a relationship until only recently, and
before that… Well, she just had the idea that he didn't
keep himself quite as cut off as she did.

He had been in a relationship until recently. That
thought hit her a little bit harder the second time through.
He had been with her *friend.* Until just a few days ago.
Touching her, kissing her.

*Of course, you already touched him. On what would've
been her wedding night.*

She did not feel like she'd betrayed Natalie, because

Natalie was the one who had chosen to leave Colton at the altar. Still, the idea of the overlap was kind of…icky.

But that was just on a philosophical level. Since nothing about physical Colton was icky. He was decidedly non-icky, all over, in fact.

Touching him felt so… So good.

He was *hot*. Which was possibly the understatement of the year. But more than that was what he made her feel. There were plenty of hot guys that she could admire from afar and not feel this. This was beyond hot. It touched something deep and dark inside of her. Something that she had left untouched and unexamined for… well, forever.

But she was powerless to keep it locked down with him. It was beyond her control and she found she was fascinated by that in the same way a tiger was fascinating in person.

Beautiful. Impossible to look away from. So clearly dangerous and best kept in a cage.

Even so, she didn't want to pull away. She wanted to stretch up on her toes and taste his mouth.

She didn't even care if it was a weird thing to wish you could taste someone. It was what she wanted. She was suddenly so overcome with the desire to do it that she began to shake. Had she ever wanted anyone like this before? Had she ever wanted anything like this. Anything at all?

She would never have thought she was the kind of person to lose her mind over sexual attraction. And here she was, losing it completely, wearing ridiculous shorts, T-shirts and socks in the middle of some guy's kitchen. She was not dressed to play the part of seductress. She was hungry. For Mexican food, and for him. She wasn't wearing makeup and had underwear that was the opposite of sexy.

None of that seemed to matter to her. She had officially gone insane. She wasn't sure she cared.

Suddenly, he released his hold on her, propelling her backward.

"I think that's enough for tonight."

"I'm not...I'm not comfortable yet," she said, wishing she didn't sound quite so needy.

"I think you'll do fine tomorrow. You didn't stab me with anything."

She laughed, a thin, nervous sound. "Well, good for me."

"It's going to have to do," he responded, his voice gruff.

"Good night," she said.

"Enjoy your enchiladas," he responded, turning and walking out of the kitchen, leaving her standing there with her heart pounding in her throat.

She had no idea what to do with him, what to do with this. It was impossible. It was ridiculous. She had to keep her mind on the task at hand. On winning the election so that she could become mayor. On surviving this ridiculous farce of a marriage. She could not afford to allow her brain to turn to soup just because her accidental husband was sexy. So what if he was? That didn't mean she had to act on her feelings. She had survived this many years without sex. She could survive just as many more.

And she would, dammit. On that she was determined. At least, she would survive until the election was settled. She couldn't afford any more bumps in what had already been a very pothole-filled road.

She had come way too far to be undone now.

CHAPTER SEVEN

WHEN COLTON WALKED into Beaches to see not only his mother but both of his sisters sitting at the table in the back of the dining room, facing the Skokomish River, it took all of his strength not to curse out loud.

"Hi," he said, eyeballing Maddy as he took his seat to her left. "I didn't know that the two of you would be joining us?"

"We are very surprising," Maddy said.

"And hungry," Sierra added.

"Right. Well, it's good to see you."

He looked behind them, checking out the door, trying to see if Lydia was on her way in.

She didn't seem like the kind of person to run late, so it was a little bit annoying that she wasn't here yet.

"I invited them," his mother said. "I thought we might as well make the best out of a difficult situation."

"Right," he said. Privately, all he could think was that the situation was about to get a lot more difficult.

"I didn't want to miss this," Maddy said.

He was about to kick her underneath the table like they were twelve. She seemed to be enjoying his fall from grace a little too much. All things considered, he couldn't really blame her. But she could hide it a little bit better.

"Mom," he said, watching his mother's face for indicators as to how she was doing, "I do have something to tell you."

"Sorry I'm late." He turned toward the sound of Lydia's voice, as did his mother and sisters.

She was standing there, her dark hair in a loose braid, her grip tight on her large leather purse. She was wearing some formfitting dark red dress that he imagined was meant to be classy and casual but just forced his eyes straight to her breasts. Because the fabric was soft and it shaped itself around her curves so perfectly.

And this was not what he wanted to be thinking about.

"Not too late," he said, doing his best to force a smile. He stood, moving to the empty chair and pulling it out.

That earned him not the thank-you he deserved, but a flat-eyed expression. And he realized that he had to greet her, and he had to greet her in the appropriate way a man would greet his new wife.

Well, when that man was a West.

He leaned in, brushing his lips over her cheek. And he felt the impact of that simple contact straight down, like a shot of alcohol. Burning low before firing back to his brain.

When they parted she was still looking at him, but her expression wasn't flat. It glittered like whiskey in a glass.

She took her seat, and he sat down beside her, facing his mother head-on. "Mom, I think you've met Lydia Carpenter before."

A slight crease marred his mother's forehead. "Of course," she said, clearly confused.

"She was supposed to be one of the bridesmaids at

my wedding to Natalie. But when Natalie didn't show up…Lydia and I got to talking."

He felt Lydia stiffen beside him, an obvious response to the way he was glossing over the truth. Oh well, he was not about to tell his mother that he got drunk in a dive bar before making this life-altering decision.

"We got married," he finished, realizing that he had skipped a lot of steps in between, and that—as transitions went—it was a clumsy one. But there really was no good way to tell the story. At least, there was no good way to tell it that wasn't somehow damning.

Gloria West sagged in her chair. "You…you got married."

"Yes. We flew to Las Vegas. It's an easy way to get married quickly."

His mother's gaze turned sharp. "Yes, Colton, I'm not so sheltered that I don't realize that."

"I understand that it's a bit of a shock," Lydia said, her tone suddenly as comforting and sweet as warm honey. It was not a tone she had ever used with him before, though he imagined it served her well on the campaign trail. "And I apologize that we handled it the way that we did. But I had feelings for Colton for a long time. Of course, I kept them quiet because he was with my friend, and it would have been wrong to say something. But when she left him…I didn't see any reason to keep the feelings to myself anymore. I thought at least it would be nice for him to hear that someone loved him, after being left at the altar."

He could see that Madison wasn't exactly buying Lydia's explosion of hearts and flowers. But then, Madison was cynical by nature. Sierra, on the other hand, was watching with a slightly more open expression.

It was his mother he was the most concerned about. If, in the end, Madison and Sierra didn't believe the whole story, then he would tell them the truth. His mother wouldn't understand, and he did not want to torture her with this.

You don't think your divorce is going to torture her?

He gritted his teeth against that thought. It probably would, but at least it would be later. After the dust settled on his father's scandal. After people had forgotten about the wedding. Or rather, the lack of wedding.

"That's...amazing," Maddy said.

Lydia lifted a shoulder. "I don't know if it's particularly amazing. I think I should have been braver earlier on. And, since Colton obviously had feelings for me, maybe he should have been, too. And I think we should both be grateful to Natalie."

He was not going to be grateful to Natalie. All things considered he wasn't that upset to not be married to her, but he still wasn't happy with the way things had gone.

"Does this mean that you get to attach the West name to your campaign?" Maddy asked. "I mean in a literal sense. Clearly it's added inescapably by your link to my brother. But Lydia West might stand a slightly better chance at making it into Copper Ridge's highest office."

He was tempted to jump in, but Lydia was sharp, quick. She was also unflappable. It was easy for him to forget that his new wife was an aspiring politician. Mostly because she didn't employ any of those tactics with him. No, with him she was candid. That was the nice way of putting it. But with others she had clearly perfected the art of diplomacy.

"I haven't made any decisions about my name. In part because reprinting the signs would be rather expensive. Also, pamphlets." She smiled. "I've gotten a long way with my own name. I feel like I can get all the way with it."

Maddy looked at Lydia with a measure of respect. "I imagine you can."

"Very interesting," his mother said, addressing him instead of Lydia. Her expression was neutral, but as always, he was aware of something brittle beneath the façade. "Interesting that you've chosen a woman with political ambition, Colton."

"Perfect, I think," he said.

"If Lydia wins it will make you the first family of Copper Ridge," Sierra pointed out. "And I guess that makes you the first lady, essentially."

Leave it to his younger sister. "First man," he said.

"If it were any other town I would say that would mean you were going to a lot of grand openings to cut ribbons," Maddy said, not bothering to hide her amusement.

"Actually," Lydia said, "if I'm elected, I hope that we will have more grand openings."

Sierra looked intrigued by this. "What sort of things are you thinking?"

"It will be up to the people of Copper Ridge to shape the town, but I want to encourage growth. Not the kind of growth that erases who we are, but the kind that honors the past while moving forward into the future."

Lydia was campaigning now. There would be no stopping her.

"My husband, Ace, he's interested in that sort of thing. He just opened a new restaurant and brewery."

"I've been to it," Lydia said, sounding enthusiastic now. "It's exactly the kind of thing I want to see more of here in town. Local people taking charge of the economy. Bringing in more vibrancy. Like Sadie Garrett did with her bed-and-breakfast, and the events that she hosts there. Like your husband has done."

At the mention of Ace, his mother started looking a little tense again. She wasn't exactly over her youngest daughter unexpectedly getting pregnant at twenty-five, then hastily marrying the town bartender.

Which Colton had to admit had bothered him at first, too. If only because he hadn't been prepared to face the fact that Sierra wasn't a child anymore.

That had not been the issue for Gloria West—though he knew she would tell anyone who asked that she was too young to be a grandmother. The issue had been Ace's status. Or lack of it.

One reason he imagined she found Lydia's aspiration *interesting*. Even though she had spoken the word in a not entirely approving manner. It would be hard for his mother to accept the idea of a woman with serious career goals. But she would definitely like the status having a daughter-in-law as mayor afforded, maybe even enough to forget the scandal of the wedding-that-wasn't.

And then it will all fall apart because this is going to be a hell of a short marriage.

When he screwed up, he didn't go halfway.

It wasn't that he needed his mother's approval. That wasn't it at all. It was just that no one else took her into account at all. His father was a distant tool—and a cheater, it turned out. Gage was gone. Madison had created her own perfect storm, and then seemed to disappear inside of it, retreating into an outer shell that she only sometimes shed to offer warmth. Sierra had swanned off to find herself in the wake of the news that Jack Monaghan was their half brother.

He'd been the one to make sure his mother didn't mix too many antianxiety pills with her mimosas.

He'd also been the one to take Sierra in when she'd gone on her quest for self—but hadn't had the money to finance it.

He'd been there for Maddy because their mom was too brittle, and someone else's pain would only shatter her. Because Nathan West cared only for himself and because their brother Gage had apparently taken after their father.

This was what Colton did. He was the pillar that held his family together. Even if it was a pillar shot through with cracks. And sometimes he felt like he was the only thing keeping it all from crumbling.

But he would. That was why he was here.

By the time they all got up to leave, he couldn't even remember what he'd eaten. He'd been too focused on refereeing the dynamics between everyone.

He put his hand low on Lydia's back as she stood, trying to keep his mind from zeroing in on the heat beneath his palm. On the memories that flooded back.

His hands on her curves. Good God, those curves.

He drew his hand away, satisfied he'd done enough to present a happy couple front. Even if he hadn't, too bad. He'd already nearly lost his grip on his control last night. He didn't need to push it any harder today.

"I'll meet you outside in a moment," he said to Lydia, his tone meaningful.

"Mom," Maddy said, "I'll meet you at the car."

He was glad that Maddy had driven since their mother had had more than her share of wine with lunch. Sierra gave Gloria and Maddy a hug goodbye, then patted him on the shoulder before walking out, upping her pace to try and catch up with Lydia.

He would worry about it except Lydia had proven she could more than hold her own against the West women.

"How are you doing?" he asked his mother, once they were alone.

"I'm fine," she said, forcing a smile. It was what she always did. Like she didn't think they could tell when she was quietly self-destructing.

"I know that the wedding not going through was stressful," he said. "And I'm sorry about how quickly things happened with Lydia. I'm sorry you didn't get to have the big wedding you wanted to plan."

Her shoulders sagged slightly. "It's all right. I don't think I could have handled two in a row." She brightened suddenly. "Though it would be wonderful to host a party on election night for Lydia. Especially since your father isn't supporting her opponent anymore."

"Thank God for a few things going smoothly. The last thing we need is Dad supporting my ex's father and my current wife's opponent, right?"

She tried to force another smile. "Yes, I suppose things could be worse."

He wanted to ask which things. He wanted to dig deeper. But he was always afraid she would break if he did.

"I'd like them to be better."

"That would be nice," she responded.

"I'll call you again this week," he said.

They walked out together and his mother made her way toward where Maddy was parked. He looked down the walk and saw Lydia standing there waiting, the wind catching strands of dark hair and tugging it from her braid.

The waves lapped against the shore across the street, the gray water and pale sand backdrop fading behind her. A view he normally appreciated washing into a watercolor blur as she moved more sharply into focus.

"Did I pass muster?" she asked, taking a step toward him.

"You know how to work a crowd. You just needed a baby to kiss."

"Yeah. No, I'm not kissing a strange baby," she said. "It's rude, first of all. The parents don't know where I've been. Also, I don't know where it's been."

"That's the kind of thing you probably shouldn't say during a campaign speech."

A smile tugged at the corner of her lips. "You think?"

"Sometimes. Right now I'm thinking about what Maddy said."

Lydia frowned. "About your last name?"

"Yes."

"I meant what I said. I have signs printed up, Colton. I'm not going to hijack your last name so I can ride your coattails to glory. I have my own coattails. And my own glory."

"You headed back to work?" he asked.

"Yes."

"I'll go with you. We can walk and talk."

"Walk and argue?" She started to head down the street, back toward town. He moved into step with her.

"Not too loudly," he said. "We aren't the only ones coming back from lunch break."

She paused, the corner of her lips turning down. "We should probably...hold hands or something."

He captured her hand with his, lacing his fingers through hers and drawing her closer to him. He gritted his teeth against the wave of heat that assaulted him. It was a hand. A palm. Fingers. There was nothing erotic about it.

He had held hands with more women than he could count. More women than he could remember. Hand-holding was the bare minimum of first date affection as long as you didn't hate the person you were with.

It shouldn't affect him at all. But it did. Because she did.

A car slowed beside them on the road, and Colton turned, realizing it was Eli Garrett in a marked police cruiser.

"Hi, Lydia," he called. "Colton."

Colton had the distinct suspicion that Eli was checking up on them. He knew that Lydia was friends with Eli's wife, Sadie, and that he was also good friends with Jack Monaghan, Colton's newly discovered half brother. All things considered, a West was probably high on his list of suspicious persons.

"Hi," Lydia said, tightening her hold on his hand slightly. "Were we walking too quickly? Committing some kind of pedestrian-related infraction?"

"No. I just wanted to stop and congratulate you."

"That's nice of you," Lydia said, her smile warm.

"Thank you," Colton added.

He felt like he was having an out-of-body experience. Standing there on the main street of town receiving congratulations for a different wedding than the one he had been planning for eight months, holding hands with a different woman than he had thought he would call his wife.

"Sadie was telling me she came to visit you yesterday." That was directed at Lydia.

Lydia stiffened beside him. "Oh yes. She did. She brought coffee, which was nice."

"She's good like that. Anyway, we'll have to have you over for dinner sometime. And I have to get going."

"Felons to bust?" she asked.

"I'm speaking at the elementary school about bicycle safety." He smiled. "See you around."

"I got the feeling he was about one wrong move away from tasing me," Colton said.

"I've known Eli for a long time."

"Did you ever date him?" It didn't matter. He didn't know why he had asked. And he really didn't know why a burning ball of jealousy started to roll around in his chest, leaving a trail of fire in its wake.

"No," she said, "though I did give it a pretty decent shot. But Sadie rolled into town and I had to concede defeat."

"And now you're friends with her."

Lydia lifted a shoulder. "There's no point being ridiculous about a man that isn't all that into you. I was hardly going to pitch a fit. He didn't want me."

"That is not the way most people feel about that kind of thing."

"I've never seen the point of being insane about relationship stuff. It either works or it doesn't. It either fits, or it doesn't fit. There's no reason to force anything."

"That's how I feel."

She looked sideways at him. "Really?"

"Yes. That's why I was with Natalie. We fit. We made sense. It was easy."

Lydia made a scoffing sound. "People can be so dramatic about it."

"On that I think we can agree."

They walked past the Trading Post just as Rebecca Bear was coming outside. Her eyes widened for a moment before her expression settled into a stony glare. She had never been very friendly in his experience, so he didn't think much about it.

"Hi, Rebecca," Lydia said, her tone overly cheerful.

"Hi," Rebecca said quickly, her eyes darting to Colton for a brief second.

Silence settled between them, thick and awkward.

"Well," Lydia said finally. "I'll…see you around. I'll have to stop in when your Christmas decorations arrive."

"End of November," the other woman said, looking at the ground now.

"Okay," Lydia responded. "Great."

Lydia waved awkwardly and they continued on down the sidewalk. "That was weird," Lydia said, when they were out of earshot.

"Was it?" he asked.

"Yes," she said. "She was all unfriendly."

"That's just how she is. At least in my limited experience with her."

Lydia frowned. "Not in mine."

"You have that politician thing, though," he said. "You show up and smile and it's like a switch is flipped and you're radiating charisma. It flips off when you look at me."

"Hmm," Lydia said. "So the common denominator here with women who are usually friendly, but then sometimes not, is you."

"Lydia!" Colton turned and saw Cassie Caldwell

rushing out the front door of The Grind, wiping her hands on her apron. "I wanted to make sure I congratulated you."

"Oh," Lydia said. "Thank you."

She looked as shocked as he felt. And he was almost insulted that he was clearly much less popular around town than she was. Thanks to his last name, he was one of Copper Ridge's most prominent citizens, but no one was rushing to offer him congratulations.

If he cared more, he might be wounded.

But that was possibly the sharpest contrast between himself and Lydia—she cared. Deeply. Down into the depths of her soul. At least, about Copper Ridge and becoming mayor.

He couldn't think of a damn thing he felt that way about. Except for his family.

"Thanks from me, too," Colton said.

"I didn't…realize." Cassie's face turned pink. "I mean…well, you were engaged and…"

"Nothing was going on when I was engaged," Colton said. The last thing either of them needed were cheating rumors going around.

"I didn't…" Cassie shook her head. "Never mind. If I try to correct I'll overcorrect and it'll get weird for everyone."

"There's no way it can get weirder," Lydia said. "We understand that."

"Are you going to have another meeting here soon?" Cassie asked.

"Yes," Lydia said. "I've been meaning to call you. But then…I got married instead. So we'll set up a time next week?"

"Sounds good. I'll make sure to have a peppermint mocha at the ready."

Lydia said her goodbyes and they walked on.

"Do I have a Just Married sign on my ass?" he asked. "Did you tie tin cans to my belt loop?"

"News travels fast, Colton," she said. "And you could work a little harder to be more…effusive."

"Oh, could I?"

"Yes. You sort of get…statue-like."

"Well, no one is being effusive at me. They're all being effusive at you."

She squinted. "I seriously doubt that even if they were you would return the favor."

"You've met my family. You know who they are. I'm an expert at handling social situations."

"Which is why you've been kind of a jerk to me every time we've ever met prior to this little—" she waved her free hand between them "—thing?"

"That's just you. You're special."

She smiled, but it felt vaguely more like she was snarling. "Thank you, darling."

"Are we doing pet names now?"

Her dark eyes narrowed. "We are a couple now, sweetheart."

Lydia led them down to the wharf, and to the little Chamber of Commerce building that was right over the water. It was situated between The Crab Shanty—a restaurant that let you rent your own crab pots, and offered to cook your catch—and a whale watching tours and bike, paddleboard and canoe rental stand.

It was summer, and it was still cold down by the water, the wind coming up off the ocean, sharp, slicing through his flannel shirt with efficiency.

Something about the wind whispering over their skin drew his attention back to the fact that they were still touching. That even though the rest of him was cold, her touch was keeping him warm.

Absently, he let his thumb drift over the back of her hand. She looked up at him, her eyes wide, and damned if he wasn't right back in a hotel in Vegas about to make the biggest mistake of his life.

CHAPTER EIGHT

OH...HELL.

She was remembering the exact moment when he'd grabbed her while they were in the lobby of some shiny, blinky hotel on the strip and had looked down at her with those lethal blue eyes.

She'd been giddy, and so drunk, and she'd forgotten for a minute that he made her angry. She'd just thought he was the most beautiful man she'd ever seen. She could see it like it was playing out in front of her right now on the wharf.

The rugged lines on his face, his square jaw and dark brows. Those lips. How had she never noticed how gorgeous his lips were before the past week?

She felt light, and electric. Super tipsy. They were surrounded by Sin City and dammit, sin seemed like a good idea when she looked at that mouth.

"I was supposed to get married today."

"I know. I was in the wedding. Or...almost."

"I didn't expect to end up here. I'm supposed to be in Manhattan. With my wife. And it's supposed to be my wedding night." His voice got rougher then, deeper.

She frowned. "So you're thinking about her?" And about the sex he was supposed to have, she imagined.

Oh, Lord. Just thinking about Colton and sex made her feel weak all over. So much like that time in the bar when she'd run into him, touched his hard chest. She wanted to touch it again. So badly.

His gorgeous lips tipped upward. "Not her specifically. It hasn't been her from the moment you took that first shot with me in the bar."

That warmed her even more than all the whiskey they'd had at Ace's. Maybe he was thinking of touching her, too. Normally, she would think that was nuts. But normally she wouldn't have taken off to Las Vegas on the spur of the moment with a man who drove her crazy in all senses of the word.

"It sucks you don't get your wedding night," she said, licking her suddenly dry lips.

"Kind of hard to have a wedding night when you don't have a bride."

"You..." She looked around the casino. "I mean...you could have a bride. I bet. I mean I would—"

Then the world stopped, and he started to lean in...

She blinked, throwing herself back into the present. She was not going further with that memory. The present wasn't much safer than the past, though. Because they were standing in one of her favorite places, with the wind whipping through his hair and across the front of his shirt, tightening the fabric over his masculine physique.

And he was still touching her hand. His lips were every bit as interesting as they had been back in Vegas.

She pulled away from him abruptly. "Why don't you come in?" she asked.

He lifted a shoulder, seeming unaffected by what had just happened. "All right."

Clearly, she'd been alone in her memories. Colton had probably been spacing out about... She didn't even know what he would space out about. Tenpenny nails? She was pretty sure those were a thing.

She was struck again by how little she knew him. Though that lunch with his mother and sisters had been pretty illuminating.

He felt protective of all of them. His sisters felt protective of him. His mother was worried about herself.

It wasn't an easy family dynamic.

Still not quite as messed up as her own, though.

"Come on," she said uselessly, since he was already following her into the building.

It was a simple, clean office space with mottled, commercial-grade carpet and white furniture to match the trim. The windows afforded a nice view of the ocean, and lilies added to the charm.

There was a waiting area with pale blue couches and a whitewashed table with brightly colored pamphlets spread over the top.

Marlene, who was old enough to be Lydia's grandmother, but attacked her job with the energy of a much younger woman, looked up when they walked in.

"Hello, Lydia. And oh! This must be your husband."

Lydia had done her best to prepare her small, mostly female staff for the inevitability of meeting Colton. She hadn't offered a whole lot of explanation for the hasty marriage, but then, no one had acted terribly shocked when she'd broken the news.

Of course, a wave of tittering that rivaled a tree full of birds could be heard beyond her office door after she'd told them, but as long as they didn't bother her with gossip, she didn't care if it was going on.

"Yep," she said, "this is him."

"Oh, you're the West boy," Marlene said, smiling. "I

think your company came and did new kitchen cabinets in my house a couple of years back. My birthday present from Al."

"I hope we did a good job," Colton said, treating Marlene to a smile that hollowed out Lydia's stomach and made it difficult for her to breathe. So. He did have charm.

"Excellent work," she said. "I hope you take as much care with our Lydia."

He wrapped his arm around her waist and all the air gusted from her lungs. "Of course. My peaches is pretty precious to me."

Peaches.

Oh, screw him. She was going to punch him in the stomach when they were alone in her office. Provided her knees didn't buckle. She was feeling a little wobbly at the moment.

"He's…he's doing fine, Marlene," she said, patting the center of his chest, then immediately regretting it. She pulled away like his pecs were on fire and she was in danger of a third-degree burn.

She put her hand down at her side, rubbing her palm on her dress. "Just… We're fine." She cleared her throat. "Colton, I want you to see my office."

"We'll talk again soon, Marlene," Colton said, pouring on more of that charm she'd certainly never gotten from him.

They continued on down the hall, and to the end, where her office was positioned, looking out over the little harbor. She loved her view of the fishing boats, the horizon line, and then, off to the side, the glimpse of dark green mountains. Like she could see everything that made this place her home all at once.

Normally, her office was neat, her desk perfectly arranged to help her get her work done without anything cluttering her up.

But that was not the case right now. She had stacks of pamphlets rubber banded and arranged in the corner; there were campaign signs stuffed behind her potted palm.

Her drink station was still neat, her single brewer coffeemaker and mugs, along with a selection of tea and coffee pods, arranged neatly on a table at the back of the room. Next to that was a cream-colored chair that had somehow managed to avoid any sort of beverage stain.

"Peaches?" she asked, shutting the door behind them.

"I panicked," he said. "You said that we should use more endearments, and I couldn't think of one."

She rounded to the back of her desk, planting her hands on the smooth surface. "You did not panic."

"Maybe social situations make me uncomfortable."

She narrowed her eyes. "You are basically the least panicked person I have ever been around. You barely panicked when you woke up married to me in a Las Vegas hotel."

"There isn't any point to panicking, peaches."

"I'm going to throw something at you."

"You won't."

She turned away from him, bending down and picking up a stack of pamphlets. No, those were too heavy. She tugged one pamphlet out from beneath the rubber band and flung it in his direction. It floated feebly in the air before drifting back down to the ground.

They looked at each other, and the corner of his mouth twitched.

"Don't say anything," she warned.

"What could I have possibly said? That was an incredibly fearsome move. I was concerned for my personal safety. In fact, I think I should call Sheriff Garrett and let him know that you're not the one he has to be worried about."

"Okay," she said, holding up a hand. "You can tone it down a little bit."

He bent down, picking the pamphlet up and opening it. She nearly choked when he started to read it. Which was silly—she wanted people to read it. And he was people. Mostly.

"I like your slogan. Protecting the Past, Embracing the Future."

"I thought it would resonate," she said, knowing she sounded a little bit snippy.

"It's very mayoral."

"Right. Well, I am. It's why I'm running."

"Excluding when you tried to throw a pamphlet at me."

"I didn't try. I succeeded. I threw it."

"Yeah, it didn't get very far."

She tapped her fingers on her desk. "Okay, fine. My pamphlet-throwing skills aside, I did need to let you know that in two weeks I'm having a campaign fundraising dinner at the Garrett Ranch."

"And that pertains to me…?"

"Because you're my husband. You know you're going to have to be my date."

He frowned. "Black tie?"

"Don't panic. It's casual. We're having it out in the barn."

He laughed. "Don't forget, I'm pretty professional at

black tie. My mother never met a gala she didn't like, and my father throws fund-raisers more than once a year."

Of course. And she knew that about him. In fact, her predominant thought about him when Natalie had introduced her was that he was another one of those spoiled rich kids who had had everything handed to him.

But actually spending time with him made it hard for her to think of him that way. Yes, sometimes it was impossible to ignore the fact that he was rich. Well, most of the time. His house was a testament to that. As had been traveling with him to Las Vegas and back.

But he wasn't ineffectual or lazy.

He had a partly functioning ranch that he ran with help, but he also had a construction company that he went to work at every day. And she wasn't exactly sure what portion of the physical labor he took on, but judging by his physique he didn't spend his day sitting behind a desk.

He was complicated. She didn't like that. She wanted him to be easy to dismiss. Easy to dislike.

He wasn't really either of those things.

"Of course. I should have known. You probably have custom fitted suits for every occasion."

"And specially tailored jeans."

"Are you serious?"

"No," he said, smiling, a ghost of the smile he had given to Marlene, but still a little friendlier than she usually got. "I buy them at Fred Meyer."

"Okay. Because the next thing I was going to have to ask you is if your underwear was specially tailored too."

Well, she should have known that was a mistake before she even said it. Talking about Colton's underwear was a clear path to insanity.

The silence that settled between them was awkwardness unrivaled. It was like that with him. Fine for a moment, and then the next…all that tension would settle down between them.

"I would have thought you might know the answer to that one," he said, his voice dropping a degree.

"I…I…don't," she stammered, wanting to punch her own stupid face for stammering.

"Because you don't remember."

"Nope."

"That's kind of hard on a man's ego."

She busied herself fiddling with things on her desk. "Well, you know, I think life does enough to prop up the male ego. I'm not all that concerned with its health, generally speaking."

"What about my personal ego?"

She looked up, but did her best not to focus on him. "Even less concerned."

"I think you verge on protesting too much, Lydia."

"I…" She inhaled sharply, then coughed, gripping the back of her office chair and trying to steady herself so she didn't have a full-on respiratory episode in his presence. Speaking of his ego. "I am not," she finished weakly.

"You don't remember anything, though, so you can't be certain. Maybe you're responding to instinct."

She released her hold on the back of the chair and waved a hand. "I… No. I feel like if anything were… egregious or notable I would remember."

He crossed his arms and leaned against the wall. "So, I'm neither egregious nor notable."

"Neither thing."

"Which is why you don't remember if my underwear needs to be specially tailored or not."

"Ha!" She nearly howled. It was either that or slink under the desk in embarrassment. And she would not do that. "No, I would most certainly remember if the contents of your underwear were such that special alterations were required. Again, either way."

"So you're saying…"

"You were inoffensive," she said quickly, "clearly."

"My penis is…inoffensive."

"Yes." Her ears were burning. She couldn't recall ever being so embarrassed in her life. Well, okay, not since they woke up in bed together.

"Well, that's…something."

She pinched the bridge of her nose. "This is terrible. You are terrible." She released it and slapped her hand back down at her side. "Can we just…try to get through this without any more innuendo?"

"Since my body is inoffensive to you it should be pretty easy."

"You would think."

"Well, I'm going to take my inoffensive appendage back to work."

She snorted, reaching for the back of her office chair and missing, stumbling slightly. "Fine. Where are you I mean, what are you working on?"

"Building a new retirement community in Tolowa. Slightly cheaper bay-front property. Copper Ridge has gotten a little steep. Also, we're building a house on a hill overlooking the ocean."

She was interested, in spite of herself. "Do you actually…build?"

"I am a contractor."

"You own the company, though," she pointed out. "Most people would maybe sit in the office."

"I've never liked sitting behind a desk. It's not for me. Anyway, my dad owns the company. My family. It was my uncle's until he passed away ten years ago. And then my dad folded it into his empire. Someone needed to run it."

"And you…love building things?"

"Does anyone *love* building things? It's a thing you do. A man has to do something."

Lydia looked around her office, at her little space that felt like an extension of home. "I love what I do. I believe in it really passionately. I love this town and I want to serve it in every way I can. I don't just do it because I have to work."

"I think that's a one-in-a-million thing, Lydia," he said. "Anyway, I have to get going. I'll see you tonight."

He turned and walked out of the office, closing the door behind him and effectively cutting the tension off. She sagged with relief, all the way down into her chair, her heart thundering in her ears.

She would see him tonight. And every night thereafter for an awfully long time because they lived together and how had she gotten herself into this mess?

She groaned and laid her head down on her desk.

She needed to get a grip. Not on Colton. She mentally scolded herself ahead of the prurient thought that she knew was about to pop up. Maybe she was reaching her sexual peak. Women did that in their thirties. And, granted, she was only recently thirty, but it seemed like it was potentially likely.

It had been a good long while since she'd been in a

relationship. Testosterone exposure was starting to go to her brain. Masculine carbon monoxide. He radiated it.

And she did not have time to worry about it.

She straightened, waking her computer up and getting back into the spreadsheet she'd been working on before she'd gone to lunch. Immediately, a sense of calm came over her. Yes, this was her domain. She was good at this. In this, she was confident.

Spreadsheets were the source of all sanity. And she was going to get as much sanity as she possibly could before she returned to Colton's home later.

CHAPTER NINE

SHE WAS STARTING to feel like she lived with a ghost. Over the past week she had barely caught sight of Colton in their shared living space. Really, it shouldn't bother her. Really, it didn't. Except that they were going to have to present some kind of unified front at Eli and Sadie's house next week for her fund-raiser dinner. So, it would help if they weren't presenting as total strangers.

Colton seemed like a decent human being. Well, mostly. So while they rubbed each other the wrong way, and definitely carried around a little bit of tension, ultimately she didn't see why they couldn't come to some kind of understanding.

With that in mind, she had called ahead and told his housekeeper that they wouldn't be needing dinner tonight, and she had picked up fish and chips from the crab shanty on her way home from work.

When she pulled in the driveway, she could see Colton's truck was already there, but when she got into the house, she couldn't find him. He was elusive. At least, as elusive as a man who was well over six feet tall could be.

She set the brown paper bag on the dining room table, then walked into the living room. He wasn't there. He had a home office, but she had never ventured into it. Mostly, she stayed in the bedroom she was sleeping in, the nearest bathroom, the kitchen, living room and dining room. Common areas.

She avoided his office. She avoided even going in the neighborhood of his bedroom. These were common-sense practices. Much like avoiding a bear's den.

She supposed she could shout and see if he responded. Or she could text him.

She pulled her phone out and opened a new message box. She hadn't ever texted him before, but she had gotten his phone number because it seemed highly impractical not to have your husband's number.

I come bearing dinner.

She waited, watching the bottom of her screen to see if those three telltale dots appeared showing that he was composing a response. Nothing.

She sighed heavily and wandered out to the front porch. It was a beautiful evening, a cool breeze blowing in off the ocean, rustling through the evergreen trees, making them look as though they were shivering from the cold.

She walked down the stairs, her steps on the gravel blunted by pine needles that had fallen into the driveway. She hadn't done much exploring of the property, she realized. Not only had she localized herself indoors, she had done the same outdoors. She always parked her car in front of the house and took those few steps up to the front porch and inside. From there, she carried out her well-worn routine.

Okay, maybe she couldn't exactly blame Colton for the distance. Maybe she was cultivating some of the avoidance. Or a lot of it.

She sighed heavily, walking down the dirt road, wishing she had brought a jacket. It cooled down sharply in the evenings, especially when the sun dipped below the tall trees and the mountains. And now she was walking in the shade, and she was definitely feeling it.

Dressed in only a short-sleeved top, a pencil skirt and sensible flats, she was really feeling the lateness of the hour. She gripped her elbows, rubbing her arms vigorously with her own hands as she continued to walk.

She knew that the barn was somewhere this way, and she felt absolutely ridiculous for having not seen it before now. It was like she was just trying to keep tunnel vision and get through this weird detour she was on.

She didn't do detours well. She liked everything to go according to plan. She liked control. And in this situation, with this man, she had so little of it.

Sometimes, she got the sense that he felt the same. But most of the time, he just seemed to go about his day with a kind of smug assurance.

Irritating bastard.

She paused when she came around the corner and the tree branches gave way, revealing a large red barn bathed in golden light from the sinking sun.

There was a fence connected to the side of it, and field beyond it. She could see horses in it, grazing as though they had all the time in the world and night wasn't about to descend.

She could hear a sharp, staccato sound echoing off the buildings, but she still didn't see Colton. She walked across the neatly groomed gravel clearing, taking in her surroundings as best she could.

It was a much bigger operation than she had imagined. There were tractors, other heavy equipment that she couldn't name. A large stack of hay bales was just inside the barn, giving off a sweet scent that mingled with the smell of horses. It wasn't an overly familiar scent to her. It was something she had only experienced in special events, and on those rare occasions she had gone to visit Eli at his family ranch.

She associated it with good things. Solid and steady things. Deep roots and hard work.

It was challenging her assessment of Colton yet again.

He had told her the other day that he actually did the physical labor at his construction company. And along with that, that he didn't particularly enjoy it, but that he liked sitting behind a desk less. And now, she was being confronted with all this. This evidence of further hard work.

She followed the strange sound that was echoing through the air, around the side of the barn until she saw a rustic, natural woodshed. And, in front of that, wearing nothing but a pair of low-slung jeans, was Colton.

Chopping wood.

It was like a cologne commercial. Like the promise of something rugged and woodsy that could be bottled and possessed. Except it was real. *He* was real.

For a full thirty seconds she couldn't even move. All she could do was stand there and watch. Watch the play of his muscles as he raised the ax high into the air before bringing it down hard on the piece of wood he had stacked on top of a shorn-off tree stump.

Suddenly, she forgot why she had been cold a few moments earlier. Suddenly, she felt as though she were in the throes of a hot flash. She wanted to strip layers off, not put any on. She was actually sweating.

He raised the ax again, the muscles in his chest straining, his ab muscles shifting and bunching.

Good Lord, she was thirsty.

"Hi," she said, because she really couldn't stand there just staring any longer or it was going to get weird.

Okay, it was already weird. But he didn't have to know how weird it was.

He paused, dropping the ax down to his side and resting the head on the dirt, drawing his forearm over his forehead.

"I...I came to find you," she said, feeling like her voice sounded dull and rather obviously affected.

"Here I am."

He was breathing hard from all the exertion, and that was making his muscles move in yet more interesting ways. Sweat was beaded across his skin, and she imagined she should find that repellent in some way. Unhygienic.

She did not.

"Yes," she said, waving her hand in a broad gesture, "here you are."

"You haven't been out here to see the barn, have you?"

"No," she said. "It's nice."

"Yeah," he said, "it is."

"Modest at all times, Colton."

"I'm not. I'm honest. Anyway, you don't downplay your achievements. And you shouldn't."

She bristled, mostly because all of this felt a little bit like telling her what to do. "No, I shouldn't. I agree with you. Because I'm very accomplished."

"You are."

For some reason, that didn't feel like a compliment.

She should just tell him that she had dinner, and then they could go back and eat it. Or he could stay here, and not eat with her. He could continue to avoid her. Really, that would be fine. But for some reason she didn't do that.

"Is this where you've been spending all your time in the evenings?"

He nodded. "Pretty much."

"What all do you… What all do you do?"

"A lot of things. I have horses, which you can see. I've been selling livestock to the rodeo circuit. Pretty specialized breeding."

"So you own rodeo horses?"

"I retain ownership to a few of them. Others I sell. But it's kind of cool to own one of the horses that's competing. There's decent money in that. I don't want anyone to get hurt, of course, but I do like to root for my horses, not the cowboys."

"Is this…is this what you love doing?"

"I would rather do this than hammer nails, let's put it that way."

"Rather do what? I mean, specifically. Just the rodeo horses or…?"

He leaned his ax up against the stump, putting his hands on his lean hips. Her eyes were drawn to the muscles on his broad chest, and she had to force herself to look up and meet his gaze. "I think it would be pretty cool to get some bulls, personally. Or sheep. Whatever. I think I would just rather work on my own lands than just about anything else."

"Why don't you?"

He laughed, shaking his head. "Because that isn't how it works. I know a lot of people see the West family name as some kind of trophy. But the fact of the matter is there's a lot of responsibility with it. Yeah, we have a lot. Privileged as hell. But the thing is, I have to do something with that. I didn't build any of this. The reason I have money is that my father was able to put me in charge of a business that was already lucrative. That's the reason I have this land. I owe it to him to keep working the business. And after that, I owe it to him to keep the family business going. I can't just step aside to do what I want to do."

"What about your siblings? I know your younger sister is involved in the rodeo, when she isn't pregnant."

"Yeah, she's pretty much it as far as rodeo affiliation goes. Madison is into dressage. Which is mostly what my father breeds horses for. Dressage and hunter/jumpers."

"I've never been to your family ranch. What's it look like?"

He lifted a shoulder, and that small motion set his muscles into play again. She blinked hard. "It's different than this. Lots of open space around the house, fields everywhere. My parents' house is like an Italian villa."

"Which sounds like nothing you would be interested in inhabiting."

His dark brows locked together. "You think so?"

"I'm not blind, Colton. I've been living in your little cabin in the woods for the past few weeks."

"Little?"

She felt a smile tugging at her lips and even though she knew it was ill-advised, she couldn't resist. "Inoffensive?"

He laughed. "Okay."

"The point is, this—" she gestured to the barn "—is not an Italian villa."

"It doesn't matter. Anyway, I can't put too much into it, and I can't get too much into the breeding part of it, because then I'm in competition with my dad."

"So what?"

"Spoken like someone who doesn't have to deal with her parents on a regular basis."

She couldn't argue with that, but it still hurt. And it made her want to lash out.

"So, you somehow imagine that because I don't see my parents all the time my relationship with them is any easier?"

"I'm just saying, you don't have to negotiate your personal life and choices around them. Or your position in the community."

"The reason I don't see my parents has nothing to do with my relationship with them being easy. Trust me. I didn't move away from them for fun or just on a whim. I needed distance."

Her mother and father's brand of smothering, controlling, never satisfied love was something she wouldn't wish on anyone. And she knew it made her a terrible person to remove herself from them when she was all they had left, but she hadn't known what else to do for her sanity.

Phone calls and occasional holiday visits were much easier. It was much simpler to listen to her mother drone on and on about how Lydia needed to start focusing on getting married, because of course Frannie hadn't been able to live to see a wedding day. Much simpler over the phone, where her mother couldn't read her facial expressions.

But, of course Colton wouldn't know about that.

His brother left.

Yeah, as if that was remotely the same.

"That doesn't change the fact that you don't have the same considerations that I have. Plus, it's up to me to do what my brother isn't here to do."

And that hit a little too close to home.

"Why? He chose to leave. Anyway, you can't make your entire life about fixing what somebody else broke."

"That's what everyone does, Lydia."

"What do you mean?"

"Everything we do is a response to something. If you do the exact opposite of what your parents want you to do, you're still doing it for them in a way, aren't you? Whether you work to please them, or you work to piss them off. Either way, you're doing it for them."

"Not me," she said. There was almost no one on earth doing less for her parents' benefit than her. Except for maybe a crack addict.

"All right," he said, "I forgot. You're a special snowflake who does everything better than everyone else."

"Damn straight."

"Do you go out of your way to be impossible to deal with?"

"Do you go out of your way to be the most high-handed man on the planet? Seriously, Colton. As if you have the world completely figured out?"

"I thought I did. Until I wound up married to you."

"Oh right, after your fiancée left you at the altar, which most definitely happens to men who have everything on lockdown."

Suddenly, she found herself being advanced on. She froze completely as Colton closed the distance between them, wrapping his arm around her waist and pulling her up against him. Her palms made contact with his bare chest, her heart lurching into her throat as his skin scorched hers.

He was hot, impossibly so. She felt as though he might burn her at the first touch. Incinerate her completely where she stood and turn her into a little ash pile formerly known as Lydia Carpenter.

That was ridiculous. He did not possess the power to change her, or to alter her molecular structure in any way.

Even if it seemed like, in this moment, he might.

"What are you doing?"

"Something we both want."

Before she had a chance to protest, his lips crashed down on hers, claiming her fiercely, intensely.

She knew she should pull away. She knew that she should stop this. But the fact of the matter was, whether she knew she should or not, she didn't want to. Because he was right, this was something they both wanted. This was something that she craved.

It didn't make sense. But it was slick, and hot, and sweet, and she didn't really care if sense was involved at all.

He angled his head, deepening the kiss, his tongue sliding against hers. And her knees buckled. Thankfully, he was holding on to her tightly or she would have slid right down onto the ground.

She slid her hands up to his shoulders, reveled in how muscular he was beneath her palms. She didn't care if this was like any of the kisses they had shared before. She didn't even try to reach back in her memory to see if she could remember. She didn't care. She didn't care about anything but this.

He grabbed hold of her hips, propelling her backward until her shoulder blades butted up against the wooden building just behind them. Her face was hot, flushed, her entire body starting to feel the same way.

She had kissed a few men, but none like this. No man had ever just grabbed hold of her and pushed her backward. No man had ever made her quite so aware of how feminine she was in contrast to how strong and masculine he was. No man had ever made her quite so acutely aware of the differences between men and women, and he was still dressed. Well, mostly.

She moved her hands over his bare skin, over the muscles on his back and down over his chest. She had never thought much one way or the other about chest hair. But she was thinking very positive thoughts about it right now. It was all a part of that contrast that she was enjoying so very much.

He rocked his hips against hers, bringing her into contact with the evidence of his arousal. He wanted her. He wanted this, as badly as she did. It didn't matter that he thought she was annoying, and he most certainly did. He still wanted her.

He slid his hand down to her side, down farther, grabbing the hem of her skirt and pushing it upward. Then he gripped her leg, drawing it up over his hip, before repeating the motion with the other one, pressing her back yet more firmly against the wall as he kissed her harder, deeper.

Driven by some instinct she hadn't realized that she had possessed, she rolled her hips against his hardened length, gasping as her sensitive bundle of nerves made perfect contact with him.

Blunt fingertips dug into her thigh, holding her more tightly to him as he continued to kiss her. He rocked against her, heightening the reckless heat that was raging between them.

She readjusted her hold on him, grabbing his shoulders, her fingernails digging into his skin. She wasn't sure she cared. About anything. About what might happen in five minutes, ten minutes, three hours. The only thing that mattered was this.

She had expected she might flash back to Las Vegas, but she was too present. Too caught up in what was happening now. So sharp, so utterly consuming she could do nothing else but exist in it.

He nipped her bottom lip, then sucked it deeply between his own, and an arrow of pleasure shot down unerringly between her thighs. She gasped, letting her head fall back, and he angled his head, taking the opportunity to blaze a trail of kisses down her neck and her collarbone.

She had always thought that Colton West was arrogant. And it turned out he had a very arrogant mouth, and he knew how to use it. In this instance, she could only be grateful.

Because she did not know how to handle chemistry like this. And he, apparently, did.

Something about that thought brought the first invasion of reality prodding through the hazy veil that had drawn itself over her brain. Oh yes, he knew, and he had experienced it with her friend. Ex-friend. Whatever. It didn't matter.

As if this betrayal was any worse than running for mayor against her father?

Okay, so it wasn't really that that she cared about. It was comparisons. It was being found lacking.

She pushed against him, regretting it even as she extricated herself from his hold. "This is crazy," she said.

He jumped back as though he'd been scalded, his chest heaving with the force of his breath. "Completely."

She made the mistake of looking down. And when she did, she saw the outline of his *inoffensive penis* against the front of his jeans. Inoffensive indeed.

She looked back up, but, it was a little too late since he had already realized what she was doing. "It's…it was nothing," she said. Then she could have bitten her own tongue off because she had not intended to say that out loud.

"That was not nothing," he said, which, all things considered was one of the least horrifying things he could say.

"But I'm going to pretend that it was," she said.

"You think you can?"

"Alternate question—is there any world in which we shouldn't?"

"Probably not," he said, stepping away from her. "But that doesn't mean it was nothing."

"Fish," she said, for some reason the image of the brown paper bag still sitting on the counter in the house floating up to the top of her mind.

"What?"

"I bought fish for dinner. It's sitting on the counter."

"Oh. That's a strange anticlimax."

"There are French fries, too," she added, as if that was somehow going to make up for the fish.

"Well, okay then."

"Don't act so irritated. You know as well as I do that it's a good thing I put a stop to this. Otherwise we would have...we would have... You know."

"We would have had sex?"

"I don't see any point in discussing it now. We came to our senses."

This time, he was the one who looked down at the front of his own jeans. Heat lashed her cheeks. "Kind of," he said.

"I'm sorry about...that." It occurred to her then that she had never really had to apologize to a man for giving him an erection before. Mostly because she couldn't remember being in this kind of situation.

Not that she'd never given a man an erection. Obviously she had. She'd had sex before. It was just, it had never been so fraught. She had never really tried to resist it before. There had been nothing to resist. Always before she had been in relationships. Relationships with very nice men—okay, two men spaced very far apart. And there had been a very steady timeline. And things happened with planning and a lot of discussion beforehand.

She had never been carried away on a wave of desire. Had never been remotely tempted to sleep with someone she wasn't in a relationship with, much less someone she didn't even like.

You're married to him. That's a relationship.

She wanted to beat that wicked little internal voice of hers. Because this was not a relationship. And falling back on the excuse that they were married was pretty thin. Considering they weren't actually married. Well, they weren't going to stay married.

"Don't worry. It should remain inoffensive," he said. "It won't trouble you while you try to eat your dinner."

"Good," she said, refusing to smile, or to act like his words had bothered her in any way.

She realized then that her skirt was still hiked up partway, exposing way more of her thighs than she was comfortable with.

She tugged it back down, trying to look somehow like it was a calculated move. Like maybe it was even smooth, or kind of sexy rather than a belated realization executed clumsily.

"Well," she said, trying to keep her tone arch. "I'm going to go back and eat dinner. So, maybe I'll see you."

"Yeah, I'll be back in soon."

But she knew that he wouldn't. Because now he was going to start avoiding her again. Which was for the best. It really was. She should not feel crestfallen about it. Or disappointed in any way. She needed him to ignore her. She needed one of them to be sane, since she had clearly lost her mind.

"Great," she said, turning and walking away.

She had a feeling she knew now why she kept her well-worn paths. And she was more than a little determined to keep to them again in the future. No more detours for her. None at all.

BY THE TIME Colton walked into Ace's his mood was somewhere way past foul. He had not gone in to eat fish and chips with Lydia, because if he had done that he would have ended up laying her over the counter and finishing what they had started down there by the woodshed. Common sense and questionable breath be damned.

So instead, he was here probably looking as vile as he felt. Which would be great for the rumor mill. Actually, he hadn't thought about the rumor mill until he'd walked in and seen every eye in the place pinned to him.

He chose to ignore them. He walked over to the bar and sat down on one of the stools, pounding the top of it. "Bartender, who does a man have to shoot to get a little service around here?"

His brother-in-law turned to face him, a broad smile on his face. "There has not been a single shooting in this establishment since the 1800s. And you know it."

As much as Colton had questioned his sister's association with Ace initially, he couldn't deny that the other man was actually a great match for Sierra.

"Not down at the brewery today?" he asked, talking about Ace's new venture down by the waterfront.

"Some days I just like to get back to basics. Anyway, if I was never here anymore we would have to change the name."

"Good point."

"I hear congratulations are in order," Ace said, putting a glass beneath the tap and filling it up. He slid the beer across the counter, and Colton grabbed hold of it.

"Congratulations and a beer is all I get?"

"Sorry, I didn't realize marriage was a hard drinking occasion."

"If marriage isn't, then what is?"

His brother-in-law regarded him closely. "Right. Well, you start with the beer. I would hate to have to call your wife and have her come pick you up. We don't want her to find out too much about you this early into things."

"True enough," he replied.

"I sense there's a story here. And I would really like to hear it."

"I didn't offer to tell it."

"I noticed. But, I'm asking. My bartender hat is on, not the married-to-your-sister hat."

Colton frowned. "If that's your way of asking for explicit details I'm going to decline."

"No," Ace said, "you got left at the altar. I think that's a pretty good story."

"*Good* is not the word I would use."

"But you ended up married to the right woman."

"Yeah," Colton said, "so I did."

Footsteps alerted him to someone else walking up to the bar and he turned, recognition hitting him like a blow to the jaw. This was not what he needed right now.

"Colton, this isn't your usual hangout."

Colton couldn't say anything for a moment. He was too preoccupied looking at the person in front of him. He didn't normally examine another man's features, but when they look so much like your own it was difficult not to.

"Jack," he said, looking at his half brother.

The two of them had barely spoken since they had found out that they were half siblings. Really, there wasn't much to talk about. It didn't change much. It didn't change anything. Not really. Jack, for his part, hadn't gone spreading it all around, but it was pretty much an open secret at this point.

"Yeah," he said. "Do you mind if we talk?"

Colton bristled. "We're talking right now."

"That isn't what I mean. I want to go outside and talk for a minute."

"If you want to punch me in my face, Jack, why don't you just do it here?"

"I don't have any interest in punching you. Well, I don't have any interest in punching you anymore. I might have a couple of years ago."

Colton would have honestly preferred a fistfight to a conversation, at least tonight. But he couldn't very well deny his half brother's request for a conversation without looking like a dick. Not that he really minded looking like a dick.

But doing the right thing was ingrained in him. If it hadn't been, when Lydia pushed him earlier outside the woodshed he might have just pulled her closer. Might have rolled his hips into hers once more. She wouldn't have protested. Not again. Not when she wanted it just as badly as he did.

But no. He did the right thing.

He was starting to hate that.

"Fine." He stood up, then turned back to look at Ace. "Don't let anyone roofie my beer."

Ace didn't say anything; he just stared at the two of them, as did everyone else in the room, while they walked out to the front of the bar. It was damn cold outside, especially right here by the water. And he hadn't brought a jacket because he'd been in too much of a hurry to get well away from Lydia.

"Okay, what's up, Monaghan?"

"Sierra is due soon," Jack said, "which I only know because Kate is due soon. And I understand why you didn't come to our wedding. Hell, I didn't go to yours."

"Well, no one did," Colton retorted.

"The other one," he said.

"Right. Okay then."

"It's just…my kid and Sierra's kid are going to be cousins. Any kids you have…same thing. I don't know what our relationship is going to be. I don't blame you for having reservations about me. And I think I'm well within my rights to have them about you. I understand why your parents are never going to welcome me with open arms. Your dad is never going to be grandpa to my son. And I get that. I don't like it, but I get it. The thing is, I don't think I want him cut off from the rest of the family."

Jack's words hit Colton hard. He'd never really considered the long-reaching familial connection they had. Or what it would mean for their children.

Of course, God knew when he would be having children now. He and Natalie had had a two-year plan. She had been more than ready to start a family with him, after they had been married an appropriate length of time. But where did that leave him now? All of this put him at least four years away from having children. Which meant he would be… No. He wasn't going to do the math on that.

But he didn't know how he hadn't really considered any of this before. He was going to be an uncle to Jack's children. And either they got it together and dealt with each other, or Jack was right. Those kids would continue to be cut off from a huge part of their family.

"It's one thing for us," Jack continued. "I mean, we're in our thirties. We've made what we could out of what we got. But I want better for our kids. I want better for my son. The Garretts are a great family. They were a family to me when I didn't have one. And I know they'd be more than enough family for my and Kate's baby. But this is in our control. So let's just do better."

Colton didn't really want to do better. Not right now. He had done all that he could for one day. Hell, maybe for one lifetime. He felt stretched and pushed, and all he wanted to do was walk away from this right now. Go straight back home, lose himself in something. Lydia's arms would be his preference, but that had pretty much been ruled out for the day.

And she was right—they shouldn't touch each other. There was no future in it. He didn't have casual sex. And he most especially didn't have this kind of casual sex. The kind that was loaded and difficult to deal with.

Still, it didn't change the fact that he wanted it.

It also didn't change the fact that he had to deal with this. Even if he didn't feel like it. Damn responsibilities. There was never any end to them.

And there was something strange about standing there, looking at someone who looked so much like him. A brother.

He hadn't seen his other brother, the one he had been raised with, in seventeen years. And then there was Jack. Which was strange, because Colton had spent so many years feeling like he was the only one. The last man standing in the West family. At least, in his generation. But there was Jack.

Jack, who had their father's eyes. Colton's eyes. Jack, who was so obviously Nathan West's son once you knew what to look for.

"Yeah," Colton said finally. "I agree. And I'm...I'm happy for you. The baby. And Kate."

"They're the best thing that ever happened to me."

"And here I thought that was me."

Jack smiled. "I guess we'll find out."

He stuck out his hand and Colton just looked at it.

Finally, he extended his own, shaking it. "All right. I guess...I guess we're going to do this."

"Right. Well," Jack said. "I guess I'll see you around."

"Yeah."

Okay, at least one interaction had gone well tonight. As for Lydia...well, he would just continue to avoid her. Eventually, his body would chill out.

Unfortunately, since he wasn't one for casual sex, it meant there would be no sex with anyone else. Also, they were technically married. Which presented a problem. Not just because they lived in a small town, but because for some reason his conscience didn't like the idea of sleeping with anyone else while they were still bound by a marriage license. As ridiculous as it was to feel bound by a license he couldn't even remember signing.

Nothing about this made sense. It hadn't from the very beginning.

And more and more, he was starting to wonder why exactly he thought it was such a bad idea for the two of them to be with each other, at least for a little while.

Because you don't like her.

Right. Of course, he liked her a whole lot more when her breasts were pressed up against his chest and her tongue was in his mouth.

He gritted his teeth. He was going to have to forget that. Because he did the right thing. Even when it felt terrible.

CHAPTER TEN

HER STOMACH HADN'T stopped fluttering all day. She trusted her campaign volunteers to see to the details of the dinner. But it was still all she could do not to show up early and micromanage.

She liked micromanaging. That was the truth.

But she didn't have time. She was still acting president of the Chamber of Commerce while running this campaign. That meant working full-time and trying to get votes. So, she had had to finish out the workday, then she had to go back to Colton's place and get dressed. Which was what she was currently stuck in the middle of.

It wasn't black tie, but she needed something that looked polished. Now she sort of wished it was formal. Then she could've put on an awesome dress. As it was, she had decisions to make.

She ended up deciding on a navy-and-white checkered top, a colored vest and a pair of skinny jeans with ankle boots. That was appropriately rustic for the surroundings. She did the kind of loose, effortless braid that actually took almost an hour and transformed her fingers into claws, but the end result was adorable if she did say so herself.

She added a berry lipstick and some navy-colored

eye shadow that complemented the shirt. And with that, she felt slightly ready to face her potential constituents.

Sometimes, it dawned on her that she was officially a politician. And she wondered how on earth she had gotten here. She supposed it was an achievement. But it was kind of a strange one. An exhilarating one.

Really, the only one she had ever aimed for because of how much she loved her town. And that was the real reason people should get into politics, anyway. The desire to serve. For the love of a place and its people.

With that little internal mantra firmly in place she headed down the stairs and almost ran right into Colton.

And oh, sweet Lord, tonight was going to be a slow descent into madness.

Colton was… Well, there were words for what he was, but all she came up with was a strange, inarticulate squeak.

He had a cowboy hat on, which did things to her insides that weren't decent. He was also wearing a red plaid flannel shirt, tucked into a pair of dark jeans, accentuated by a belt with a very large…buckle. Of course, her eyes had drifted a little bit south of said buckle.

Inoffensive…

Inoffensive was not the word.

His sleeves were rolled up to his elbows, displaying those incredibly enticing forearms. Seriously, who would have ever thought forearms could be particularly enticing. Well, maybe a lot of people had. But she hadn't.

He was wearing black cowboy boots, and a black cowboy hat, and she felt like she was having some kind of very strange Westerngasm, which she would have said previously that she was absolutely not prone to.

She really needed some water. Just so very thirsty.

"Does this meet your criteria?"

"It's fine."

If by *fine* she was really meaning damaging to her sanity, then she was being completely honest.

"You look like…you look like you should be carrying a basket of apples."

"Okay, that's weird. Why apples?"

"I don't know. You have a wholesome country girl thing going on."

She frowned. "You have a very strange idea of what a country girl is."

"I feel like I would be a better expert on the subject than you. Since you're an import."

"Yes, from the greater metropolitan area of Seattle."

"Fake country girl," he said, his tone filled with mock scolding that she strangely found her body responding to.

She swallowed. "Well, you're going to have to deal with me, sans apples. I hope you can manage the disappointment."

A smile curved his lips, and she felt her own lips tug into an even deeper frown in response. "I think I can handle that." He gripped the edge of the counter and she was powerless to keep herself from admiring his hands. They were workman's hands. Large, rough. She could remember easily the way he had held her as he'd kissed her up against the woodshed.

And it was all flooding back to her now. And along with it, heat was flooding into her face.

"I'm not exactly sure what you need me to do," he said, shifting his hold on the counter, drawing her eyes straight back to those fingers. Those hands.

"You're my basket of apples," she said.

"Come again, peaches?"

"If you call me peaches I might kill you."

"Not at a political event you wouldn't."

"I feel pretty confident I could get acquitted."

"Okay, expound on the basket of apples."

She sighed heavily. For some reason fruit metaphors were abounding. "You're my accessory." As soon as she said that, she got a little giddy kick in her chest. She was enjoying the idea a little too much. "The arm candy."

"I'm your arm candy?"

"My trophy husband." And then she smiled, because this idea she actually enjoyed. Not only because she usually did this sort of thing alone, but because Colton was Colton, and she knew that he was used to being the center of…well, everything. She also knew that Natalie had been prepared to step into that role. To be his arm candy at any given event. But the tables were turning. And she wasn't even going to pretend she wasn't enjoying it.

"Does that mean I have to get Botox?"

"You are a little bit…rugged around your mouth. But, with men that's often a plus. One of the great inequalities in society." Except, she couldn't really complain about it because she liked him rugged. The lines next to his mouth, little ones feathering out from his eyes. It gave him character. A little something extra to look at.

"I'm rugged? Rugged around the mouth. Excellent. I'll add that to my list of qualities. It goes underneath *inoffensive penis*."

Heat streaked across her face. "Well, you do that. I'm not going to keep a list. But if you must."

"I'm just learning a lot of new things about myself. You know, from you."

"That's funny, you've taught me nothing."

He moved forward, and she felt faint. Was certain that she was going to find herself hauled up against that hard chest again, wrapped tightly in his embrace, that firm uncompromising mouth kissing her until neither of them could breathe.

But that didn't happen.

Lydia, calm thyself.

She was breathing hard, her cheeks were most certainly red, and she had little doubt that Colton knew exactly what she had been thinking he might do.

Instead of grabbing her, he slowly looped his arm through hers, sliding his palm down her forearm, over the back of her hand, before gradually lacing his fingers through hers. She held her hand stiff, straight. Because she couldn't move. If she did, she might do something humiliating. She might run out of the room. Or worse, she might lean in and smell him.

He smelled so good. Even from where she was standing. Pine and salt from the air outside, wood and hay.

She felt herself sway slightly, and she jerked herself back.

"You're going to have to hold my hand, peaches. Otherwise this isn't going to look real."

"I don't know. Maybe I have a strict policy on public displays of affection and professional events."

"No politician does, Lydia, and you know that."

His blue eyes were locked on to hers, and she found she didn't want to look away even though she should. It made her unbearably conscious of everything. Of the fact that her mouth was dry, and her lips were dry, and she desperately wanted to lick them, but if she did it would seem provocative. Or maybe it wouldn't seem that provocative. She wasn't much of a seductress.

She could feel the challenge radiating from him, could see that he was going to keep persisting until she gave in. Well, she wasn't a coward. And she had held hands with him before. She had done a lot more than that.

Slowly, she curved her fingers over his, the warmth of his touch burning through her, making her stomach tight.

"There," she said. "Is that convincing enough?"

"It's a start," he said, his voice suddenly a little bit rougher.

"Okay, dearest husband. Are you ready to go to the hoedown?"

His smile widened, and a corresponding sensation unfurled in her stomach. "I'm ready to show the whole town what a good trophy I am."

It was kind of an incredible experience, to see how many people had come out to support Lydia. He had only ever really looked at her through his own lens, and Natalie's. Natalie had definitely not been her biggest fan for the past few months.

He remembered listening to her going on and on ad nauseum about the betrayal. And, being a guy, he had asked why on earth she still had Lydia in the wedding.

She had explained to him, very slowly, as though he were stupid, that it was too late to change the bridal party. That Lydia already had her dress, and that expelling her from the group would only look petty. Which would look worse for her father.

And so, Lydia had remained, and Colton had been forced to endure a great many rantings on the subject.

Not that he'd objected on a personal level. Because he hadn't exactly been Lydia's number one fan.

Well, now here he was, standing in the middle of the Garretts' barn all but wearing a campaign badge.

Just as he had that thought, Sadie Garrett breezed by and handed him a button. "You have to wear this," she said, smiling, her expression dazzling.

"Thank you, Sadie," he said, taking the red, white and blue button emblazoned with Lydia's name and pinning it to his shirt.

"It matches," she said, looking far too cheerful. It made him wonder how much she knew.

"Why, so it does."

Sadie bounded off after that, continuing to hand out buttons and straighten centerpieces on the various tables set up throughout the space. There was going to be a dinner, a barbecue, and everyone was shelling out mass dollars a plate.

He supposed, given that his own bank account was relatively flush, he should probably make a donation. But then, wasn't standing in as her husband donation enough? He had essentially donated his body to the cause.

Lydia was fussing with chair placement and a clipboard over next to a staging area that had been set up. He supposed he should go stand with her. Or maybe it wasn't appropriate. He wasn't really sure. He didn't want to loom.

The fact of the matter was he didn't know anything about politics and Lydia seemed to know a lot. There wasn't much he could contribute.

Maybe he would seek out a beer.

But he didn't want to look disinterested, either. Okay,

it was more difficult to be a trophy spouse than he had given credit for.

Colton watched the entire Garrett family file in. Kate was about as round as his sister, though not wearing the flowing maternity dresses that Sierra favored. Kate was wearing jeans and an oversize flannel top, untucked. It looked like it was probably Jack's. Jack was standing with her, holding on to her elbow, playing the part of solicitous husband much better than Colton ever could.

After them came Connor and Liss, who seemed to have a slight bump herself. Colton hadn't heard that they were expecting a new addition to their family, but then, he didn't really seek out that kind of gossip.

He looked up at the lights that were strung overhead, giving the whole space a warm glow. Really, it was pretty perfect. Lydia was smart, steering clear of the formal affair. He had experienced his fair share of them, but that didn't mean he liked them.

That kind of stuff was old money. Old politics. Old, dusty family names like his own. Lydia was trying to separate herself from that, and this event would do a great job.

Eli came in a few moments later, obviously scanning the room for Sadie.

"She's running around," Colton said.

"That doesn't surprise me," Eli said.

"Can I get you something? A beer?"

Eli shook his head. "No, thank you. I'm not allowed to drink."

For a full second, Colton wondered if it was because Eli actually got rowdy when he drank. Rowdy Eli Garrett would be a sight indeed. If there was a more uptight, staid individual in the entire town, well, Colton was married to her.

But then, he knew pretty quickly that couldn't be why. "Not allowed?" Colton pressed.

"Sadie says I can't until she can again."

"Oh," Colton responded. "You Garretts are prolific."

"Pretty much anything that looks like permanent commitment terrifies Sadie. So, I had to wait much longer than I wanted to to marry her. And we are jumping into the family thing a little later than everyone else. And I had to make trades."

"No alcohol."

"That's just the tip of the iceberg. I'm not allowed to do anything she can't do." Eli smiled. "Of course, I don't really mind."

"Marriage," Colton said, not really sure if that was the appropriate response.

But all of this made him wonder exactly what he would've been in for if he were actually married. If he and Natalie had actually gone through with it. He would have had to deal with pregnant Natalie. Though he couldn't imagine her asking him to forgo alcohol, or anything like that. Their lives hadn't been like this. They hadn't been all meshed together.

"Right," Eli said.

Colton still had the sense Eli would happily use him for target practice if need be.

"I should go see if she needs something."

"Soon she may need you to abstain from alcohol."

Colton nearly choked. "I doubt it. If you haven't noticed, Lydia is a touch ambitious. I think I'll just be an assistant pamphlet distributor for a few years." Months. Until all of this was over.

The barn was starting to fill up with people he didn't know quite as well, and folks were beginning to fill up their respective places at the table.

He walked over to where Lydia was standing and put his hand on her elbow. She jumped, nearly losing the campaign buttons she was holding in her hand. "What?" she asked.

"Where are we sitting?"

Much like Sadie, her smile grew strangely wide. "Kind of everywhere."

"What does that mean? How hard am I going to have to work to get my barbecue?"

"Well, we're going to have dinner at every table. We are going to rotate while we eat."

"That sounds exceedingly friendly of us."

"You said yourself, you're used to this kind of thing. You should be really good at it." She smiled yet more unconvincingly. "In fact, I know you are. Because I saw the way you charmed Marlene at my office the other day."

"I am good at it."

"I mean, not with me...but with other people. So as long as we don't talk everything should go well."

For some reason, that devil that lived inside of him, previously undiscovered, really wanted to prod at her. Because there was something intoxicating about it. It was this. The fact that he felt like he didn't have any control. That he was effectively being neutered, and yeah, taking the position of a trophy spouse. Whatever the reason, he couldn't quite resist.

"I don't know, peaches. I think I'm pretty damn good with you."

She flushed, just like she had back in the kitchen before they had come here tonight. She had turned a pretty compelling shade of red when she had first seen him, and then, when he had gone to take her hand she had taken on the color of a poppy.

Of course, it wasn't as though he was unaffected. He had touched that soft skin on her hand and had gotten hard as a rock. Kissing her down at the woodshed had been a mistake, there was no other word for it.

He had been doing okay controlling himself where she was concerned ever since she had moved in. But then they had kissed. And after that? Well, after that he had gone to bed every night with a hard-on that wouldn't quit. And he'd woken up with it, too. Persistent bastard.

"Not dignifying that with a response. Because peaches isn't my name."

"That's going to make socializing at dinner a little bit difficult."

"Oh no," Lydia whispered, her gaze on something just past him. He turned, and she slapped him on the forearm. "Don't look," she admonished him.

"I'm sorry, but I wanted to see exactly what we were upset about."

"I'm upset about it. Not you. You don't have to be upset." She sighed heavily. "Actually, *upset* isn't even the word. It's just I didn't really need to deal with Nolan tonight. I have guilt."

"Who's that?"

"My ex-boyfriend. It's been a long time since we dated. And, we do have to deal with each other since he's involved in the Historical Society. But I'm not usually married when that happens."

Colton bit back a rising tide of jealousy he had not been expecting. "And that's a problem because you... still have something going with him? Chamber of Com-

merce and Historical Society shenanigans. Which, inci-
dentally, sounds like the dustiest sex imaginable."

She frowned. "His sex was not dusty."

"But was his penis inoffensive?"

"I'm not having this conversation with you. Not right
now." She looked behind him again. "And to answer
your question, no, nothing is still going on between the
two of us. But I kind of broke up with him because I
didn't want things to progress between us any further
than they already had."

"Meaning...what? Role play?"

"Meaning he wanted to move in. And eventually get
married. And I said no. I told him I didn't think that kind
of commitment was for me."

"Oh. So you think he's going to be mad because you
did get married."

"Probably. I kind of broke his heart."

"Lydia Carpenter, I didn't realize you were a Jezebel."

"I ran off with my friend's fiancé. You should have
known."

"I guess that was the warning."

"Okay, we have to sit now. And, you have to behave."

"We've been through this already. I always behave."

She looked at him, studying him closely for a moment. "Except for sometimes with me."

That struck him straight in the chest. "Same goes."

"Sometimes," she replied, her voice scratchy.

And then it was time for him to take her hand. Because dinner was being served. He reached out, slowly
taking hold of her, lingering a little overlong as he let his
fingers drift over the back of her hand. He didn't need
to touch her like this. He didn't need to make an event
out of it. But also, it seemed wrong not to.

Partly because he had been celibate for three months before that night in Las Vegas. Partly because casually touching Lydia didn't seem right.

Not when he was only allowed to do it so briefly. Not when he was preventing himself from having what he wanted most. It was like taking a sip of something you wanted to drink in deep. But sips were all he was allowed. So he would take them slowly. Indulgently. And yeah, maybe that wouldn't do much of anything for his craving, but if all you got was a taste you better relish it.

And tastes were all he felt like he was getting all night. Not just of Lydia, but of his dinner. There were more tables than there were courses, so he found himself taking a bite, attempting to make casual conversation, and then getting ushered off to the next table. Lydia seemed to have boundless energy for the whole thing.

It was strange, following her lead in a social setting. That was not his usual default. For anything. He had gone to a great many events with Natalie over the years, and it was like a well-worn imitation of what his parents had done before him.

His father forged business connections and made conversation while his mother clung quietly to his side.

Natalie was more than happy to assume that position. And he had been more than happy to have her there. This was…this was something else. Lydia would never do that. Lydia would always be out there trying to achieve her own ends during an event.

Lydia seemed to be entirely comprised of ambition and good intentions. And what he had seen as being uptight was…well, she was uptight. But also, she was enthusiastic, and she cared a lot. So when things weren't going her way she didn't have the best of reactions.

If he was being completely fair, it was a little like him.

She tensed, and he realized that little silent timer on her watch had finished counting down. And that their next table was very likely the one she had been dreading.

They got up, and shuffled over to the next table, which was a slightly larger one. Most of the people there were probably over the age of sixty, but there were a few closer to their age. And only one that was male.

For some reason, Colton's first thought was that he could easily win in a fight. Which was possibly his testosterone talking.

"Hi," Lydia said, sitting down. "Nolan." She greeted the man by name. He didn't really blame her, getting it out of the way. Trying to make it less awkward. Though, in reality, nothing would probably make it much less awkward. Because Lydia looked like she was about to vibrate out of her skin.

"Hello, Lydia," the man said, adjusting his glasses, pushing them up higher on the thin bridge of his nose. Everything about him was thin. He was reedy. And pale. And, in spite of what Lydia had said, clearly dusty. In a bookish way, not in a working outside way.

Not that he cared that Lydia had an ex—of course she did.

It was just that Colton objected to everything about this guy on sight. First of all, he made Lydia uneasy. And pretty much no one made Lydia uneasy. Therefore, anyone who did was automatically suspicious.

"I'm very interested to hear what the Historical Society is working on right now," Lydia said, addressing the table.

"Well," one of the women said, tucking a strand of hair behind her ear, "the farm isn't quite up and running yet, but once it is, we have plans to do farm-to-table dinners, tours of the original house, a corn maze, and talks from local historians and archaeologists."

"That's so interesting, Jenna. And I feel like it's going to be a big draw. Both for locals and for tourists."

It never failed to amaze him the way that Lydia remembered people. He had never listened to a single person the way Lydia seemed to listen to everyone she came into contact with. More than that, she remembered them. She knew this woman's name. And clearly had some idea of her interests.

It was either that, or she was very good at what she did. Either way, it was amazing.

"We have some new initiatives at the museum, as well," Nolan said, sounding every bit the stuffy librarian type Colton had figured he was. "This quarter, we'll be doing displays in the museum that focus on the native peoples of the area. And we will also be doing portable displays, for the schools." He looked at Colton, in a way that Colton felt was a bit too meaningful for two men to be looking at each other. "I'm going to be giving some talks at the school."

"Great," Colton said.

"Yes," Lydia said, sounding much more sparkly than he did. "That is fantastic. I'm very excited to hear about all of these new initiatives. And, of course, if I'm elected I'm going to offer support for these things, as much as I possibly can."

"It seems like being mayor would be an awfully big commitment," Nolan said. "I felt like in the past you had some issues with that."

"I've changed," Lydia said, reaching across the space

between them and taking hold of Colton's hand. "And my commitment to Copper Ridge has always been real."

Nolan didn't look like he had a comeback for that. Instead, he sat back in his chair. Lydia continued to make small talk with the rest of the women around the table, and, much to his chagrin, Colton accidentally caught Nolan's eye.

"I can't believe you convinced her to marry you," the other man said, clearly regarding Colton as competition of some kind.

"You know," Colton said, knowing he was just being a dick, "it wasn't actually that difficult."

"Well, that's different," Nolan said.

"I just feel like when it's right, it's right." And when you were Jack Daniel's drunk, you were Jack Daniel's drunk. Also, Las Vegas made it way too easy to get married. He would say neither of those things out loud.

"I felt like it was right with us. But she's weird about her space. She wouldn't even let me have a drawer at her house. And when I wanted to move in... I've never had a woman run when I wanted more of a commitment."

"I'm not entirely sure why you feel comfortable discussing this with her husband, even less with her husband at a professional event," Colton said, not quite sure where the righteous indignation was coming from. "But whatever was between you and Lydia is in the past. It has no bearing on what kind of mayor she's going to be. I think you know that Richard Bailey has no interest in what the Historical Society is doing." Colton was basing that entirely on having been in a relationship with the older man's daughter. "Lydia is going to do the right thing for the town, and if you let your personal feelings get in the way of that…well, I really believe you love history as much as you say."

He adjusted his spectacles again. "I care about the history of the town more than I care about anything else."

"Then you should take that into account when you vote. Not just the fact that you were spurned."

"My connection with Lydia was built on how much we both cared about the town. I'm surprised that she felt connected with you, all things considered."

"Reason being?"

"Your family has a lot of money, but I've never gotten the impression the West family cared much about the heritage of the town."

"Lydia makes me care about a lot of things," he said simply.

Nolan didn't have anything to say after that, and then, thankfully, their time was up.

When they stood, he wrapped his arm around Lydia's waist, resting his hand low on her hip. He was doing it mostly for Nolan's benefit. It was also a slightly longer, cooler sip.

Idly, he let his thumb drift across the denim, until he felt her shiver beneath his touch. It was a bad idea. He was full of bad ideas when Lydia was around.

The next table was much easier, as was the next. Pretty much any table that didn't have an irritated ex-boyfriend at it was easier.

As dessert and coffee were about to be served, Lydia stood. "I have to make a speech. I think you're supposed to stand to the left."

He leaned in, whispering in her ear. "I think that's only sex scandals."

"Is it?"

"I don't know. But is there one? Nolan would certainly like for there to be."

"We'll discuss that later." This time, she was the one that grabbed his hand, the contact of her soft skin against his an unexpected shock.

He felt slightly ridiculous moving to the stage, standing off to the side as Lydia took her position at the center and picked up a microphone that had been set up earlier. But then, he supposed he never really questioned it when wives did the same for their politically-minded husbands.

In his defense, it wasn't really sexism that was the issue, so much as this not being a real marriage.

"I want to thank everyone for coming out this evening," Lydia said, her voice steady. "Your support means so much to me. Without you, I wouldn't be anything. Without your support, my campaign doesn't go anywhere. You are here because you believe in the things that I believe in. You're here because you believe in Copper Ridge. So do I. More than that, I love it. It's my home. I know that traditionally small towns have a reputation for not accepting outsiders easily. But each and every one of you accepted me, and I never once felt like I didn't belong. I want to pay you back. All of you. Copper Ridge doesn't need to change—it just needs to move along with time. But while we do that, I feel it's important to respect our roots. To honor what it is about our small town that we love while building a better tomorrow. Thank you, and enjoy your dessert."

She began to step down off the stage, and he grabbed hold of her hand, drawing her forward. He wasn't sure why. He only knew that it seemed like the right thing

to do. Because she had made a great speech, and she'd
had every single person in the room riveted on what
she had to say.

He was…he was proud of her. Even if he hadn't
earned that feeling. And he was playing the part of trophy husband who was proud of his wife, so even if he
hadn't earned it, he had to act like he felt it and he had
to show that he did.

He curved his hand around the back of her neck,
drawing her in. Her dark eyes widened, her pupils expanding, and he saw panic there. But he also saw desire.
For a split second, there was a chance to turn back. To
figure out which message he saw on her face he was
going to take.

But then, he caught a wave of her scent. Floral, feminine, and there really was no more decision-making
time. Really, there was no decision.

He leaned in, pressing his mouth to hers. It was light,
because he wasn't going to get overly passionate in front
of a room full of people. Also because he needed to
prove to himself that light was possible with Lydia.

But light didn't mean easy. It didn't mean feeling any
less scorched from the inside out. It didn't mean that it
left him without that hollow ache that started deep in
his stomach and slowly scooped out every other part
of him, leaving him feeling weaker and stronger at the
same time.

When they separated, he was breathing hard, and so
was she. Their response was definitely a little bit over-
blown for as chaste as the kiss had been. But in truth,
nothing with Lydia was chaste, ever. Not a touch of her
hand against his, not an arm around her waist and most
certainly not a kiss. Hell, even a glance was filled with

the dirty, deep memory that neither of them seemed to have entirely. It was the wondering that made it so powerful. The fact that the blank space was full of infinite possibility.

All they knew was desire, and beyond that, neither of them remembered how they'd satisfied that desire. It was a strange sensation for Colton. To know there was a section of time when he'd been with Lydia, when he'd been beyond himself.

And all at once, he wondered if resisting was pointless. If it was doomed to fail.

It took him a moment to realize that people were still cheering. Probably for the kiss. If they had ever been in doubt that their relationship would be well received by the community, there was no doubt now. At least, not by this contingent. Of course, he had been engaged to the daughter of her rival, and he imagined that for Lydia's camp that made for a very interesting bit of gossip.

He imagined he was less popular in the Bailey camp. Even though Natalie had been the one to abandon him. He imagined there was a story being told over there that didn't flatter him at all.

He'd been the one abandoned at the altar. He didn't need a story or an excuse. Because he married someone else, because he wasn't the one who had stopped the wedding. He hadn't really appreciated what a convenient position that was until just now.

He had a little more control over the gossip than Natalie.

Not for the first time, he wondered if he needed to get in touch with her. Personally, not just through a moving service.

"It was a great speech," he said.

"Thank you," Lydia said, her words tight.

"I think I make a pretty good first lady."

"Yeah, you do," she said, her eyes never leaving his.

He wondered if she might be thinking the same thing he was. If she might be thinking it was a lost cause and that there was no point in fighting.

He damn sure hoped so. And if she wasn't, then he was ready to try and bring her around to his way of thinking.

CHAPTER ELEVEN

Lydia was more determined than ever to resist Colton.

Resist was a strong word. It implied that it was hard. It implied that she was actively doing battle with her desire for him. No. She wasn't. In fact, the kiss from the fund-raiser last night had all but been forgotten.

She grabbed her peppermint mocha off the counter at The Grind and took a sip, letting the comforting warmth settle inside of her, making her feel calm. That's it. She was calm.

And, if she had retired quickly to her bedroom after the dinner last night, and had decided to go into town to do some campaign work on her computer on a Saturday just because she couldn't concentrate at Colton's house, it was all a coincidence.

"Thank you," she said to the barista behind the counter.

She walked back to her seat, where her laptop was already set up, her purse slung over the back of the chair. She imagined that was something you couldn't do in most towns. But, in Copper Ridge, she didn't worry much about leaving her belongings for a few moments.

She hummed as she pulled up an Excel spreadsheet, examining the takeaway from last night. There had been the expected money earned per plate, which had been discounted for people from various organizations, such as the Historical Society, where she was looking to get a group on board with her vision. But then there were donations on top of that that had been incredibly generous.

She opened up the new pamphlet she'd been working on. She would be able to get those printed up and distributed, and probably get a radio ad, too. The good thing about politics in a small town was that it was a bit more budget friendly than it would be if she were in a larger area. Of course, that meant that she had to tailor her fund-raisers to small-town budgets. So really, you ended up working within the economy you had.

She didn't have scads of her own cash to throw around, unlike her opponent. But her campaign had been going well regardless.

She curved her fingers around her cup, looking out the window at the view of the town. It was gray out, mist hovering behind the little row of buildings outside. An American flag blew in the breeze, as did the wind socks hanging outside of Rebecca's store. Brightly colored nylon ribbons swinging in the breeze like fish on a trout line.

She leaned in, smelling her coffee before taking another sip. And then nearly choked on it when she saw Natalie through the glass door of the coffee shop.

She gritted her teeth, sitting up straighter. She seriously considered hitting the floor and doing an army crawl into the bathroom.

Damn small towns.

Instead, she sat there frozen, clutching her cup like it was some kind of lifeline. Or maybe a cloak of invisibility. It was neither. So when Natalie opened the door and stepped into the coffee shop, of course the first thing she did was make eye contact with Lydia.

Natalie froze, her blue eyes going wide. "I…" She turned, as though she were about to leave.

"Wait," Lydia said. Oh, why did she ask her to wait?

Natalie turned, arching a pale brow. "Oh, are you speaking to me?"

"Okay, that's weird. I was never not speaking to you. You're the one who's mad at me." Lydia could have bitten off her tongue. "Also, you were never not speaking to me, even though you were mad at me."

"Well, I'm just surprised that you would talk to me, seeing as you married my fiancé."

"You kind of left your fiancé at the altar first."

Neither of them were talking all that loudly, but Lydia could feel every eye in the room on them. They said all the world was a stage, and Lydia had never been very convinced of that. But a small town was most definitely a stage when drama was going on.

Out of the corner of her eye, Lydia saw someone lean over and whisper to another person across the table. Probably giving backstory. Lydia had done it a time or two herself. And she knew, had she been in the audience for this particular moment, she would have been glued to the action, too. It didn't mean it wasn't strange and irritating to find yourself being watched by a roomful of people.

"I still wanted to talk to him," Natalie said. "I wanted to explain. And I didn't want things to be over between us. But they definitely are now." Her voice was vibrating with anger, and Lydia felt a pinprick of guilt needle her back. She had never intended to hurt anyone. Honestly, she had never intended anything. And of course, she and Colton weren't even real.

Sure, they were attracted to each other, and yes they

had—physically. But they weren't staying married. And Natalie was hurt. She could be difficult, but she wasn't evil.

Lydia bit back a hundred replies that verged into cutting territory. There was no point in having a fight about it. There was no point in trying to one-up her.

It was weird, though, being in a position where she clearly had something someone else wanted. That just wasn't... That wasn't her life.

"You still can," Lydia found herself saying instead.

"Oh, and can I still marry him?"

"Legally, obviously not," Lydia said, feeling a little more irritated now. "But I can't answer for him. I can tell you that I think he was probably having similar doubts as you, or he might not have...done what he did."

"Well, thank you for your assessment on that," Natalie bit out. "How long were you waiting in the wings to grab hold of him? It wasn't enough you want to take my father's position in the community, you had to take my fiancé?"

"Unattended fiancés may be married by other people, Natalie," Lydia said, immediately regretting the sharpness of the statement. She was supposed to be benevolent. Everybody in the coffee shop was watching her. And all of this was going to get back to...well, eventually everyone.

"It's not like leaving your car in the wrong parking space. I did not want my fiancé to be towed away."

"Nothing was happening between us before the wedding—that I do want you to know. It was a sudden thing. Impulsive. But we are trying to make it work." That was close to honest.

Natalie's eyes suddenly filled with tears. "This wasn't how it was supposed to go."

Lydia was caught between the desire to hug her and slap her. Because she did feel bad, because she didn't want to hurt anyone. But Colton had been hurt. Colton had been left in the lurch. And Natalie was clearly under the impression that she should have been able to have her own private freak-out and then waltz back into his life as though she hadn't just ruined a wedding that had been a year in the making. As though she hadn't just left him standing there, humiliated in front of the whole town.

"I know," Lydia said. Oh, did she know. "But Colton isn't a thing, Natalie. He's a person. He's a man. And he was never going to respond to being left at the altar in a positive way. Even if... Look, even if he and I hadn't... I don't know that he would have wanted to put himself through that again. I know you're used to getting your way. And I know you're used to being able to move people around like dolls. Even knowing that you were furious at me I agreed to still be in your wedding. Even when you're kind of terrible, you are the kind of person that people can't help but want to be around. But people have their limits. And I think Colton hit his."

Natalie looked like she'd been slapped. "I made a mistake," she said, her voice low. "With someone else. I didn't feel like I could show up at the wedding after that. But he's not someone that I can... He's not the kind of person I can marry."

Lydia frowned. "You cheated on Colton?"

Natalie's cheeks turned bright red. "It isn't that simple. I mean, it is. It's why I couldn't just marry him without talking to him. But you know Colton. Obviously. He's not passionate. And neither am I. We cared for each other—I care for him. But we made a lot more sense than we made sparks." She looked away. "It was strange to meet someone I felt differently about. Someone who made me feel different. I didn't know how to fight against it."

Lydia could strangely relate to what Natalie was saying. Because Lydia felt much the same about Colton. The moment she had met him there had been sparks of one variety or another. And it was always like that. If they weren't fighting they were kissing.

She also felt a lot less guilty, hearing what her friend was saying. Natalie didn't love Colton. It was that obvious. Because anyone who thought Colton wasn't passionate...

Well, obviously that person didn't have very strong feelings for him.

Lydia didn't even like him and she thought he was the most passionate man she had ever known.

She blinked, dragging herself back into the present conversation. "I don't really know what to say to you," Lydia said. "You're angry at him, you're angry at me, but you're the one who didn't show up at the wedding. You're the one who cheated on him. And yes, he and I jumped into marriage, but he was never unfaithful to you. I had no idea he was even attracted to me until we got married in Las Vegas."

Natalie snorted. "I knew."

"What?"

Natalie plopped down in the chair across from her, clearly somewhat defeated by the exchange. Her righteous anger had dimmed to a very dull vibration. But then, that was Natalie. She could be hideously mean one moment and kind of delightful wrapped inside of it, then act like all was forgiven, and should be forgiven in return in the next.

"The moment I introduced the two of you. He was mean to you. He was a jerk. He's never a jerk. And you bristled like a cat backed into a corner. Which I had never seen you do with anyone. You're unfailingly diplomatic. You've been diplomatic with me through this entire conversation. You were not diplomatic with him."

"You think he was…attracted to me?"

"You thought he married you the moment he was free of me for fun?"

Actually, Lydia had thought he did it all for the alcohol, but she wasn't going to say that. "I don't know."

"You two had a weird magnetism the moment you met. And I was jealous. I mean, I was upset when you chose to run against my father, don't get me wrong. But I was more upset that he looked at you like that."

"That he looked at me like he wanted to push me into the ocean?"

"Kind of. I never got that strong of an emotion out of him either way."

Lydia turned that over. She supposed it stood to reason that anger and attraction were two sides of the same coin. Passion. The emotion they had just been discussing.

"I think maybe all of this is for the best," Lydia said, beginning to pack up her things. Because this had just gone past the point of uncomfortable, and while she was sort of glad they'd had this conversation, she really needed to go put her thoughts in order. "I'm not sure that you should be with him." She stuffed her laptop into her bag. "Well, I know you shouldn't be with him. Since we're married. And he's my husband. You know, 'til death do us part."

She felt like she was kind of waiting for a bolt of lightning to hit her for that one.

"Right," Natalie said.

"But, if you need to talk to him, then talk to him."

"You aren't going to chase me off the property with a pitchfork? Because, I'll be honest, I maybe would have done that to you."

"Yeah, no. I don't like to run. So, you can rest assured that you will not be chased."

"Okay. Well, I'll at least call him. Which is maybe better than texting. Which is all I did when I didn't show up at the wedding." She winced. "I really don't like having to admit that I'm at fault for things. I find it very uncomfortable."

Lydia laughed. "We all do."

"But you do it so much more than I do. I assumed it was easier."

"No, everyone hates it."

As she finished saying goodbye to Natalie and walking out of the coffee shop, Lydia did have to wonder if it was slightly easier for her because she was so used to it. She sighed heavily, continuing down the street to her car. She drove over to the copy shop where her pamphlets were already done. Another plus to a small town.

She was going to need to fold them, but a little bit of menial labor was actually welcome. Of course, to do the whole task, she would have to enlist her team, but she could get a start on it.

And since she was already in town it was tempting to just stop by her house. Just for a little bit. Maybe she would fold her pamphlets there.

She pulled into her driveway, a feeling of relief washing over her. She hadn't been back here in a few weeks.

Mostly because she was afraid that when she walked into the door, she would burrow down deep and never come back out. And, when she walked inside, she couldn't deny that she definitely had that desire.

She set her box of pamphlets down, then took a stack out of them, taking a seat on the floor and spreading them around her. She stood up, putting her phone in her speaker dock, something she had left here by accident that she would absolutely be bringing back with her, and she turned on some country music.

With Dierks Bentley to guide her through pamphlet folding, some of the weirdness of her previous encounter began to slide away.

She worked steadily with songs in the background, until her back began to ache and she leaned backward, trying to ease the tension in her spine. And then she began to fixate on the song lyrics that were filtering through her living room. And they were kind of sexy, and about moonlight and kissing and things that she didn't really want to think about.

She looked up, and realized that it was dark outside. She had been sitting on the floor for hours—no wonder she was in pain.

She looked around the room. The familiar room with everything in its place. She was comfortable here. She really wanted to hide and pretend that this whole thing with Colton wasn't happening.

There was a knock on her door and she startled. "Just a second," she said, pushing herself into a standing position. It was probably one of her neighbors. Because the house had been empty for a few weeks, and everyone knew she wasn't staying there, it was probably strange to see a light on inside.

She opened the door, and her heart stalled out. "Colton. What are you doing here?"

"I could ask you the same question."

"I mean, you could. But I live here, so it isn't really that big of a mystery that I should be here."

"Except, that you don't live here, not right now. And you left the house early this morning, and you didn't say anything about when you'd be back. I called your phone. I couldn't get a hold of you."

She cringed. She probably had the app set so it wouldn't interrupt the music. "Sorry. But, I don't think we're really in a position where we keep tabs on each other, are we?"

"Whatever our relationship is, I don't want you dead in a ditch."

"Well," she said, waving a hand. "Here I am. Undead and not in a ditch."

"Are you *not* dead, or are you *un*dead? Because those are two different things. If you're undead then you're a zombie, and at some point you were dead. Probably in a ditch."

"If I were a zombie I would have eaten your brains by now. So your rescue mission would be a huge failure. It would be too late to save me, and too late to save yourself."

He pushed past her, into the living room.

"I didn't invite you in. Even zombies need their personal space."

"If you were a zombie, technically this would be meal delivery."

"Great. If I give you a tip will you take your body away and leave your brain behind?"

He arched a brow, crossing his arms over his broad chest. "No. I'm not going to do that."

"So, you just came to collect your wayward wife?"

"I came to make sure you were okay. I figured that if you were anywhere it would be here. Your office was my next choice."

Well, both guesses were logical, and showed that he had a basic understanding of her. Which made her feel strangely warm in her chest. As opposed to feeling warm in her stomach, and lower, which was a little bit more typical of her Colton feelings.

"I'm glad you don't want me dead. That's... Well, it's not really the highest praise, but I'll take it."

"Is everything okay? I mean, are you hiding from me?"

"Why would I be hiding from you?" She kind of was.

"I don't know, but I haven't seen you since last night."

"It was a big deal, and it takes me a little while to wind down from things like that. It's kind of intense." That much was true. An event like that where you were the sole focus was more than a little enervating.

"Fair enough. I wouldn't know. I go to a lot of events, but I'm not usually the star of the show."

"And I just want to do a good job." She shut the front door and moved back to her pile of pamphlets, standing where she'd been sitting before. "I want to win this election. It's really important to me. I want to do the best job. I want to be the best person for the job."

"Most people only care about the winning."

"I know. But I really do care about this town."

"I know. You probably care about it more than anyone I've ever met."

She drew in a breath. "Because I... Do you know

what it's like to feel like you're walking on eggshells in your own house? Like every corner of it belongs to someone else, and you're just kind of there."

He frowned. "No."

"I wasn't allowed to have friends over. And I was just weird. I cared about things, but not the things that other kids cared about. And I never had anyone to talk to about how alone I felt. I couldn't do anything to fix it. To top it all off, at home I just felt like I didn't belong. And when I moved here everything changed. It was like I found this place where what I was good at mattered. Where who I was mattered. I bought this house. And everything in it is mine. And I can be as loud as I want, or as quiet as I want. Let's face it, it's not like I go through the place turning cartwheels. But, either way, it's mine.

"To finally feel like you have a place is the best thing. The most amazing thing. So yes, I do love Copper Ridge. And maybe it's even kind of a selfish love. But I would still do anything for this town."

She had never said any of that out loud to anyone before. She didn't like talking about her past. She didn't like talking about her family. And everything she had just told him was vague enough.

It had hardly been a tell-all. Really, who didn't have a little bit of dysfunction in their past. It was her experience that everybody was a little bit messed up, no matter how idyllic a childhood they might have had. So, confessing that was not exactly groundbreaking.

"I never really thought of it that way. Of the town being a support system." He shifted his stance. "I've kind of always seen it like living under a microscope."

"I guess it can be that way." She hesitated, knowing that the subject of Natalie really should come up. "Speaking of small towns…I talked to Natalie today."

"Really? What rock did you find her under?"

"No rock. Just a coffee shop. For what it's worth, she seems kind of broken up about everything that happened."

A muscle in his jaw ticked. "Good."

"You're happy that she's unhappy?"

"Yes. To a degree."

She sort of envied that pure, petty emotion. Because even when she'd been faced with Natalie's cheating confession, Lydia had been so reluctant to feel or be too negative.

You're always afraid of losing people.

She swallowed hard. "She said…well, she said that the two of you didn't really have a…conventional relationship."

He looked thoughtful, but not surprised. "I guess not. I mean, I wasn't wildly in love with her. She wasn't wildly in love with me. But we both knew exactly where the other stood. At least, I thought we did."

"What's the point of getting married if you aren't in love?"

"Marriage is stability. It's everything that I wanted. When I look into my future, that's the kind of man I see. Married, children."

"But the only thing that makes that good is love. Otherwise, you're stuck in a house with people that you have to endure."

"I liked Natalie. And I know that a lot of people don't. But I do. She didn't hesitate to speak her opinion, but ultimately, she always supported what I wanted to do."

"Damn. *I* should have married her. She sounds like she's the perfect politician's wife."

"Yeah," he said, "she kind of is. And when you spend a lot of time going to various charity events and other community functions, all throughout the state, she's valuable to have. When I take over the family ranch, I'm going to need somebody by my side to fulfill the role that my mother has now. She could do that for me. I knew she could."

"It just sounds…well, it sounds chilly."

She didn't like the expression on his face. The one that clearly said she should talk about chilliness. Whatever. He didn't know her. Not really.

"What about you? Your ex-boyfriend tells me that you didn't want to get married. That you didn't think marriage was for you. What kind of a future is that. You're going to spend it alone?"

"I'm not alone. I have the whole town." Oh, good Lord. Even she knew that sounded sad.

She sat back down and started to fold her pamphlets again. She did not need to justify herself to Colton. To a man who was willing to get married to somebody he didn't even love just so he could have a wife.

"That's not the same, and you know it. You don't want kids? You don't want companionship?" Those words made something uncomfortable settle in the pit of her stomach. She didn't look at him. "Sex?" That time, she did look up at him, but mostly because she couldn't control the reaction.

"Just because I'm not married doesn't mean I can't have sex," she said, her tone crisp.

She sounded like a pearl-clutching maiden. Not

someone who would be jumping on the casual sex band-wagon anytime soon.

"Okay," he said slowly. "So you're going to be the mayor of a small town by the sea with a rather conservative constituency and you're going to remain an unmarried spinster who takes lovers?"

"Copper Ridge is not a Regency romance novel."

"I didn't say it was. I'm just saying you knew that you couldn't get divorced in the middle of an election because of what people would say. What if you were just carrying on sexual liaisons? You think they would be any kinder about that?"

"I think saying I didn't want to get married four years ago is not the same as never actually wanting to get married. But, unlike you, I would have to be in love. And I really just haven't met that man."

"I don't know what love has to do with anything. My mother is in love with my father. All he does is hurt her."

"But you see the value of love. I've seen you with your sisters. I've seen you with your mother. You love them."

"I do. And they love Gage, who pissed off into the mountains somewhere. We all love him, for all the good it does us. But when the other person doesn't love you back in the right way it doesn't mean much of anything. And if I would rather have a transaction where both people are going into it with cool heads and an understanding, I'm not going to apologize for that."

"Okay, I can't really blame you for that." She folded another pamphlet and set it into the finished stack. "But, now you get to revisit your plan. I mean, I have a feeling that Natalie would take you back, when we're finished."

"Well, I'm not going to take her back. I thought we

had an understanding. I thought she was on the same page I was. Clearly she wasn't."

"She said she was with someone. Before the wedding. She said that was why she couldn't marry you."

"With someone? What do you mean by that?"

"I mean, she cheated on you."

His eyebrows shot up. "She *cheated* on me? That is... well, it's almost hilarious, considering she was the one who enforced months of celibacy before the wedding."

"She *what*?" Lydia was struggling with a few weeks of celibacy around Colton. She could not for the life of her imagine what Natalie had been thinking. She had the man on a string, ready to marry her, she had access to his body whenever she wanted, and she had enforced celibacy?

"Yeah." He laughed, shaking his head. "I guess I was the one being celibate. Alone."

"She felt bad about it," Lydia offered, not sure how she'd landed in the position of being apologetic about Natalie's crazy behavior.

"Oh, great. She got laid, and she felt sorry for me."

"I just mean, she thinks that she threw away something real for something that didn't matter." The words felt wrong on her tongue. Was it real if they didn't have passion? Was passion pretend? It felt real when Colton touched her but honestly she wouldn't know. It lasted as long as his hands, his lips, were on her. But then reality set in and it all faded away. She swallowed hard. "But she did say that the two of you didn't have very much...passion."

"I guess we didn't. But I don't see what that has to do with anything."

"No love *and* no passion."

"I'm sorry, you're judging me? Do you have either of those things in your life?"

"I guess not."

He huffed out a laugh. "You guess not. I'll take that as a *no*."

"Just… You know. Stop it," she said, frowning. "My life is not open for dissection."

"If you really think that, you're the most naive political candidate ever. You're public property."

"On the campaign trail. Not in my freaking house."

"But in your house, my life is up for examination?"

"Well, the issue at hand is your fiancée."

"Ex."

"Sure," she said, folding another pamphlet a little bit angrily.

Colton settled across from her, grabbing another pamphlet off the stack. "Trifold?" he asked.

"Obviously."

"Let me help with your obvious trifolds."

She waved a hand and started to work on another piece of glossy paper.

"I get the feeling you're ungrateful."

She looked up and met his gaze, an electric shock piercing her body. "Um. No. Ungrateful is not…me. Undead is the only un."

She was tongue-tied and ridiculous and she just didn't do either thing. So what on earth was wrong with her?

"Zombies need help, too. And they can say thank you."

"You're so fixated on manners," she said, keeping her focus on the picture of her own face on the pamphlet she was folding. "Well, my manners."

"Fine. Don't thank me, rude zombie bride."

She looked up at him that time, curling her lip. "I am not your zombie bride."

He shrugged and went back to folding, and she didn't know what possessed her next. Didn't know what exactly made her want to poke at him when they could easily sit on the floor and fold pamphlets in peace.

Maybe because they really couldn't fold pamphlets in peace. Because no matter what she pretended was happening, the fact he was here with her like this wasn't a stagnant event leading to nothing. It was electric. And she knew exactly where it was headed.

"Natalie said…that she was always a little jealous of me," Lydia said, watching Colton out of the corner of her eye.

"The only thing Natalie has ever been jealous of is a Pegasus. Because they're magical and have wings. Also they don't exist so the jealousy is theoretical."

Lydia laughed at that, and recognized her chance to turn back. But she didn't. Maybe a little bit for her pride, but also because she just wanted to keep pushing. For once, she didn't want to test something gently and retreat the moment it turned intense. For once, she wanted to push through and see what might happen.

What happened to resistance?

Well, nothing had happened yet. So she would just see.

"I mean, thank you for thinking it's ridiculous that Natalie could be jealous of me."

"I just don't think she possesses enough humility to be jealous of anyone," he said. "It has nothing to do with you."

"Except this does." Lydia took a deep breath. "She

said she was jealous because she could tell that when we met, you were attracted to me."

He went still. "Did she say that?"

"Yes." Lydia looked back down and pressed the paper down, making a deep, straight crease, then going over it again. "That is exactly what she said. That she knew there was…something between us."

"Irritation?"

"But why?" she asked, her ears ringing, her cheeks burning. "Why do we irritate each other so much? Nothing actually happened."

He said nothing, but she heard him shift. And suddenly, he was grabbing hold of her chin, tilting her face up so that she was forced to meet his gaze. His blue eyes burned into hers, his thumb sliding across her skin, leaving a trail of sparks behind.

"Because," he said, his voice rough, low. It was intimate and so enticing she could feel herself leaning toward him, leaning into his touch. "From the first moment I saw you I wanted to kiss you. When you looked at me, I felt like I got slapped."

"You did?" she asked. She was pretty sure she'd managed to form the words correctly. It was hard to say because her lips were numb so she couldn't feel them moving, and then on top of that her ears were buzzing and she could barely hear herself speaking.

"Yes."

"Then why were you mean to me?"

"Nobody likes to get slapped in the face, Lydia."

The words settled between them, settled in her. He was right. And it was the same reaction she'd had too. Seeing Colton for the first time had felt like an assault, and no one responded positively to an assault.

Especially not people like them.

Yeah, people like them. They weren't so different, she and Colton West. They both wanted to do the right thing for the people they cared about. They both guarded themselves. They both prized control.

For Lydia that meant carving out her own space in her home, for Colton it meant, well, it seemed to mean building up walls of respectability all around him. The semblance of a life without ever letting anyone too close.

They were the same, and they handled it in different ways.

They didn't like their territory threatened. They didn't like to be challenged. And they really, really didn't like their control being tested.

But was it a loss of control if they *decided* to lose it?

Her blood was running hotter, faster, and much like when she'd been drunk, she wasn't entirely sure if she was capable of making a smart decision right now. Apparently Colton was a lot like alcohol.

Maybe it would be different if she could remember the sex. If she could remember then maybe she would have enough shower-fantasies to get her through the hard times. She'd pretty much decided before Colton that sex was nothing more than a bit of nice companionship. It was fine, but she'd never felt the need to be crazy about it.

Now there was a little kernel of what if. Hope restored. Maybe the fuss was about something. Maybe it could be earth-shattering. If she knew, then maybe she wouldn't feel so needy now.

But she didn't know. She couldn't remember. So that made this...well, it was unique.

"Do you think maybe we fight to keep from...this?" she asked.

He chuckled, his breath fanning over her cheek, sending a shiver down her spine. "No, I think we fight because we annoy each other."

She laughed, helpless, trying to keep from dissolving into giggles there on her living room floor with Colton West holding her chin in his hand. "I suppose that's a fair enough assessment."

"You're uptight," he said.

"You're arrogant. High-handed. Is that the same thing? Well, maybe it is."

"I'm going to kiss you."

"I'm supposed to be resisting you," she said, the words almost a plea.

"You are?" he asked, his brows shooting upward.

"Yes."

"And here I made it a point to stop resisting you."

"What a surprise. We're disagreeing again," she said, another laugh escaping her.

He made her breathless. He made her giggly and weird and she had no idea what on earth to do with it. He made her tremble. He made her want.

"I'll make a deal with you," he said, his voice the richest of seductions, dark and warm as it poured through her like a potent drink. "I kiss you, and you can decide where you stand on your resistance."

She nodded slowly, and he barely waited for her to finish the gesture before he leaned in, closing the distance between them entirely. He had kissed her last night, though it had been for show, but still, it felt as if she had been waiting for this for weeks. Months. Maybe all of her life. She felt like Sleeping Beauty, asleep until

Colton's lips touched hers. And now, parts of her body she had never fully engaged with were starting to wake up. Were starting to ache. Were starting to need.

He slid his tongue along the seam of her lips, gently encouraging her to open for him. She complied, because there was nothing else she could do. His kiss was gentle, soft, so unlike the kiss he'd given her last night in front of everyone, which had been firm, but dry. So unlike the kiss at the woodshed that had been fierce and full of regret and anger. This was a tease. This was him drawing out every bit of her desire that he could. Coaxing it from her slowly, stroke for stroke, with each wild, delicious pass of his tongue.

When he pulled away, it was too soon. Her heart was thundering hard, her whole body shaking. Her stomach seemed hollowed out, and she felt a deep emptiness, something like being ill. A strange thing, because she never would have associated desire with sickness. But that was how she felt. Sick for him. For this.

"This isn't a good idea," she said, her voice thick, drugged.

"What's the worst that could happen? If the two of us make love again, what's the very worst thing that could happen?"

She closed her eyes, trying to ignore the beating of her heart in her temples. Trying to rise above the heat that was washing through her. Trying to find some sanity.

"The earth could crumble into pieces and fall away," she said, her eyes still closed.

He leaned in, his lips brushing her ear, his hand cradling her cheek. "Okay, and if the earth crumbles and falls away, we still had sex. And I think that kind of takes the sting out of it, don't you?"

"Well," she said. "We would be dead. So, it would be difficult to say."

"Would we?"

"Us. All of humanity."

"All of humanity? All because we took our clothes off?"

She nodded, the motion creating friction between her cheek in his palm, sending a delicious shock of sensation through her. She pressed her knees together, trying to minimize the ache at the apex of her thighs. It didn't work.

"That's a lot of responsibility," he said.

She swallowed hard. "Too much. So, we should just stop this. It's crazy."

"Or, we do it anyway." He shifted, moving nearer. And oh, she could smell him. All masculine and clean and perfect. "Because the earth isn't going to fall away."

"What if it does?" she asked.

All she had were wild theories that she knew weren't true to keep herself from leaning in and kissing him again. It was the only thing keeping her clothing firmly in place. Catastrophes. Made-up catastrophes that would result if the two of them ever touched again. But she was finding it hard to remember why she needed that. Finding it difficult to recall why she was resisting in the first place. When they could just have each other. When they could just have this.

"I still don't remember," he said, his voice rough. "I don't remember what happened that night in Las Vegas. And I want to. Do you know how much that tortures me? To have you walking around in front of me all the time, knowing that I've seen you naked, knowing that I know, somewhere inside of myself, what you look like without your clothes on, but not being able to recall the image? Do you know what it's like to know that I've tasted you, that I've touched you, that I've had my hands all over your beautiful, bare skin, but that there's just a big blank space in my mind where it should be." He laughed. "The damn ironic thing is that it's because of the alcohol that we did it in the first place, and it's because of the alcohol that I can't remember."

She sucked in a deep breath, looking down. Needing a reprieve from his face. It was too much. Too tempting. "But it's for the best that we don't remember. Because then we're not…we're not tortured."

"You're not tortured?" he asked, sounding incredulous. "You don't feel completely tortured right now?"

"I mean…okay, it's a little bit of torture."

"Honey, you might as well have me on the rack."

"But I…I don't know myself when I feel this. I don't know what's happening to me. I don't want men that I don't like. I don't have casual sex. For me it's always been part of a relationship. Something to make me feel… companionship. It's not about…this crazy attraction."

"So, how's that worked out for you?"

She looked up at him again, frowning. "I'm single. I mean, apart from being married to you."

"Sure. Apart from the whole marriage thing," he said, his tone dry.

"You know what I mean."

"All things considered, maybe it isn't working out that well for you. Maybe there's nothing wrong with trying this."

She wanted it. She wanted it so badly. But wanting

wasn't having. And she wasn't that woman. She wasn't the kind of woman who made a man lose his cool, who made him beg to be with her. And even if she were, she wouldn't be the kind to say yes.

"One more time," she said, the words rushed, reckless as she felt inside. Tumbling out of her with all the subtlety of a rock slide.

There was no turning back now.

"One more time?" he asked.

"I feel like you do. I feel like it's torture to not remember. I feel like maybe if I did…maybe this wouldn't be quite so torturous. Then maybe we could just finish this marriage thing and go on with our lives. Maybe we won't be completely tormented by the what-ifs."

It made sense. Because in Lydia's experience the promise of sex was a whole lot hotter than sex itself. She was usually more turned on by kissing than she was by the whole nudity/penetration thing. Not that it didn't have its merits, it's just that she was usually a whole lot hotter imagining what might happen, than actually dealing with what did happen.

Maybe it didn't make sense. Maybe she was so deep into justifications she just started to buy whatever sounded vaguely logical because she was desperate.

Either way, she didn't really care. All she cared about was what might happen next. Where he might touch her… Where he might kiss her.

She let her eyes flutter closed, and she waited. She waited, and nothing happened. Then, she felt the brush of his thumb over her bottom lip, slow, steady.

"You're going to have to open your eyes, peaches."

She did. The electric shock of his blue eyes boring into her was almost too much to bear. Making her shiver inside. Ratcheting up the tension between them to an almost-impossible degree.

He continued to trace the line of her lower lip, his movements purposeful, exquisite. He was touching her with his thumb. That was it. Touching her on the lip, not even anywhere salacious, and she was melting. It wasn't difficult to understand why she had succumbed to him so easily on their wedding night.

It had been easy to imagine that it was some kind of madness contained inside the shot glasses at Ace's. It was easy to pretend that it had been a one-off. The glorious friction, the delicious slide of his hand over her face, was proving that it was probably more than a onetime deal.

She was starting to think it was something that lived inside her. Buried down deep. Something that only he could call up. Colton West, who was supposed to be just as dispassionate as she was. Just as controlled. And yet, they tested each other.

Opposites attracted—she'd heard that over and over. But they weren't magnets. They were people. And while she would have said only a few weeks ago that they were opposites, opposites that wanted each other dead, she understood now that neither of those things was true.

At the moment, same, opposite, it didn't matter much. The only thing that mattered was want. Want and have.

That thought made her feel giddy. Made her shake. She lived her life with so much rigid control that wanting and having were never the same thing. She weighed every option, every consequence. Overthought everything to death. It had taken her a year to decide what kind of car to buy. Had taken hours of reading *Consumer Reports*.

But there were no consumer reports to read on Colton. And even if there were, she wouldn't care.

She felt…suddenly she felt unprotected, exposed. Without all the little rules and walls that she imposed on herself surrounding her, there was nothing to keep her safe. Nothing to deflect his intense gaze. Nothing to hide the desire that she felt for him. She just had to own it. And follow it.

Her day usually looked a lot like a multiple-choice test. All of the options neatly laid out before her, predictable and simple. But this…this just felt like a wide, dark chasm of unknown. She was just going to have to jump into it, consequences be damned. She was ready. She was giddy.

Just this once. And then you'll leave it behind and everything can go back to normal.

That made it feel manageable at least. Made it feel a bit less scary.

"Kiss me," she said. No, she demanded. She didn't think she had ever done that before. She had always waited for a man to lean in. Had always just kind of waited, accepted.

But this was different. Because he was different. And it made her feel different.

He complied. No, that was too safe a word. Too gentlemanly. Too much…not this. He consumed. He parted his lips over hers, kissing her deep, hard, reaching up to take hold of her face, keeping her steady as he devoured her.

He leaned in, pressing her back against the couch, sliding his hands through her hair. She shifted, and found herself parting her thighs, allowing him to settle between them. She let her head tilt back, separating their mouths, a soft sigh on her lips. Colton angled his head, kissing her neck, his teeth scraping over her delicate skin.

Teeth. Who would have thought that could be erotic? She certainly hadn't. She had certainly never been with a man who would do something so feral. She liked it. So maybe something inside her was feral too.

Under other circumstances that might have disturbed her. Not in these. Not at all.

He wrapped one arm around her waist, pressing his palm against her lower back, encouraging her to arch against him. She did not need much encouragement.

He rolled his hips against her, allowing her to feel the evidence of his desire for her. Suddenly, that wasn't enough. Suddenly, she needed to know more. She reached between them, curling her fingers around his arousal, gasping as she felt him. All of him. She moved her palm slowly up and down his length, relishing the rough groan that rumbled in his chest as she felt him through his jeans.

He reached down, grabbing hold of her wrist and pulling her hand away from him, bringing her arm up above her head, before taking hold of her other wrist and doing the same as he claimed her mouth again.

She groaned as he kissed her, didn't even bother to hold it back. She had never made noise during sex before. It always seemed embarrassing. Even if she'd been tempted, she had held it in. But she didn't possess the capacity to hold it back now. Not with him.

What was the point of making an ill-advised decision if you didn't go all the way? Embarrassment had no place in fantasy. Regret had no place. This was all about what she wanted. All about what felt good.

This was… It was a contained moment in time. Something that would never go beyond this space. That made it both safe and dangerous. A kind of controlled burn. Something that wouldn't destroy the whole mountainside, just this one little room. This one little moment.

She curved herself against him, pressing her breasts against his chest. Opening herself to him, she rocked against his erection. He growled, moving his hand down from her lower back to cup her butt, his fingertips digging into her flesh. Suddenly, their clothes felt like too much of a barrier.

She struggled against his hold, and he released her. She pulled at his shirt, trying to get it over his head, but with him holding on to her rear, that made it difficult.

"I demand nudity," she said.

He pushed backward, on his knees, between her thighs as he stripped his T-shirt off. She reached out, pressing her hand flat to the center of his chest. "Stay like that," she said, "just for a second."

She wanted to look at him. And she wanted to watch herself. Watch as she allowed her fingertips to trail over his skin, down his rippling ab muscles. Then back up again, grazing his nipple as she relished the feel of his heat. Of his chest hair. The fact that she was touching him. She, Lydia Carpenter, was touching a man who looked like this.

She had wanted to defend Nolan when Colton had besmirched him. But *dusty* was kind of a good word for the sex. Bookish. Not in a well-studied, *Kama Sutra* kind of way. Just in a very dull, pale sort of way.

He was nothing like this. That was for sure.

"I want you to…" She nearly bit her tongue. She hadn't meant to start talking without fully thinking through what she was about to say. But she was looking at Colton, thinking he had the body of every bad-boy fantasy a girl could have ever have, but knowing that he wasn't really a bad boy. He was a good man. Which was worth everything in real life.

But tonight she wasn't interested in good, responsible Colton and she wasn't interested in being Lydia Carpenter, small-town politician and quite levelheaded lady. Tonight she just wanted.

"What do you want, peaches?" She didn't even mind the nickname. It felt intimate. It felt specific to her. To their situation and to this moment. She held it close to her chest, savored the momentary warm glow that she felt.

She had always been highly susceptible to things that felt like they were only hers. And peaches was only hers. She might not like the fruit, but she would never look at the word the same way again.

"I want you to do whatever you want," she said, her voice shaking a little bit as she spoke the words.

The light in his eyes turned dark. "What exactly do you mean by that?"

"Exactly what I said. Whatever you have always wanted to do. Do it with me. Do it now. We've been way too well behaved."

Too well behaved for all of her life. Quietly tiptoeing through the halls so that she never disturbed her sister. Quietly grieving, so quietly because it would never top her parents' grief. Because how did losing a sister, even a twin, compare to losing a child? Quietly making love to quiet men on quiet blankets in quiet positions.

He moved his hands to his belt buckle, slowly undoing it, working the leather free and tugging it through the loops on his jeans. He undid the top button, drawing the zipper down slowly. He didn't say anything as he pushed his jeans and underwear down his narrow hips, tossing them to the side.

She felt like she had swallowed a handful of sand. Her throat was so dry she couldn't swallow, so tight she couldn't speak. But that seemed fine because she was pretty sure they were done talking now. And that was okay with her.

"Now it's your turn," he said, his tone commanding.

With shaking hands she grabbed the hem of her T-shirt, tugging it up overhead. She wasn't insecure about the way that she looked. She dressed nicely, she was happy with her sense of style. And she knew how to wield a makeup brush. Those things combined left her feeling pretty confident.

But this was different. This slipped down into the ugly places that demanded she consider all potential comparisons. How many other women he'd been with, what they looked like without their clothes on. Because there was no barrier of makeup and perfectly flattering dresses here.

She didn't like this. This insecurity that was bubbling up inside of her. It wasn't usually an issue. She had managed to compress her life down to a routine. To things that let her feel confident. She didn't have to face these kinds of things. Feeling lost, feeling inexperienced, feeling naked.

It was always like this with someone new. At least in her experience. Limited though it was. But, with the other guys she had just moved things to the bedroom, shut off the lights. Had comfortably gone about the business of things with darkness to cover it all.

She supposed she could do that now. But she didn't want to. Not really. She was caught between two things. The desire to protect, the desire to break out.

So, she simply reached behind her back and quickly undid the clasp on her bra, pulling it down her arms and flinging it to the side. She didn't stop to look at his face. Didn't stop for anything. Instead, she unsnapped her jeans, unzipping them quickly and pushing them down her thighs.

She was not wearing seductress underwear. She didn't even really own seductress underwear. She had never felt the need to. She wished she had them now. Something red lace and sexier than she was. She wanted to be someone else with him. Wanted this to be something different.

She gritted her teeth, gathering her courage before she looked up at his face. And then her heart plummeted straight down into her stomach. He looked hungry. Like a predator. His every muscle was tense like a big cat just before it pounced.

And then, he made his move. He reached down, wrapping his arm around her, drawing her up against him, her bare breasts pressing against his chest. She gasped, grabbing hold of his shoulders, almost overwhelmed by the heat of him, the feel of him pressed against every naked inch of her.

He moved his hand down beneath the waistband of her panties, the sensation so intense her internal muscles clenched in response. He squeezed her tightly, then moved his hand away slightly before bringing it back down sharply over her skin. She squeaked, jumping slightly. It wasn't painful; it just stung a little bit. And as it dissipated, left an even-sharper ache between her thighs.

"Was that okay?" he asked.

"More than okay," she said.

He looked…not quite insecure, not quite shocked, but definitely concerned. And the fact that this was maybe uncharted territory for him too made her feel a little bit better.

Made her feel special even.

He shifted, divesting her of her panties. She helped him get them down below her knees, throwing them into the corner with the rest of their clothes. Finally he kissed her again, moving both of his hands down to her ass, gripping her tightly, pressing her up against the hard, hot length of his arousal.

He slid his hands up, holding her hips tightly, still pressing her up against him. She wrapped her arms around his neck, kissing him with every bit of desire that was inside of her. She abandoned his mouth, kissed his cheek, the feel of his whiskers beneath her lips making her stomach tight, a sharp thrill twisting it.

She shut her brain down, focused on what she felt. On what she wanted. What she wanted was to trail her tongue over all those perfect muscles. So she did. Down the center of his pecs, to those amazing abs. Until she was down low on the floor in front of him. She knew that her butt was sticking out behind her, up in the air, on display. She didn't even care.

Didn't care that this was probably the most provocative pose that she'd ever been in in all her life. That she was playing the part of a seductress when she wasn't entirely sure she'd ever felt like one.

He reached back, grabbing hold of her rear and

squeezing her again before landing another light slap against her skin. She gasped, then groaned, a reckless jagged pleasure pouring through her. Spurring her on.

She looked up at him, then back down at his arousal. She leaned in, flicking her tongue over the head before sliding it down his length. He growled, grabbing hold of her hair, his fingers tangling with it, curling into a fist. He tugged against her as she lowered her head again. And she ignored him. Little pinpricks of pain dotting her scalp, spreading over her arms in a rash of goose bumps.

She looked back up at him as she took him deep inside of her mouth.

"I can't... Lydia, I'm not going to be able to control it."

The admission, tense and helpless, sent a surge of power through her. She had done that. She was pushing him to this place. She was the one who was making him act out of character. Making him do and say things he wouldn't normally.

A rush of confidence flooded her, and she shifted her position, curling her fingers around him as she continued to pleasure him with her mouth. He kept his hold on her as she did, tugging a little bit tighter when she did something that felt particularly good. This was him, trying to cling to some control. He didn't have to tell her. She just knew.

She pleasured him like that until his thigh muscles began to shake, until he tugged on her hair a little more intently. "Stop, Lydia," he said, his voice strained. "I want to be inside of you."

She lifted her head, feeling dizzy, feeling dazed. "You are," she said, smiling.

"You know what I mean," he said, hauling her up

against him again. He lifted his hand, tracing her lip
again, his blue eyes electric. "I want you. I want to feel
you all around me. Tight. Wet. Are you wet for me,
Lydia?"

"Y-yes," she stuttered, his words touching her, stok-
ing the fire of her arousal.

"Tell me," he said, his expression like granite.

She took in a deep breath, nerves sparking through
her. "I'm wet for you."

She had never said anything like that ever in her entire life. She felt desperately exposed. She felt afraid that
she had done it wrong. But when he moved, sliding his
hand between her thighs, drawing his fingers through
her slick folds, she forgot to feel nervous. She forgot to
feel embarrassed or self-conscious.

"You want me?" He stroked her, sending sparks
crackling along her veins.

She nodded, biting her lip, unsure if she could speak
now even if she wanted to.

"You want me inside you?" His voice had grown
deeper, huskier.

"Yes," she said, the word trembling, almost shattering.

He moved away from her then, and she groaned in
disappointment when he took his hand from between
her thighs.

He moved to the far side of the room, where he had
discarded his jeans earlier. He picked them up, pulling his wallet from the back pocket, producing a condom. All the breath rushed out of her lungs, and all she
could do was stay where she was, on her knees on the
floor, held captive by his movements. By how beautiful he was.

She had never really given much thought to a man's thighs. To the way his full-body profile looked when he was naked and aroused. She was looking now. At the enticing hollow on the side of his ass, the tight muscles in his legs. That thick, glorious erection. She wanted him. She wanted him so badly that she could hardly wait. She had never felt like this before. Had never felt like she would die from wanting.

But this wasn't just wanting. It wasn't just longing. It was about to be having. A fact punctuated by his quick application of the protection.

He moved back to her, claiming her lips in a kiss, pushing her backward until she was flat on the ground, and he was over the top of her. For a moment, they simply looked at each other. And then she touched his face, tracing the line of his jaw, dragging her fingertips over his stubble.

The she kissed him. Because she wanted to be as close to him as possible. Because she didn't want to wait anymore.

"Are you ready?" he asked, his words rough and tender. She had a feeling that he couldn't wait anymore, either.

"I'm ready," she said. "I want you. I want you inside me."

He groaned, testing her entrance with the blunt head of his cock before inching into her slowly. She let her head fall back as he filled her, deeply, completely. She grabbed hold of his shoulders, her fingernails digging into his skin. But if she didn't cling to him, then she would fly away completely. Come completely unglued from the earth and float into space.

When he began to move, it wasn't tentative. It wasn't

slow. He thrust hard inside of her, pushing her. Testing her. He was so much. He was in her, he was over her. He was making her feel things she couldn't control, things that she couldn't begin to understand or quantify. It wasn't simple. It was rough, it was messy. It was everything she had never imagined sex could be.

He didn't hold back. And neither did she. She arched against him, meeting his every move. Bringing that sensitive bundle of nerves into delicious contact with him every time he went deep. She could feel herself getting closer to the edge. Without any effort at all, pushing up against climax. Against completion.

It had never been like this before. She had never, ever managed to come with a partner. She didn't even know she could. She knew that plenty of women had difficulty with that kind of thing, and she'd just assumed she was one of them.

Colton made her wonder if maybe her only real problem had been choosing the wrong guy.

But then she couldn't think, she couldn't wonder about it at all. She felt like a thin pane of glass that was on the verge of shattering. Little cracks spreading out over her, in her, making her feel perilous, fragile. And then he flexed his hips one more time on a growl, and she shattered completely. Into a million crystalline pieces. Broken. Beautiful.

If there was one thing she was certain of in that moment, it was that she was beautiful. In his arms, disheveled, with absolutely no clothes, with no protection whatsoever, she was beautiful.

Slowly, very slowly, she began to come back to herself. Slowly, she began to realize that she was lying on her living room floor. In her home that she had set aside as a kind of sanctuary. A place she didn't share with anyone. And here she was, sharing it with Colton. A man she had barely let in the door the first time he had come over, because she didn't want memories of him filling these spaces that belonged to her.

Well, it was safe to say this room would forever be associated with this moment.

The thought made her chest tighten. And on the heels of that realization, she gradually became aware of the fact that she was lying on top of her pamphlets.

"I can't send them out *now*," she said, looking all around her at the dark green pieces of glossy paper that were effectively spread all around, their neat little stacks destroyed.

"That's your first thought?" He looked bemused, pushing up into a sitting position. "Clearly I did something wrong."

She shook her head. "No," she said. "You just… I didn't know what to say. I still don't know what to say. I should just not say anything."

"Probably."

Without the haze of arousal to shield them, she felt… well, she felt very, very naked. And a moment ago that feeling had been empowering. Right now, it was just embarrassing. Right now, she had to contend with the fact that she was Lydia Carpenter, the Lydia she had always been. Not the one that was aroused and half-insane with need, who could easily push aside thoughts of embarrassment and acting out of character.

No, she was just firmly herself at the moment. And she did not have the right equipment to deal with something like this. She couldn't believe she had said all those things to him. That they had done those things.

She'd never gone down on a guy before. Which was weird maybe. But her past boyfriends hadn't ever asked for much, and she'd never felt like she wanted to do it.

This time she'd just wanted to do it. It hadn't felt weird, or wrong, or embarrassing with Colton. But now she was feeling all insecure. Now she was feeling a little like she might have done it wrong. Or like it was something she shouldn't have done.

It was a whole weird world of—not regret, exactly, but feeling like she'd been peeled and left open for Colton's perusal of her soul.

Ick. No. She did not want any soul perusal happening.

Now if only she could get up and go get dressed. Cover herself—metaphorically and physically. But she was just shell-shocked.

And something was burning in the back of her mind. Something...

She looked back at Colton, at his naked body, at the expression on his face. Another shiver washed through her, an aftershock of pleasure that wasn't like anything she'd ever experienced before.

She could believe that in Las Vegas she hadn't felt this exposed. But what she couldn't believe was that she'd forgotten this kind of pleasure.

And that was when she knew with absolute certainty that this was the first time she'd ever had sex with Colton West.

CHAPTER TWELVE

THEY HADN'T HAD sex in Las Vegas. Colton was completely certain of it now. Because there was no way he'd forgotten *that*.

Absolutely no way in hell.

That begged the question of what the hell he had done with the condom—

Holy shit.

"I made a balloon animal out of the condom," he said. "In Vegas, I mean. I really did. I thought I was joking when I said that, but I guess...I was remembering."

Lydia froze, her posture going stiff, her eyes getting round. "Well. You... That... No, you... Yes, you did." She frowned, clearly remembering something. "I mean, granted, Colton, it wasn't much of a balloon animal. I think you said it was a snake."

"And you laughed so hard you fell onto the bed," he said, "and then..."

"I crawled under the covers and you complained. And then...okay, then I really don't remember anything else."

"You fell asleep," he said.

"Did I really?"

"Yeah. And I did too, I think. We were going to and then... Apparently drunk us is a bunch of idiots."

She frowned. "With more willpower than sober us."

He wasn't really sure it had anything to do with willpower. He hadn't wanted to resist. Not at all. He'd just wanted her. He'd come over to the house—worried, like he'd said—and he'd…well, he'd been intent on kissing her the moment he found her.

He'd had a condom in his wallet for a reason.

Lydia looked at him, her cheeks turning pink before she looked away again and started to push herself up into a standing position. Maybe the polite thing to do would be to look away, since she was clearly feeling a little uncomfortable.

He wasn't feeling polite.

He wasn't sure what he was feeling. He wanted to keep on looking at her beautiful body, though. So, he did.

"I'm just going to go to the bathroom," she said, turning away from him, giving him a full view of her bare back, her bare ass and…

"You have a pamphlet stuck to your rear," he said.

She slapped her hand over said body part, then squeaked before brushing it off. It fluttered to the ground like a falling leaf being shed from a very indignant tree.

"Bathroom," she said, her voice sounding strained as she walked through the house and back toward where he knew her bedroom was.

He took that opportunity to seek out a second bathroom and take care of practicalities while Lydia was in retreat.

He imagined she would be happy if he left. But he wasn't going to do that. Instead, he collected his clothes and put them on, because he wasn't going to hang out in her living room bare-ass naked.

A man had to have some limits, even if he wasn't quite sure where his were at the moment.

He'd never…he'd never lost it with someone like he had with her. Everything he wanted, *everything*, he filtered before he let it out. He didn't act without thought. Except for with Lydia, it seemed.

Sure, the sex had been somewhat premeditated on his part. But not what had actually happened. He'd…well, he'd been a little rougher than he'd ever been before. He wasn't sure what had possessed him.

Except, he'd definitely thought about doing that before. But he'd never wanted to shock, never wanted to be offensive. He didn't say words like he'd said to her, didn't do the things he'd done to her, because when he thought it through, the risk didn't outweigh the benefit.

He'd weighed nothing when he'd been with her. He hadn't thought at all. He'd just felt, and he'd acted, and that was not like him at all.

He was still trying to decide if that bothered him.

It was tough to be bothered by much of anything when his orgasm was still buzzing through his system.

Lydia reappeared a moment later, a much softer version of Lydia than he was used to seeing. More like the Lydia he'd seen in his kitchen that night before they'd had lunch with his family. In frilly shorts and socks up to her knees.

This time, she was wearing some sort of thermal outfit. A pair of pants that clung to her long slender legs and had a cuff around the ankle, with a top that matched.

"That's…interesting," he said.

She looked up at him, her expression fierce. "Most of my clothes are at your house. All I had here were a few extra pairs of pajamas."

"How many pairs of pajamas do you own?"

"Several. Coziness is next to godliness."

He cleared his throat. "Well, I wouldn't know since I sleep naked."

Her cheeks turned bright pink, and that forced his mind back to the other thing he'd been pondering since his ears had stopped ringing.

Lydia was not very experienced.

Not that it was a commentary on how good it had been, or even on her skill. There was just something in her touch. Something about her hesitancy. About the ease with which she blushed. He wasn't exactly a renowned playboy, but he'd have considered his a pretty normal healthy level of experience. He wasn't usually very long without a relationship.

He had the feeling that Lydia was different, and considering the fact that they both now realized they hadn't actually slept together in Las Vegas he felt a little bit... Not guilty. Okay, maybe a little bit guilty.

It was just the previous sex had been a part of the rationale for the recent sex, and without the previous sex, he wondered if she would have made a different decision.

He wouldn't have. He confidently and definitively stated he wouldn't have. He was only a man after all. And she was a temptation that had proven beyond his abilities to resist.

"Are you...are you okay with everything that happened?" he asked finally.

"No," she said, looking down at the floor, her hands planted on her hips. "My pamphlets are ruined."

"Aside from your sexed-up pamphlets. I mean are you all right with what happened between us."

She tucked some of her hair behind her ear, looking down. Suddenly, she seemed very young. And he felt like an ass. "I think all right is a little bit of a stretch. I'm not really sure where to go from here."

"I guess I don't know how you feel about things like your number. Or, whatever it is that people seem to obsess about when it comes to sex and partners. It was different maybe when we thought we had done it before..."

"Are you concerned that you just made me a slut when you hadn't already?"

He frowned. "That's not what I said. And you know it. But I feel like maybe it was a little bit of sex under false pretenses. And, it wasn't on purpose, but I'm worried."

"Worried that I'll have a spiral because I've now had sex with three men instead of two? However will I go on?"

"You don't have to be sarcastic about it."

"Yes, I kind of do, because it's either that or punch you in the face, or maybe curl up on top of my pamphlets and have a mental breakdown."

He took a step back. "Well, don't do that. Because, while you have doubts about the viability of your promotional materials, I think you could probably still send them out. Unless you make a nest in them, in which case all bets are off."

"I am not a burrowing animal." She treated him to an extremely angry expression.

"I didn't suggest you were. Only that maybe you were melting down."

"I'm not melting down. You're the one who's kind of having a meltdown, actually. Quizzing me on the number of men I've slept with. How many women have you slept with?"

"I don't keep track." Of course he did. He knew exactly how many women he had slept with, because it was the exact number of women he had dated seriously. Except for Lydia. He was married to her. But, not permanently. So that put her in her own weird category. He imagined it was the same for her.

"BS. Of course you keep track. How many women have you slept with? Did I compromise your number?"

"My number is fine."

"What is it?" She continued to badger.

"Six. Counting you. All women that I've dated seriously."

"Oh," she said, blinking. "I guess, I just assumed..."

"That's kind of a lot."

"Is it? I mean, I honestly have no idea. I'm kind of out of touch with this sort of thing."

"Well, as long as you aren't upset."

She crossed her arms, looking as though she were trying to shrink. "I'm not upset. We did exactly what we said we were going to do. We had one more time. Or I guess we had the first time."

"Right," he said.

"Right. So I'm not damaged. My pamphlets are a little worse for wear, but otherwise, everything is fine."

"Right. Fine. So are you going to come home?"

"I'm going to go to your house, if that's what you mean. It isn't my home."

"Good," he said.

"Yeah, it's great. Because now, all the tension is diffused. And, we'll be...normal. Completely normal."

He resisted the urge to ask her what the hell normal

was for them. Since it seemed to be either fighting, getting married, or tearing each other's clothes off.

He felt it was probably best to not discuss the tearing off of clothing. Especially since the image of her naked was still fresh in his mind. He had a feeling it would be the top thing in his mind for the next...foreseeable forever. Because, of all the six women he had ever slept with, Lydia was the only one who had ever tested his control. He still wasn't sure he liked it. He didn't think he did. But it had certainly left the strongest impression. Of that there was no doubt.

"Just let me... I need to get my things. I need to try and salvage however many pamphlets I can. And then I'll be right behind you."

"I can help you. I'll wait for you to be ready to leave," he said.

"No," she responded. "That's fine. Honestly, I need a few minutes."

And if he were in character, if he were acting with any kind of sense, he would let her have it. But, apparently, he was still acting a little bit out of his mind.

"What if you spend a few minutes talking to me. Because I'm trying to figure out exactly where I stand here, and I have to say, I'm not entirely sure."

"Well, excuse me for not feeling all that sorry for you," she said, her tone verging on ferocious. "I am... I don't do things like this."

"This is starting to feel a lot like a rehash of the day after our wedding."

"Except, I think what we just remembered kind of underlines my point. Even drunk, I don't do things like this."

"You were going to. It was just that you passed out."

"Okay, we don't need to split hairs. My point is, I'm a very self-contained person. I act responsibly. And no, I'm not going to get all bent out of shape because I slept with someone else. I don't have an issue with that. It's just that…I'm not entirely comfortable with what happens when we…"

His stomach twisted in horror. "This is why I want to talk. Did I…did I do something that you didn't like?"

She lifted her hands, rubbing the back of her neck and squeezing her eyes shut. "No. I'm just…horrified. And I don't know what to do with all of the feelings. Because I've never had an orgasm with a man before, and I've never gone down on… Anyway, I can't have this conversation with you right now because I'm very delicate."

Her words washed over him in a rush, leaving him stunned. "You're delicate?" He had no idea why that was the part of her little speech he had chosen to comment on, except maybe because it was about the only thing he could focus on in the middle of all that information.

"Birdlike."

"And you've never had an orgasm with a man before?" He was not even going to touch the blow job issue.

"No," she said. "But I don't want to talk about that."

"You can't introduce the fact that I was the first man ever to give you an orgasm and expect me to not talk about it. At length."

"If you were a gentleman you would honor my request."

"You didn't want me to be a gentleman a few minutes ago."

"Yeah, well, things change. When I'm hungry I want French fries. When I'm not hungry, I don't want French fries. That's not being fickle. That's just… Things change when appetites have been satisfied."

"First of all," he said, "you're a liar. You don't not want French fries just because you ate French fries and aren't hungry anymore. You still want French fries. It's a constant state of being. You would take French fries again immediately after already having had French fries."

Maybe he wasn't talking about French fries. Well, it was true about French fries, but mostly he was thinking about sex.

"Maybe that's true of some people, Colton. But, some of us aren't gluttonous."

"Well, that's just a damn lie," he said. "Some of us might hide it. Some of us might do our damnedest to keep it very down deep. Some of us might even lie to ourselves about it," he said, leaning closer, assaulted by the delicate, feminine scent of her. "But all of us are gluttons, Lydia."

Tension stretched between them like a band, and he knew that when it snapped it was going to hurt. But he didn't care. He wanted to push, and he didn't know why. Didn't know what that made him. What she made him.

"For punishment, maybe," she said, finally, sniffing, her manner haughty.

"Yeah," he said, thinking back to the way she had responded when he had given her something a little bit rough. "Some people do like that."

She curled her lip. "You're disgusting."

"You don't think I'm disgusting. That's your biggest problem with me. It has been from the beginning."

If she had been a cat, all of the hair on her back would have been on end, and she would have been arched as high as she could possibly go. "You don't get to say things like that to me." She bent down, beginning to gather up her pamphlets.

"No? Who does get to say things like that to you, Lydia? Do you have anyone who gives you honesty? Or do you hold everybody at a distance?"

"Again, none of your business."

"Have you only been with two men because you're discerning, or is it because you don't like to let people close to you?"

She sputtered, dumping the handful of pamphlets she had back into the box they had come out of. "I can't imagine why I don't pursue more relationships. Because this one is so much fun."

"You were having fun a few minutes ago."

She whirled around to face him, her expression furious. "Colton, I like you best with your zipper down and your mouth shut."

Her words hit him like a flame, burning over his skin. "That can be arranged."

"No," she said, picking up the box of pamphlets, leaving the rest on the floor. "It can't be."

"You think you can resist me?"

He had no idea what he was saying. He had never attempted to seduce a woman before. He'd never had… this. Whatever this was. It was some kind of insanity that he had never known existed inside of him. Some kind of ridiculous drive that he would have said he was above.

Impulsiveness, recklessness, that was his brother Gage's MO. Colton had never been that; he had never done those things. He had never had the luxury.

You have it now. With her.

It was true. In a weird way, it kind of made sense. They were married, which gave whatever this was more legitimacy than any other relationship he'd ever been in. And sure, it was fake. And they both knew it. But no one else did. They could have this. This pure, hot, sexual thing, and no one would ever know. They could both lose control, in a very controlled way.

It was irresistible as far as he was concerned. He could tell that his potential partner in crime was not similarly convinced. Risky behavior for the risk averse.

"I *know* I can resist you," she said. She began to walk through the living room, heading toward the front door.

"Like you did just now?"

"Like I did in Las Vegas, asshole." She opened the front door, then slammed it behind her, leaving him standing in her living room.

He charged after her, flinging the door wide-open again. "Are you just going to leave me in your house? Because I don't have a key. I can't lock up or anything."

"I was going to come back," she shouted, opening up her car and putting her box in the trunk. "Darling," she added for good measure, in case the neighbors were listening, clearly. Because what couple didn't scream endearments to each other from the driveway?

"Well, I would be happy to do whatever you need me to do, peaches," he retorted.

"You're always thinking of me."

"I always make sure you come first," he said, speaking heavily of the orgasm that he'd treated her to a few moments before. And obviously, Lydia picked up on that. Not that hard, since it was as subtle as a drunken Vegas wedding.

She growled, walking up the steps, her posture so

divergent from what he usually saw, from Lydia, the staid and steady politician, that he could have laughed. She looked a whole lot more like a recalcitrant teenager.

She went back inside for a moment, then reappeared with her purse. Then she closed the door, locking it behind them. "The lights are on a timer," she said.

"Never let it be said that you aren't efficient."

"It would never be said, Colton. Because it would be a lie."

She walked back down the steps and got into her car, starting the engine and slamming the driver-side door shut behind her. He walked over to the window and tapped the glass. She narrowed her eyes, evil intent glittering in them. He didn't really care. He was past the point of common sense. He was past the point of control. He was at least ten miles past Colton West, and he had no idea who the hell he was right now.

"You didn't give me a kiss goodbye," he said as she rolled the window down.

"How silly of me," she said, clearly reluctant to tell him where he could shove his kiss, just in case. The picket fences had ears in this part of the world.

She looked around, probably aware there were likely people sitting on their front porches, or any manner of small-town nonsense. Walking their dogs, watering the rhododendrons late.

Then she looked back at him. "I'm waiting," she said. The challenge in her eyes spurred him on.

But it wasn't only the challenge in her eyes. It was just the fact that he wanted to kiss her again.

He leaned in, closing the short distance between them and claiming her mouth with his. It was hot, it was fast, it touched him all the way down deep. Grabbed hold of his cock and squeezed tight. He would have her again now. Right now. If she would have him.

He could tell by the flush in her cheeks that she would. It was only her pride that wouldn't let her admit it.

"Good night," he said, turning away from her and heading back to his truck.

She wasn't going to resist him; that much he knew. And he was determined. If he was going to be trapped in a marriage, then he was going to have his cake and eat it too.

He wasn't the kind of man who did things like this. At least, he hadn't been.

As far as he was concerned, for the next couple of months, all bets were off.

LYDIA SLUNK INTO her bedroom, box of pamphlets in her arms, hoping that she could handily avoid Colton for the rest of the evening.

What had she done? Her head was spinning; she didn't know how to process anything. Didn't know how she felt about the fact that they hadn't had sex in Vegas, and that they *had* had sex on her living room floor. Or rather, half on the living room floor, half on her campaign materials.

She groaned, crawling into bed and feeling a spike of humiliation when she realized that she was wearing her thermals.

What the hell was wrong with her? She had retreated like a terrified rodent after they'd made love, then she had appeared in what had to be her most embarrassing pajamas. She should have just brazened it out. Walked into the living room naked and grabbed her clothes. It could not have been more embarrassing than prancing around in this.

Or maybe it could have been. But really, she was kind of at max capacity with humiliation, so did it even matter at this point? Fatal was fatal. And this was definitely fatal.

One just might have killed her slightly quicker.

She grabbed hold of her cell phone, tapping the screen, debating whether or not she should make a phone call. She could just marinate in her humiliation alone. She wasn't used to having humiliation, so she didn't really know what to do with it. There really was no standard operating procedure for ill-advised sex. Not in her life.

But she knew someone who would know. That just meant confiding. It meant doing an actual, intimate friend thing.

She let out an exasperated breath and dialed Sadie's number. The phone rang twice before she picked up.

"Lydia? Is everything okay? It's kind of late."

Lydia groaned. It was late. And she was a self-centered ass. "I'm sorry. I didn't think to check the time."

"That's okay. I'm not normally in bed this early. But I'm kind of wiped out."

"Is everything okay?" Lydia asked.

"Yes," Sadie said, "everything's fine. I thought maybe Colton might have told you, since my loose-lipped husband let me know that he told Colton at the dinner last night."

"He didn't tell me anything," Lydia said. Mostly because she'd done her very best not to talk to him at all, and even when they'd been together this evening, talking had been minimal. "What's going on?"

"I'm pregnant."

"What?" Lydia nearly shrieked into the phone. "That's great!"

On the heels of the initial euphoria came a strange kind of weight. That was what happened now when people she knew were pregnant. Or engaged. Because she was thirty. Because, even though a large portion of her wasn't entirely certain she wanted those things for herself, there were parts of her that ached for them either way.

"Yes, it's pretty exciting. I'm not very far along, so we weren't really going to tell people yet. But the chatty sheriff can't seem to keep a secret. So the information is leaking out in strange and disorganized ways. I wanted to tell you myself. And, I wanted to tell you *not* at tenthirty when you were clearly calling about something else, but I couldn't wait. And now I feel like I've coopted whatever's happening with you."

"Co-opt away. A baby is a lot nicer of a topic than what I'm calling about."

"What's wrong?" Sadie asked. "Now you're freaking me out a little bit."

"There's no reason to be freaked out. I'm not dying or anything."

"Did you slip in the polls? Did all of the money that we raised get stolen? Are you running away to join a rock band?"

"You're ridiculous. And no. It's just…I slept with Colton again."

"You slept with him like you two had a slumber party, or is this euphemistic?"

"It's euphemistic," she whispered. "There was no sleeping at all."

"Excellent!" Sadie chirped in her ear.

"Nothing is excellent about this. It was a terrible decision. Colton and I are... We are nothing, with a marriage license. I have an election to worry about and I can't afford to be dealing with whatever this is."

"Was the sex good?"

"It was amazing, but I fail to see what that has to do with anything."

Sadie made a scoffing sound. "That has everything to do with *everything*. If the sex sucked then I can see you being disappointed. Of course, if the sex was terrible I guess you wouldn't be conflicted about it." There was a slight pause. "But I'm not really sure why you're conflicted about good sex."

"Sadie, I have been very celibate. I think you can figure out with that little bit of information that I'm not really the kind of person who does *just* sex."

"While I was not...inactive in my day, I was more one for relationships myself," Sadie said, "but I hear just sex works."

"When does it work? What does it work for?"

"Orgasms."

Lydia's face flamed and she turned over onto her stomach, nuzzling her pillow. "Well, yes, there was that," she said, her words muffled.

"Then why are you so distressed? Recently orgasmed women should not sound so distressed."

"Because! This just isn't the kind of thing that I usually do."

"Why?"

"Because. I don't... I like control. And this is kind of the opposite of that. Also, it's potentially messy."

"So let me get this straight. You've found a guy who

makes you, *you*, Lydia Carpenter, feel out of control, when I'm pretty sure driving your car through a patch of black ice won't do that. And somehow this is a bad thing?"

"Yes. It is my version of crawling into a cage with tigers."

"I think you should embrace it," Sadie said.

"Why do you think I should embrace it, Sadie?" Lydia asked, even while realizing this was basically the sole reason she had called Sadie in the first place. Because Sadie would support the decision to have sex with Colton again. Unless it was a really, really terrible idea, Sadie would definitely fall into the *have fun* camp.

And that was obviously what Lydia was looking for. Someone to validate what she couldn't find it in herself to validate.

You didn't want advice. You wanted Sadie to be your shoulder devil.

She couldn't even let herself get away with sneaky behavior. She was internally calling herself out for it already.

"Because embracing a hot guy while having doubts is more fun than embracing your pillow and feeling horny?"

Lydia pushed herself up and brushed her hair out of her face. "You know this how?"

"I'm not a saint, Lydia, as mentioned."

"Yes, but you said you were a relationship person."

"Yes," Sadie said slowly.

"So this…the sex-only thing was you and Eli."

Sadie all but hooted into her ear. It was not the most genuine hoot. "Can you imagine? Can you imagine Eli…

doing only sex. Just sex and no…promise ring or whatever? Ha."

"That was not convincing." She and Sadie hadn't been friends when Sadie and Eli got together, and then, Lydia imagined out of concern for her feelings, Sadie had never really talked much about the circumstances of them getting together.

But Lydia was post-Eli and had been for a while, so it really didn't matter to her. And her friend was being conniving.

"You know how he is," Sadie said.

"A man."

Sadie made a tsk-tsking sound. "Okay. Fine. So he was my one attempt at a sex-only relationship."

"Sadie!" Lydia scolded. "You can't advise me based on the fact that you think I'm going to marry Colton for real if we start having just sex."

"But you're so cute together."

"We're not cute. He calls me peaches. And I think he's the most annoying man ever."

"Because you like him. Because this kind of thing makes you eleven again and sticks you right back onto the playground. Of love. Chasing each other around and him trying to pull your pigtails."

"There is no playground of love, Sadie," Lydia said fiercely. "This is a terrifying parking lot carnival of lust. Full of danger and bad decisions. The Ferris wheel is being run by a guy with a neck tattoo and, sure, you might make it all the way to the top, but also the whole basket could fall and burst into flame and that's how you die. In a mall parking lot in a ball of fire."

She flopped onto her back and threw her arm over her eyes.

Sadie sighed heavily into Lydia's ear. "Okay," she said. "Do you want to know what I think?"

"No. What you think is devious and riddled with secret motives."

"I think that no matter what, you should just sleep with him again. You're going to do it no matter what. There's ample evidence to support that. You have to keep touching him, kissing him and living in the same house as him, and you're going to give in eventually. The only real decision is—are you going to plan it and enjoy it, or are you going to call me in a panic every time?"

Lydia chewed her lip, irritation spiking inside of her. She'd been looking for help excusing her behavior and Sadie was giving it. But she was just indecisive enough to want to argue with every possible scenario.

She wanted Sadie to acknowledge that this was impossible and nothing could be done at all to ease her terrible suffering. Instead, Sadie was offering solutions like they were simple. It was so annoying.

"But I just... I..." She was out of arguments. She really was. She and Colton were on a timer. Neither of them wanted a relationship.

Yes, the things he made her want, the way he made her feel. The absolute, hellfire levels of shame she'd felt when her orgasm had died down and she'd had to replay all the dirty things they'd said to each other in her head—that was hard. It was exposing and she didn't like it.

But it was also so good. It was everything she'd never known she wanted. And if it was only sex then she didn't have to worry about the other stuff. His eventually wanting her to move in, or be more, or share about her childhood and all the other things about relationships that made her feel like she was being slowly dissected under a microscope.

"I'll be distracted if I'm having sex while I campaign," she pointed out.

"As if you won't spend all day every day obsessing about his body if you're not getting all up on it," Sadie replied.

"You shouldn't have sex before a big game," Lydia protested. "I'm pretty sure that was on *Friday Night Lights*."

"You're not a football player."

"Still. The principle applies."

"No," Sadie said.

"I want him."

"I know you do."

"I have so many pamphlets to fold, though, and I feel like sex will distract me from that. That and talking to constituents and things."

"I don't know one person on earth, including my husband, who's more organized than you, Lydia Carpenter. I don't see any reason why you can't be the mayor of Copper Ridge, replete with both perfectly folded pamphlets and good sex with a good guy."

Lydia chewed her fingernail. "That *does* sound nice."

"That's my vote. But you have my vote first and always, and you know that." Lydia nodded silently, as though Sadie could see. "Now. I have to get some sleep because I already know I'm going to have an early-morning wake-up call in the form of nausea."

"Oh no. That's terrible."

"Pregnancy. The miracle of life is sort of a drag, but I hear it's worth it in the end."

Lydia smiled, feeling that little twinge around her

heart again. "You and Eli will be great parents. You have the best family ever, and I know you're going…" She took a deep breath, trying to ease the pain in her chest, trying to loosen up her throat. "I know you're going to make your child feel like they can do anything. You do it to me and I'm just your whiny single friend. Think how much more you'll do it with your kid? They're lucky to have you."

"I'm sure I'll also be a huge embarrassment. And Eli will show up at all functions in his uniform and give the kids a stern glare and tell them not to do drugs."

Lydia laughed. "I hope he does."

"And you'll be there, giving speeches and cutting ribbons. Because you'll be the boss lady."

Lydia blinked, suddenly having an image of herself all alone. She'd never really come to an internal conclusion on if she wanted to be married. She hadn't really felt like it was something she had to choose. Because it was a not-right-now kind of thing and she didn't have to.

She was starting to wonder when she'd choose. And she was starting to have to face that she'd have to at some point.

Or maybe she didn't because she would never actually have the chance to have something like Eli and Sadie did.

Even if she could, she really didn't know if she could handle it. If she wanted it at all.

You can have good sex, though. That you can have. And avoid thinking about the future.

She liked that option more and more.

She ended the call with Sadie and tossed her phone

onto the vacant pillow by her head. Determination burned in her stomach.

She wanted Colton and she was going to have him, pamphlets be damned.

CHAPTER THIRTEEN

SLEEP HAD BEEN HELL. Work had been hell. Colton had no desire to do either. What he'd wanted to do from the moment he'd left Lydia last night to the end of work today, was find her and drag her to his bedroom and explain to her—with his hands—exactly what they should be doing during this little enforced relationship.

But he hadn't done that. He'd been respectful of her space and responsible with his time.

Which really was terrible.

What he'd actually wanted to do was storm off the job site, stalk straight downtown to her little office, slam the door and bend her over her desk so she could get a good look at the ocean view while he screwed them both into oblivion.

But he hadn't done that. Because of respect. Of space and time and blah blah—he hated all of it now.

There had been a lot opportunities for resentment to burn inside of him. When he'd been forced to get a business degree in college—never even being given a chance to think about if he wanted to do something else—because he would need it for the inevitable *someday* when he would be put in charge of a ranch he didn't want to operate. When he'd been placed in charge of West Construction after his uncle's retirement. Or hell, he could take it all back to the day his older brother had walked out and left all of this for him to manage.

He'd never let the resentment fester. He'd just done what needed to be done.

Today he hated it.

As soon as he closed the front door behind him, he turned and walked back out onto the porch. He really wasn't in a frame of mind to be dealing with Lydia. She had made it clear that she didn't want this to happen again between them.

But she's a liar.

Yes, she was a liar. And he was pretty damn confident of that fact. Still, he was not going to be the jackass that chased after her. He had been a jackass enough over the course of the past month. Actually, he was pretty sure that being left at the altar was the lifetime limit of being a jackass.

He growled, stomping down the front steps and stalking across the driveway, heading down the dirt road that led to the barn. He would just chop some more wood. Because what the hell else was a man supposed to do in this situation?

He supposed he could put his forearm muscles to work in a different way. Taking hold of himself and working himself to oblivion with the fantasy of her in his mind, but he just couldn't bring himself to do it. Not when he could still taste her on his lips.

He gritted his teeth, trying to shove that memory back down deep. It didn't work. Instead, he was consumed with it. The way her lips had felt, soft and slick beneath his own. The sounds she had made when she'd found her release.

When he had found out he was the only man to ever

give her an orgasm. It made him feel like a man. In the most basic, elemental way.

"Not helpful," he said, grabbing his ax from against the side of the woodshed. "Not helpful at all, West."

He propped a log up on top of the stump he used as a stand, and brought the ax down hard over the top of it, splitting it cleanly in two. There was something immensely satisfying about hard labor. At least for him.

It was clean. It was honest. And, any work that he did here was *his*. That thought, as always, sent a rush of satisfaction through him. Too bad it was more of a philosophical sense of satisfaction. That wasn't exactly what he was after. He would have preferred the physical. The sexual.

Since when did he become so basic? He wasn't sure he cared. Lydia made him feel obsessive. One time. She expected them to limit it to *one* time?

He recognized the irony in that. Since it was supposed to be this one *more* time, so that they could remember the *first* time, so that they could put it behind them.

All they had remembered was that there hadn't been a first time. So now, it had only been once. Somewhere in his brain, he felt that made it logical to try and do it again.

Or maybe there was nothing logical to be had in any of this. Maybe he just wanted. It had never really happened before. Not like this. He wasn't a stranger to sexual desire, but he was a stranger to this all-consuming, specific lust that he knew could only be satisfied by one woman. That he knew couldn't even be tricked with a few moments in the shower and his soaped up right hand.

So, he would burn it out. Chop wood until his body

ached, until he couldn't move. Maybe it would reduce the chances of him walking down the hall and knocking on her bedroom door tonight. Putting himself out there again, getting on his knees and begging.

Or he could make her beg.

She wanted him. Even if she wished that she didn't. The thought made his stomach twist, made his blood rush south of his belt.

He picked up another log and put it on the stump, chopping it mercilessly, trying to expend some of the frustration that was tensing his muscles and making him feel restless. Aroused.

Somehow, this was his life. He had gotten to a place where he had never experienced this kind of lust before. Ill-advised, pointless. He had gotten to a place where he was building a business that he didn't care about, where his future would involve running a ranch that didn't have his heart.

Somehow, there was a woman who would beg for him, when he knew none ever would have before. Somehow, he was considering making her do it.

He slung the ax again, bringing it down hard on the stump, abandoning it with the head buried halfway into the solid block of wood.

"Are you trying to destroy yourself?"

He turned and saw Lydia standing there, her hands clasped in front of her. She looked…she looked prim and proper, and like she had not spent the day in sexual agony. She made a mockery of all the fantasies that were rioting through his head.

She was wearing a skirt that fell down past her knees and a top that was buttoned up to her throat. And he wanted to tear it all away. Pop the buttons off her blouse.

He had never done anything like that in his life. But he wanted to do it so badly his fingers itched.

"I can handle a little wood chopping." He gripped the handle on the ax and leaned up against it.

She arched a brow. "You must have a lot of wood."

Those words made a mockery of the hard-on pressing up against his jeans. He looked down, then back up at her. "You may want to consider or rephrase. As a politician you should be aware of the power of words."

She looked down, then her eyes widened. She looked back up in his face. "I'm sorry. Most of my constituents are not thirteen-year-old boys."

"You and I both know that I'm not a boy."

Good intentions be damned, he had just walked them both off the pier and into the deep end.

"You are cranky today," she said, crossing her arms beneath her breasts, drawing his attention to those perfect little temptations that he'd had under his hands, under his tongue, just last night.

He could respond to that. He could tell her that it was her fault he was cranky because he was sexually frustrated. That he was cranky because she had given him the best sex of his life, and then cut him off completely. Yeah, he could say that. But frankly, he was done talking.

He released his hold on the wooden handle, striding across the empty space between them. He didn't care that his hands were dirty, or that she was wearing nice clothes from a day at work. He didn't care that she had decided they couldn't do this anymore. He didn't care that it couldn't go anywhere.

All he cared about was the arousal that was roaring

through his bloodstream. All he cared about was how much he wanted her, how much he needed to have her.

Her eyes widened as he wrapped his arm around her waist, drawing her up against him. Then he lowered his head, claiming her mouth with his. He wasn't asking; he was taking. He wasn't seeking approval; he was demanding. And he knew that she would rise to the demand.

He wasn't disappointed. She wrapped her arms around his neck, kissing him back with all of the frustration that was pouring out of him. She matched it, amped it up. Kiss for kiss, thrust for thrust of his tongue, she met him.

He propelled her back up against the woodshed, as he had done just a week or so ago. Pressed her hands above her head, holding her steady as he continued to ravage her mouth. She didn't protest. She didn't try to stop him. Instead, she arched her back, pressing her breasts more firmly against his chest, a needy sound escaping her lips. Yes, she wanted this. Yes, she wanted *him*. He was insane, but so was she. It was a common madness that wove itself around them both, that made him feel somewhere beyond control, somewhere beyond common sense.

And since he knew that both of them firmly existed within the realm of common sense on a good day, it had to be magic. Some kind of dark spell propelling them on. But if it was witchcraft, then he was happy to burn in hell. As long as she was with him.

He pressed his hand between her thighs, edging beneath the waistband of her panties, drawing his fingertips through her damp flesh, feeling the evidence of her desire as it spread over his skin. She was so hot. So hot for him, for this. He pushed one finger deep inside of her, and her head fell back, a raw gasp on her lips. He just wanted to watch her as she came, as he teased her clit with his thumb, adding another finger to the first, stretching her, teasing her. The color in her cheeks mounted, her lips parting slightly, short, sharp gasps of pleasure escaping her mouth.

"Come for me," he demanded, the rough words on his lips. "Come for me, Lydia. I need you to. I want to watch."

She began to roll her hips in time with the movements of his fingers, the dark slashes of color on her cheeks growing even more pronounced as she did. Her dark eyes were glazed over, and he could see that she had surrendered herself to this completely. There was no resistance. There was no evidence of doubt. There was nothing but desire. She was as lost in this as he was, and he loved it.

He could honestly say that he had never once before taken so much pleasure in watching his partner come undone. Could honestly say that he had never taken the time to watch a woman reach her peak. Yes, he always felt triumphant when his partner did, and he considered it a must. He never left a woman unsatisfied. But this was *different*. This wasn't about his ego, this was about her satisfaction becoming his own.

She clung to his shoulders, sobbing now with her need, her fingernails digging into his skin. He pressed harder, his movements going faster. And then she let out a broken cry as her internal muscles tightened around his fingers, as she gave herself up to her release.

"Good girl," he said, the words soft, unintentional. She made him unintentional. Made him, a man who did everything, took every breath with purpose, feel like he didn't know himself. Feel like he didn't know what he might do next.

It was a damned abomination. And a damned miracle.

She was breathing hard, still holding on to him. Her whole face flushed. "I don't feel so cranky anymore," he said.

She didn't say anything. Instead, she grabbed hold of his face and pulled him in for a kiss, one that was so fierce, so intense, he feared she might knock them over completely. He held her hips as she kissed him deep, as her tongue slid over his. Then he reached into his back pocket, grabbing hold of his wallet, and some protection. He worked at the front of his jeans, freeing himself and sheathing himself quickly.

Then he pushed her skirt up her hips and pulled her panties to the side, testing the entrance to her body, testing her readiness, before he thrust in deep, pinning her up against the side of the woodshed.

She tightened her hold on him, deepened his kiss as he began to drive them both toward oblivion. It was fast, it was raw, it was like nothing he had ever experienced before. He didn't have sex with women outside of bedrooms. Didn't take them quick, didn't take them hard. He lit candles, he set the mood. He made sure that it was right, and that they were ready. But none of that had happened here.

She wanted it, and he knew it. He had read her body. He felt more connected to her desire then he had ever felt with his own before. Much less another partner.

She bit his neck, clawed his back. Whispered in his ear. *Harder. Faster. Now.*

He gave. He gave as much as he took. *Harder*, until his thighs burned. *Faster* until he couldn't breathe. And *now*, when he couldn't control himself any longer.

His climax came fast and furious, and so did hers. Hit them both at the same time like a bolt of lightning straight from the sky. She convulsed around him and he pulsed inside of her, as the electric tendrils wound around them both. He took her mouth, deep and hard, while still fully seated inside of her body, staying deep until the very last jolt of release shocked his system.

And when it was over, he wrapped his arms around her, and pulled her down onto the ground with him, so that she was sitting on his lap. And he wasn't sure what the hell had just happened.

"I don't—"

"If you say that you don't do things like that," he said, his voice a growl, "I'm going to have no choice but to prove you wrong again. Fact of the matter is you do things like that. *We* do things like that. At least, we do them together."

He was surprised he had been able to get his voice to work. Was surprised that he had been able to speak at all. Especially when his heart was still thundering in his head and his muscles were still shaking from the aftereffects of his release.

"Well, then I have no idea what to say," she said, leaning even more firmly against him, as though she was trying to melt away completely.

"Maybe don't talk, peaches." He gathered his strength, moving up onto his knees, then into a standing position. His jeans sagged, and he remembered belatedly that they were still open.

He looked down and noticed that Lydia still had her shoes on. "I have to put you down."

He set her down gently, then set about to putting his pants back in order. He made a quick trip into the woodshed, where there was a wastebasket, to deal with the condom.

When he returned, he half expected her to be gone. But she wasn't. She was standing out there in the dirt, looking completely incongruous. Tumbled, and yet somehow still as sleek and polished as ever, a refined little thing in the middle of nature.

"I know we agreed not to do this," he said. It wasn't an apology. He wasn't sorry.

"I was going to tell you that I changed my mind anyway."

His eyebrows shot up. "Really?"

"Yes. I was going to seduce you, actually. It's just that you kind of jumped the gun."

"I guess I kind of did."

"I'm not complaining."

He cleared his throat, crossing his arms over his chest. "So, you were going to seduce me."

Lydia wrinkled her nose. "Do you think we should go inside to have the seduction discussion?"

"It doesn't matter to me either way."

She sighed heavily, walking toward the fence that corralled the horses. She leaned up against the rough wood, looping her forearms over the top of it. "I think that this is a losing battle. Actually, I'm not really sure there's anything for me to say, since you just proved my point so handily."

"What exactly was your point going to be?"

"We can't resist each other. Like, can't. At all. I

walked up to you, and then you kissed me, and now we've had sex again. That easily. And, now that we have, I realize how ridiculous it is that we thought we had before. When we obviously hadn't. Because now that we have…I haven't been able to do anything all day but think about last night. Do you have any idea how impossible it was for me to be at the office? I felt like everyone could read my mind. And my mind was very dirty today, Colton. And I'm rarely dirty."

"That…" He moved where she was standing, copied her pose at the fence. "That seems like it could be a problem."

"I work with a bunch of octogenarians. I feel like they're even more insightful than most when it comes to matters of the…pants."

"Matters of the pants?"

"It's not a… This is not a heart feelings thing. It's feelings located in a much different place."

He laughed. "Okay. I guess I should be flattered by that."

"You should be. This is kind of uncharted territory for me."

"Me too. I guess we were sort of stupid. Thinking we were somehow immune to this thing that seems to eventually get everybody."

"What thing?"

"Sex madness. People have affairs with unsuitable people all the time. They break up marriages, destroy careers… And I've never once thought that I could even remotely understand why someone would do it. So, I'm wondering if we were just naive."

"I'm not sure that's it. But, maybe we have behaved a little too well for a little too long."

She laughed. "Okay, maybe that's it."

"How are you feeling?"

She sighed heavily. "Why do you always have to ask about my feelings? I don't want to think about my feelings."

It was his turn to laugh. "Okay, how's your body?"

She tilted her face upward, the waning sun washing over her features. She was glowing. He would like to take credit, but he had a feeling that was just Lydia. "Satisfied."

"I like that."

"I think that while we're married, while we're living together, there just isn't any point in us resisting. But I think this is perfect. I don't want a relationship, Colton. I know that you were on the verge of getting married, but I wasn't. I have too much of my own stuff to figure out before I ever get involved in a relationship."

"Is that why you broke up with the dusty museum guy?"

"Yes." She looked down, picking at a splinter on the top rail of the fence. "He wanted things that I didn't know if I could give."

"And you still don't know?"

"No, I still don't know. Because unlike you, I tend to think that if I ever get married I want it to be because I'm crazy in love with somebody. And I just never have been."

"And I still think that love is overrated."

It was a strange thing to have a conversation about love with a woman he had just screwed senseless up against the side of a woodshed. He felt kind of like a jerk, saying he didn't believe in love right then. But it was also a much more honest conversation than he ever could have had with anyone else.

They were bolstered by the fact that there were no expectations between them, by the fact that they weren't even supposed to like each other, but seemed to be beginning to understand each other.

"*Sex* is a little less overrated than I thought."

"Now," he said, leaning toward her, brushing a strand of hair out of her face, "I am glad to hear that."

"Then it's settled," she said, licking her top lip, a motion that he felt all the way down in his cock. "You and I are going to have a reckless, physical-only marriage, which we will conclude after the election. Sex only. No judgment, no feelings."

The words gripped him tight, settled down low inside of him. Yeah, he wanted that. He wasn't even going to hesitate.

"Lydia Carpenter," he said, reaching out and wrapping his fingers around hers, shaking her hand gently. "You have yourself an affair."

CHAPTER FOURTEEN

AGREEING TO AN affair was one thing, but actually dealing with what that meant was another. It reminded her a lot of when she had first moved into Colton's house, and everything had seemed simple until she was hungry and wondered who exactly would be paying for the food.

So many things had been left unresolved. So many hairs left unsplit. She didn't like that. She needed to split hairs. She needed to know the details. The nitty-gritty. The bottom line.

But they hadn't discussed it. They'd just…shaken hands like they'd embarked upon the world's most torrid business deal, and then he'd asked her about work.

She had no idea what happened next.

Now she was hungry, metaphorically, and wondering exactly how often she would be allowed to eat in this little arrangement. Metaphorically.

They had already *done it*, out at the woodshed earlier, and then they had gone inside and had dinner, and Colton had claimed to have work to do after that. So he was outside somewhere being rugged and cowboy-esque, and she was pacing the halls.

She didn't exactly want to reveal herself as a sex-starved maniac. But she was basically feeling like a sex-starved maniac. Before Colton it had been years since she'd been with anyone, and it had not been anywhere near as good as being with Colton was. He had opened up an entire new world of pleasure to her, and now she just wanted more. It was like discovering the existence of cake. Or peppermint mochas.

Either way, it was all she wanted now.

But she imagined that if he wanted to have sex again, he would come to her room. Yes, she would wait for him in bed. She scampered back to her bedroom, looking in the closet for something that wasn't too dowdy.

She emerged with a nightgown that wasn't exactly lingerie, but it was silky, and it did just barely cover her butt, so she supposed it was better than flannel.

She slipped it on, then climbed into bed, tugging the covers up to her chin and waiting.

Sometime later, she heard the front door open, heard Colton's heavy footsteps downstairs. She held her breath, waiting. And she kept waiting. And waiting. He didn't come.

"Oh good, you're the woman and of the two of you, you're the one who wants sex every couple of hours."

She threw her arm over her face, her stomach twisting tight. The longer she lay there, the more she felt…the more she felt completely and totally put out. They had begun an affair earlier today, the first thing he should have done was storm into her bedroom and take her like a marauding outlaw. Otherwise, really, what was the point of hooking up with a rough country boy. Okay, so he was one of the more sophisticated rough country boys around, but still. He spent his days working construction and chopping wood, he should be a testosterone-laden man-beast who could scarcely contain himself around delicate women such as herself. Especially when they had verbally agreed not to contain themselves anymore.

She huffed, rolling over onto her side and curling her knees up to her chest. She was fine. She did not need him to come in here. She did not need him at all. She had spent the past four years sex-free, and the past thirty years Colton-free. She was fine. She did not need his hands, or his mouth, or his...

"Wargh!"

She let her own frustrated scream get absorbed by her pillow.

She was fine. This was fine.

So fine, that she found herself getting up out of bed without fully thinking the action through. So fine, that she found herself opening her bedroom door and pattering down the hallway. So fine that before she knew it she was poised in front of Colton's bedroom door, ready to knock. And then she just decided to hell with that.

To hell with everything.

All she did was tiptoe. All she did was knock and behave appropriately. The only person she had ever broken apart for was him. And she wanted to keep doing it, again and again, as long as she could. It was safe. The first safe space she had ever found to act on those secret places inside of herself.

So, she opened the door, and she barged in. Colton was standing at the foot of his bed, and he was completely naked. She was not going to apologize.

"I expected you to come by my room."

He turned to face her, most of his body a dark shadow in the unlit room. "I didn't want to hassle you."

"I thought we agreed that we were going to hassle each other for the foreseeable future. No judgment. No feelings. Concern over hassling me is a feelings thing. Stop it."

"A man doesn't like to feel like he's forcing himself on a lady, Lydia."

"Was there something about my enthusiastic response to all the sex that you found ambiguous or confusing?" she asked, sounding every bit as exasperated as she felt. "Was my orgasm a source of consternation for you?"

"I don't..."

"You were *supposed* to come into my room and take me, because you couldn't wait another second," she said, advancing on him.

"Was I?" There was a thread of dark humor in his voice, laced with heat and something that was undeniably Colton.

She moved closer, sliding her hand up his chest, the hair there scraping against her palm. "Yes," she said.

"It seems like I've come after you an awful lot, peaches."

She tried to swallow, but her throat was too tight. Why did that stupid nickname on his lips make her whole body *want* in ways that she hadn't known were possible?

He was perilously close to making her like a fruit she would have said grew on the trees in hell only a few short weeks ago.

The man was a problem. But right now, he was her very own, very big, very muscular problem.

"I mean... I don't... A woman wants to be wanted."

He leaned in, his breath fanning over her cheek, his whiskers rough against her skin. "You don't think a man wants the same?"

"I...I..."

"You were lying there aching for me. Wanting me. And now I forced you to come after me." He nuzzled her neck, his skin so hot she was ready to go up in flames. "It must be hard to have to show how much you want me."

She realized as soon as he said the words, that he had been the one to pursue all of the encounters between them. That she really had managed to protect herself. Even today, when she had intended to let him know that she wanted things to progress between them, he had been the one to ultimately take the last step. She had been spared.

"If you want me now," he said, his voice as rough as that delicious stubble on his jaw, "you have to tell me, peaches."

She took a deep breath, and she felt like something cracked in her chest. Something she kept buried, something she tried to keep hidden. She was shaking, and it had nothing to do with the sex. Sex with Colton, at this point, didn't intimidate her at all. It was what he had just said. Showing him how much she wanted him.

She lifted her other shaking hand, brushed her fingertips against his cheek, against the rough stubble on his jaw.

"I want you," she said, testing the words out, waiting to see if she would feel completely stripped, completely bared for having spoken them. She managed to survive them.

He caught hold of her wrist, drawing her hands down, and pushing them behind her back, tugging her forward so that she was pressed hard against his chest. "Do you?"

"Yes," she said, the word coming out in a rush.

"Tell me," he insisted, "how much you want me."

Her stomach tightened, and she tried to pull away, but he held her fast. "A lot."

"You can do better than that, Lydia. I know you can."

"I… It aches. It hurts. How badly I want you."

"And?"

She looked down, even though it was dark and she knew he couldn't see her face anyway. "I'm…I'm wet for you."

"I'm going to have to check that." He put his hand between her thighs and she gasped as he slipped his fingers through her slick flesh. It felt so good. It felt better than anything had a right to. He made her want. He made her want so badly she could scarcely breathe, scarcely think.

"You are," he said, his voice husky. And if she weren't so turned on she was ready to collapse, she might have laughed. Because this was the same man who she had once imagined was high-handed and uptight in the worst ways. Well, she still thought he was high-handed, she just enjoyed it in the right context. And uptight? He had done such a great job of unraveling her, there was no possible way he could be uptight.

She fought the urge to let her head fall back, to sink into his touch and surrender to him. She didn't want to simply follow. Didn't simply want to give herself up. She wanted to give as good as she got. She wanted to make him feel what he made her feel. Even if it was only a portion of the ecstasy he brought to her.

While he stroked her, she leaned in, angling her head and scraping her teeth along his neck lightly, then retracing the line with her tongue. He jerked beneath her touch, and she could feel him, hard and insistent against her hip.

That made her bold. The simple fact that he wanted her to. That he was as close to the edge as she was.

She slipped her hands down to the front of his chest, down over his abs, skimming her fingertips across his rock-hard thighs. She drifted inward, teasing his sensitive flesh, then moved to grip his shaft, squeezing him until his breath hissed through his teeth.

"I want you," she said again.

She felt bolder now, stronger. More excited. She squeezed him again, and he grabbed hold of her wrist, flipping their positions so that her legs were backed up against the mattress.

"I'm not convinced," he said, grabbing hold of her hips and lifting her up off the floor, depositing her back on the bed. "I'm going to have to make absolutely certain."

He dropped to his knees, gripping her hips even more tightly and pulling her toward him, draping her legs over his shoulders.

She felt panicky. A fluttery sensation spidering all over her chest like a terrified creature. She felt completely powerless. At his mercy. And more than a little exposed in spite of the darkness of the room. More than that, she was fascinated. Desperate. For what came next. For it to be over. For it to never end. She was a mass of contradictions and want, and she knew that only seeing this through to the end could solve that.

Or maybe it couldn't. But it was better than not being satisfied.

"Damn, baby," he said, the words rough and unfamiliar. Unfamiliar to him, too. She could tell. Could tell that this wasn't him any more than it was her. Could tell that this madness was something he'd never experienced before, either.

That got her even hotter, which she would have said

wasn't possible if asked. Truthfully, if asked, she would deny all of this because good girls didn't marry strange men and then agree to stay married for a political campaign.

Good girls also didn't engage in physical-only affairs with their fake husbands, she was pretty sure.

So if asked, she would probably deny everything. But no one was asking now. No one else was here.

He leaned in, drawing his tongue over her sensitized flesh.

"Oh, Colton," she gasped, grabbing for him, and coming up with air. She moved her hands to the bedspread, curling her fingers around the fabric, gathering handfuls, trying to do something to root her to the mattress.

"I like you like this," he said, his voice rough. "Mindless for me. Begging for me."

"Yes," she said, "I'll beg. I'll do whatever you want. Just please."

"Please, what?"

Heat spread over her skin like a rash. "You know what."

"Maybe I don't. Maybe I need you to tell me, peaches."

"Now you're being a jerk," she said, gasping as he flicked his tongue over her clit.

"Tell me what you want," he said, his mouth hovering just above her core.

"I need to come, damn you."

"Say please, Lydia."

"Bastard."

"Never," he responded. "I'm an upstanding citizen."

For some reason, that got her even hotter. For some reason, it was the one thing that made her want to actually give in to his demands. Because it was true. Because he was normally the most upstanding citizen in town, other than her. Because he would never normally torture a woman like this. That made her special, in a weird way. Just like he was special for her. Because no other man had ever made her feel this way. No other man had ever made her want like this. It was dangerous, but it was intoxicating. Lydia had never wanted dangerous. She had never wanted intoxicating. But she was neck deep in it now, and she didn't regret a thing.

"Please, Colton. I need to come."

He chuckled, low and deep and wicked in a way that he almost certainly never was. "That wasn't so hard, was it?"

Then she felt his hot breath on her, just before he leaned in and began to pleasure her again with his mouth. She was lost in it, in him. Surely, this made her some kind of extraordinarily wanton type woman. They had done this earlier. She should be satisfied. At the very least, she shouldn't be so desperate. But, God help her, she was desperate. In ways she hadn't known she could be.

She arched her hips up off the bed and he held her tight, bringing her in even more closely, forcing her to submit to his devastating sensual assault.

He tasted her until she was shaking, until she was boneless, until she could not have gotten up and walked away from him even if she wanted to.

One last deft flick of his tongue over that sensitized bundle of nerves and she lost herself completely, gave herself up to her pleasure. To him.

And for some reason, somehow, she still ached. Still wanted more. Still needed more. She needed to be joined to him. Needed him buried deep inside of her.

"Please," was all she could say. But the light in his eyes had changed, and she knew, instinctively, that forcing her to say please had been letting her off easily.

He had tested her, and she had passed. But he was going to test her again, of that she was certain.

"You want me?"

"Yes," she said, no hesitation at all.

"Then you have to tell me."

"I already have," she responded, breathless.

"I'm going to need you to ask me to fuck you."

She was already naked, but his words stripped her bare in a way that nothing else ever had. It should be easy—it was just a word. But for some reason, it felt to her like she was being asked to open up her chest and show him everything she kept hidden away.

She'd never heard him say anything like that before, and it was exhilarating and terrifying. So damned sexy she could hardly stand it. She wanted to say it. Wanted to give it right back to him.

It hovered on her lips, and yet it terrified her. Because if she said it, it would change things. It might even change her. It was only a word, and yet, it was one of the more powerful words in existence.

He had said it the last time they were together, and it had been rough, thrilling. She had relished that look inside of him, beneath the veneer. And because it had meant so much coming from him, she knew it would mean even more coming from her. And what would happen then? The world might fall apart, and she would be revealed. Lydia Carpenter, in all of her shattered, messy glory, wrapped up in a tight little ball and squished down deep inside well-ordered, reinvented Lydia Carpenter, who controlled her life in a way that was a lie, because life couldn't be controlled.

Who looked so smooth and serene, like she could never be broken when deep inside she already was.

If she asked Colton West to do that to her then he would know. He would know that deep down she wanted those things, that she fantasized about those things. That she was no more the perfectly kept and well-ordered person she presented to the world than he was.

Then he would have her. Have his hand wrapped around her every vulnerable piece. He would know just where they were, and just how to destroy them.

"You have to ask for it, Lydia," he said, his voice still, firm. "Otherwise, I send you back to bed now, alone."

It was the stillness, the steadiness of the words that betrayed how important this was to him. How much he needed her to say it. To prove herself. To prove her desire for him. That wasn't why she hesitated. It was because of all it would expose. To him. To herself.

Like removing limitations she hadn't realized she had set there in the first place. She was only just becoming aware of them now that she realized how difficult they were to shake off.

She swallowed hard, her throat dry.

"Please," she said, her voice soft, hoarse. "Fuck me, Colton."

He growled, and she found herself being propelled back on the bed, her head resting on a pillow, Colton above her, his gaze intense. He reached over, opening the drawer to his nightstand and pulling out a condom. He made quick work of the protection and positioned himself at her entrance.

He pushed inside her slowly, filling her, inch by exquisite inch.

"Yes," she said, the word a prayer of thanks that he was finally inside of her.

Then she was lost, in the all-consuming rhythm that he set, pushing them both toward release. He was above her, around her, deep inside of her. So deep. And she was undone. Now that she had said the word, she said it again. And again. She made demands of him that she had never made of another man; she said things she had never even said in the dark, private silence of her own room.

It was as if he had begun an exorcism of all of these dark secret things inside of her that not even she had ever known existed.

Never in her life had she wanted so deeply, and had so completely. Never had she felt so completely needy, and so completely satisfied all at the same time. But Colton made her feel that. Colton made her feel entirely too much.

But before she could seriously worry about that she was swept away on a tide of pleasure, lost beneath the surf as her release swept through her. As wave after wave of sensation rolled through her.

He gripped her harder, his thrusts growing erratic as he lost his hold on that control she knew he prized as much as she valued her own. "Yes," she said, encouraging him. "Take me. Take what you want."

He turned his head, growling against the curve of her neck as he stiffened, his release racking his big body, making him shudder, making him tremble. She had done that to him. She had made him lose his control again. Again, and again. Just as he had done for her.

He moved away from her, getting off the bed and walking into the bathroom. Leaving her alone.

She stared up at the ceiling, trying to make out if there was a texture, if it was wood. If it was anything other than a witness to her sweetest downfall.

Slowly, her pleasure began to wear off. And then, she just sort of saw everything, and heard it, without the misty veil of arousal around it. She kept hearing her own words, replayed over and over again, but she heard them flat. Far too loud. Far too *her*.

She had not magically transformed into some sort of temptress, who could get away with saying those things. She was still just Lydia. She was not a temptress of any kind. And she had shown him so much of herself. She didn't know him all that well, but now she felt like they might be strangers. Or, at least, that she might be a stranger to everybody.

Suddenly, she just wanted to cry.

She most definitely wanted to get off the bed and go hide in her own room. But she was rooted to the spot, unable to move. She was having a mental breakdown, she was certain of it.

He returned a moment later, and it was too soon for Lydia's taste. She didn't want him to join her in the bed. But she still didn't move, so maybe that wasn't true.

She stayed on top of the covers, and he got underneath them. He didn't say anything.

She supposed it didn't say anything good that she now felt tongue-tied and completely uncomfortable with a man she had just done the most intimate things with. Or maybe that was normal. Maybe it was normal to want to retreat back into yourself when you had laid so much of yourself out there. Either way, she was certain of a couple of things. The first being that while she'd had sex before, she had never actually been intimate with anyone.

Intimacy wasn't easy. It cost. It definitely wasn't comfortable.

Her last relationship had been exactly that. Companionable. Easy. She had been able to hide so many pieces of herself away, and he had never even looked for them. And with one rough, crude command, Colton had demanded more of her than a two-year relationship with Nolan ever had.

He had asked for more over the past few encounters than anyone—friend, boyfriend, family member—had asked of her in years. Either because they accepted who she was at face value, or they simply didn't want to dig too deeply. And she had been happy with that. It was why she was here. It was why she had chosen Copper Ridge, instead of opting to stay in the neighborhood she had grown up in. Because she didn't want to be known.

Because she didn't want to pass people on the street every day who knew the details of her grief. Who knew that she was the remaining half of something, rather than a whole person.

That thought gave her pause. It made her wonder if she was actually a whole person anymore, or if she had squished and squeezed herself down until she really was just that half.

"I should go to bed," she said, rolling off the mattress.

"Wait," he said, catching hold of her arm.

"If you want another round, I think I might have to disappoint you. I'm exhausted." Not physically, but emotionally. She felt like she'd been divested of her shell, leaving only a tender, vulnerable thing behind that she had to protect at all costs.

"That isn't what I want," he said. "Okay, I would take it. But I just thought you might want to stay."

"I have my own room. I think I need it."

"Okay," he responded, releasing his hold on her, not pushing the issue. Because he was so decent. Because, at the end of the day, he was Colton.

A few minutes ago, he would have demanded she stay. And a few minutes ago, she would have obeyed. But it wasn't a few minutes ago. It was now. That was the damned ridiculous thing about time. It always moved, even if you didn't want it to.

"Good night," she said.

And when she was safely closed back in her room, she curled into a ball and gave in to her misery. But at least, after all he had seen, Colton West didn't see her dissolve.

CHAPTER FIFTEEN

COLTON KNEW HE had messed up with her somehow. But it had been back to work the following day, so he hadn't gotten a chance to see her at all from the time she fled her bedroom the night before to the end of shift the next day.

Not that he thought she had contrived it that way, but he was pretty sure she had contrived it that way. Not that he should care. Because it was a physical-only affair, and he was happy enough to be balls deep in that without adding conversations and feelings.

Right. You can't even think something that crude without feeling apologetic.

Dammit. It was true. He couldn't.

He had lost his head a bit with Lydia last night. He had never even dreamed of talking to another woman like that. But the whole idea of their relationship was supposed to be to push their personal limits. He had to wonder if he had found hers.

You don't wonder that. You know that isn't the problem.

He did. It was just that it was much easier to blame coarse language and potentially crossing a sexual line than it was to try and delve deep into feelings.

He didn't want to care about her. He didn't want to understand her. But she wasn't the cold, obnoxious creature he had first imagined her to be. He could remember thinking of her as a yapping dog, who never let go once she had gotten a hold of something. Usually his ankle.

Now he saw her as being determined. She was a woman who set a goal and went straight for it. He had to admire that. Mostly because it was so different to how he did things. Oh, he was as hardheaded and determined as she was, but he had never set his own goals. His determination came from putting his head down and fulfilling the goals his father had set out for him.

Taking care of his family, when the easier thing to do would always be to take off and do whatever he wanted. Like Gage had done. But he refused to do it. Even when it sucked. Even when it meant turning away from all of the things he actually wanted.

Yeah, hardheaded stubbornness. They had both accused each other of having it more than once. They were both right.

He noticed her car in the driveway as soon as he got home, but when he went inside the house, he didn't find her.

He wandered around the back, tempted to head toward the woodshed, since that seemed to be where she wandered when she got the bug to explore the property. But then, considering what happened yesterday, and considering how handily she had been avoiding him since, he changed course.

He walked around back behind the house, across the manicured lawn and through a field that was growing too tall. The grass was wet, lashing against his jeans as he walked through it. He came through a little grove of trees, and that was where he found her.

She was sitting on the swing, the swing that he was

pretty sure not even Natalie knew about. It was tied to a thick oak branch, the leaves making a canopy overhead. Her dark hair was backlit by the sinking sun, casting her in a golden glow. She was swaying back and forth slightly, her green dress fluttering in the breeze with each motion.

"Fancy meeting you here," he said.

"Okay, this is a very big property. How did you find me?"

"I decided to go to a place you didn't know about, because that meant that we had never encountered each other, and it was the most likely place you'd go to hide from me."

"Wow. That is some Sherlock Holmes stuff, right there."

"I might have missed my calling." He walked closer to her, taking up a position behind the swing. He wrapped his hands around the rope, just above hers.

"Why do you have a swing?" she asked.

"For my kids."

She planted her feet on the ground, her shoes skidding in the dirt. "You don't have kids."

"No," he said. "I don't. But I mean, future kids."

"Oh."

"I thought this would be the perfect place for them to come out and play on summer days. This is a great field to run barefoot in. That's just my expert opinion."

"On running barefoot through fields?"

He gave the swing a little push. "Yes. I'm an expert. At least, I used to be."

"Not anymore?"

"Things change."

"Like what?"

He laughed. "Okay, now you're going to pry when you and I both know you don't want me asking questions about you?"

"Yes."

"Things changed when my older brother left. It's a funny thing, growing up in a family like mine. Who thinks they're some kind of royalty, when they're just rich ranchers. But it was very much that whole heir and the spare thing. My brother was supposed to take over the operation. He was supposed to do everything that I'm doing. My father rested everything on his shoulders from day one. But Gage was never interested. He was rebellious. And he got into a lot of trouble, I guess. I don't know the whole story. Or any of it really. I only know that one day…he left. He left, and he never came back. I was sixteen. And suddenly, my father turned and looked at me. And I mean, he really looked at me. That was when I realized he had never done it before. Not really. Not like that. He was depending on me. I knew I couldn't let him down."

It had been that and more. That and the fact that Gage leaving had splintered his mother when she was fragile already. The fact that he was all that his sisters had. Because their dad had never given a damn and their mom just couldn't.

"You don't know where Gage is?" she asked.

"No."

"Have you ever looked?"

"No," he said, his voice rough. "I hope he stays gone. After everything…he better stay the hell away."

He'd never said those words to anyone else.

"Why?" she asked. Though, he had a strange feeling she already knew.

"You ever heard the story of the prodigal son?"

"I do believe I've seen it acted out with flannel characters before, yes."

"That's what would happen," he said, shocked at the bitterness in his own voice. Shocked that he was saying this out loud at all. "They would kill a fatted calf for him. Because it doesn't matter which son is there at the helm as long as there is one. And it would be like nothing ever happened. Like he didn't waste years off in the wilderness with his dick in his hand. Or in a city with his dick in his hand, I don't know what he's doing."

"And everything you went through would be for nothing," she said.

"Yes."

"But you'd have your life back. I mean, the one you were supposed to have."

"It's not mine anymore," he said. "I mean, I gave everything up. I moved on. I did other things. I don't even know what I would do."

"This," she said, as though it were the most obvious thing on the planet.

"Peaches, I have better things to do than to push your pretty ass in a swing."

She made a scoffing sound. "Not the swing, cowboy. The cowboying."

That struck uncomfortably close to his heart. He looked out over the spread, the tall grass rustling in the breeze, an old barn in the distance he never used, but liked the look of. It was completely different to the West Estate. With its perfectly kept grounds and Mediterranean-style buildings.

Like his dad thought he was some European duke in the middle of Oregon.

This place was his. Only it could never be something he worked with his whole heart because he had to give so much to the family land. To the family name.

"The cowboying," he repeated.

"Yes," she said. "You could do this full-time."

He had just wanted to hear her say it. She was the only person on earth who knew. The only person who had any clue that he'd be happiest here, working his own land. Never putting a suit on again. That he'd be happiest—in many ways—if he would just let go of the legacy his father had built. Let it wither and die out when the older generation did.

Immediately, a wave of guilt threatened to crush him. It would never be that simple. He had the money for this place from his father. He had the know-how from working the family spread. To act like he'd be here without it was a lie he couldn't get himself to believe.

"He won't come back," he said.

"He could." She took a deep breath. "My sister won't ever come back."

"Your sister?"

She looked away, her eyes downcast, her posture tense and somehow small. Like she was trying to shrink. "Frannie. Francesca. Because my mom didn't want to do alliterations. That was too trite, you know?"

"Was it?" he asked, a strange tightness stealing through his chest, making it hard for him to breathe. For some reason, a cold sense of dread settled deep inside of him.

He'd heard her talk about family. About them being difficult.

But he'd never heard her mention a sister.

"Yes. She did dress us alike a lot, though. Because

we were identical, and you can't pass that up. I guess."
She cleared her throat.

Colton stopped the swing.

"You were identical," he repeated.

"Yes. We were. They always talk about twins being
like…halves of the same whole, or…closer to each other
than normal siblings anyway." She turned and looked
up at him, a strange, flat look in her eyes. "I'm just the
half now."

LYDIA HAD NO IDEA why she was telling him this. She
shouldn't tell him this. She didn't tell anyone about Frannie. No one here knew.

But he'd just told her about the swing. The one he
wanted for his kids. The kids he didn't have because he
was left at the altar. The swing that wasn't being used,
on the ranch he couldn't really run because he was so
busy cleaning up after his older brother, who didn't have
an ounce of the sense of duty that Colton had.

She suddenly felt like she was drifting, and not just
because of the breeze, or the fact that she was sitting on
the swing. But because she and Colton were two powerless control freaks who were truly at the mercy of the
world, and everyone in it.

They were the two most together people in town. That
wedding, that wedding that never happened was like
a loose thread. And they'd tugged on it and the whole
damn world had started unraveling around them and
now there was just no hiding the fact that they were as
ragged as everyone else.

If not more so.

So why not tell him this? She'd told him to fuck her;
she could certainly tell him about Frannie.

"When we were eight, Frannie got sick," she said, feeling a little colder now. She shivered.

Colton shifted, coming to sit beside her. She wanted to tell him not to do that. It was too nice. It was too intimate.

That terrible *I* word again.

She cleared her throat and pressed on before she could get too emotional. "She had cancer." She took a deep breath and tried to move forward. But it was just so hard. She had never told anyone, she realized then. It wasn't just that she didn't like to talk about it. She had never, ever told anyone. The people around them knew, of course. Because Frannie was sick for years and by the time she slipped away, everyone knew it was coming.

Then, after years of still living there, still living with it, she had moved and she hadn't brought any of it with her.

Why are you doing it now?

She wished she weren't but it was too late to go back.

"It was so strange," she said, her voice getting thicker as her throat got tighter, "watching her change. Watching as she started to look less and less like me. It seemed wrong. Like she was moving further away from me, on this road I couldn't follow her down. One I wouldn't have wanted to—" She blinked and shook her head. "But it didn't seem right. Or fair. It's just not fair. But nothing about life is. I learned that when I was eight. To be like someone in every way…and to watch as they get betrayed by this body you both share while you're just fine is… There's nothing natural about it."

He didn't say anything. He wrapped his arm around her waist and pulled her back against his chest. She looked down at his forearm, at the muscle revealed there by his rolled-up shirtsleeve. She could feel his heart beating against her shoulder blade, and it felt good in the strangest way. To sit here with another person who knew the truth.

"It changed everything," she said.

"Losing her?"

She took a sharp breath, and it caught in the center of her chest. She thought about telling the truth, but she didn't think she could. Not when he was giving her an out. "Yes."

The sickness changed it all first. Took her friend. Her playmate. Took the smiles from the house, and everything else along with it. Everything big. Everything that mattered.

"How old were you?" he asked.

"We were fifteen when she died." She swallowed hard. "That's ridiculous. It's terrible. She never even got t-to drive or go on a date or…" Lydia blinked hard, and a tear rolled down her cheek, splashing onto Colton's hand. "It doesn't make sense," she said finally.

"And you left home when?"

"Well, initially when I was eighteen. I went to Oregon State University, which put me a few hours from home. And on a road trip, I drove through Copper Ridge and I thought…I thought this place looked like an old black-and-white movie. I thought I could be happy here. I thought maybe it could be that other half of me. And it has been," she said, pressing on, her tone determined. "It has been."

"You don't like to go back," he said. She was afraid that there was a little bit of accusation in his voice, but she understood it. Her parents had lost a child, and then she had left. She had to contend with that guilt already.

The fact that Colton might judge her...well, she understood. She judged herself sometimes. Even though, ultimately, she felt like she had made the right choice.

"No," she said, "and it gets harder, not easier. That's the thing about running away." She hated to call it that, but she supposed it was honest. "You think that maybe distance will clear your head. But it just continually reminds you why you left in the first place. So you leave again. And then you leave again. And that part gets easier. Every time."

"Maybe that's why my brother never comes back."

She knew him well enough to know that he didn't mean to hurt her with that comparison, but all things considered, it kind of stung. "Maybe. You don't know what happened with him?"

"I just assume that he left because he didn't want to fall in line with my dad. Which I imagine didn't go over very well. You don't oppose my father unless you don't want him in your life."

"But you don't know why?" she asked, pressing gently. "I mean, not for sure."

"Now you're making this about me."

"Full circle," she said. "It started about you."

"But you... I'm sorry. We should be talking about you."

"I don't particularly want to talk about me. There's a reason that you haven't heard that story before. There's a reason it doesn't make it into campaign speeches. I'm not interested in a pity vote. I'm not interested in using my sister's life or death to enhance my life in any way." That was only part of the truth, but it was good enough.

"Regardless, you told me." He cleared his throat. "I feel like...I guess, that we should discuss it."

"Why?" she asked, feeling almost like she had found some of her composure again. "So that I can cry? Get it all out? It's been fifteen years."

"It still hurts," he said, and she knew that he was talking about his loss too. The abandonment of an older brother that he didn't even want to come home.

"Nobody tells you that emptiness is so heavy," she said. "But it is. Losing somebody carves this hole out inside of you, and it's so useless. This void that lets you know something is missing, always, but somehow adds weight to your every step. But, while it never goes away, you do get used to it. You get strong enough to walk with the extra burden."

He didn't say anything. He tightened his hold on her and pushed the swing slightly with his foot. She didn't need him to say anything, anyway. It was just nice to have someone understand for a second. At least, she would pretend that he understood. She knew he didn't understand all of it. That part that he perceived as abandonment. But he was still there. Still sitting with her. So she supposed that he didn't find her completely reprehensible.

"It's amazing how much the lack of someone can change things. How someone being gone can make you see just how much they did when they were here." Colton's voice was soft, low in her ear. "I don't think I ever felt my brother as much as when he wasn't there."

Lydia took a deep breath, trying to banish the tenderness in her chest. She felt like she had been opened up, and that something of Colton had gotten inside. It was exhilarating and terrifying. She wasn't sure she liked it. Feeling close to someone. Feeling like someone knew. Like someone had an insight into who she was.

Not just *anyone*. *Colton*.

She didn't particularly want to be vulnerable in front of anyone, but only a few short weeks ago she would have said he was probably the last person on earth she wanted to show any weakness in front of. And here she was, presenting herself to him without barriers in place.

It was an extension of the madness from last night, she knew. But knowing that didn't mean there was anything she could do to stop it. She was bleeding out emotionally and she had no idea what to do to stop it.

She wanted to make it stop. Wanted to make it so she was somewhere else. Or so she was at least thinking a little bit less.

She angled her head and reached up, running her fingertips along his jawline. His dark gaze met hers, and she saw the same thing there. The desire to pull back. Regret, because he had said more than he wanted to. Because they had both revealed more than they normally would have.

She rescued them both. She closed the distance between them, kissing him. She intended to blot out the emotion with physical desire, but there was something different about this kiss. She waited for the fierce current of need to sweep them both under. It was there. There was no chance it wouldn't be. But it simply swirled around them, didn't drag them under. She was firmly in the present, caught up in the need that he made her feel, but far too aware.

Aware of who she was. Aware of who he was.

She closed her eyes tight, deepened the kiss. She lost herself in the sensation, determined to drown in it. The velvet slide of his tongue and the masculine scent of him. The sweet ache of desire that built down low inside of her. Drowning out some of the pain in her heart. Stripping an edge from it, leaving it dull, rather than lethally sharp. But it was still there. Radiating outward, competing with her desire now.

"I think we had better take this inside, don't you?" he asked after a few moments.

"I think you're right."

CHAPTER SIXTEEN

When his sister's frantic texts called him off the job site the next day, Colton was less than amused. Still, he got in his truck and drove down to the Chamber of Commerce, as directed by an overenthusiastic Sierra.

When he got there, the two of them were already in the parking lot. Sierra was carrying a binder that was large enough to obscure her baby bump, and Madison was simply standing there, looking as placid and unreadable as ever. Which meant that something shocking was likely to come out of her mouth. Although, with Madison, that was usually the case.

"What exactly are the two of you doing here? And why did you need me?"

"Planning your wife's party!" Sierra said.

For once, it didn't seem strange at all to have Lydia's image in his mind when someone said the word *wife*. He didn't think of Natalie much at all.

"I see. And does my wife know that you're coming?"

Maddy waved her hand. "No. But since the West family is so generously allowing her the use of our property, I don't suppose she can be too bent out of shape over planning it on our time."

"My dearest lady of leisure," Colton said, "not all of us spend a very small amount of time teaching riding lessons and the rest of our time polishing our nails. Some of us have work that's a little more demanding."

"Bite me, Colton," Madison said, flashing him a brilliant smile. "I work more than forty hours a week, you degrading jackass. Anyway, your sister could go into labor anytime over the next couple of weeks, so we have to plan it around her and her cankles."

Sierra scowled and looked down. "I do not have cankles. They're a little bit swollen. But there is still a calf and an ankle. But Maddy has a point. I've been having a lot of Braxton Hicks. And given the things that they say induce labor, I have a feeling I'm going to go early."

"What things?" he asked.

Sierra arched a brow. "Things you don't want to hear about, dearest brother. Things concerning my husband and the fact that he doesn't mind my cankles."

"Okay, you're right, I don't need to know. Now, let's go ambush my wife with your binder." Colton followed his sisters across the parking lot and toward the building. "So you have a plan now?"

"Yes," Maddy said. "Dad is paying for everything. It's his contribution."

"I see. And why hasn't he called me about any of this?"

"Have you been pestering him? Because I have."

"No," he said, "I haven't talked to him at all."

They had one hell of a weird family—there was no denying that. His father depended on him to do his bidding, and yet, rarely made contact. His mother, on the other hand, was in frequent contact, and it was unusual for him to go more than a week without talking to his sisters.

And then there was the half brother.

Yeah, he didn't really want to think about his family right now.

When they walked in, Marlene was sitting at the front desk, as she had been the last time he had come into the Chamber. "Hi, Marlene," he said.

The older woman smiled, then blushed. "Well, hello, Mr. West."

"Colton. And these are my sisters, Sierra and Maddy."

Marlene made all the requisite comments about Sierra being ready to have the baby any day now, asking for the gender and the due date, and all of the things that people seemed unable to hold back in the presence of a pregnant woman. Sierra, for her part, was long-suffering and friendly.

The extricated themselves as quickly as possible and went down the hall, toward Lydia's office.

"You've obviously been here before," Maddy said, treating him to an assessing look.

"Yes, I have been to my wife's office before." He knew that his sister was still a little suspicious about the circumstances of his marriage. He would love to be defensive about that, but in this case, the suspicions were correct, so there really was no ground for him to stand on.

"Very supportive."

"I am supportive, Madison. As you should well know."

Madison made a jerk off motion with her hand. And then turned and knocked on the door to Lydia's office.

"Come in." At the sound of Lydia's voice, his stomach twisted tight. He wanted her, that easily, that simply. He wished that he was not with Sierra and Madison, because he wished that they could be alone. He wished that he could fulfill that fantasy he had had about taking her over her desk.

Madison was eyeing his face speculatively, and that killed his fantasy a little bit.

"What?" he asked.

"Nothing," she said, twisting the doorknob and pushing the door open. "Hi." Her voice turned instantly cheery. "We thought it might be a good time to come and plan your election night party."

Lydia tilted her head to the side. "Okay. I mean, it is, but usually I have appointments…"

"I called ahead," Madison said. "Not you, but the woman who works at the front desk, Marlene? She said you were free."

Maddy took her seat in front of the desk, and Sierra took the other available chair. Colton leaned up against the back wall, only shrugging his shoulders when Lydia looked up at him with about a thousand questions in her dark eyes.

"I brought some ideas for setting. And theme," Sierra said. His sister was making a little bit of a name for herself with interior design, after having done her husband's new brewery. Obviously she was now extending this skill to planning family events.

"That's very… That's very nice of you," Lydia said, looking more scared than excited.

"You're family. And of course we want to support your campaign."

Maddy tapped her fingers on the desk. "Of course."

"Thank you," Lydia said, shooting him another look. He treated her to another shrug.

They started going through guest lists, and practicalities regarding setting up screens so that they could watch as the news of the election results was announced.

"Oh," Sierra said. "Do you have any family from out of town you want to invite? We'll make sure we give them a table of honor."

Lydia's expression went stony. "No."

Sierra frowned. "No one?"

"She said no," Colton said, pushing away from the wall and walking toward the desk, his chest tightening. "Just leave it."

Lydia shot him an irritated look. "It's fine," she said to Colton. "Thank you for thinking of everything." She directed that comment to Sierra.

Truly, he did not feel like she was grateful enough for his intervention.

"Well," Sierra said, her tone conciliatory, "you will have family there. Because we'll be there. You're part of our family now." His sister sounded like she was getting choked up, which was kind of par for the course with her hormones at the moment.

Lydia reached across the desk, patting Sierra on the hand. "Thank you. That's…very sweet."

"I think that covers everything important," Madison said, standing, and encouraging Sierra to do the same.

"I'll call you if I have any more questions but I would like to make it so that I handle as much as possible. I don't want to make this any more work for you," Sierra said.

Lydia eyed Sierra's stomach. "I'm pretty sure I'm more worried about your workload."

"I'm ready to pinch-hit should she go into labor before the party," Maddy said.

"I'm not worried about the party. I'm worried about exhausting a pregnant woman."

Sierra waved a hand. "I'm young."

Maddy nodded. "Obnoxiously so."

"If it gets to be too much for you…"

"I've got it," Maddy said. "Everything will be fine. This won't make more work for you."

"I don't mean to sound ungrateful at all. I just… Why are you doing all of this for me?"

"Because you're family. Because this matters to Colton if it matters to you, and that makes it matter to us," Sierra supplied.

"I hated that bitch Natalie," Maddy added.

Lydia's eyebrows shot upward. "Okay then. I accept either way. Thank you both."

"Goodbye to you both," Colton added.

"Eager to get rid of us?" Sierra asked.

"Very," he said, looking at Lydia, and that wasn't even part of the show. It was just the truth. He wanted to grab her and pull her into his arms and give her a kiss. He wanted to do more than that, but he wouldn't, because she would probably get mad at him if he interrupted her workday further.

"Bye," Maddy said, grabbing hold of Sierra and leading her out of the office.

Once they left, Lydia let out a hard breath and grabbed hold of her temples. "I feel like such a jerk."

"Why?"

"They think I'm family."

"Mostly, it's the thing about how much they hated Natalie."

"Whatever. I don't really like tricking your sisters."

"I don't, either. I mean, obviously I'm not perturbed enough by it to not do it."

She huffed out a laugh. "Eli and Sadie know."

"Eli knows?"

"Well, I had to tell Sadie, because there's no way she would believe that I just ran off and married you in a fit of passion, since I don't do fits of passion."

"I beg to differ, but go on."

She quirked her mouth to the side and treated him to an unamused look. "Anyway. I had to tell her, and she said she tells Eli everything, so I can only assume he knows. But he was also sworn to secrecy."

"I'm lying to my sisters," he said. "And you apparently have a whole posse of people who know what's going on with us."

"But you're the only person who knows much of anything about me."

Those words hit him in a strange place, somewhere in the center of his chest. Made him feel like he'd suffered a crack in the retaining wall around his heart.

Her cheeks turned pink, and he could tell that she regretted the moment of sincerity. He wasn't sure if he did or not.

He decided not to say anything. Instead, he decided to give in to what he'd been wanting to do since he first walked into the room. He moved to her desk, reaching out and taking her hand, drawing her up and pressing a kiss to her lips. "Hi," he said.

"You greeted me already," she said, her voice breathless. He didn't think he had ever made Natalie breathless. Or anyone else, for that matter. It did something to him. She did something to him.

"Yeah, but not properly."

"Now I forgot what we were talking about."

"For the best, probably."

She laughed. "I can't argue with that. So, I guess there's going to be a party at your parents' house."

"Yeah," he said. "I guess so. That will be interesting."

"You don't talk to your dad very often, do you?"

Her words echoed his earlier thoughts. "Not really. Unless he's issuing edicts or laying out complaints, Nathan West doesn't have much to say to his kids. I suppose this party for you is his approval. Or it's just revenge because he's still angry about Natalie humiliating the family."

"You got left at the altar and he never even called to check on you?"

It was Colton's turn to laugh. "Why would he do that? That would imply that he was concerned my feelings might be hurt. Or that I had emotions wrapped up in this in any way at all. He wouldn't get why I wasted any time feeling bad about a woman."

"That seems…"

"Cold? Unfeeling? You have to remember, this is the man who had a secret affair years ago that resulted in a child. And that same man kept it a secret from his wife, from his whole family for more than thirty years. My father is not a man terribly in touch with his emotions."

"Unlike you?"

"Next to him I look like a damn Care Bear."

She pressed her hand to his stomach and pushed against his abs. "Aren't you supposed to have some kind of rainbow light that shoots out of you or something?"

"I regret my choice of simile. Stop pressing on my stomach."

"It pretty much doesn't press. Your abs are crazy."

"Dusty enough for you?"

She pushed him. "That isn't fair. I don't make any jokes about the other women you've slept with."

"I know. Because you're way too nice."

"I am not nice."

"Nice as peaches."

She scowled. "Peaches aren't nice. They're gross."

"Yours taste pretty sweet."

He really was just a few seconds away from pushing her over that desk and having his way with her. He'd had her twice last night. It had done nothing to take the edge off his need. Here it was the middle of the day, he should be at work, and yet, all he could think about was her. It was like he was having some kind of delayed adolescence. The one he had never really been able to afford to have, because he had been too busy trying to be the shining example next to Gage's tarnished one.

"That's filthy," she said.

"You like it."

She looked away from him. "A little bit." She took a breath, and met his gaze again. "So, I assume that you're going to talk to your father at my dinner."

"About the weather?"

"More than that. I thought you might talk to him about…about your ranch."

He frowned, extricating himself from her hold. "Why would I do that?"

"Because it's important to you. I understood that the first moment you showed me your barn and your horses, but yesterday…yesterday I really understood. That place is your dream, Colton. That's where you see your life headed. Kids on that swing. That property. It isn't at your parents' ranch, and you know that."

"I've spent more than thirty years not discussing any of those things with him. I don't know why I would start now."

"Because you were just talking yesterday about how—"

"I mentioned it to you yesterday. That doesn't make it new. Just because you heard about it for the first time doesn't mean it's anything but business as usual on my end."

"So what was the point of telling me? Are you just going to invest in something you don't even care about for the rest of your life?"

"I'm going to do the right thing. Because sometimes you have to stand by your family even if it isn't comfortable."

His words had been chosen carefully to silence her. He knew that phrasing it that way would tap into her own guilt. And he felt like an ass for doing it, but really, there was no other choice.

"Your dad can't put someone else in charge? I don't believe that for one second." Lydia, it turned out, was not so easily cowed.

"That isn't the point. It's the West family legacy. It can't be handed over to someone who isn't a West."

"Your sister Madison isn't available?"

"He's not going to put Maddy in charge of the construction."

"As if she couldn't do it? I've only met her twice, I grant you that, but I'm pretty sure she could order men around on a job site if she really wanted to."

"Even if she could, my father wouldn't allow it. That isn't how it works. My family has been in Copper Ridge ever since the town's inception. Our ranching operation has passed from father to son over all those years. My father is hardly going to change it."

"So what?" She said the word so easily, as if they could simply dismiss generations of tradition. As if they could wipe away an entire legacy.

"So, it's up to me to keep everything together. If I don't carry on the family legacy, then no one else will. If I don't stay and take care of my mother, my father certainly isn't going to do it. If I ostracize myself from him, then my sisters have to have another brother that's outside of the family. And we'll be splintered even more than wc already are."

"So you have to sacrifice everything for everyone else's happiness?"

He curled his hands into fists. "Yes. Absolutely. And it isn't like I'm unhappy. It's all ranch work. It's splitting hairs to care about whether it's at his property or mine."

"It's not splitting hairs. It's splitting your dream."

"Fine for you to get principled, I guess. You left your family." He was pushing hard now. He was being something far beyond an ass. And he couldn't stop himself. Not now. "You left, so you don't see why it shouldn't be simple for me to do the same."

"You think it was simple? You think it was easy to leave home? To gradually decrease contact with my family because every conversation was like walking back into the past? Because walking around my own home was like wandering through a mausoleum? If you think that was easy, if you think losing my sister to a terminal illness that ate away at her slowly somehow made my choice to try and find my own life simple? You're kind of an idiot."

Her words hit him like a slap, echoed in the room,

made him feel every bit the small, mean jackass that he was. "I'm just saying it isn't an option for me."

"You're making it sound like talking to your father about you doing what you want is the same as cutting him out of your life forever. Which, by the way, is not what I did with my parents. I moved away. A lot of people move away."

"Opposing my father does mean cutting him out of my life. Worse, it means cutting my mother out of it. And that's what I care about more than anything. She's lost enough. That's why we're involved in this marriage, in case you forgot. On my end? It's about protecting her. She can't lose another child. She can't have the family upset any more than it already is. You expect me to cause a giant rift while she's dealing with finding out her husband had an affair?"

"There's always going to be a wound, Colton."

He pushed his hand through his hair, pacing the length of the room. "What the hell is that supposed to mean?"

"You're using yourself as a Band-Aid. Trying to cover everyone's pain, everyone's injury. But there's never going to be a point where everything is magically okay. There's always going to be another wound. But at some point you have to stop."

"I can't listen to this. I have to work."

"Oh, that's hilarious. I just have to sit here and braid my hair. I have to work too, but I feel like this is something we should discuss."

She was getting too close to something. Something that he couldn't quite put a name to. Something he didn't want to think about too deeply. He clenched his jaw, taking a step back. "You seem to be forgetting, Lydia, we don't need to discuss anything. You're not my damn wife. Not really. Just because we're having sex doesn't mean it's different."

And then he turned and walked out of her office, and he didn't look back.

CHAPTER SEVENTEEN

SHE WAS BAKING revenge zucchini bread. She had no idea if that was mentally balanced or not, but Marlene had brought five zucchinis into the office this morning, and Lydia had left with her arms full of the offending green vegetable.

And now she was in Colton's kitchen, up to her elbows in flour—flour she had purchased with her own money—putting together loaves of sweet, cinnamon-infused bread. Because Colton had said she wasn't his wife. So her very logical, noncrazy response was to go straight into his kitchen and act as much like a housewife as possible.

"You're crazy," she muttered, pulling the first pan of finished bread out of the oven.

Yes, she was. It didn't stop her from baking.

She heard the front door slam shut. So obviously, her husband, who didn't think of himself as her husband, was home.

"Hi, honey," she said, making her voice as singsong as possible. "I'm just in the kitchen." Something evil entered her mind just then. "Barefoot."

As suspected, he appeared very quickly after that. "And?" he asked, looking very concerned.

She smiled, letting the silence stretch between them.

"And nothing," she said finally, after he had gotten a little bit pale.

Were she in the kitchen, barefoot and pregnant as she knew she had just made him suspect, she would be the one who was pale. He had a swing. She didn't want to swing, so to speak.

"What are you doing?"

She smiled even wider. "Baking."

"Did you put arsenic in the bread?"

"Just cinnamon. That you know of."

"Why are you in my kitchen baking me bread? I was an ass to you earlier."

She threw a dish towel on the floor. "Because. I wanted to have you come in and see me being a 1950s housewife. I wanted to give you a heart attack."

"Well, I don't believe you're here being domestic, so my first thought is that you're going to poison me. Congratulations, I do feel a little bit unsettled."

She stamped, bending over and picking up the dish towel.

"You are horrible. And vile." He crossed the space between them, advancing on her, wrapping his arm around her waist and pulling her up against him. Which he had a bad habit of doing. She narrowed her eyes. "Don't you dare," she warned.

He didn't listen. His mouth crashed down on hers, his kiss hard, swift. Toe curling. "I'm mad at you," she hissed.

"I'm mad at *you*."

"Why? All I did was give you advice. Good advice. You…" She poked him in the chest. "You were mean and you said mean things."

"And that was different to the way we interact usually how?"

She wiggled out of his arms. "I know that I'm not your wife, you moron. Not in a real way. I get that. That isn't where my advice was coming from. I thought that maybe we were... I don't know. Friends, maybe?"

"I'm not sure that I would call us friends."

"Well—" she threw her hands up, then slammed them back down on the counter "—nobody else here knows about Frannie. You're the only one. And then, when I tried to help you out with your issues, you use that against me. How dare you do that to me? How dare you?"

His face changed. His expression suddenly looked... contrite. At least, she thought that's what it might be. She had never really seen Colton contrite, so it was hard to say.

"I'm sorry," he said. "You're right. I shouldn't have used that against you."

Her head was spinning. Because not only had he looked sorry, he had said sorry. One was rare enough; the other was basically unheard of. "Good," she said, "you should be sorry."

"Everyone in town knows that Gage left. So it isn't like you're the keeper of any of my deep dark secrets. But I've never talked to anybody about the position I feel that puts me in. So no one has ever tried to give me advice about it. It turns out, I don't like being told things that I already know, but don't want to do."

"Well, nobody likes that."

"Is the zucchini really poison?"

"It's revenge bread."

"How is it revenge bread? Does it have itching powder in it, laxatives... Will it kill me?"

She let out an exasperated sigh. "It's revenge bread, because I was trying to unsettle you with my housewifely ways."

"You realize that's a really unappealing name for a baked good."

"Then don't eat any. And my revenge will be complete."

A smile curved his lips upward, and something in it drained the rage straight out of her. That smile, that slightly cocky, arrogant grin, used to wind her up like nothing else. It certainly wouldn't have defused her anger a month ago. Was the sex making her mushy? Was it just impossible for her to have a sex-only relationship? Maybe.

Except she knew that was selling it short. They didn't just have sex. They shared secrets on a swing, and he had told her about what he really wanted. About the children he hoped to have. It reluctantly made her understand why he had been willing to enter into a marriage that was less than a wild and crazy love match.

He hadn't seen much in the way of love being demonstrated. Not in his family. She understood what it was like to turn away from strong emotion. And she knew what it was like to grow up in a situation that was less than functional. So she could see why he had opted for something else. Why he had thought maybe the answer would lie in a sensible union. One with someone he was compatible with.

So that he could have kids to use that swing. So that he could have his home the way that he saw it, at least, as much as he could without feeling like he was betraying his family.

She really didn't want to understand him. The problem was, she did.

"I would like some of your zucchini bread," he said.

"Fine. If you die it's coincidental."

He only smiled again and everything inside of her sighed. He crossed the kitchen and retrieved a knife, cutting a slice of bread off the fresh loaf, and then another. Suddenly, her plan was backfiring, because she had a sexy man serving revenge zucchini bread to her. And it was not being served cold.

"Coffee?"

"Do you have anything sweet to put in it? I'm kind of a wimp."

"I actually noticed that. I bought some peppermint syrup the other day at the store."

And that right there made her internal organs feel like they were about to take flight. "Oh. That's...very nice."

He flipped the switch on his electric kettle, bringing some water to a boil and starting a French press. Suddenly, she felt like the one who was getting a joke played on them.

This felt like the kind of domestic bliss she had spent years trying to avoid. Sharing space. Peppermint syrup in his house because she liked it. And he was preparing everything for her.

He pushed the plate of zucchini bread toward her, along with a small fork, and she accepted it, trying to ignore the warm sensation in her chest.

"Did you learn this recipe from your mom?" He was pushing for more information about her, and the fact that he cared made her want to give it.

"No. Marlene. My mom didn't cook. I mean, she never did. But, we did used to bake sometimes, before Frannie got sick. But not after."

"I'm sorry. Again. For what I said."

"No. You don't have to apologize. Everything you said…I've thought it. You're right. They lost a daughter, how could their only remaining child pull away so completely? I mean, I still speak to them. I call my mother once a week or so. But I just can't… All of the dreams that they had for Frannie and me ended up focused on me."

"I can imagine that. I mean, to a smaller degree."

"I needed to go to prom because Frannie would never get to go to prom. I needed to carry an extra rose at graduation for my sister who couldn't be there. And you know, before your wedding, when I was supposed to be a bridesmaid, my mother was angry, because I hadn't gotten married yet. My sister is never going to have a family, Colton. She's never going to get married. She's never going to fall in love. It's somehow up to me to do all of these things for her, and for her memory.

"And at the same time I'm not ever supposed to be too happy because we're missing someone. I'm missing a part of myself. I don't know how to be all of those things. So I had to come here where I didn't have to be anything. I had to come here so that I could find out who I was. Because nothing there was ever going to be mine. Not my life. Not my grief. I felt like I was half, but that was what I was always going to be for them, too. Like I had this vacant space they could pour into, to try and make up for what happened."

She felt drained, saying all of that. Putting words to what had been inside of her for so long. That weight, that responsibility that had been placed on her, it was a part of everything.

"But you're right," she continued, "I left. I decided that what they were asking was too much. And I don't know if I had that right. She's gone. Doesn't she deserve all of those things in her memory? Who am I to decide that it isn't important? Who am I to decide that I can move on if they can't?"

"I don't… I can't actually speak to loss like that. My brother left. He's still alive. As far as I know he's off doing exactly what he wants without giving any thought to the pain he's caused our mother, or to anyone else. I get to be angry at him. That helps a lot with the missing. So, if I'm wrong, and I might be, feel free to tell me to go to hell. But what does your sister get out of these monuments to her memory?"

"I…I just think it…it means so much to my parents… and it…" Everything inside of her felt frozen, completely seized up.

"I can't imagine the grief they must have gone through. But if the way they're handling it affects your life, what's the point? I understand you have guilt over being the only child remaining, the one that left. But it sounds to me like they're putting more into the child they lost than the child they have."

He was speaking the words that she had felt deep inside for so long. The things that made her feel guilty. The anger that made her feel like a child on the verge of throwing a tantrum over something she didn't deserve to have. How could you be angry at people who were grieving? How could you be angry that a sibling was sick? How could you feel sorry for yourself?

"I just…" She felt like she was cracking apart inside,

and there was nothing she could do to stop it. "I wish that I could be strong enough to do everything they needed me to do. I wish that I could have been enough. That I could have filled both spaces. Instead, I couldn't even fill one. I had to leave. I couldn't... I just couldn't live that life."

"You shouldn't have to."

"That's as simple as me saying the same thing to you. Meaning, it isn't simple at all."

"It sounds to me that you weren't allowed to have anything of your own," he continued, ignoring what she had just said.

That was exactly the truth, and he had hit it head-on. Nothing had been hers. Not anymore. Not her happiness, not even her grief.

A memory pushed at the back of her mind, one that she tried to keep at bay. That day when Frannie had died, and she had been inconsolable. She hadn't even had the strength to fling herself across the bed and cry, she had simply gone to the floor where she'd been standing, weeping as though she'd lost a part of herself, because she had. Because she was destined to spend the rest of her life as an incomplete half. And she had known then as clearly as she knew it now.

"My father told me that I needed to hide my grief in front of my mother," she said softly. "He told me that my grief couldn't compare to theirs. Because I had lost a sister, but they had lost a child, and that was the worst pain in the world. He said that my mother didn't need to be worried about me on top of dealing with her own pain."

"Lydia," he said, his voice tense, "that isn't fair at all. That doesn't... It doesn't work that way."

"Maybe it doesn't. But that's the thing, Colton. Grief

isn't rational. And in that moment, my father had lost his child and had a wife that had fallen apart. I think he couldn't handle me being devastated. He would never say that, but that's what I think happened. I think he panicked. Because the entire world was resting on his shoulders and he was in pain. And I had to...I had to be stronger for them. But that's... Nothing was mine. Not anymore. Not even my grief. I needed to go somewhere where things could be mine. Copper Ridge is mine. My house by the ocean, that's mine. It's my space. To feel what I want, to say what I want, to be what I want. And I guess that all seems pretty childish, but it's all I have."

"I don't think there's anything childish about taking control of your life. Or realizing that you need something different than what you have."

She shifted, feeling fragile, brittle. Everything felt like it hurt. She felt tender. New and strangely hopeful. Speaking these words out loud and having the world not fall around her. Telling someone and having acceptance, rather than judgment... It changed so much about what she thought. About how she felt.

It also made her want to hide, but she supposed that was nothing new.

It made her want to go to her house, her house that was her sanctuary, her self-created sanctuary that belonged to only her, and hide away from this man who seemed to be able to see down deep into her soul. Who saw parts of her that she didn't even know were there.

Parts of herself she had done a pretty good job of keeping hidden even from herself. But she had a tendency to want to show herself to him. Had a tendency to open herself up and let him see the dirty, messy things that she normally swept under the metaphorical rug.

"But maybe there is something a little bit childish about hiding most of your past from everyone you know, so that you never have to deal with it at all," she said, looking down at her bread.

He turned and pressed the plunger down in the French press, then poured her a cup of coffee, adding cream and peppermint. She didn't even yell at him for doing it for her, even though she doubted he had gotten the ratio right. He was being too nice. She would take her slightly wonky coffee, just because it had been such a thoughtful thing.

That thought disturbed her. That she was willing to take potentially gross coffee just because she was having soft fuzzy feelings for him.

Still, she accepted the coffee. And actually, it was good.

"Everyone is hiding," he said finally.

"Everyone?"

"Yeah. I think so. I think it's easy to pretend you're doing the hard thing, that you're making the selfless decision, when you're really doing what will keep you safe. Or, I guess, the simple truth is there often isn't an easy thing. It's just that one decision protects you, and the other doesn't." He took a deep breath. "I don't think staying with your family would have been easy. I don't think leaving was easy."

"Maybe it was the same for your brother."

He laughed. "Okay, Gage may have taken the only true easy way."

"But you're assuming that it was easy. That he didn't go through anything. That it didn't cost him to walk away." She swallowed. "Or that he doesn't care about leaving you with the consequences. Maybe he does.

Maybe, he just thought it was worth it. I didn't leave consequence-free. It required adjustment for my family, and I know they weren't happy for me to leave, but they adjusted. Unlike your brother, I didn't cut them off completely, but I didn't make it easy. And it didn't make it wrong."

"So it was all right for him to leave me with everything?"

"He didn't leave you with everything. He left. And you chose to be the one to pick it all up."

Colton pushed his hand through his hair. "What's the alternative? To just let it go?"

"To trust that everyone in your family is an adult and they can take care of themselves. And to realize there's a lot of ground between abandonment and having your own life." She straightened, taking a sip of her coffee, and looking at him square in the eye. "Do you think I'm weak, Colton?"

"Of course not. That's ridiculous."

"I left. I left because as difficult as it was, as much as I want to support my parents, I can't be everything for them. My life is not in existence solely for me to devote myself to them. And you don't think there's anything crazy about that, do you?"

"No," he said.

"Good. I don't, either. And there wouldn't be anything easy, or crazy about you doing the same. About you being up front with your dad and telling him that you aren't going to give your entire life to the family name when you want something for yourself."

"I don't know if I can do that."

"I want you to. You...you have no idea how amazing it is to finally tell someone. To be able to stand here and talk to you. I have never said most of this out loud. I've never had this conversation, not with anyone. Not with Sadie, not with Natalie, not with anyone. You're the only person who knows all of this about me. Telling you, having you hear me without judgment… You have no idea. You really don't. I want to give you something."

"I can think of something," he said, his gaze turning sharp, intense.

"I was thinking emotions," she said, "not sex."

"But I like sex. Emotions are terrible." He leaned in, nuzzling her neck, sending a streak of lightning through her body. "This seems better."

"I was mad at you," she said, her tone faint.

"I know. But you aren't mad at me now." He kissed her neck.

"I'm smart enough to know that you are trying to change the subject by getting me hot and bothered."

"Is it working?"

She let her head fall back on a sigh. "Yes."

"Good." He kissed her again, and she started to forget what they were talking about.

"No," she said, fighting against the fog that was crowding her brain. While at the same time wanting to latch on to it. There was something magical, something completely unique about the way that Colton made her feel. About the way that he commanded all of her focus, all of her control and all of her attention in a way that nothing else could. Her brain was a busy place; it was always working, always two steps ahead of the moment. Colton forced her to be in the moment. Something she had been avoiding for years, ever since she had first existed in a moment that was too painful to stomach. She had practiced being somewhere else. Practiced planning the next thing.

It was an effective block against dealing with strong feelings. And it had become a habit. To be somewhere else. To have one foot in the future in order to shift some of the weight from the present.

Colton stole that from her, and it was both a blessing and a curse.

"Colton," she scolded, "we are talking."

"I don't want to talk." He kissed her lips, snatching the next words right from her mouth.

"Tough luck," she said.

"Story of my life."

"Yes," she said, "I feel really sorry for you."

"Not sorry enough." He put his hand on her waist, his fingertips sliding up toward her breast, making her shiver. All of her focus went to that touch, to him.

"You're helping me become mayor," she said, and for some reason, those words made him freeze. "I want to help you. I don't want to help you keep your mom happy. Although I do care about that. I want to help you with more. I want you to have this ranch, the way that you see it. Take it. Don't you think you're worth that?"

"You sound like a shampoo commercial."

"I'm serious."

"So am I."

"If you're not man enough to take the ranch," she said, hardening her tone, "I'm not sure you're man enough to take me."

COLTON COULDN'T LET that go unanswered. He had no idea what to do with this moment, how to classify this conversation. It was anger, baked goods and desire, mixed with a generous helping of soul-baring secrets. Only Lydia could ever bring all those things together. Only Lydia could make him feel like this.

When she talked about claiming the ranch, she made him feel like it was possible. When she talked about hiding, he felt like she was chipping away at his own defenses, at his own stronghold, built to protect him from all manner of things.

Things he didn't even have names for, because he didn't do this kind of weird self-examination stuff.

But then, he didn't do what he was about to do, either. Except, Lydia made him break all of his rules. Lydia made him into something different.

How the hell had that happened? How had the only person he'd ever met who was more uptight than he was managed to set him free? Who knew that somehow, they would be combustible together, when they had never combusted before in their entire lives?

He wrapped his hands firmly around her slender waist and lifted her off the ground, settling her on the counter, knocking her coffee cup to the side, sloshing some liquid over the edge. Her fork clattered off her plate. He was on the verge of causing a serious kitchen accident, and he simply didn't care.

"You want to say that again, peaches?"

"If you aren't man enough to take hold of your aspirations, I don't know if you're man enough to grab on to me."

"I think I and my inoffensive penis could change your mind."

She tried to keep a straight face, but he saw the corner of her lip turn upward. "*Inoffensive* isn't the word I would use anymore."

"Oh yeah? What word would you use."

She reached down, cupping him through his jeans, squeezing him tight. "*Big*, for a start."

"Cliché. But I'll allow it because my ego likes it," he said, his voice tight.

"*Hard.*"

"Uh-huh."

She leaned in, her teeth scraping over his jawline, the feral little action sending a rush of pleasure down his spine, settling at the base and jetting to his cock. "*Mine,*" she finished, squeezing him even more tightly.

That left him completely undone. Incapable of response. Incapable of anything but submitting to her touch. He braced his hands on her thighs, pushing her skirt slowly up her hips, parting her thighs so that he could step between them. She didn't release her hold on him.

"I'm yours?" he asked, wrapping his arm around her waist, kissing her chin, adding his teeth, as revenge for what she done to him earlier. "I guess that makes you mine."

She shivered beneath his touch and he gloried in it.

"You think?"

"I'm going to need you to say it, peaches."

"I'm yours," she said, giving the words easily, simply, as though they were the most natural thing in the world. And they left him feeling like he was in a free fall.

"Am I allowed to take you?" He slid his finger along the edge of her panties, feeling her wet and ready for him beneath his touch. "Or do you have more ultimatums?"

"How about I put it this way," she said, her voice husky. "If you're man enough to take me, you're sure as hell man enough to take the ranch."

He felt…unmanned. Completely and totally unequal to the gift that was spread out before him. This home, this land, this woman. He'd never done a damn thing to deserve any of them.

But that didn't mean he wouldn't take them. She made him feel like he could. Made him feel like he should.

But then, she made him feel like sex on the counter in his kitchen was a great idea. Lydia, possibly the only person on earth as sensible as he was. Somehow, together, they were wild.

She made him want to drop everything and have her all the time. She made him crazy. She made him something that went way beyond control, that went way beyond common sense and every other pillar that supported his life. Wanting her, being with her, it didn't benefit anyone. Anyone but him.

It had nothing to do with a staid, sensible future. Had nothing to do with carefully laid plans. It was heat, it was fire. It was destructive and it was restorative. It was absolutely everything, and whether or not it was a good idea, he couldn't turn away from it.

He pressed her more closely to him, holding on to her tight, pulling her off the counter before depositing her back on the floor, grabbing hold of her hip and turning her away from him. She gasped, and he leaned in, pressing a kiss to the top of her shoulder. "Trust me," he said.

He unbuttoned her top, letting it flutter to the floor before making quick work of her bra. He cupped her breasts, teasing her nipples, marveling at the perfect, soft weight of them in his hands. There had never been anything so perfect, not in all the world. Not a sunset, not a swing, not a ranch spread. His entire world right now was Lydia Carpenter's breasts and their unmatched perfection.

Reluctantly, he slid his hands downward, reveling in the soft silk of her skin as he blazed the path down to her skirt, pulling her panties and all down to the ground. She was still wearing her shoes, which was the only thing that made her tall enough to do what he did next.

"Trust me," he said again.

He protected them both, then tested the entrance to her body with the blunt head of his arousal. She gasped, her shoulders tensing. He pressed his palms flat between her shoulder blades, until he felt her relax. He reached around, one hand firm on her stomach, the other braced on her back as he pushed deeply inside of her.

"Good?" he asked.

"Good," she responded, shivering delicately.

He moved his hand between her thighs, teasing the source of her pleasure with his every thrust, trying to push her higher before he reached the edge. Because he was so close, so desperately close. She was so tight, so hot, so undeniably his. No other woman had ever responded to him this way before, and he had never desired another woman like this. This was theirs. It was only theirs. It was intimate in a way sex had never been before. Intense in a way he hadn't known desire could be. And it was all wrapped up in things he normally would have turned away from. But he was turning into them now. Embracing them. Needing them. Needing her.

He was lost in her. In the soft sounds of pleasure she made with his every thrust deep into her body, in the sweet, floral scent of her that was so deceptive in its fragility, then wound itself around him like a creeping vine, threatening to strangle him with all of its feminine magic.

Just like Lydia.

From the first moment he laid eyes on her she had grabbed hold of something deep and unknown inside of him. And from that first moment, she'd had him. He'd convinced himself it was annoyance. That she was an irritation. Nothing more. And then she had continued to burrow her way under his skin, completely undetected. Until, when he was drunk, the first thing he'd done was haul her off to Vegas and marry her. Because that was how powerful it was. That was how powerful she was.

She'd said he had to prove he was strong enough to take her. But he knew for certain, he didn't possess enough strength, enough self-control, to do anything but take her. The road had always been leading here. From that first moment they'd met in Ace's bar, it had always been leading here.

He stroked her, moving his fingers over her slick flesh, responding to her every sound of pleasure, to her every command. Until he felt her lose control, her internal muscles gripping his body tight as she went over the edge. Then he gripped her hips, losing himself in her completely, losing his control entirely. He came on a ragged, uncivilized sound, his entire body shaking as his orgasm raged through him like a freight train.

He held her against him, his chest pressed against her back, still buried deep inside of her. He had started this to avoid talking about feelings. To avoid uncovering yet more uncomfortable, vulnerable things that he didn't want to deal with. And that plan had backfired spectacularly. Because this had left him feeling raw, exposed in a way he never had been before. He had no control. He had no strength. If she were to turn around and push him over he would fall straight onto his ass, and he wouldn't be able to get back up.

Lydia Carpenter didn't just test his control, she destroyed it.

She made a small, kittenish sound, and he released his hold on her, withdrawing from her. She turned toward him, resting her head on his chest, her palm placed right over his heart. And he felt like she was touching him there. Beneath his skin, beneath his muscle, like she had managed to achieve direct contact with his most vital organ.

It was far more affecting than when she'd grabbed on to his cock.

He wrapped his arms around her, holding her against him, resting in this feeling. Memorizing the way she fit against his body. The way it felt to be pressed against her, skin to skin, from head to toe.

He hadn't seen it coming. He was a man, after all. Orgasm was supposed to be the be-all and end-all. It was when sex was finished. But this was something. This moment. When the intimacy of everything they had done settled around them like a blanket, wrapping around both of them, binding them together.

"Let's go to bed," he said, his voice rough.

"I didn't finish my coffee," she said.

"I don't care about your coffee."

"I don't know if I have energy for more sex," she said.

"No, I mean let's go to bed and sleep."

She froze against him, and he knew why. Because, for all the nights they'd made love, she'd gone back to her own room when they were finished. Because they didn't sleep together, since that would blur lines and make it more like being a couple.

Dammit, he wanted to blur lines. He didn't know to what end, only that he wanted to.

"Okay," she said, her voice soft, small. "I did still have more mix for my revenge bread."

"I guess you'll have to finish getting revenge on me tomorrow."

"I can do that."

So, even though they hadn't finished their conversation, and she hadn't finished baking her bread, Colton and Lydia went to bed.

CHAPTER EIGHTEEN

COLTON WAS STILL lost in the pleasure of the night before when one of his workers came and found him while he was installing cabinets in the kitchen of the house they were working on.

"There's someone here to see you," he said.

"Who?"

The guy lifted his shoulder. "A woman."

Colton's heart hit the front of his chest. Lydia.

He set his nail gun down, walking through the house that was still in various stages of being assembled and out to the front of the property. But it wasn't Lydia standing there. Instead, it was a pretty blonde he hadn't seen in quite some time.

"Natalie," he said. "What are you doing here?"

She shifted in place, adjusting her purse two or three times before letting it settle awkwardly on her left shoulder. "I thought it was time we talked."

"About what?"

"About the weather. Or maybe about our wedding that I didn't show up for, Colton—you could pick the topic if you want."

Oh, Natalie. "I assume you want to talk about the wedding."

She let out an exasperated sigh. "I'm not sure that I want to, but I think that we have to."

"We don't have to if we don't want to. It may have escaped your notice, but I've moved on." The moment he said it, he realized how true it was. It didn't feel like a lie. Didn't feel like a carefully constructed phrase in order to make her think that his relationship with Lydia was more than it was. He didn't know how his relationship with Lydia could be any more than it was. They were married, after all. And he…well, he'd never felt more for anyone than he felt for her.

"Right," she said, her tone clipped. "And, honestly, I'm not surprised. I saw the way you looked at her when I first introduced you. I'm actually shocked that you didn't run off with her then."

It was strange, that someone like Natalie—someone he would have characterized as being exceedingly self-centered—seemed to have more insight into his initial feelings for Lydia than he did.

It had taken him a lot longer to untangle exactly what it was he felt for her, why he felt on edge and restless when she was around. But, regardless, she did have a few things wrong.

"I didn't run off with her the way that you're implying. I never touched her before you left me at the altar, which I kind of figured meant we were done."

She looked down, angry color flooding her cheeks. She couldn't deny it, but he knew that she hated being called on the carpet when she did something wrong. When they'd been together, he'd been more than willing to let a lot of things slide. They had constructed a relationship made of convenient fictions and carefully accepted deceptions.

He, for his part, pretended that Natalie was every bit as delightful as she *could* be. Even when she was being decidedly nondelightful. For her part, she had ignored the fact that he clearly wasn't completely invested in the relationship on an emotional front. Both of them pretended that everything was okay, even while they both knew it wasn't.

"I thought we might have a chance to talk," she said.

"You slept with someone else."

She looked up at him, her eyes wide. "I guess Lydia told you."

"Of course she told me. That's not something you keep from someone, especially not your husband."

"I didn't want to hurt you," she said. He believed that. Except, the thing was, she hadn't. And that was maybe more notable than anything else.

"I'm not hurt. I was angry. I chose you to be my wife because I thought that you understood what was important. I thought that you would make the perfect final puzzle piece to my life. That if I married you, everything would kind of fall into place and be easy from here on out. We didn't fight. We had an agreement."

"I know," she said, her voice catching.

"But you didn't hurt me. And I don't think that's a good thing. I think that's every sign we ever needed that getting married was a mistake."

"But it's not...it's not fair," she said. "We should work. This should have worked."

"Maybe. But it couldn't. Because I didn't choose you because of the enormity of what I felt for you. I chose you because what I felt for you was manageable. You told Lydia that you and I didn't have passion. You told her I wasn't passionate. And I wasn't with you."

"I didn't know that you were going to spend our entire conversation insulting me, Colton."

"I'm not meaning to insult you. Because it isn't you. It's me. It's us. Don't tell me you were passionately in love with me, Natalie."

"Well," she said, "no. But you're perfect. And our wedding was going to be perfect. And our children would have been perfect."

"The guy you're with now?"

Her face turned an even deeper shade of pink. "He's not perfect."

"But he makes you feel things."

She blinked rapidly, gripping her purse strap even tighter. "Awkward topic. But yes."

"We were too good for each other, and that was bad. We would have let each other go on and never challenged each other at all."

"Still sounds perfect to me," she said, her voice hushed.

"Of course. Because it's easy." And he had wanted easy. He had gotten it into his head that if he married Natalie everything would be fine. That he could ease up on his control. That he would maybe stop wanting so many other things; that it would make going forward, transitioning into the man he was supposed to be easier.

God knew, being with Natalie would've been easier. She would never have pushed him to defy his parents. Would never have ripped him right out of his comfort zone, made him lose his mind with her touch, with her kiss. Would never have baked him revenge zucchini bread. And he would never have taken her on his kitchen counter.

Natalie had been what he'd wanted. What he'd needed, in many ways, to continue on down the path he'd set his foot on more than fifteen years ago. When he had decided to pick up every piece of slack his brother had left. She was a part of that. Something that he had acquired to help enable him to continue on.

Lydia didn't enable him in any way. Lydia made his life feel claustrophobic; she made it feel too small. She made him realize that he wanted more, that he wanted different. Because the man who couldn't control himself when she was around, the man who said rough, dirty things to her in the dark, who had found a passion inside of himself he hadn't imagined existed, could never be content with a life that had been designed for another man. Could never be content with a future that was simply stepping into the shadow of his older brother.

He understood now. Why he had chosen Natalie. And why he wouldn't choose her now.

And he understood that he wanted Lydia. For more than a month. For more than just an election, or to keep his family happy. He wanted more. Because of her, he wanted more.

"I really messed things up," Natalie said. "I really did. And I…"

"You don't want me," he responded.

She shook her head. "No."

"Don't feel bad about that. Don't waste time being sorry that you've found something better."

"But it isn't better. My father will never—"

"Your father isn't the one who has to sleep with your spouse for the rest of your life. You are. You're the one who has to live with the guy for the rest of your life."

"I'm not sure it's as serious as that."

"You're clearly terrified of what he makes you feel. Enough that you were going to see if I would take you back. I would say it's that serious. At least for you."

She let out a heavy sigh. "It's awful."

He agreed. He really did. This was uncomfortable. It reminded him of that year he'd been in tenth grade or so, and he'd grown too many inches all at once and each and every limb had felt stretched. Growing hurt. That was just the damn truth.

"It's pretty terrible," he agreed.

"Lydia does that to you?"

He took a deep breath and looked out across the property, toward the mountains. They were the same mountains he looked at every day, but today something felt different. He was different, maybe.

"Yeah," he said finally. "She does."

"For what it's worth I'm sorry."

"Don't be. Okay, I'm still not exactly thrilled about being left at the altar in front of the entire town, but thank you. For not marrying me. You had sense when I didn't."

"I think that might be the first time anyone has ever accused me of being sensible."

It was strange looking at the woman he'd thought he would share his life with, knowing that this was it. That it wasn't happening. And feeling more grateful for her leaving him at the altar than he'd ever felt for anything in his life.

"Be happy," he said.

And he meant it with everything he had.

"You too," she said.

She turned around and walked away from him then, and he watched her until she got into her car. Then he took a deep breath, looking back at the mountains. He felt like he was having an out-of-body experience. To understand so clearly why he had done something, and how ridiculous it was, wasn't exactly typical. He had gone through life reacting, doing whatever he needed to do to keep his family together. Assuming every single responsibility to prove that he would never be like Gage. And he had been using Natalie as a literal ball and chain. To keep him tethered to that responsibility. To ensure that he carried on as he had started.

And the very thing that had irritated him about Lydia from the beginning wasn't even so much the attraction as what it signaled. The fact that she was a woman who wouldn't let him do this. A woman who didn't want to chain him further, but who insisted he be set free.

He had a feeling he was the only man on the planet who had wanted marriage to imprison him further. Damn Lydia and her insight. Damn Lydia and the way she made him feel. The way she made him want.

But God bless her too, because she wanted him and he had never wanted anything or anyone as much as he wanted her.

It just didn't make it any less terrifying.

He had a feeling she had grabbed hold of him that very first moment they'd met, but he hadn't realized just how deep she grabbed hold of him until years later.

Like a bomb with a long fuse.

And it had just ignited inside of him. Now he had to figure out what to do with the wreckage. He didn't have a clue in hell. But things seemed to make more sense when he was with Lydia, so he figured that was a good place to start.

LYDIA EXAMINED HER reflection in the mirror, thinking that it was interesting how different this political event had been from the last one. The dinner that she'd had at the Garretts' a month ago had felt very Copper Ridge, at least, Copper Ridge as she knew it. This was an entirely different subset of people. While she had definitely done her share of rubbing elbows with them, they weren't exactly the constituents she had initially set out to appeal to. Seeing as she expected them to vote for Richard Bailey. But that had changed when Nathan West had officially given her his endorsement at the country club.

Anyway, it was a much easier thing to think about than the fact that it was actually election day, and the results would be in soon. She and Colton had dropped their ballots off this morning, and she could only assume the rest of the town would be doing the same soon.

Imagining the lines in front of the drop boxes gave her a twist of excitement and anxiety. She wasn't watching any of the early numbers. It was just too much to handle. She didn't want to know. Well, she did want to know, but she had to somehow get through tonight with grace and poise. And, seeing as she was currently in a dress that required foundational garments and high heels, she really had to work to find grace and poise.

She looked back at herself, examining the way the black dress fitted to her figure, hoping it was appropriate for the new mayor. Assuming she was the new mayor. If not, it was going to be one sad party. Wow, she hadn't fully considered that. That would be kind of awful.

She grabbed a bracelet off the nightstand and slipped it onto her hand, jiggling her wrist and watching it glitter in the mirror.

Her bedroom door opened, and Colton walked in. She just about had a full-fledged heart attack. As sexy as he was in his T-shirts, jeans and cowboy hats, he all but knocked her on her rear in a suit.

"All right?" he asked as he reached up, adjusting his tie. Her eyes went to the wedding band on his hand, and her heart turned over.

There was something hot about that. His hand with that outward symbol of their connection. Except, they weren't really married. Not really. They weren't. And maybe if she repeated those words to herself over and over again they would mean something. Maybe she could convince herself that the marriage license, the sex and the living together wasn't real. That the terrifying feelings that were beginning to grow inside of her weren't real, either.

That was the other thing the election symbolized. Not just the end of her run for mayor, but the potential end to their relationship. If she won, they would certainly stay married for a while longer, to avoid any kind of serious shake-ups. But if she lost…there would be no point. Beyond dealing with the emotional issues of his family. And that was a more open-ended deadline.

New anxiety churned through her. Broader than the anxiety she had just been feeling about the election. All-encompassing. Her whole life suddenly felt too big for her to carry and all out of her control.

She had two choices. Either she kicked Colton out of the room, or she closed the distance between them, clung to him, since everything else felt impossible to hang on to. She chose the second one, because it meant touching him.

She wrapped her arms around him and rested her head on his chest, listened to the sound of his beating heart. Suddenly, she felt more grounded. More present. Happy.

A pang of discomfort hit her hard. And she found herself pulling away.

"Are you ready?" he asked.

"I'm about a thousand times more ready to get put on a rocket ship and sent to Mars then I am to deal with tonight's election."

"Well, they did find water on Mars. But you can often find wine at events thrown by my family. So I feel like maybe you're better off just coming tonight instead of leaving the planet."

Darn him. He made her chest feel all tender and soft.

"Okay, I promise I will stay earthbound. But I'm not entirely certain what's in it for me other than the wine."

"Potential electoral victory?"

"I don't know."

"Cake. Because any party planned by my sisters will have cake."

"Okay, that's a little bit more enticing."

"And," he said, his blue eyes filled with humor, "we can make out afterward."

Everything inside of her honest to God quivered. "I hope you do a lot more than make out with me."

"Remember when you used to hate me?"

A jolt of nerves rocked her. "I still don't like you very much," she lied.

"If you're going to lie, you have to do a better job than that."

"I never lie."

"You're a politician."

"That's insulting. Also, bad stereotyping."

He reached out, capturing her chin between his thumb and forefinger, his blue eyes going sharp. "You would beg for me, and we both know it. You *more* than like me, Lydia Carpenter."

The worst part about his words was that they sent a giddy little shot of recklessness straight through her. Hot and straight up, like the shots they'd downed the night they got married.

It added to the suspicion that it had never been the alcohol at all. Sure, the alcohol had lowered inhibitions, had made a lot of the worries and general common sense they usually carried around go away. But it had a lot more to do with him than with Jack Daniel's.

"I don't want to be late," she said, moving away from him. Some of the heat in his eyes cooled. And she knew that she had ruined a moment. She didn't know why she had felt so compelled to ruin that moment, only that she had done it with swift, incisive purpose.

"Of course not, peaches." He extended his hand and she reached out, taking it. He was her husband, and they were attending this together. So, as much as she needed distance, she couldn't actually have it. But breaking some of the tension a moment ago had at least helped. Or, hurt, which in its way was helpful.

And now, when he said *peaches*, it didn't have any of the warmth it had had last time. That hurt. It shouldn't hurt.

"Okay," she said, taking a breath. "Let's go see if I won an election."

CHAPTER NINETEEN

LYDIA AND COLTON were greeted by Maddy and Sierra. The latter was looking fatigued, which was unsurprising, given her current state. As if Lydia didn't feel guilty enough. Both of the other women were being so kind to her, and Sierra was at the very tail end of her pregnancy, doing things for her she would never do if she knew that Lydia wasn't her actual sister-in-law.

The unsettled, awful feeling that had taken root inside of her earlier expanded. Grew.

"This is so exciting," Maddy said, treating Lydia to what she thought might be the first genuine smile she'd seen the younger woman hand out. "Last I checked you were ahead in the polls by quite a bit."

Lydia's stomach dipped. "Oh, I hadn't been checking."

"Seriously? I would be checking every two seconds."

"Honestly, these things change so many times before the actual results are announced. I just don't think I can subject myself to watching any kind of live speculation."

Colton tightened his hold on her, his hand large and warm on her waist. She was such a lost cause. The fact that he affected her so deeply, simultaneously turning her on and calming her down with just the touch of his hand.

"No matter what happens, this is going to be a great party," he said. "But she is going to win."

"Assuming everybody is as tired of having the same person running the town as I am," Madison said. "Anyway, it will be nice to have a woman in charge."

"Which is probably also going to play against me," Lydia said. "People are probably afraid that I'm going to start painting things pink."

Maddy waved a hand. "That's ridiculous. You have much better taste than that."

"If I were running for mayor it would be a genuine concern," Sierra added.

"You should sit down." Sierra's husband approached them, placing his hand on his wife's stomach. "You're worrying me."

"Stop it," she said, swatting Ace on the arm. "I can stand up. I'm pregnant, I'm not an invalid."

"You look precarious. Like you might be prone to tipping over."

"Wow. That's very flattering, honey," she said. "Now, do I need to worry about the youth of Copper Ridge playing a new game? Instead of going cow tipping, they'll go Sierra tipping?"

He leaned in and kissed the top of her head. "No one is going to tip you. Anyway, if they did, I would refuse to serve them alcohol. If we let that threat get around, you're safe for sure."

There was something in their easy affection that made her feel a deep, gnawing envy.

Then Colton touched her hand, and the combination of this real, deep relationship in front of her and that casual contact that wasn't casual at all, but engineered to carry out their fiction in a believable way, sent her stomach into a free fall.

You are being crazy. It's the night of your election.

The night where you find out exactly what the next four years of your life are going to look like, and you're fixating over a man.

Yeah, it would be fine if it were that easy to trivialize. If he were *only* a man, in the general, broad sense, and she were a teenage girl being silly. But this wasn't kids playing with matches. This was two adults with kerosene and a flamethrower. The scope for devastation was real.

So there was nothing *only* about him. No way to reduce him because this was romance, and not the career milestone she had been working toward. There was no way to tell it to get in line, so she could deal with it in an orderly fashion.

This wasn't even actually supposed to be romance. It was supposed to be a ruse in service of this election. Sex in service of her long-neglected needs.

It was not supposed to be a roiling mass of confusion, insecurity, jealousy born just from seeing a couple who had genuine emotion between them.

Not that she wanted emotion between herself and Colton. But what she wanted and what was actually occurring in her chest were two different things.

She swallowed hard, letting go of Colton's hand. "I think I'm going to circulate."

It was strange, how much easier it was to grab hold of her purse, rather than Colton, and breeze her way through, making casual conversation with people she had barely had any interaction with before, than it was to stand there with Colton's family and pretend to be something she wasn't. To pretend to mean something to him that she didn't.

Probably because this sort of thing came as second

nature to her. She could make small talk on autopilot. And meanwhile, her brain could weave tales of woe regarding everything that was happening with Colton, everything that was going to happen tonight and what her life would look like when the dust had settled.

This night was a much bigger deal than she had let herself imagine. If the election didn't go her way then everything really ended. Or rather, it all went back to the way it had been before. Nothing would *change*.

That was disconcerting on multiple levels.

She would continue serving at the Chamber of Commerce, continue serving the people of Copper Ridge much the way she had been for the past several years. She and Colton would divorce, and they would go their separate ways, and scandal and public perception wouldn't really matter.

But if she got elected then things would change. Her function in the community would change, and, yes, they would be changes that she wanted, but still, it was change. She and Colton would have to continue to pretend to be married until they decided that the dust had settled enough for them to end their union. And if they continued pretending they were married, then they would obviously continue to sleep together. Or, maybe not obviously. Maybe she was making assumptions that weren't entirely accurate.

It was suddenly quite surreal to be standing there on the glittering, well-decorated lawn at the West Estate imagining what it might be like tomorrow if she woke up in her bed, alone. At her own house, as though none of this had happened. As if it were all just a dream.

Not a mayor. Not a wife.

Not a lover.

In the safe little cocoon she'd woven for herself, still an inert caterpillar determined to never become a butterfly.

She couldn't decide if it sounded horrible, or wonderful.

Colton came and found her again when the buffet was served, and they made their plates and took their seats at a table together. It was the first time she had come face-to-face with Nathan West since their marriage. And she knew it was the same for Colton.

The older West didn't seem at all put off by the situation. In fact, he was surprisingly warm and friendly to Lydia.

"I'm glad to see that my son married someone with ambition," Nathan said, looking at Colton as he spoke. Lydia wasn't entirely certain which one of them he was addressing, or if he was aware of how closely his words echoed what his wife had said when she'd first learned of the marriage.

She chose to assume his sentiment had been aimed at her. "I'm very appreciative of you opening up your property for tonight," she said.

"Well, if it puts me in favor with the mayor's office it will be worth it. Of course, if it pits me against the mayor, we may have a problem. Depending on the outcome."

She had no idea if he was joking or not. But if she lost the election he wouldn't be her father-in-law for very long, so she imagined it didn't really matter.

"I'm sure that Lydia prefers to be optimistic," Colton said.

"Lydia is mostly nervous," she said, earning a chuckle from Nathan and the others at the table. She couldn't help but notice that Colton's mother was very quiet. She had a nervous energy about her, which Lydia had gathered based on the fact that Colton wanted to remain in their marriage in order to protect his mother's mental health. She had also had it reinforced that day at lunch. Still, seeing her seated next to her husband—a husband that Lydia knew had betrayed her in the worst way possible—so pale and silent gave her a deeper understanding of exactly what Colton was managing at home.

Colton put his hand over hers. "Don't be. You're the best person for the position."

The gentle contact, and the nice words, sent a rush of warmth through her. Of course, she had no way of knowing if he meant them at all, or if he was just doing his part to reinforce the facade of the marriage. And it shouldn't matter. She had no idea why she was suddenly having a breakdown about their feelings for each other. Maybe because recently it felt like they had grown closer. But she kind of liked that.

It was good to have a friendship with the guy you were sleeping with, at least, at a minimum. Of course, she hadn't imagined that she and Colton could ever be friends. And, that was part of why she imagined she would be safe sleeping with him. Because there was no chance for any sort of feelings to grow out of the animosity that had once existed between them.

That was before she had gotten to know him. Now she knew that they were more alike than they had originally imagined. Now she knew that he wasn't just a stubborn, pigheaded jerk. He was a man with too much on his shoulders. A man who carried the weight of the world, at least, the weight of his world, and the weight of several of his family members' worlds.

It was impossible to remain immune to him when she knew all that.

Plus, he was amazing in bed. There was no way she could remain neutral through that. In bed, on counter, against woodshed. His sex game was on point.

But that had nothing to do with warm, fuzzy feelings and wishing that their marriage could be real.

Her breath caught in her throat. No, she did *not* want their marriage to be real. If there was one thing she was even more certain of after her confessional to Colton about her sister, it was that she was not prepared to be in that kind of relationship. To have children, to have people depend on her emotionally.

She was just freaking out because of everything that was happening. That was it. The beginning and end of it. Her brain was like a tornado right now, swirling around and picking up concerns, adding them to the column of doom twisting in her brain.

Actively looking for yet more things to obsess about.

"Just thinking of the kind of legacy the two of you can have is…well, it's better than I anticipated having for this family." Lydia bristled as Nathan West spoke. She had a feeling this wasn't going anywhere good. "My children have been difficult, as I know you know," he said, addressing the entire table. Lydia could only be grateful that Sierra and Madison weren't sitting here, because she had a feeling it would not stop him from saying everything he was about to say. "So when Colton was left at the altar by Natalie Bailey, I thought we were in much the same situation with him as we have been with the others. But I have to hand it to him. Marrying the most likely candidate for the next town mayor was a better choice than simply marrying the daughter of the irrelevant incumbent."

Strangely, Lydia felt indignant on behalf of Natalie. Though not only on behalf of Natalie. She had heard that Nathan West could be the very thing he'd just accused his children of being—difficult. And obviously, she knew that he had fathered a love child during his marriage that he had never acknowledged, and that the situation had been difficult for everyone involved, so she wasn't sure what she had expected. Not this. She wasn't entirely sure that you could expect…this.

She also noticed that Nathan was very comfortable listing the sins of his children, but had left his own scandal out of the mix. She noticed, but she wasn't surprised.

"With Colton committed to taking over the ranch after I retire, and Lydia at the helm of the town, the West name has most definitely assured its place in history."

The other old men at the table raised their glasses to that, because clearly, they wanted to be in the good graces of the people who would continue to run the town so that it benefited them. She could see that was what they imagined. That, because she had married Colton, she was becoming some kind of establishment candidate. Such as the establishment was in Copper Ridge.

Truly, the election was over so there was no point in correcting them, but she was tempted to. It was only out of deference to Colton that she didn't. Out of deference to his mother, and to what she knew was a precarious situation.

She looked at Colton, hoping he would say something. Hoping that he would comment on the fact that he was going to focus on his own operation, and not on the West family legacy. Of course, that was a completely impractical hope. Because even in his position she wouldn't do that. Not at this venue. It was a conversation he was going to have to have with his father in private, and Lydia knew that. Still, she couldn't help but think that his father going on like this was going to make things more difficult. And she resented that.

For the rest of the meal they mostly listened to Nathan West talk, which seemed to be something he enjoyed. She decided that if she were going to stay married to Colton for the rest of her life, dealing with his father was probably going to be the most challenging aspect of that. She could see why he didn't seek out conversations with the older man.

She could also see why his allegiance to his mother and sisters was so strong. He was doing his father's bidding in many ways, but also, he was committed to keeping a kind of peace so that he could stay close. So that he could still be involved with the family. He'd told her that if you crossed the patriarch of the West family, you were forbidden from being involved with the rest of them.

She had no doubt that Colton was strong enough to oppose that. Colton was the strongest man she had ever met. It wasn't weakness that kept him where he was, it was actually an unimaginable strength. Self-sacrificing. Giving. She imagined him standing there, physically holding his family members together, keeping them from breaking apart, using everything he had in order to keep them whole.

But he deserved more. That was the bottom line. Eventually, everyone would have to support themselves. She stood by that.

As the meal wound down, and the hour came closer to the election results, Lydia could scarcely breathe.

Suddenly, the insulation provided by the gathering felt claustrophobic.

She edged to the periphery of the crowd, keeping watch to see if anyone noticed as she slipped away from the well-lit area and into the darkness. She took a deep breath as she walked across one of the expansive fields, headed out toward a clearing where she could see the moon shining on the ocean down below. This truly was a beautiful place to live. A beautiful place for a ranch. But it wasn't Colton's.

She wondered if he would do it. If he would fold himself into that little box his father had prepared for him. If he would do everything that was expected of him, continue to sacrifice at the expense of himself.

"Are you okay?"

She knew it was Colton before she turned around. Part of her thought maybe she had felt him before she heard him. That she was just that connected to him now, whether she wanted to be or not. That was the real scary thing. That no matter what happened, even if she did go home to her own house tonight, even if she did wake up just Lydia, not the mayor, not Colton's wife, things still wouldn't have gone back to normal.

She was changed. Fundamentally, from the inside out. He had changed her. Had taken all of the spaces she had carved out for herself, to simply be Lydia, and somehow imprinted his name all over them.

That was terrifying. On a soul-deep level nothing else had ever been.

"I'm fine," she said, taking a deep breath and turning to face him. He was a stark, dark silhouette against the brightly lit party, broad-shouldered and slim-waisted. Basically, the hottest man she had ever seen. "Did I win?"

"No announcement yet. You look like you're going to win." He took a couple steps toward her, and her lungs contracted, all of her breath disappearing into the velvet night. "I thought you might actually want to hear that before you went back for the announcement. I thought you might need a minute to prepare."

She felt dizzy all of a sudden. Both with the revelation that she was actually pulling this off, and with the simple truth that Colton knew she would need this. That success was going to be almost as terrifying as failure. "Several minutes," she said, putting her hand flat on her stomach. "Actually, a few hours, a drink. That would be nice."

He grabbed hold of her chin, tilting it upward. "A kiss?"

She swallowed hard. "I guess so."

He leaned in, the press of his mouth against hers warm, comforting, sending a wave of sensation through her body. She could exist like this forever. Then she wouldn't have to worry about the future. Wouldn't have to worry about what it meant to realize that she would never go back to how she'd been in her pre-Colton existence. Wouldn't have to worry about all of the changes that lay ahead.

It was so tempting to sink into him completely. So tempting to just melt into him. When had she started to depend on him so much? That was what all of this came down to. The scattered, strange emotion she had been having ever since they arrived suddenly crystallized, forming one clear picture.

She was dependent on him. She had come to Copper Ridge to make an independent life for herself, and she had managed to do that for close to a decade. Now, suddenly she found herself utterly welded to this man, afraid that she would never be able to separate herself from him again.

She was going to win. She was going to win and she was going to have to stay with him like this. And it was only going to get worse. More intense. She didn't possess any self-control where he was concerned—she knew that beyond a shadow of a doubt. If she did, she wouldn't be married to him. If she did, she wouldn't be sleeping with him. Suddenly, getting everything she wanted seemed like it might actually be a disaster.

Lydia pulled away from him, her heart thundering in her chest. "Colton—"

A scream rose up from the direction of the party. Not a party kind of scream. A terrified scream. Colton's body jerked toward the direction, then he turned and looked at her. "Go," she said, lifting the front of her dress and following him as quickly as she could back toward the lights, back toward the crowd.

Sierra.

That was Lydia's first thought. That Sierra had gone into horrible, hideous labor now, at this party. Sweet, wonderful Sierra, who was being tricked just like everyone else and was now probably in pain.

The TV was playing loudly, the election results being read out now. And, at the same time, the guests had all crowded around a person who was lying on the grass. It was not Sierra, who was standing on the edge of the tight group of people, her hand resting on her stomach, her face full of concern.

Lydia could see Maddy, down on her knees in front of the inert figure. And when Lydia moved to the side, she could see that the person who had collapsed was Nathan West.

"Has someone called an ambulance?" Colton asked, breaking through the people and kneeling down beside his father.

"Yes," Maddy said. "And Mom is inside, lying down. Genevieve is with her."

Lydia had no idea who Genevieve was, but she supposed it didn't matter.

It didn't take long for the paramedics to arrive. When they did, they had everyone take a step back, including Colton, who came to stand beside her. The TV was still going in the background, and as Nathan West was taken away from the party on a stretcher, Lydia dimly heard that she had been declared the winner of the election. That Lydia Carpenter was the new mayor of Copper Ridge.

Her head felt fuzzy; it felt like everything around her was echoing. She had no idea how to process any of this. Had no idea how to exist in a moment that had her feeling so torn in two.

"I have to go to the hospital," Colton said.

He didn't say we. He said that he had to go. And she supposed that this was her out. A chance to establish some distance. To take stock of what had just occurred. But she couldn't. She couldn't leave him.

"I'm going with you," she said.

He just looked at her, his blue eyes filled with fear. "Thank you."

LYDIA HATED HOSPITALS. Hated them. She avoided them at all costs, though she supposed everyone did. But she really, really hated them. It was still hard for her to set foot inside. It always reminded her of the last time Frannie had gone into the hospital. Of how she had never come home. Of how they had left the hospital forever changed. A family of three instead of a family of four. Of how she had left feeling like half of herself was missing. A half that would never be regained.

But this was for Colton. She was here for Colton, and she couldn't back out now.

When they arrived, Maddy was already there, having ridden in the ambulance. A few moments later, Ace and Sierra arrived. "Is Mom coming?" Colton asked.

"Tomorrow," Sierra said. "I didn't think it was a good idea for her to come tonight, and she agreed."

Lydia couldn't fathom letting your husband lie in a hospital bed by himself. But then, she supposed, given the fact that this particular husband had had a child with another woman and kept it from his wife for years and seemed to treat his wife more like an accessory than a partner, it was safe to say they didn't have a conventional union.

Sierra took a seat and her husband stood behind her, rubbing her shoulders. She put her hand over his, the gesture so casually caring. They were like that all the time. Lydia had to wonder what it would be like. To have someone care about you like that, constantly. To have someone look to you first when the world was in turmoil. To have someone reach out to you as the storm raged around you.

Lydia had spent so many years alone in the storm.

Her family fought through the wind and the rain in isolation. And here the West family was, all together in this, even though they had differences and a million disagreements.

She was very aware of the fact that she wasn't touching Colton. If Sierra or Madison noticed, they certainly weren't going to say anything. Not now. Likely, they didn't notice at all.

She thought about reaching out and taking hold of his hand again, but then she just couldn't. Her hand felt like it was made of lead, like she couldn't lift up her arm.

"Did they tell you anything, Madison?" Colton asked.

Maddy shook her head, gripping her elbows, looking as though she wanted to fold in on herself. The incomparable Madison so rarely looked at a loss. But now she looked small and pale. "Nothing yet. He's stable. But I'm waiting for more information."

"Did he have a heart attack?" This question came from Sierra.

Madison frowned. "I just said I didn't know."

"I'm speculating," Sierra said.

"I'd venture to say the speculation isn't all that helpful," Maddy responded.

Ace looked up at Madison, his gaze sharp. "I think that's enough."

"Killing each other is maybe not the best course of action at the moment," Colton said, his tone even and steady. "We just have to wait and see."

His words seemed to calm both of his sisters. She imagined they were used to looking to him for guidance. That was his position. The place that he assumed in the family. She had gotten an even closer look at the dynamics tonight than she had over the past weeks of living with and interacting with Colton.

Their father was thoroughly self-absorbed. He was a self-described pillar of the community, and while a good portion of the town had bought into that, she felt that no one bought the myth of Nathan West more than Nathan himself.

Their mother was something beautiful and breakable to be protected at all costs. And someone had to stand strong for Maddy and Sierra.

She could see that Colton was bound and determined to stand in every gap.

And that he had done so perfectly, admirably for all these years.

Minutes turned into hours, and Lydia began to feel like her rear end was welded to the pink hospital chair she'd been sitting in ever since they arrived. Colton was leaning forward in his own seat, his chin resting in his hands. He was radiating weariness, the lines on his face more pronounced than they usually were. She wanted to reach out and smooth them, to find a way to relieve some of his stress. To take some of this burden from him.

At some point, a doctor appeared, and asked if she could talk to Colton privately in the hospital room.

Sierra and Maddy watched him leave, their eyes glued to the door, waiting for him, and news, to appear. Lydia could hardly stand it. It was too reminiscent of the night her sister died. Too awful and tense, and most especially egregious because this wasn't actually her family. Because she was here under false pretenses, because she was sitting here like she was a part of something that she just wasn't.

The doors to the emergency room slid open, and Lydia looked up. It was Jack Monaghan. His blue eyes were filled with concern and matched Colton's in a way that she had not fully appreciated until this moment. Until Colton's eyes had become so intimately familiar to her.

"I heard what happened," he said, stuffing his hands into his pockets. He hung back, clearly uncertain about whether or not he should be here.

"Sit down," Maddy said.

He nodded once, crossing the space and taking his position with the family. Now she felt even worse. Even more of an interloper. These moments, these difficult, crushing moments that they were experiencing didn't deserve to have a witness who was nothing more than an imposter.

"I don't know if he would want me to be here," Jack said. "But I felt like I needed to be."

"Thank you for coming, Jack," Sierra said.

He forced a smile. "I told Kate not to come until morning. She's...well, in about the same boat you are."

"Exhausted?" Sierra asked.

"Yes."

Colton was in the hospital room for about forty minutes, and when he appeared, he looked grim. Sierra, Maddy and Jack all stood. Lydia stayed rooted to her seat.

"He had a stroke," Colton said, moving closer to the waiting area. "They're doing what they can to minimize the damage. It's a good thing he made it to the hospital right away. But it was pretty massive. They don't know what he'll recover, and what he won't. It's just too soon to say." He looked like he wanted to say more, but didn't. His eyes landed on Jack. "Thanks for coming." He echoed what Sierra had already said.

"Family is a helluva thing," Jack said. "But it is a thing."

"True."

"Whether or not he wants me to be, I'm his son."

There was no ignoring Nathan West's sins, not even now as he lay unconscious in a hospital bed. His sins were real, living, breathing. They had affected everyone here. And yet, they all stood by him. A testament more to them than to him. The strength of this family overwhelmed her. Awed her.

"We could probably all go home," Colton said. "I'm not sure there's going to be any other changes tonight."

Nobody made a move to go. And as long as Colton was here, Lydia would be here too.

The doors to the emergency room opened again, and Lydia felt like she was experiencing a moment of déjà vu. Because this was another man who looked startlingly similar to Colton. The same height, breadth and blue eyes. His hair was darker though, and he didn't have the same sort of civility that Colton carried himself with. There was something raw about him, and it wasn't just his torn jeans, black cowboy hat or the dark band tattooed on his forearm.

Something in Colton tensed, his manner changing completely. Like a dog who had spotted danger, his hackles were raised, his hands clenched into fists. "This has to be a joke," he said, his voice low.

"I'm not here to have a fistfight with you in the emergency room of a hospital," the other man said.

Based on the family resemblance and Colton's anger, Lydia could make a fairly educated guess about who the newcomer was. It didn't seem possible. Not after he'd been gone for so long. But this could only be Gage West.

"Then why are you here?"

"I was contacted by Dad's lawyer," Gage said.

Lydia looked at Maddy and Sierra. They were both white-faced, their lips blue around the edges. For his part, Gage barely flicked them a glance. His younger sisters, who had to have been children the last time he'd seen them, and he was barely giving a nod to their existence. But then, based on what Colton had said about him, she couldn't be too surprised that Gage had a self-absorbed streak.

"How did he know where to find you?"

"I've kept in contact."

"Not with us," Colton said.

"With Dad's lawyer."

"Well, great. I hate to break it to you, but Dad's still alive. So if you were expecting to show up and collect some money…"

"I'm sure you would enjoy that," Gage said. "But I don't have any interest in Dad's money. I do have an interest in a few things, though. But I'm not going to discuss them here, not with you."

"I don't think you've earned the right to be cagey with me," Colton said. "It may have escaped your notice, but you walked into a situation that was being handled. A situation that has been handled for the past seventeen years. We didn't need you to come back in to handle things. I'm not going to apologize for assuming you're here for money."

"If I gave a damn about Dad's money I never would have left in the first place."

"Then why are you here?"

"Responsibility."

"That's a joke. You haven't cared about responsibility at all from the moment you left. You left all of us to deal with life on our own, so don't barge in here now like some busted-ass savior ready to rescue us. If we waited around for you things would have fallen apart a long time ago."

Lydia felt like she was on the verge of panicking. It wasn't fair. She knew it wasn't fair. This was something major and terrible that was happening to Colton; it wasn't happening to her. But she shouldn't be here. She shouldn't be here witnessing this. She wasn't anything to him, wasn't anything to them.

It was just too much. It was too big, too real. It had nothing to do with her and still it reached beneath her protective layer and squeezed at her heart, threatened to crack her open completely.

She couldn't do it. She just couldn't do it. She should never have been here in the first place. This was for the West family, and she had inserted herself into it, under the guise of helping Colton keep the peace, but really just to serve her own ambitions.

Now she was mayor. She had accomplished everything she had set out to accomplish, maybe because she had ended up getting the endorsement of Nathan West. Possibly because of her marriage. She would never know.

And now she was here, taking up space during this tense moment between family members. Taking a space she didn't deserve. A space she wasn't equal to.

She stood up, and no one seemed to notice. Then, she slowly extricated herself from the group. It was Madison who saw her. Madison who made eye contact, whose expression spoke loudly. With accusation. With understanding. Lydia ignored it.

She turned and walked out of the emergency room. The early-morning air was sharp, cutting into her like glass. She wrapped her arms around herself, trying to hold herself together. It was up to her to hold herself together. Colton had enough on his plate, was preserving enough things. He didn't need to preserve her too.

She swallowed hard, scanning the parking lot for her car. One of his siblings would take him home, he would be fine. But she had to go.

So she did what she did best when things got too painful. She ran.

CHAPTER TWENTY

COLTON FELT LIKE he was living in a bad dream that wouldn't go away. He kept waiting to wake up in his bed, next to Lydia, and find that he was not in fact in a hospital with his father lying incapacitated in the other room. That he was not facing his brother, who he had not seen for nearly two decades.

He refused to wake up. This seemed to be real. He was pretty pissed about that.

This evening had been waves of change, rolling over and over. When Lydia had won the election it had become clear that the two of them would be continuing on with their marriage. And he had been…happy with that. He had seen a future there. Maybe one that he didn't deserve, or one that would be difficult, but he had seen it.

For Lydia, he wanted to do the bigger things. The harder things. He had seen a life where he grew the ranch for them. Where their children went out to that swing to play. And he had been…happy. Then it had all come crashing down when his father had been lying there on the ground. Colton had realized then that freedom was never going to be in the cards for him. The West Ranch was going to pass into his possession; there was no doubt about that. He couldn't abandon it. Couldn't abandon his family.

And as he had been grappling with that, and with

fear over what exactly his father was facing, Gage had walked in. He was claiming that he was here to handle things. His brother who had been away all this time. The reason that Colton was where he was at. In every damn way.

Because of Gage, Colton worked the family construction business. Because of Gage, Colton had seen nothing more than a future building his father's legacy. Because of Gage, Colton had thought he needed to marry a woman who would help keep him in his place. Because of Gage, he had chosen Natalie. Because of Natalie, he had gone off and married Lydia.

His older brother had set off a chain of events that had been continually rolling for the past seventeen years, and he hadn't been here to witness any of it. And now, he simply was. And all Colton wanted to do was haul off and punch him in the face.

Hell, they were at a hospital. If he was going to get into a fistfight with someone who matched him in size and strength, this was the place.

Instinctively, as his anger threatened to overwhelm him, he looked for Lydia. And discovered she wasn't there.

"Where's Lydia?" It was entirely possible she had gone into the bathroom, or something.

"She left," Maddy said.

That made him feel like the wind had been knocked out of him, like he was in danger of tipping over. He hadn't realized until that moment just how much having Lydia there really meant.

How much she meant to him.

He looked around the room, at his family. It was the worst time for him to leave. Gage was here. It was also three in the morning. They were all exhausted. They weren't solving anything tonight. And he needed to go see his wife.

"I'm going to go," he said.

"You're just going to leave?" Maddy asked.

"No, Maddy," he said. "I'm not just going to leave. It's difficult for me to leave. But I need to figure out what's going on with my wife. That's just something I have to handle. And it can't wait."

"I can't believe you're being so selfish."

Her words nearly knocked him on his ass. "I'm sorry you feel that way," he bit out. "But the way I see it, everyone here is an adult. I want to support you. I want to support the whole family, of course. But sometimes you have to stand on your own feet, Madison. I have an issue that isn't going to take care of itself, and I can't send anyone to take care of it for me." Lydia. The most important thing was Lydia. That was where he needed to be; it was who he needed. He hadn't been willing to stand up to his family, not for himself, not for the ranch. But for her? He would lay it all down for her. That was what you did when you loved somebody.

And dammit all to hell, he loved her.

"Go," Sierra said, squeezing Ace's hand. "We can deal with…this. In fact, I might go home too. I'm exhausted." She looked at Gage. "And I don't even know what to do with you. I probably won't until I sleep for fourteen hours."

"I'm staying here," Maddy said, thrusting her chin forward.

"So am I," Gage said.

"I would rather you didn't," Maddy said.

The hardest thing that Colton had ever done was turn

away from the confrontation. Not intervening. Not trying to solve it. They were adults, and they would make
their own decisions. He couldn't do it for them.

If he did it now, he would do it forever. Apply a se-
ries of temporary fixes to the cracks that made up his
family. And he would never get around to dealing with
his own life. Ever.

As he walked out of the hospital and into the cold
night, he realized that not dealing with himself was
probably a huge part of why he did this. Why he poured
himself into solving everyone else's problems when
things went south.

Because they were easier than solving his own.

Whatever the hell his own were. He looked around
the parking lot, and realized that he didn't actually have
a car there. He had come over with Lydia, and she had
left without him. He pulled out his cell phone and called
the lone cab service in town. Fortunately, it was about
that time for them to be ferrying drunks home from the
bar, so there were drivers out and about. Copper Ridge
was not the kind of place where you could stand on the
corner and grab an easy ride.

It took about ten minutes, but the car did show up,
and Colton instructed the driver to take him back to his
house. Hopefully, Lydia was there, but if she wasn't,
he could take his truck over to her house. Because that
would be the next guess on his list.

When the car pulled up to the front, he saw that the
kitchen light was on. And then he saw her slight figure
moving around inside. And he realized beyond a shadow
of a doubt that this was what he wanted. That no matter the time of day, no matter the situation, he wanted
to come home to this. To her. It didn't really matter if it

was here, if it was her house, if it was his parents' home. As long as she was in it.

Yeah, he still had his other dreams. But she was the big one. He didn't know how that had happened. Only that it had. Sometime between waking up at a hotel in Vegas married to the last woman on earth he would have ever claimed to want, and this moment, standing in his dark, cold driveway watching her make tea in the kitchen.

Lydia Carpenter had become his dream.

He paid the driver and walked up the steps, heading into the house.

"Lydia?"

He got silence in response. Which he imagined wasn't the best sign. Still, he didn't care. He was in the middle of a damn revelation, and she had to listen. He didn't do this kind of thing. He didn't do mad, crazy revelations and over-the-top declarations at three in the morning. But he was about to.

Because he also didn't storm out on his family when they were in the middle of a crisis. He didn't do any of this. He did it for her.

"Glad I found you here," he said, walking into the kitchen.

She turned, clutching a mug in her hands, her dark eyes wide. "I wasn't hiding."

"You didn't say goodbye."

"You seemed like you were in the middle of something."

"Yeah, well. Gage coming back was a little bit unexpected. Or a lot unexpected. But it isn't something that I want to deal with right now. Just because he stormed back in doesn't mean that he gets all the attention now.

I don't have to drop everything just to deal with him. I have my own life."

The corner of her mouth tilted upward. "Yes, you do."

"I've had a lot of…revelations over the past few hours. It's actually all kind of surreal."

She nodded slowly. "I can relate."

"I haven't helped my family. The way that I've handled things. I've been…I've been trying to hold everything together since Gage left. And tonight I just… stopped. Not because he's back, because honestly I don't care that he's back. I mean, I'm angry at him, but we're going to have to deal with that later."

She took a sip of tea, her eyes never leaving his. She didn't speak. So he continued.

"It will never end. This thing that I'm doing. It just doesn't end. And you can't… I can't keep doing it."

"I hope you told them that," she said.

"I didn't really. But I did kind of leave them to handle all of this by themselves. And hopefully everyone will still be speaking to me tomorrow. Later today. I don't even know what day it is."

"It's tomorrow."

He nodded slowly. And then he felt like he was out of words. So he just did the thing that made the most sense. He wrapped his arms around her and pulled her in for a kiss. Her tea sloshed over the edge of her cup, burning his chest through his shirt, but he didn't really care. He just kissed her, because it was the only thing that made sense. Because she was the only thing that made sense. And on the other side of this kiss were revelations and confessions, things he didn't want to say, but that he knew he had to say. But right now, there was just this kiss.

And so he kept it going, long and slow, and not caring that there was a ceramic mug between them.

Then, it had to end. He let her go reluctantly, taking a step back.

"We should probably talk about that," she said, tucking a strand of hair behind her ear.

"About what?" He knew, but he wanted to make her say it.

"About the kissing. About all of that. Because I got elected and…"

"I know. And so you're going to keep living with me."

"I mean, that was the original plan."

"And you're questioning things now?" he asked.

She pushed her hand through her hair. "It's just… tonight, with your family. Everyone that was there is part of you in some way. And I'm not. I'm your fake wife, and I can't keep tricking your sisters. Your mother is only more vulnerable now than she was before, your father is… And now your brother… Like you said, it doesn't stop."

"If it's too much for you to handle, I can understand that. I mean, it's borderline too much for me to handle, but they're my responsibility, so I do it."

She frowned. "That isn't it. It has nothing to do with handling your family." She looked away, and he knew she was lying.

"So you left tonight because you felt guilty."

She lifted a shoulder. "Yes."

"That's bullshit."

"It is not," she said, her voice raising half an octave with the protest.

"It is. Something freaked you out back there, and I want to know what."

"I don't like hospitals, okay. Can you understand that? The last time I spent any significant time there was when I ended up leaving my sister behind, because she died. I'm sorry. But I couldn't stay."

Her words hit him with the force of a punch. "No," he said, "I'm sorry. I should have thought of that."

"Why? Why should you have thought of that? As you reminded me not long ago, Colton, you are not my real husband. It isn't your job to deal with my emotional crippling."

He took a sharp breath, the intensity of it stabbing him in the chest. "Actually, I should have thought of that, because I care about you. Because all of this *not your real husband* stuff, that's what isn't real."

"What do you mean?"

"Nothing about you is dumb, Lydia Carpenter. Don't play stupid now. You are my real wife. I married you, I sleep with you every night, I damn well love you. Tell me what isn't real about that?"

She took a step back, her dark eyes wide, and unless he misinterpreted the emotion in them, she was afraid of him. Afraid of what he had just said. "Don't. Don't act like our drunken marriage that only happened because you got left at the altar by the woman you actually wanted to marry is real just because suddenly you're comfortable in it."

"That isn't why. I said that I loved you. Are you just going to ignore that?"

"Yes," she said, exploding. "I would like to ignore that. I would like to pretend that you never said anything of the kind. I...I don't love you Colton. I really don't need you to love me."

Her words hit him with the impact of a bullet. "You don't love me?"

"I never wanted any of this. None of it. I didn't want to marry anyone. Never. You met my ex-boyfriend— you know all about that. I'm possibly the only woman in Logan County that has no interest in a husband and children." She drew in a shuddering, shaking breath, evidence that she was not unaffected by this, no matter what she was saying. "I never wanted this. This was supposed to be something convenient, something that kept my campaign running smoothly. It was supposed to just be a little bit of sex on top of that. It was not supposed to be feelings, and hospital rooms, and family drama."

"Yeah, well, I was supposed to marry a woman who made me comfortable. I was supposed to happily take the helm of my family legacy. I was supposed to fall in line with what everyone asked of me. I wasn't supposed to fall in love with you. So, I'm real sorry that plans didn't go the way you wanted them to, peaches. But I'm not really in a better position. I'm just not running scared."

"That's what you think this is? You think that I'm scared?" She laughed, borderline hysterically.

"Yes, I think you're scared. I think that's why you left the hospital tonight. I think strong emotions terrify you. I think that's why you've been running all this time."

"How dare you?"

"What? How dare I make you examine yourself? How dare I ask you to answer a question honestly?"

She flung her arms wide, releasing her hold on her teacup, sending it crashing down onto the ground. She looked startled by her own actions, by the shattered ceramic on the floor and the dark tea stain spreading over the tile.

Then she looked up at him, breathing hard, her breasts rising and falling with the motion. "I'm not afraid," she said, her voice trembling. "Is it too much for you to imagine that I simply just don't love you?"

"Yes, yes it is. Because I think from the moment you met me in Ace's bar, you wanted me. I think it's why we couldn't stand the sight of each other, because we knew that all we really wanted was to tear each other's clothes off. To disappear into our desire and never come out of it. I think we both knew it from moment one. I think we loved each other then."

"Lust," she said, "that's all it is. And lust isn't love."

"Right. So it was only lust that had you losing your mind up against the woodshed with me? That was lust? Simple lust ruins all of your carefully cultivated control? I don't believe that." He took a step closer to her, the broken mug crunching underneath his shoe. "It certainly takes more than that for me."

"I guess it doesn't take more for me. You're hot in bed—I'm not going to deny that—but that's not the same thing as…feelings."

"I know what you're doing. Because it's what I've spent my whole life doing. You're running away from the hard things. From the big things."

"We've already been through this, Colton. I was brave enough to change my life. I didn't cling to my family and get involved in some kind of codependent mess the way that you did."

"No. You ran away because you felt like they were crushing you. And it was good that you did. But did you ever set yourself free after? Or did you keep on living the way that they wanted you to? How long has it been since you were really happy, Lydia? How long has it been since you really cried?"

"Is that what you want? You want me to cry, Colton? Well, I'm not going to cry over you." She tried to brush past him and he grabbed hold of her arm, pulling her back against him.

"I don't need you to cry for me," he said, his chest feeling full of broken glass, digging into him with his each and every breath. "But maybe you should cry for you. Maybe you should try to feel something. You pour everything into this town, Lydia. Everything. Because it isn't a person. It can't love you back. It can't hurt you."

"Right, because you know me better than I know myself. After a month and a half of marriage, you're an expert on me," Lydia said, pulling away from him again.

"Tell me I'm wrong."

"You're wrong," she said, turning away sharply.

"You do all these things so that you can pretend you're being brave. Running for mayor looks brave on the surface. It makes you feel like you're a part of something, a part of Copper Ridge, but it just distances you even further from people. You stay busy, you make yourself important. But it's not the same as loving someone."

"That's a really nice story. And it's pretty convincing. The thing is, I care about a lot of things. I risk a lot. None of this is a story I tell myself—this is a story you're telling yourself. Because you can't deal with the fact that I have feelings, I just don't have them for you."

Then she turned and walked out of his house, leaving him there with a broken mug, and a broken heart.

CHAPTER TWENTY-ONE

LYDIA DIDN'T KNOW where she was going. She thought maybe she would go to her house, but she passed on by. She continued driving down the winding road that afforded a brilliant view of the ocean during the day. Right now, everything was blanketed in gray. Including her.

She parked her car in one of the small lots above wooden stairs that granted beach access, got out, letting the salt air blow over her skin. Cautiously, she walked down the stairs and down to the sand. Her feet sank in immediately, and she kicked her shoes off. The ground was freezing cold, the coarse grains wrapping themselves around her feet, making her skin ache. But she didn't care. She carried her shoes down to the water's edge, closing her eyes and listening to the invisible waves crashing in front of her.

She was numb. Scenes from a few moments ago playing through her mind. Colton telling her she was scared. Telling her she was protecting herself.

Telling her that he loved her.

Her knees felt wobbly all of a sudden, and she gave in to the weakness, sinking down onto the sand, not caring when the cold and moisture seeped through her jeans.

She didn't know what was happening to her. She didn't know what had happened tonight. Colton was never supposed to love her. Why would he? He was

Colton West. And she was not a woman who made men lose their heads. She certainly wasn't a woman who lost her head over a man. And yet, here they were.

Her shoulders shook, a sob catching in her chest. What was she doing? She had been elected mayor less than twelve hours ago, and now she was sitting on the beach, by herself, on the verge of an emotional breakdown. She had everything she had come here for.

The full and total acceptance of the town, the position she had wanted... And she felt...nothing.

She was hollow. A kind of echoing hollowness that radiated aching pain all through her body. She wanted to lie on her face in the sand all of a sudden, feel the coolness pressed up against her, see if it would take away some of the hideous restlessness rioting through her.

It was as if a lifetime of pain suddenly rolled over her like a sneaker wave from the sea. Pure misery gripped her, swamped her, made it almost impossible to breathe.

Something cracked inside of her, and from there it all just poured out. Her pain. Her misery. Tears. A deep, unending grief that shook her. Rocked her.

She had never cried for Frannie. Not really. She'd shed tears, but she hadn't cried from her soul since the moment she found out her sister was dead. Not since her father had told her she had to bottle it back up because it was far too upsetting for her parents to witness. But there was no one here to see now. And there was nothing but that aching, vacant place inside of her that made her feel like half.

It was bleeding now. As though she had suddenly removed the tourniquet and reopened a wound she'd long thought healed. It wasn't healed. Not even close.

She thought of what Colton had said earlier, about

temporary fixes. That's what she had been doing. Putting Band-Aids on deep, fatal wounds and hoping to ignore them for the rest of her life, while they killed her slowly.

She took a deep, shaking breath, tears slipping down her cheeks. She wiped them away, leaving behind grains of sand that had been stuck to her hands. "Stupid town," she muttered, the words breaking as her insides continued to shatter. "You were supposed to fix me. You weren't supposed to break me."

She was supposed to find quiet here. A place to hide. She was not supposed to find Colton West.

Wasn't supposed to find a man who dragged her out into the open, who insisted that she didn't hide. She clutched her chest, trying to push the pain that was radiating from her back inside. Trying to push it back down deep. But it would not be contained. It hurt. It physically hurt.

She sobbed, deep and long, harder than she could ever remember crying. For everything. For Frannie. For herself. For her parents. And most especially because she was such a hypocrite. Because she had pushed Colton to take things that he wanted while she continued to hide. Because she had told him he had to go for his dreams because that's what she believed she had done. She hadn't. She was a coward.

Hiding from grief. Hiding from joy.

Using a community to fill empty spaces inside of her because, Colton was right, she didn't have to love it in a personal way. She had taken her parents' issues and made them her own. Had taken their fear of pain, of strong emotion, and owned it. Even while she pretended she was going off to make a life of her own.

Because this was scary. It was horrible.

And she was so afraid to reach for more.

She closed her eyes, replaying in her mind the moment she had told Colton she didn't love him back. The hurt, the naked, unguarded pain in his blue eyes reverberating through her.

She did love him. She did. And he was right, she probably had from that first moment she'd seen him in Ace's. No wonder she had hated him so much. Because underneath it, she had known what could be. Because she had known that he would challenge everything, that he would breach her defenses, scale the walls that she had erected around her heart, around her soul.

He was an enemy to her quiet life. Her safety. That was why, instinctively, she had shut him out of her home, of her sanctuary in the beginning.

She had been smart. Because if she had wanted to stay safe, she should have stayed away from Colton West from the beginning. But here she was, on the other side of safety. She couldn't go back. That deep foreboding she had felt at last night's election party was true beyond a shadow of a doubt. She had been changed by Colton. She could try to pretend that she wasn't. She could try to go back and reclaim that quiet existence she'd once had. That didn't contain deep grief, deep happiness, deep pain or deep love.

But, looking at that, looking back at the person she was, at the half, she knew she couldn't do that. Knew she couldn't go back to the gray.

She stood up, her eyes fixed on the horizon line. She could see an orange glow starting around the edge of the mountains, spilling over and out across the ocean, illuminating the whitecaps, brightening the gray.

She watched as the sun rose higher, wrapping the trees in a golden wreath, the glow extending down over the large, jagged rocks that dotted the shoreline, and the mist that rose up above the sand. The light mixed with the slate-gray waves, turning them a velvet purple.

It had always been there. All of it. Shrouded in the gray. It only needed the light to be revealed.

It made her wonder. It made her wonder for the first time if perhaps she wasn't a half at all. If maybe, just maybe, she had always been whole.

She just had to let the light in to see it.

DRINKS WERE ON his brother-in-law that night at the brewery, and Colton was in no position to say no.

His father's health was stabilized, but there was still no way to know how he would recover. Only the coming weeks would really tell. Additionally, his disgraced brother was skulking around town.

Worst of all, Colton hadn't seen his wife since she stormed out of his house early that morning.

She didn't love him. She had made that clear. And whether or not Colton believed it, she did. And that was all that really mattered. At least at the moment. He'd never had his heart broken before. He had done such a damn good job of insulating himself against anything like that, that it had never been a factor.

This was what happened when he stepped outside of what was expected. He realized now that this was what he had been avoiding for years. It was jarring. Being faced with Gage's return, his father's failing health and the loss of Lydia. It made him take a good, long hard look at himself and the reasons he did things. He didn't like any of it. He didn't particularly care for introspection. What man did? But it was difficult to avoid in this situation.

The real reason he worked so hard to do exactly what his parents needed him to do, the real reason that he did everything he could to hold it together for Maddy and Sierra, was because he was afraid of losing them too. Simple as that. If things got too hard, someone else might leave. If he failed in some way, someone else might give up.

As pissed as he was at his older brother, he had missed that bastard. Seeing him had driven that point home. He wasn't ready to hug it out with him. He wasn't even sure he wanted to talk to him. But the first emotion he'd felt when Gage had walked through that door was relief.

He'd made that speech to Lydia about the prodigal son stuff. About resenting the idea that Gage would be given a hero's welcome if ever he returned home. The real issue was, Colton had always known he would be tempted to give Gage a hero's welcome if he ever came home. Colton would be tempted to forget the past seventeen years had ever happened and embrace his older brother as if nothing had ever gone wrong.

And then he would be hurt all over again when he left.

A lot of good this bit of self-actualization had done. He had lost Lydia. He was living his worst fear. He had lost the person that had come to mean the most to him the moment he had demanded too much.

He closed his eyes and took another sip of whiskey, imagining the first moment he had seen her back in Ace's bar. She had gotten to him then. It was her. And it always had been. He had held it off for as long as possible, and look what had happened.

"More?" He opened his eyes and came face-to-face with Ace.

"Yes. I would like to drink until I can forget the last couple of days."

"I'm the right person to see about that. But I do feel like I should remind you the last time you did that you ended up married."

"Yeah, maybe this time I'll end up divorced." He picked his glass up and tipped it back, draining the rest of the contents before setting it down hard on the bar. "Keep it coming."

"That bad, huh?"

"That bad."

"Drinking for the whole family?"

Colton turned and saw Jack Monaghan coming up to the bar.

"Unless you want to help," he said to his half brother.

"I would. But, I need to stay sober in case my wife decides to go into labor. Any day now. Really, any moment now. She's overdue."

"Then I guess the drunken debauchery is up to me."

"What happened with Lydia?" he asked.

"What makes you think something happened with Lydia?"

"Well," he said, sitting on the stool next to him. "You left the hospital after her in a hurry last night. None of us have heard from you since and now you're here getting shitfaced."

"First of all, are you on the family text chain now or what?"

"Madison agreed that I should be kept in the loop."

Colton snorted. "Madison did? That's something."

"She's…prickly."

"She's been hurt."

"Who hasn't been?"

Colton had to laugh at that. "Good question. Maybe I'm getting drunk because I'm worried about my dad."

"No. I recognize this. This is woman related."

"Had your share of female drama?"

It was Jack's turn to laugh. "You don't think Kate made me work for it? She made me work for it hard."

"I told Lydia that I loved her. And she said she didn't love me." He must have been a little further into the bottle than he had originally thought. He didn't bother to explain exactly why his wife might not love him, or why confessing his love to her meant something.

"I've been there."

"Kate rejected you?"

"Big-time. And I kind of deserved it. I mean, I had never shown her a reason to trust me where women were concerned. And she'd been hurt too many times, lost too many people."

"What did you do?"

"I went after her."

"Okay, and what would you have done if that didn't work?" Because he had gone after Lydia last night, dammit, and she had still rejected him.

"I would have made sure she knew I was there. No matter what. I would have waited for that woman 'til the day I died. Because if your life is empty without them, there's no point in pretending you're going to move on. She changed me. Everything I was. Everything I am."

That was true for Colton too. Somehow, in the past month and a half Lydia had taken him from a place where he had been willing to marry a woman he didn't love and continue on in the life he didn't want, to a man who loved passionately, and couldn't imagine going on without it.

"I might be waiting for a long time," he said.

"Is she worth it?"

"Yes." Ace set another glass down in front of Colton and he took a drink. "She is," he finished, setting the glass back down on the bar.

"Check that out," Ace added, gesturing to the other side of the restaurant.

Colton turned and saw Lydia getting up onto the stage that was normally reserved for live music. His heart stopped. Was this where she was making her acceptance speech? Had he unwittingly decided to drown his sorrows in the middle of her victory party? That would figure.

"Hello," Lydia said, her voice trembling as she bent down and spoke into the microphone. "Most of you know me. I was elected mayor last night."

A short cheer went up from the crowd and Lydia raised her hand to stop it. "Thank you. But that's not why I'm here." She took a deep breath. "Most of you also know that I married Colton West. After he got stood up at the altar. Which a lot of you also witnessed."

He felt most of the eyes in the bar turn to him, and he shifted on his stool, his hand wrapped firmly around his drink.

"Sorry," she said. "I promise, Colton, I have a point," she said, addressing him, putting his concerns about this being her victory speech to rest. She knew he was here. And she was talking to him. "It's just that from the beginning this relationship has been very public. In fact, I know that you only stayed married to me to help my odds of winning the election. Which is probably a terrible thing to admit now that I've won, and I guess if that's going to get me in trouble we're going to have to deal with that. Or I will. But, since all of this has been so public, from the wedding that didn't happen, to our surprise wedding, I thought this needed to be public too. I made a mistake last night. When you told me that you loved me and I walked away, I did it because I was afraid. I did it because you're right. I'm afraid of big emotion. Of things that will devastate me if I lose them. I'm afraid of caring about something too much, and wanting to hold on to it forever in case it gets taken from me. Well, my fear is stupid. It isn't going to protect me. It's just going to keep me living the kind of life I left Seattle to get away from to begin with. I don't want that."

She hopped off the low stage, leaving the microphone behind. "I love you," she shouted, throwing her hands wide. "I'm going to say that publicly. I want to be your wife for real. Not for an election. And I wanted you to have this be the thing that everybody sees. Because no matter whether you still love me, or if I ruined it, I don't want people to remember you being left at the altar. I want them to remember that time the mayor made an idiot out of herself because she just loved you that much."

He hopped up off the bar stool, knocking it over onto its side, leaving his drink behind. "You love me?"

"Yes," she said.

"I knew it," he responded, "you little liar."

"Not so much a liar. More a coward."

"Okay. Coward."

"That isn't really helping me out here." She swallowed, looking up at him with glittering eyes. "Do you still love me? Or did I ruin it? Because I am so ready to give you everything. Everything. My heart, my soul, my house. Everything."

He bent down and kissed her lips, not even remotely interested in making her suffer. They had suffered enough. "Of course I love you," he said against her mouth.

A cheer went up from the brewery, led by Jack and Ace. Colton lifted his hand in a halfhearted wave. And then he took hold of Lydia's hand, and led her quickly out of the restaurant, down the stairs and onto the beach that was just outside.

"We need some privacy," he said.

"I agree," she said, breathing hard.

"So, you love me?" he asked, still feeling a little bit disbelieving. "You really love me."

"You know how I told you that I was half a person. I was. I kept myself that way. Kept everyone at a distance. But I just… I don't want to be that anymore. I had it all inside of me all this time. I just had to stop being so afraid. I had to stop hiding. Well, I'm done with hiding. I don't need to be this perfect, well-ordered person with a perfect, well-ordered life. I just want to be yours."

"You are," he said, his voice getting husky. "And I'm yours."

"I can't…I can't even express everything you've done for me, Colton. All the ways that you've changed me. The strength that you showed me I had. You made me want…you made me want something more than easy, quiet control. You made me…you made me passionate."

"I made you say dirty words."

"Yes, you did that."

"Lydia, I hope you understand you did the same for

me. I'm tempted to say that you made me a new man. I think you just made me the man I was always supposed to be."

"Yes," she said, a tear sliding down her cheek, that easy display of emotion coming from Lydia touching him all the way down to his soul. "That's exactly how I feel. That you found some way to uncover everything that I would have been if loss, grief, fear, hadn't made me hide it all in the first place. I guess I just had to want something more than I wanted to be safe."

"Love certainly isn't safe."

"No. I expected it to be a little bit warmer. A little bit fuzzier. Instead, it kind of ripped me out of my hiding place. But for the first time in years I'm standing in the sun. It's worth the risk."

"Who would have thought it took someone as buried as I was to find me."

She smiled. "I guess it takes one to know one?"

"I'm going to set things in motion so that I'm not running the construction company anymore. And, even if it means dealing with Gage, I'm going to work it out so that it's clear I'm not the one taking over the ranching operation when my father's unable to run it anymore. I'm going to help. I mean, I'm not going to abandon them completely. Given his health, that isn't possible."

"I understand."

"But I'm not going to hold back on what I want to do, either. I want that ranch to be ours, Lydia. I want to push our children on the swing. I want to make a home with you. To make a life with you. I want it to be about us, not about duty to a family name."

"I want that too. But, you know that whatever support

you need with your family, I'm here to give it. Because if we're together, then we're family."

"Thank you." He bent down and kissed her again. "I'm not just going to do things anymore because I'm afraid. I was always afraid that I had to go above and beyond or I would lose my family. Lose more than just Gage, and I couldn't face that. So I did my very best to make myself indispensable."

"Well, you are that. Just because you're you."

Colton smiled, warmth rolling over him. "I can honestly say," he said, echoing the first words he had said to her on the morning after their wedding, "this is the last situation I ever expected to find myself in."

"Is it?" she asked, smiling back.

"The very last," he continued. "And absolutely the very first thing I needed."

He leaned in and kissed her, as the night breeze wrapped itself around them, mixing salt and pine in with the kiss. Approval from the town, he supposed. The thought made him smile.

It would have been tempting for him to describe his life as a run of tough luck. From his brother abandoning the family, to his fiancée leaving him at the altar.

Standing here, kissing Lydia Carpenter, he knew that he was the luckiest man alive.

EPILOGUE

LYDIA WEST'S BEDROOM ceiling had wooden beams running across it, just like the ceilings in the rest of the house. And when she opened her eyes in the morning, that was what she saw. Just like every morning.

And, just like every morning, her husband was beside her.

Since that morning in Las Vegas, they'd had a whole year of waking up married. And every day had been better than the last.

Being with Colton, finally taking steps to move forward, had helped her begin to repair things with her parents. Making a family with Colton had somehow made family seem a little bit easier.

"Good morning," he said, a sleepy smile on his face.

He was so beautiful it hurt. Colton was nothing but big emotion. Loving him was everything she'd feared for years.

But she wasn't afraid of it now. Now, she embraced it. And him.

"Good morning." She kissed his lips, then rolled over and slipped out from under the covers.

"Where are you going?" he asked, adjusting his position, putting his arm up behind his head, a cocky smile on his face.

She wanted to get back in bed with him then. But, she had a plan. It was their anniversary, after all.

"I'm going to make you breakfast."

"No way," he said, moving to a sitting position. "I should make you breakfast."

"I'm very particular, Colton. I like my breakfast the way I like it." Her heart started pounding a little harder. "Anyway, you wouldn't do it right."

"What?"

"You don't know how much I want."

"Oh," he said, getting up out of bed and advancing on her. "I know how much you want."

She shook her head, and she knew that the cute little card that she'd designed to go on his pancake tray wasn't going to get used, because she couldn't hold it in anymore. "You don't know. Because I need a little more than usual. Since I'm eating for two."

There was a certain symmetry to it. Looking at Colton's completely shocked face and letting him know he was going to be a father, exactly one year to the day since he'd discovered he was her husband.

Before she knew it, she was being swept up in his arms, and deposited back into bed. "Are you serious?" he asked, his smile so bright she thought it rivaled the sun.

"Yes. I am definitely Copper Ridge's first pregnant mayor."

"I guess I know what that makes me then."

"What?"

He kissed her, deep and long. "The happiest man in town."

* * * * *

Don't miss Ace and Sierra's story,
ONE NIGHT CHARMER,
available now from
Maisey Yates and HQN Books.
And read on for a sneak peek of
Gage's story,
LAST CHANCE REBEL.
Can the black sheep of Copper Ridge
find redemption—and a love
to call his own?

CHAPTER ONE

REBECCA BEAR FINISHED PUTTING the last of the Christmas decorations onto the shelf and took a step back, smiling at her work.

Changing seasons was always her favorite thing to do at the Trading Post. Getting the new stock in and arranging it on her antique furniture, adding appropriate garlands and just the right scented candle to evoke the mood. It was the kind of thing she could never do in her own house, since all of her money was poured straight back into the business. But she got it out of her system here.

The air was filled with pine, apples and cinnamon spice. She inhaled deeply, a sweet sense of satisfaction washing over her.

Her store was tiny. Rent on Copper Ridge's Main Street was most definitely at a premium. Which was likely why every decent building on the block was owned by the richest family in town.

But she liked her modest space, stacked from floor to ceiling with knickknacks of all varieties. From the cheesy driftwood sort tourists were always after when they came to the coast, to art and furniture handcrafted by locals.

Beyond that, she tended to collect anything that she found interesting. She turned, facing the bright blue

sideboard that was up against one of the walls. That was
her bird display. Little ceramic birds, teaspoons with
birds engraved on the handles, mugs with birds, and
superfluous little statues made of pinecones and driftwood to be placed anywhere in your home. All of them
arranged over a beautiful handmade doily from one of
the older women in town.

She kept that display all year round, and it always
made her feel cheerful. She supposed that was because
it was easy to identify with birds. They could fly anywhere, but they always came back home.

The bell above her door tinkled, and she turned
around, a strange, twisting sensation hitting her hard
in the stomach as a man ducked his head and walked
inside.

His face was obscured by a dark cowboy hat. His
shoulders were broad, and so was his chest. In spite
of the cold weather he was wearing nothing but a tight
black T-shirt, exposing muscular arms and forearms,
and a dark band tattooed on his skin.

He straightened, tilting his hat backward, revealing
a face that was arresting. It really was the only word.
It stopped her in her tracks, stopped her breath in her
lungs.

She had never seen him before. And yet, there was
something familiar about him. Like she had seen those
blue eyes before in a slightly different shape. Like she
had seen that square jaw, darkened with stubble, in a
different context.

It was so strange. She wondered for a moment if
maybe he were famous and it was just such a shock seeing him in her store and not in pictures that she couldn't
place him. He was definitely good-looking enough to

be a celebrity. A male model. Maybe a really hot baseball player.

"The place looks good," he said.

"Thank you," she responded, trying to sound polite and not weirded out.

She wasn't used to fielding random compliments on the look of her store from men who towered over her by at least a foot. Occasionally, little old ladies complimented her on that sort of thing. But not men like him.

"You do pretty good business," he said, and it wasn't a question.

"Yes," she said, taking a step backward, toward the counter. Her cellphone was over there, and while she doubted this guy was a psychopath, she didn't take chances with much of anything. And he was being a freaking weirdo.

"I've been looking over some of your financial information, and I'm pretty impressed."

Her stomach turned to ice. "I... Why have you been looking at my financial...anything? Why do you have access to that information?"

"It's part of the rental agreement you have with Nathan West. He's the owner of your building." She knew perfectly well who the owner of her building was. It felt a lot like making the deal with the devil to rent from Nathan West, but he owned the vacant part of Main, and she'd done her best to separate her personal issues from the man who held her potential financial future in her hands.

Anyway, she'd figured that if she didn't rent from him—if she found a place off the beaten path—and took a financial hit for it, then she was allowing the West family to continue to injure her.

So she'd swallowed all her pride—which was spiky, injured and difficult at the best of times—and had agreed to rent the building from him.

Also, it wasn't Nathan West she had cause to hate. Not really.

It was his son.

Suddenly, she felt rocked. Rocked by the blue eyes of the man standing in front of her. She knew why they looked familiar now. But it couldn't be. Gage West had taken off years ago, after he'd ruined her life, and no one had ever seen him again.

He couldn't be back now. It wasn't possible.

Well, it was unless he was dead, but it wasn't fair.

"I reserve the right to refuse service to anyone. I've never cashed that chip in before, but I think I just might."

"Rebecca," he said, his voice low, intense. "We need to talk."

"No, we don't," she said, her throat getting tight. "Not if you're who I think you are. You need to get the ever-loving hell out of my store before I grab the shotgun I keep under the counter."

"Gage West," he said, as though she hadn't spoken. As though she hadn't *threatened*. "I'm acting as my father's executor. I don't know if you heard but he had a stroke a couple of days ago."

"I'm sorry," she said. Mostly because it's what she was trained to say when someone gave bad news, not because she felt all that sorry for him. "I don't need to do any business with you, though."

"That's not the case."

"Yes, it absolutely is. I've managed to rent this building from your father six years. And in all that time I saw him face to face only a couple of times, otherwise we went through a property manager. I don't see why it has to be any different now."

"Because things are different now."

"Okay. Do you want to talk about things being different? I assume you know who I am." Her voice was vibrating with rage, and she resented him. Resented him for walking into this little slice of the world that she had carved out for herself. This beautiful, serene place that was supposed to be hers and only hers. And in had walked her own personal demon in cowboy boots...

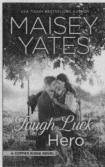

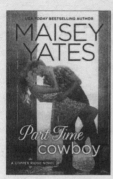
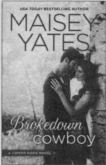

REQUEST YOUR
FREE BOOKS!

2 FREE NOVELS
FROM THE ROMANCE COLLECTION
PLUS 2 FREE GIFTS!

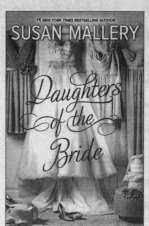

#1 NEW YORK TIMES BESTSELLING AUTHOR

SUSAN MALLERY

Daughters of the Bride

$26.99 U.S./$29.99 CAN.

- ✂